✳✳✳

This series is dedicated to all
U.S. military veterans of all branches
who served in times of peace and war,
for your families who stood by you,
for all of you now serving our country,
for all now waiting for a loved one to return,
and for all those whose wait has ended in tragedy.
God's love is for you.
The Homeland Heroes Series is for you.

✳✳✳

Other Books by Donna Fleisher

Wounded Healer (Homeland Heroes — Book One)
Warrior's Heart (Homeland Heroes — Book Two)

HOMELAND HEROES

★

Book Three

DONNA FLEISHER

VALIANT HOPE

ZONDERVAN™

GRAND RAPIDS, MICHIGAN 49530 USA

ZONDERVAN.COM/
AUTHORTRACKER

ZONDERVAN™

Valiant Hope
Copyright © 2006 by Donna Fleisher

Requests for information should be addressed to:

Zondervan, *Grand Rapids, Michigan 49530*

Library of Congress Cataloging-in-Publication Data

Fleisher, Donna.
    Valiant Hope / Donna Fleisher.
        p. cm. (Homeland heroes ; bk. 3)
    ISBN-13: 978-0-310-26396-8
    ISBN-10: 0-310-26396-4
    1. Abused children—Fiction. I. Title.
PS3606.L454V35 2006
813'.6—dc22

                                                            2005032055

Interior design by Michelle Espinoza

Printed in the United States of America

06 07 08 09 10 11 12 • 12 11 10 9 8 7 6 5 4 3 2 1

Lord Jesus, this one is for You.
Yes, they all have been for You. Without You,
they would not exist.
But this one especially. You alone made this one happen.
I don't know what everyone else did in April of 2004,
but I know what You and I did.
Who am I, Lord, that You would ...?

ACKNOWLEDGMENTS

Precious Lord God, thank You. This has been such an incredible journey. Thank You for encouraging and strengthening me along the way. No matter where this journey leads, I go with You. Thank You for all those who go with me. We go together, Lord, following Your Son. Thank You for ...

★★★

My family: Mom and Dad, Chris, Thess, Christine, and Mario.

My Zondervan family: all editors, typesetters, cover designers, marketers, salespeople, publicists, check signers, web designers, author care specialists, and everyone who acquired, approved, read, reread, proofread, formatted, sold, printed, and delivered each book. Thank You for all their efforts. We gladly place this work of our hands into Your hands.

My Mount Hermon, Oregon Christian Writers, and ACFW families.

My Sandcastle family: who share so much of themselves with me.

My best friends and all their families: Shannon, Susie, Vickie, Heather, Melisa, Trish, Steph, Jeanna, June, Lynn, Jacci, and Brooke.

My examples and teachers: Margaret Becker, Gayle Erwin, and Francine Rivers. Thank you so much for Margaret's beautiful song, "Who Am I," and for her allowing me to use it in this story.

My readers. May we all courageously hold fast to our hope and faith in Your Son, our Savior, Jesus Christ.

VALIANT HOPE

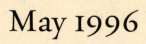

May 1996

ONE

I DON'T THINK I CAN be a Christian anymore.

The words sliced Chris McIntyre's heart. The Bible in her hands shook.

I'm sorry, Lord. Rinny said to take it slow. But I can't get away from it. I mean, it says it again, right here. If I don't forgive others, You won't forgive me. Jesus, You said it so many times. In so many different ways. In Your prayers. In Your teachings. You said, "If you don't forgive . . ."

With Erin's help, Chris had forgiven Rich. With prayer and the passage of time, she had even forgiven Del. But Del was a moron. Sometimes it was easier to forgive morons.

She had even forgiven herself.

It was so much harder to forgive the one she had dared to love, the one whose love for her had caused so much pain.

He did love me once. Didn't he? When I was really young?

The memory of that day returned to haunt her. The day she had climbed on her father's lap and leaned against his chest, then rested her head against his shoulder. His strong arms encircled her and tenderly pulled her against him. He spoke soft words in her ear. Words she would always treasure. His voice, she would never forget. "You're a good girl, Chrissy. You're a good girl."

But, Lord! What did I do? Did I suddenly turn bad? Did I cause him that much grief that he grew to hate me?

Only hate would drive a father to beat his child so viciously.

Chris jumped off her bed and tossed her Bible on the nightstand. Quickly headed for the kitchen. Ran her fingers through her hair as she walked, as she let out a long, deep breath.

Later, Lord. Later.

She grabbed the gallon of milk out of the refrigerator and poured herself a glassful, then quickly lifted the glass for a long drink. She closed her eyes as the milk left a cool, soothing trail from her throat to her stomach. She waited another second, hoping it would soothe the burn there.

If the milk didn't work, she knew something that would. It had been months since she'd taken her last drink of Jack Daniel's whiskey. Since that night at Dandy's Pub. The night that jerk pushed Erin down. The night Chris, for the first time in her life, cried out to Jesus for help.

Her eyes closed as she remembered that night. The night Erin would not let her leave. The night the Lord Jesus Christ heard her cry.

Please hear me again, now. I don't want to hurt You. Help me know what to do.

Well, that was a dumb prayer. She knew exactly what He wanted her to do. The question was, would she do it?

Lord Jesus, I know You're asking me to forgive my dad. If I refuse to forgive him, how can I expect You to help me forget? I know it's true. I need to forgive him.

She took another long drink of milk. Swallowed. Slowly opened her eyes and blinked.

But there is no way.

Her throat tightened. Started to ache.

I'm sorry, Lord, but there is no way I can ever forgive my dad. If You know anything about me, You know I can't.

Tears burned her eyes.

And if You know me, You know that isn't true. It's not that I can't forgive him, it's that I won't. Ever.

She grabbed her keys and left the apartment, slamming the door behind her, leaving her jacket hanging on its peg, her half-empty glass and the gallon of milk on the counter.

From inside the Kimberley Street Medical Clinic, Erin Mathis heard the door of the apartment above her slam. Chris and Cappy's apartment. One of them stomped down the outside stairs. Angry stomps. She hoped it was Cappy.

Past the front windows of the clinic, Chris McIntyre, Erin's dearest friend, made her way down the long porch. Erin held her breath, hoping Chris would stop at the clinic's door and peek inside to say a quick hello.

The door didn't open.

More angry stomps.

Erin peered out the big front window and waited. Chris, head lowered against the spring rain, walked down the sidewalk, down Kimberley Street, probably toward the new gymnasium. On her way to work.

With a deep sigh, Erin relaxed in her chair, then rubbed the back of her neck. She had never felt so bloated, so positively monstrous. Her weight gain, her bulging belly, her increasing impatience, being pregnant so long, so ready to be over and done with it—

"Are you all right?" Hot breath tickled her ear.

She smiled at her husband's words, then squirmed as his lips nibbled her earlobe.

"Hold still. You taste good."

His hands gently massaged her shoulders as his lips found the side of her neck. Erin squelched her immediate desire to hum with pure delight. Instead, she asked him, "Aren't you supposed to be at the hospital?"

"Yes." More nibbling. "Just wanted a taste before I left."

"You're getting more than a taste." She turned to face him. Gazed into his light brown eyes. Watched the light dance in them.

"You are so beautiful."

She grunted. "Please. I look like I swallowed a beach ball."

Her husband grinned. "Three more weeks, love."

"Two weeks, four days, and hopefully not a minute more."

He laughed.

"Don't laugh! You did this to me."

"I'll make it up to you first chance I get."

"You better."

He knelt in front of her and gently placed his hands on her protruding abdomen, then leaned in to kiss it. "Hello there, little babe. Daddy can't wait to see you. You be good for Mommy today. Try to stay off her bladder, okay? And don't kick too hard." He looked up with laughter in his eyes.

Erin could only smile.

Standing, Scott returned her smile, then moved in to kiss her lips. He pushed back her hair and cupped her cheeks in his hands.

"You're gonna be late." Barely a whisper.

Another kiss, this one deeper, lingering. When he kissed her like this, what choice did she have? She could only fall headlong into the joy of his love, the joy of sharing life with her true soul mate, of being Mrs. Scott Mathis. She savored her overwhelming gratitude to the One who had saved them and brought them together.

Scott slowly pulled away. "Okay, you're right. Gotta go. But I'll be home around three." He traced the backs of his fingers down her cheek. Touched the tip of her nose. Then turned, wrapped his jacket around him, and headed for the front door.

Still basking in the moment, Erin's lips and cheek tingled. "We'll be waiting." She rubbed her belly with one hand and returned his wave with the other as he pulled the clinic's door closed behind him. His Mustang roared to life. Then carried him away.

"We'll be waiting, love," Erin whispered into the silence, still rubbing her belly. But then, just for a second, a wave of sadness swept over her. She sighed deeply, shook her head, and returned to her insurance paperwork.

She couldn't concentrate. Slowly looked up. Fat drops of rain splashed off the porch railing. Slapped against the leaves of the azalea bush in the front yard.

Father? I'm worried about Chris. Is she going to be all right?

Constant. Relentless. Splashes of rain.

She wants so much to learn about You. To follow Your Son. She's really struggling right now. And I don't know how to help her.

Tears blurred the splashes of rain. Erin made no effort to blink them away.

I can only pretend to imagine what she's facing. What she's been through. Only You can help her find a way ... to forgive her dad.

Bitter memories flooded her mind. Horrible things she had seen. Things she had heard. The few things Chris had told her.

Please help her, Father. Help her to put everything behind her. Please free her from all of it. For the first time in her life, Lord, please help her to be free.

★★★

Water coursed down her face and dripped off her chin. Dripped from her drenched hair to the back of her shirt. Seeped through to her skin. Chilled her to the bone.

Stupid. Leaving the apartment without her jacket.

Water dripped off her nose and landed at her feet. She glanced down at her sneakers. Wiped them on the mat just inside the door of the new Kimberley Street gymnasium.

The mat had been Isaiah's idea. And it was a good one. The new floor in the gym had fit and settled well, and though it was old and scuffed and secondhand, it suited their needs and budget perfectly. Donated by a local middle school, it had taken three days and the help of fifteen volunteers from the church to lay it out. And so far, there was only one slightly dead spot, over in the far corner, about twenty feet from the basket.

Alaina had found it.

Chris wiped her face with her hand and smiled.

After the floor had been laid and sealed, she told nine-year-old Alaina Walker and her two nine-year-old friends, Jazzy Sadler and Jen White, to dribble their basketballs over every inch of the floor. Chris had followed behind them, dribbling her own. Every time they found a squishy spot in the floor, Chris would mark the spot with a masking tape X to keep track of it, then keep score. The one who found the most squishy spots won a Pepsi. That was the deal.

It took almost a half hour for the four of them to dribble their basketballs over every inch of the new floor. Right after that, Alaina sipped her ice-cold Pepsi as Chris whispered a heartfelt prayer of thanks. Finishing the floor and finding it good-to-go had been the biggest and most rewarding accomplishment of the warehouse-to-gymnasium conversion project.

Seeing Alaina share her Pepsi with Jazzy and Jen had been the sweetest moment of all.

Pushing back her wet hair from her forehead, Chris drew in a deep breath, then let it out slowly.

So much had happened in the last five months. She had been ready to end it all. But then, drunk and passed out on her couch, she heard a knock at her door. That moment changed everything. At this moment, standing in this place, off Kimberley Street in Portland, Oregon ... all of it still seemed like a dream.

She was home. The place had become her own. Kimberley Square. And this converted old warehouse. The smell of it, the cavernous depths, the ringing echoes of laughter and bouncing basketballs.

Alaina.

Her smile faded as her heart sank. She turned and walked toward the office.

Something was wrong with Alaina. All this week, especially. She seemed down. Quiet. Even Jazzy seemed concerned.

Chris drew in another long breath to calm the ache in her stomach. She unlocked the office door and walked in, flipped on the light, then tossed her keys on the desk. She walked over to a rack of basketballs and picked one up. Squeezed it in her hands.

Her stomach burned. She closed her eyes.

Of all the kids in the neighborhood, why Alaina? Jazzy's parents were the best. Isaiah Sadler, Chris's good friend and coworker—and Jazzy's grandpa—had seen to that. Jen White's parents were the best too. Every Sunday they sat together as a family, all six of them, up front in the Kimberley Street Community Church.

Alaina had come to church once or twice with her mother. Never with her father.

Chris slammed the basketball back down on the rack.

She had seen the look in Alaina's mother's eyes. Fear. The haunted look of shame. She knew that look. Knew it well. Had seen it in her own family's eyes. Her aunts and uncles, even some of her cousins. Long ago she had turned to them for help, and they had all given her that look, then all but turned their backs on her. They knew what was going on, what she was going through, but were too afraid to stand up to Donovan McIntyre. They were all too afraid to do anything about it.

"I'm not too afraid," Chris whispered aloud. "God, please. When Alaina comes in today, please let her be all right." She picked up one of the towels on the shelf by her desk. Slowly wiped her face and hands with it. Then tried to squeeze some of the water from her hair.

Please, God. That's all I ask. Please just let her be all right.

★★★

SOME PRAYERS GOD SEEMED TO answer quickly. Some He didn't seem to answer at all. And some prayers … some prayers Chris wished she had never prayed at all. Some things just played out the way they played out. Though she didn't doubt for one second God still knew what He was doing.

At least, in this case, she hoped He knew what He was doing.

At that moment, Alaina Walker looked worse than ever.

The child didn't smile. Her normally bright blue eyes were sullen and dark. She didn't want to play with her friends. Jazzy sat on the floor beside her, leaning back against the wall, just sitting there, both of them, watching the others shoot baskets and goof around.

A tiny smile. Alaina's only response as Kelly's basketball wedged itself between the backboard and the rim. A few of the older boys tried to jump up to dislodge it, but they were about a foot short reaching it. Kelly, red-faced and giggling, asked Chris for a broom or something like that, something long enough to knock it free. But Lissa had saved the day. With a squeal, she launched her own basketball straight up with enough force to nudge Kelly's free. And not only free, but right into the hoop. Loud joyous laughter echoed across the big room.

Alaina only faintly smiled.

Chris turned to find the only other adult in the room, Kay Valleri, gave her a quick nod, then hurried to the gym's double doors and pushed herself through. Outside, the heavy cool air comforted her, then filled her lungs as she drew it in as deeply as she could.

Maybe Alaina was just sick.

Chris almost laughed. Of course, that was it. Nothing happening at home; the girl was just sick. And Chris was just overreacting. Yes, the signs were there, but did that mean Alaina was in danger?

Only one way to find out.

Her teeth clenched as she drew in one more deep breath. Then she turned and headed back inside the gym. She smiled at Kay Valleri.

"Are you all right?" Kay's eyes narrowed.

"Um ... yeah." Chris glanced at her feet. "Needed some fresh air." She tried to give Kay another smile. "I'm glad you're here. Thanks for your help."

"Well, you can't be here every minute, you know." Kay patted Chris's shoulder. "And you can't have all the fun. You've got to share some of it with the rest of us."

Fun? Chris held back a laugh. Fun. Yes. Most of the time. Five and a half days a week she enjoyed supervising the gym's activities. Watching the kids, cleaning up after them. Watching the adults too, sometimes even refereeing their pickup games. But at that moment, what she felt in her stomach and head and heart, she couldn't share with anyone. No one else would understand.

"Why don't you head on home? I'll keep an eye on things."

Chris glanced up at the clock across the gym. It was almost lunchtime. Her workweek was almost complete. "Yeah. Think I will. Thanks, Kay. I mean it."

"I know you do. And you're very welcome. See you at church tomorrow."

"Yeah. Okay. See ya, lady." Chris squeezed Kay's shoulder, then turned for her office to grab her keys. She found them where she had tossed them, though they were buried under some papers. She picked up the papers and looked them over. Two of the children had returned their parental permission forms.

Her eyes shifted to the small filing cabinet by her desk. She sat in her chair and unlocked the cabinet, then pulled out Alaina Walker's parental permission form.

It had been signed the very day she sent it home with Alaina, signed in elegant script by her mother, Laurie. No serious medical conditions were listed. Alaina did not suffer from allergies or asthma. Chris studied the home address listed. Cameron Street. Two blocks north of Kimberley. Close to the abandoned lot where she first saw the blonde-haired, blue-eyed nine-year-old. Where she stood and watched the girl dribble a basketball in a figure-eight pattern around those tiny, worn-out high-tops on the girl's feet.

She memorized the address, just in case. Then refiled the form and locked the cabinet. She stood and left her office, heading for Alaina and Jazzy to find out for herself if Alaina was sick or hurt or what.

She stopped and stared. Then bit back a curse.

Jazzy stood out on the court, laughing and playing Horse with her friends.

Alaina Walker was gone.

✷✷✷

TEARING LETTUCE FOR A SALAD, Erin glanced at the clock on her kitchen wall. Again. It was about that time, but she tried not to worry. She had set out two salad plates and made two turkey and swiss sandwiches. She would wait to pour two tall glasses of milk. There was, of course, no guarantee Chris would stop by for lunch.

But Erin could hope.

So many hopeful prayers lately. So much to talk about, so much to share. Since becoming a Christian four months ago, Chris had read most of the New Testament and asked most of the important questions a new believer needed to ask. Erin treasured every opportunity to guide Chris further into her faith. Their friendship had been born in a time of fear and war, had outlasted years of silence, then blossomed into something pure and sweet, something sent from the Lord Jesus Christ Himself. A priceless gift. Wrapped up in His love. Only because of His love. And His perseverance.

And your obedience.

She stopped tearing lettuce. Her eyes fell closed. *Thank You, Lord.*

She wasn't going to cry again, was she?

Gentle laughter worked its way up from her bulging belly. She tore the last of the lettuce and reached for a paring knife to slice up the tomatoes.

A few faint knocks on the front door startled her. She wiped her hands on a towel, then turned to see Chris McIntyre leaning around the half-open door. Erin grinned. "Hey you."

A weary smile softened Chris's face. "Hey you too."

"Are you coming in?"

Chris stepped the rest of the way around the door and pushed it closed. Then kicked off her shoes.

"You don't have to do that."

She dismissed Erin's statement with a wave.

"Hungry?"

Chris's smile brightened.

"I just have to slice up some tomatoes for the salad. Go ahead and get out the dressing you'd like." Erin picked up the knife. "Grab the Thousand Island for me, will ya?"

"Sure."

She quickly sliced up two tomatoes, then sprinkled herb croutons on both salads.

Chris moved in beside her. "How are you feeling?"

"Pregnant. You?"

Chris let out a breath of laughter.

Grinning, Erin grabbed the salads and set them on the table. Chris carried the sandwiches, then pulled the gallon of milk from the refrigerator. She filled the glasses Erin had left on the counter and brought them to the table. Erin eased herself down into the chair. Breathed a deep sigh.

Chris sat beside her. Gave her a sheepish look. "Are you sure you're all right?"

Erin pressed her lips. "I feel like I've lost my 'glow.'"

"Nah." Chris lifted her glass of milk for a quick sip. "I'd say you're just ready for the next step."

"I want to hold her. So much, Chris, I can hardly stand it."

"I know. I can see it in your eyes. You have definitely not lost your 'glow.'"

Erin's smile came easily.

"Wanna pray?"

She nodded, then gave thanks for the food. When she said, "Amen," she started to pick up her sandwich, but waited another second as she silently gave thanks for the friend sitting beside her.

Chris poured Hidden Valley Ranch dressing on her salad. Then picked up her sandwich for a bite. Erin took a bite of her own sandwich, then dribbled Thousand Island dressing on her salad as she chewed. She kept glancing at Chris, her heart growing increasingly concerned. After a few bites of salad, she couldn't take the silence any longer. She swallowed and said, "You're not all right."

Chris's dark eyes flickered. "What?"

"What's wrong?"

Chris held her gaze on Erin for another second, then looked down at her sandwich. It took a long while for her to answer. She swallowed a drink of milk and wiped her mouth with a napkin. "Rinny? What do you know about Alaina's dad?"

The question took Erin completely by surprise. "Alaina Walker?"

"Yeah. Do you know her dad, or her mom, very well?"

She slowly shook her head. "No. Not really. Why?"

"Her mom's name is Laurie, isn't it?"

"I think so." Erin had only met the woman once, maybe twice, at church.

"Do you know her dad's name?"

Where was this going? "No. I've never met him."

Chris stared at her glass of milk.

"Why do you ask? Is something wrong?"

"I don't know."

Erin put down her fork and wiped her mouth. "Chris, what is it?"

"I'm hoping it's nothing."

Silence fell heavily. Erin struggled with the moment.

Chris picked up her fork and stabbed it into her salad. Except for crunching croutons, the silence lingered.

Erin swallowed a drink of milk.

Chris finished chewing, swallowed, let out a sigh, then pushed her half-eaten salad and sandwich away. "I'm sorry, Rinny. It's really good but ... I'm not hungry."

"That's okay." Erin glanced at her own half-eaten sandwich. Maybe later, after her sudden queasiness eased, she would be able to finish it. It would keep until then. She looked at Chris. "You want a cup of tea?"

Chris's head lifted as her eyes found Erin's. They seemed to soften as she barely smiled. "Yeah. That sounds good. But sit still. I'll get it." She pushed away from the table and carried her lunch into the kitchen.

A prayer for guidance whispered up from Erin's soul.

In the kitchen, Chris tore open two packets of peppermint tea as the water in the kettle started to boil. A minute later, she carried the steaming mugs of sweet-smelling tea to the table.

"Thanks, girl," Erin said as she reached for her glass of milk. She tilted the glass and poured a few drops into her tea, then tried to restrain her smile as Chris did the same thing. She lifted the mug for a sip. Perfectly sweetened, the warmth of the mint lingered on her lips and tongue. She hummed.

Chris still stirred her tea. She gazed into the swirling liquid, but had yet to take a sip.

"If you tell me, maybe I can help."

The words brought a faint smile to Chris's face. But she didn't look up from her tea.

"Is something wrong with Alaina?"

Chris sighed deeply. "I . . . I don't know. I think she may be hurt. I just have this feeling . . ." More stirring. "You're gonna laugh at me. You're gonna think I'm crazy." She finally stopped stirring and pulled out her spoon. She watched a drop of tea fall off it into her mug, then licked it and placed it on the table beside her glass of milk. "I think, Rinny . . . I think she's being hurt at home. By her dad."

Erin's jaw dropped.

"I don't know for sure. But . . . I'm afraid for her. I can't explain to you why I'm afraid. I just am."

The queasiness in Erin's stomach sharpened. "Have you talked to her?"

"Not really. I've just seen it in her." Chris finally picked up her mug for a sip. She swallowed, then lowered it back to the table. Still did not look at Erin. "She's been . . . different lately. She's been getting winded, like she can't breathe that well. And the past few days she's been holding her arm close, like she's trying to protect her side. She's been looking . . . bad, Rinny. She's worn out. I can see it. Her eyes are . . . sad."

Erin lifted her mug but did not take a sip. It shook in her hands.

"I've been seeing it for a few weeks now. And that one time, that one Sunday when Alaina came to church with her mom . . ."

Erin waited. Steam from her mug carried the tea's sweet fragrance. She took a small sip, still waiting, praying for words to say.

"I saw it in her mom's eyes that day. There's something going on. I'm sure of it."

Erin lowered her mug. "I don't know what to say, Chris. I mean, I haven't seen Alaina since the day we opened the gym. And she seemed all right then. I've met Alaina's mom, but I have no idea what her dad is like."

"Does she have other family?" Those dark eyes finally looked Erin's way.

"She has an older sister."

"No. Does she have a grandma or grandpa that lives around here? Maybe some aunts or uncles?"

Erin shook her head. "I don't know. I'm sorry. I wish I could be more help."

Chris bit her lip for a second. "She has a sister?"

"Yes. Meghan."

"How old is she?"

"I'm not sure. She's probably in her teens. I haven't seen her in years. I first met her and Alaina at a Vacation Bible School at the church."

"When was this?"

"Oh my." Erin tried to think back. "Probably three years ago. At least. Meghan only came that one summer, but Alaina's been coming every summer since then. That's really the only way I know her. Except for when I used to see her playing in the lot. And the time we put up the hoop for her."

Chris's face hardened as she looked away. "And you've never met her dad. You don't even know what he does? Where he works?"

"No. I'm sorry."

Chris pushed away from the table and walked a few steps toward the living room. She ran her fingers through her hair. Then turned back toward Erin. "I'm sorry too, Rinny. But I can't let this go."

Chris's expression tore at Erin's heart. "What can I do? How can I help?"

Chris's eyes narrowed, then turned ice cold. "No, Erin. You are not coming with me."

"What? With you where?"

Those eyes suddenly widened. Then glanced around the room. Toward the door.

"Oh ... no." Grunting with the effort, Erin forced herself to her feet.

Chris took a step closer. "Rinny, don't—"

"Are you thinking about going over there? To see Alaina's dad?"

"Well, yeah. I need to know if she's all right."

Erin gripped the back of Chris's chair. "I know you do. But does that mean you have to go over there right now?"

"Maybe it does."

Erin shook her head. "No, I don't think so. I mean, if you suspect something's wrong, let's call the police. Or Ben." She glanced at the phone for effect. "Let's call Ben and Sonya. Right now. They may know Alaina's father. Actually, I'm sure they do. They'll be able to help us know what to do."

"I am not calling Ben." Chris's face hardened with every word.

"Come on."

"No, Rin. I'm not calling anyone until I know more. No one will believe me anyway. No one will believe me or do anything about it unless there's proof."

The words stunned Erin. "How can you say that?"

"Because I know. Okay? No one will do anything for her unless she ends up in the hospital or something."

She could only stare.

Chris turned away. Walked a few steps into the living room. "Look, Erin, I'm sorry about all this. I know you must think I'm crazy."

Erin moved closer. "I don't like what you're saying, Chris. Not one bit. I don't think you're crazy. If you think Alaina is being hurt, I believe you."

As Chris slowly turned back around, her mouth fell open.

"Of course, I believe you. And Ben will believe you too. He will do anything he can to help you."

"No." Chris raised her hand. "Rinny, this is crazy! I'm not going to call Ben or the police and accuse a man I've never met unless I know for sure. I shouldn't have said anything to you. I should have gone over there before coming here."

Erin closed her eyes and prayed for patience.

"This is no big deal. I'll just go over there and ask to see her. I'll take a look around and see what I see. I'm sure she's all right. I'm sure I'm just being stupid. I mean, maybe she has a cold or something. Maybe she's just sick."

Erin sat in Chris's chair. She let out a deep breath and pressed her lips into a firm line. "But what if you're right? What if she's not sick?"

Chris sat again at the table and gave Erin a long look. Tears slowly lined her dark eyes.

"Listen, try not to worry. Let's call Ben and Sonya. Let's talk to them before you go."

Chris wiped her hand over her eyes. "Rin, it'll take me ten minutes. I'll just go over there, ask to see Alaina, ask her if she's all right, then we'll know."

Those dark eyes ... such concern, such stubbornness. "I want to come with you."

A laugh. "There is no way you're coming with me, Rinny. Absolutely not. Nuh-uh. No way." Another laugh. "Oh man, if you came with me ... Scott would kill me."

Erin's smile wavered.

Chris patted Erin's hand. "Don't worry. Please? I know I'm just overreacting. I'm sure she's fine."

Erin swallowed deeply. Grabbed Chris's hand. And squeezed it.

"Her dad may be the biggest sweetheart of all. A big teddy bear."

"And ... he may not."

"Yeah. I know."

"You have no idea what you'll find."

"It'll be okay."

"I still think we should call Ben."

"After I come back. I promise. If I find out anything, I'll talk to Ben right away, and then we'll call the police."

Erin held on to Chris's hand, almost afraid to let it go. "Promise me? Please?"

"I promise. Soon as I come back."

"Don't do anything ... heroic."

A soft giggle. "No way."

"I know you, Chris. So promise me. Nothing heroic."

"Come on, Rinny. It'll be all right."

Erin lifted her right eyebrow as far as she could.

"Okay, okay. I promise. Nothing heroic."

But the words did little to ease the concern growing in Erin's soul.

★★★

THE RAIN HAD STOPPED, LEAVING behind slick streets and puddles in her path. The damp, dreary morning had given way to a promising afternoon. Patches of blue peeked through the gray clouds. Little glimpses of hope for a better day. And if she needed anything right now, it was a glimpse of hope.

Almost to Cameron Street, Chris lowered her head and watched the sidewalk pass beneath her feet. She dodged another puddle, then stopped at the street corner.

Did she really want to do this? What right did she have to knock on the Walker's door? What would she say when Alaina's dad or mom opened it? "Um, hello there. I was just wondering if you have been beating your little girl."

A part of her said to turn around and head back to Erin's house, to take Erin's advice and talk to Ben about it. Ben Connelly knew everyone in Kimberley Square. And beyond. He would know Alaina's dad. He would know if the man was capable of beating his daughter. Not every father had it in him. Not every dad was cruel and mean and violent.

Chris leaned against a light pole and let her eyes close as a car splashed down Cameron Street. *Lord, please let me be wrong.* She rubbed her eyes, then pushed her fingers through her hair.

She kicked at a pebble, sending it skipping across the street. Her teeth clenched.

In Erin's present state, it was insane to worry her. Because of a feeling. A hunch. What if Alaina was just sick? What if she had fallen down or something simple like that? What if all of this proved to be no big deal, when Chris was so determined to make it one?

Well, then ... so be it.

She crossed the street and headed west on Cameron Street. She stared at her feet as she walked and refused to even glance into the vacant lot as she passed it by.

Alaina's vacant lot. Her old after-school playground.

The lot that had offered Chris a refuge after the fire.

She stopped and lifted her head. Then turned around and retraced her last few steps to stand at the edge of the abandoned store. She peeked into the dirty empty lot.

Spindly weeds and garbage. That stupid rusted Safeway cart. That cracked concrete slab.

Just a child. Flyaway blonde hair. Radiant blue eyes. Cute, happy, sweet. Even when spitting on the driver's side window of Mr. Potts's car.

Tears burned Chris's eyes.

No. Alaina didn't *fall down*. And if anyone tried to say she did, they would be lying. Falling down did not cause a child's eyes to darken with sadness. And fear. Falling down did not cause a usually energetic nine-year-old to be suddenly overcome with weariness.

Chris knew that weariness. And she knew what caused it.

Cursing her tears, she wiped them away, then turned and continued down the sidewalk, down Cameron Street, quickening her pace almost to a trot. Only another block. Then she would know.

TWO

ERIN STOOD BY HER OPEN front door wanting to run after Chris, wanting to run across the street to Ben and Sonya's house to see if they were home, to see if they could help. She wanted to call her husband at work. Wanted to call the police. But what would she tell them?

Please arrest my best friend. She's criminally stubborn!

She leaned against the door frame. *Father God, be with her right now. Protect her. Help her not do anything ... crazy. You know her better than I do. You know what I mean.*

Sharp pains shot across her back. She needed to sit. To put her feet up.

She needed to be with Chris.

She needed to clean off the table. To clean out her refrigerator.

Biting her lower lip, she pushed the door closed, then turned away and headed for the kitchen, mumbling, "Lord? She needs someone to watch her back. There's no telling what she's gonna get herself into." She sealed the leftover sandwiches in plastic wrap and tossed them into the refrigerator. "Please keep her safe. Bring her back soon. And protect Alaina." She leaned against the counter and let her eyes fall closed. "Oh, dear Lord Jesus, please protect little Alaina."

Her hands made slow circles around the miracle nestled in her womb. An image danced in her mind. Six-year-old Alaina Walker, her long blonde hair caught in the wind, skipping down Kimberley Street, clutching a handful of papers she had colored that day at Vacation Bible School, humming the new song she had learned. "Jesus Loves Me, This I Know."

A smile slowly spread across Erin's lips. "Oh yes, sweetheart, He does. He loves you so much."

Cappy Sanchez.

Her heart slammed to a stop as her eyes popped open.

Yes! Why hadn't she thought of Cappy sooner?

Erin waddled across the kitchen, grabbed the phone off the wall hook, and punched in the number for Chris and Cappy's apartment. She waited as it rang twelve times. Fifteen. Then pushed the button on the handset to end the call. She checked the list of numbers on the wall by the phone. Punched in the number for Isaiah Sadler's brand-new cell phone. Waited. Praying, *Please pick up, Isaiah. Where are you guys?* Her heart thumped. *Lord, I don't even know where Cappy is.*

Two more rings. Isaiah's soft greeting.

Sounded sweet as honey to Erin's ears. "Hi, Isaiah. Is Cappy there with you?"

"Well hello, Erin. Yes, she's here. Hold on a second."

The breath she'd been holding blew out her lips.

Cappy's voice. "This is me, is dat you?" And that delightful Hispanic attitude. "It is, huh. *Hola, mamacita!*"

Erin laughed. "*Hola* to you too. Listen, lady, I need your help."

Sudden silence. "I'll be right there."

"No, wait! Where are you?"

"At Velda's."

Relief flooded Erin's heart. "Really?"

"Yep. We're trying to inspect what the contractors did this week, but Velda just got here and she brought a huge box of donuts and she's, like, trying to get us to stop and eat. Now how does she expect us to get any work done if all she wants us to do is eat donuts?"

"Oh yes. I see your dilemma." Another laugh. "Hey, do you know where the Walkers live?"

A pause. "Lainer?"

"Yes. Do you know where she lives?"

"Sure. I've been there a time or two."

"You have? Do you know her dad?"

Cappy let out what sounded like a grunt. "Not a man I'd want to know. He's a *burro*."

"A what?"

"Let's just say he's not a nice man."

Erin's blood turned ice cold. "Um … how do you mean?" Her words shook.

"What's up, Erin? Are you all right?"

"I think I need you to go to Alaina's. Right now."

"Why? Is something wrong with her?"

"Right now it's Chris I'm worried about. She went over there to see Alaina's dad. To see if he's been hurting her."

"What?"

"She said she had a feeling … and that Alaina's been acting strange lately."

"That is not good, Erin."

She swallowed deeply. "Yeah, I'm beginning to think so myself. Listen, can you go over there? Maybe take the cell phone with you? Go see what's up and give me a call. Please?"

"You bet. I'm on my way. I'll call you." The line went dead.

Still gripping the phone's handset, Erin dropped into a chair at the dining room table, waited a second, then closed her eyes and blew out a deep breath. Using her thumb, she pushed the button on the handset to hang up the phone at her end, then waited, praying it would ring again soon.

What had Chris gotten herself into this time? And what did Cappy mean by saying Alaina's dad was a "*burro*"?

She prayed for Chris. For Alaina. For Cappy. She prayed … knowing there wasn't anything else she could do.

★★★

AT FIRST CHRIS THOUGHT THE Walkers might live in one of the many apartments along this stretch of Cameron Street. But no. They lived in a small thirties-style bungalow with a nice front yard and a carport along the side. Empty carport. A beat-up Ford pickup truck, a huge Buick, and a Honda Accord were parked in the street in front of the house. Chris couldn't tell which one belonged to Mr. or Mrs. Walker. If any did.

Six or eight steps led up to a small porch barely large enough to allow the front screen door to swing open.

Not much room to maneuver ...

She wanted to laugh at her ever-analytical mind, but she cut herself a break. For as long as she remembered she had been taught to take care of herself, to anticipate any situation, to act rather than react. *Action is always faster than reaction*, she heard her heart whisper, though she knew at that moment it was mocking her.

What was she doing here? How long would it take before a neighbor started to wonder why she stood in the middle of the sidewalk staring up at the Walker's house?

This is crazy!

Her heart pounded so hard, she heard it echo against her eardrums.

Oh, Lord ...

Crazy and stupid and stubborn. Would Jesus listen to her prayers when she acted like this?

Refusing to forgive. Not loving her neighbor.

Mr. Walker was her neighbor. But so was Alaina. And if Chris discovered Mr. Walker was beating his daughter, she would never forgive him either.

Some things were simply unforgivable.

Like being stupid. Keep walking. Don't stop. Go back to Erin's. Call Ben.

A car passed by. Splashed through a puddle. Startled her out of the moment.

You walked all the way over here. Go and see if Alaina's all right.

She headed for the concrete stairs leading up to the Walker's front door. Slowly worked her way up each of the eight steps to the top. Then stood on the Walker's front porch. She reached out her hand. Pushed the doorbell. Heard it chime inside the house.

Oh, Lord ... what am I doing? Please hear my prayer. Help me!

✮✮✮

CAPPY TOOK ONE LOOK AT Isaiah's truck as she ran down Velda's front walkway but knew, if she kept running, she would be halfway to the Walker's house before the old wreck warmed up enough to even start the trip. It was just three or four blocks from Velda's house to Alaina's. Leaving Isaiah's truck where it sat, clutching his cell phone in her fist, realizing one of her closest friends may be standing toe to toe with Alaina Walker's father, Cappy took off running down Cameron Street.

⋆⋆⋆

CHRIS'S MUG OF PEPPERMINT TEA still sat on the dining room table. Holding the phone's handset close to her chest, Erin glanced across the table at her own mug of tea. Obviously cold by now. Needed to be nuked or dumped in the sink. The salad dressings needed to be put away.

Unnerved by the moment, she jumped up and returned the phone to its charger, then grabbed the bottles of dressing and put them in the refrigerator. She dumped her tea into the sink, then gathered up the rest of the dirty dishes and ran hot water into the washtub. She squirted dish soap into it. Watched the beautiful white bubbles start to build.

Lord ... oh, Lord ...

Nervous energy flooded her system. First she'd do the dishes, then she'd clean out that dirty fridge. And if Cappy didn't call soon, she'd probably clean the entire kitchen.

It needed it.

⋆⋆⋆

LAST CHANCE, CHRIS. RUN AWAY right now and it'll only be a stupid prank.

The door creaked open.

Too late.

She froze solid. And stared through the screen door at the man who had opened the door.

Whoa.

She should have ran away when she had the chance.

Her mouth gaped. She blinked.

A mammoth stood in front of her. With only the flimsy screen door between them. A wooly mammoth. Whiskery jowls hung from his scowling face.

Chris backed up a step. Licked her lips. Then swallowed deeply.

The man spoke. "Are you lost?"

I certainly hope so. Chris cleared her throat. "Um, no, sir. I mean, I don't think so." She tried to smile. "I, um ... my name is Chris McIntyre. I work at the new gym. You know. Down on Kimberley Street?"

Nothing.

"I was just wondering ... if I could ... talk to Alaina?"

Through thick plastic-rimmed glasses, the man's brown eyes flickered. "Well, you know what, Chris McIntyre? Alaina's not going down to your gym anymore. I told her she couldn't go down there anymore."

Lightning bolted through Chris's entire body. "What? Wait a minute." Words spun in her brain. "Why? I mean, she really enjoys playing basketball."

The man started to push the door closed.

"Wait! You can't do this! Please, sir, can I just see her? I need to talk to her. Can I please just talk to her?"

The door opened wide. The man's head tilted as his eyes narrowed. He stepped forward, pushed the screen door open, and peered into Chris's face.

Chris grabbed the handrail as she stepped backward, but her foot found only air. It slammed down on the top step, shooting deep pains across her lower back. Gritting her teeth, she stared at the man's eyes. They seemed to be studying her. Studying her ... ears. First the right one, then the left.

She started to tremble as her heart raced, as heat flooded her cheeks.

"Well, I can see you got 'em." Squinting his eyes, he continued to peer through his thick glasses at Chris's ears. "One on each side of your head there. But do they work?" His eyes found hers. Drilled into her. "Did you hear what I just said? Hello?"

Paralyzed, Chris could only stare.

"She's not coming back to your gym, and you can't see her. Got that?" His gaze continued to bore into her as he waited for her response.

"Um ... okay."

The screen door slammed, then the main door.

Chris stood with one foot on the porch, one foot on the top step, gripping the handrail, staring at both closed doors, each of their slams echoing through her soul.

★★★

SLOWLY. ONE STEP. THEN ANOTHER. Backward. Down the steps. Her palm squeaked as it slid down the smooth metal handrail. She stared at those doors. Hoping they wouldn't open again. Praying they wouldn't open.

She reached the bottom step. The end of the railing. She breathed. Then tried not to gulp the air in.

So. Well. Okay. Mr. Walker was not a teddy bear.

Her eyes pinched shut. Air rushed in and out of her gaping mouth.

You need to leave, girl. You found out what you needed to know. And now you know. You were right.

But what about Alaina?

Go. Go now. Call Ben. Get his help.

Ever so slowly, she turned away from the house and walked down the broken concrete path to the sidewalk. She stopped to give the house one more glance, then lowered her head and stared at the ground beneath her feet as she headed for Kimberley Street. For Ben. For Erin. For home.

Three steps later, a shout grated through her.

"I SAID NO!"

She spun around. The shout came from Alaina's house.

More shouting. Chris couldn't hear the words, only the man's voice. Then a little girl's scream.

Across the yard, up the stairs, ripping open the screen door, bursting through the front door, Chris suddenly stood face-to-face with Alaina Walker's father, right in the middle of his living room.

★★★

WET DISHES DRIPPED INTO THE drainer. She'd let them drip a bit longer, then dry them and put them away. She'd use the tub full of sudsy water to wash the inside of the fridge. But she needed to empty the fridge first. Yes. She wrung out the dishrag and hung it over the edge of the sink. Then started pulling everything out of the refrigerator and stacking it on the counter.

She needed to make a grocery list. She needed to remind Scott again not to leave just a drop of juice in the carton. Why did he always insist on leaving that last drop?

She needed to throw away the leftover corn chowder from last week. Neither one of them would eat it. Neither one of them liked it that well the first night they ate it.

She needed to trust the Lord at that moment. To trust Him to protect Chris and Alaina and Cappy.

She really needed to hear that phone ring.

★★★

NO MORE DONUTS. EVER. CAPPY peered straight ahead as she ran. Since when did a four-block run leave her winded? What happened to the days when she could run four miles in combat boots and hardly break a sweat?

A half block in front of her ... that was Alaina's house, wasn't it? She hoped so. She squinted to focus.

Yes. Good.

But who just ran into it? Was it Chris?

Cappy's stomach tightened as she slowed to a stop and tried to catch her breath. *Ahh, Lord, if that was Chris running in like that ...*

She hesitated another second, then lifted the cell phone, pressed TALK, then the numbers 9-1-1.

★★★

ON THE FLOOR BESIDE HER, just to her right, curled up in a ball, Alaina Walker whimpered, her hands over her head, face hidden from her father.

Chris turned to glare into the man's eyes. The rage she saw there mirrored her own.

His broad shoulders lifted as he sucked in a deep breath. Loud curses suddenly ripped across the room. "What are you doing here?" Fists clenched, he took a step forward.

Chris raised her hands and held them out in front of her, palms out, fingers spread.

"Get out of my house!"

Teeth clenched, she forced them apart. "Back off, mister. I'm not going anywhere." The words wrenched her throat.

Bulging veins lined the man's forehead and neck. "Get out. NOW!"

Chris glared at him, yet softened her voice. "Alaina? Sweetheart? Come around behind me, right now, and get out of here."

"Don't you talk to my daughter."

The child didn't move.

"Alaina? Come on now. I need you to get up." Chris took a step to her right, trying to situate herself between the father and daughter. "Get up, Alaina. Now! Run out of here!"

The child's father pressed his lips into a firm line. "She won't listen to you. She knows what she'll get if she does."

Bile burned Chris's throat. She struggled to swallow it.

"The question is, missy, if you don't listen to me, what will *you* get?" The man's upper lip curled in a vicious sneer.

Icy fear slipped into the rage searing Chris's blood. Keeping her left hand up and her eyes on the man's chest, she reached blindly behind her hoping to connect with Alaina's arm, to grab the girl and pull her quickly out the door.

The man's fist flashed toward Chris's face.

Leaning back just enough, she dodged it, then stared. Stunned. A strong right hook out of nowhere.

The man was quick.

Stunned stupid. The backhand caught her square on her right cheek. Turned her knees to jelly. Sent her sprawling away from Alaina across the living room floor.

★★★

WITH ISAIAH'S CELL PHONE PLASTERED to her ear and the 9-1-1 dispatcher hanging on her every word, Cappy regretted the string of curses she let fly when she heard the back of the big man's fist connect with Chris's face. Spanish curses. One after the other after the other.

But then the man turned his gaze—and the full force of his rage—toward her. Through the screen door, Cappy felt skewered by the man's eyes.

She heard a whimper. A little girl's whimper. Alaina. Weeping.

Then a voice in her ear. "Ma'am? Are you there?"

"Um, yeah. I'm still here. And you'd better get someone here right now." She pushed the TALK button to end the call and slipped the phone into the front pocket of her jeans.

The man still glared at her.

Cappy whispered a Spanish prayer, then pulled open the screen door and slowly stepped inside the house.

★★★

TEARS. THE STUFF ON HER cheek? Had to be tears. The man flat-out rung her bell. It was still ringing. She allowed herself a few tears. But enough to wet her entire cheek?

She willed her hand up to wipe them away. Blinked. Something thick, sticky, smeared across the back of her hand. She pulled it away to look. Blinked. Struggled to focus.

40

Blood.

Ahh, man! The fool cut me!

She rubbed her eyes. Heard the man shouting. Then someone shouting back at him. A very upset woman. Alaina's mom? Not unless she spoke Spanish. This irate woman was shouting in Spanish. Sounded almost like one of Cappy's tirades in the desert. Chris suddenly wanted to laugh.

Cappy Sanchez on the rampage. All hands, stand clear. This means you.

Wait a minute. That voice.

Chris shook her head to clear it, blinked to focus, then gazed at her friend.

Cappy? What are you doing here?

Ears ringing, she pushed herself up to stand. Blinking deeply, she shifted her gaze from Cappy to Alaina to Alaina's dad, then back to Cappy again.

Cappy's glance Chris's way lasted only a second. "You okay, girl?"

Chris lifted shaking hands and ran her fingers through her hair, pushing it back away from her face. "Never better. You?"

Cappy's eyes fixed on Alaina's dad. "I don't know. Things seem a little . . . loco around here."

Chris glared at him as well. The man's face shone brilliant purple.

"He's quick, Cap."

"So I saw."

"Get Alaina out of here."

As if ignited by the words, Alaina's dad took a step toward his daughter, but Cappy fell to the floor on top of the child, covering her completely. Chris stepped closer but could only watch as Alaina's dad lifted his foot and stomped it down over Cappy's back.

That did it. Chris ran and jumped on the man's back, hooked her feet around his waist, then dug her forearm into his throat, so tight his whiskery jowls fell over her entire arm.

He grabbed at her and bucked backward, but Chris held on. He stumbled backward and slammed her against the wall by the dining room table. Something jabbed into her shoulder as the back of her head smacked the wall, as the man's head butted the corner of her eyebrow. Eyes pinched shut, she held on. His elbow connected with her ribs. Breath gushed out of her. Connected again. And again.

Breathless, insane with rage, Chris held on.

The man finally swayed. Then fell to one knee. He pulled at Chris's arm, but still she held on. He swung his elbow back once more, though it carried half the force of his previous blows. Hands flailing, he slowly toppled backward.

Hitting the floor beneath him, his weight crushed whatever breath remained in Chris's lungs. Stunned, she felt one last slap on her arm. Then nothing. The man fell limp, his arms flopped out to his sides.

Desperate for air, Chris unhooked her arm from his throat and struggled to push herself out from under him. Finally free, gasping, coughing, she knelt beside him, then lowered her ear against his chest. Over her own pounding heart, loud thumps radiated across the man's sternum. She lifted her head, closed her eyes for a second, then reached up to slap the man's face. "Wake up, you fat jerk." Her words shook as she trembled. She slapped him again. "Come on. Wake up and breathe."

Cappy slowly lifted herself off Alaina.

"You okay?" Chris could only whisper the words.

Cappy reached around to rub her back. Then winced. "He kicked me!"

Yes, he certainly did. Chris slapped the man's cheek hard.

"I can't believe it. He actually kicked me!"

Her hand shook. *Please, God, don't make me have to breathe for him.*

"Oh, man, he is gonna live to regret that!"

A cough. The downed mammoth sucked in a ragged breath.

"He is gonna live, isn't he?"

Another cough.

"Yeah, Cap. He's gonna live."

Deep down, Chris despised each breath the vile man once again breathed into his lungs. She closed her eyes and pushed away from him as he coughed, as he slowly reached up to rub his neck.

Yes. Some things were unforgivable.

And some people just didn't deserve to breathe.

"It's all right, Alaina. Easy now, sweetheart."

Hearing Cappy's voice, Chris forced her eyes open. It was difficult. Winding down, her rage spent, the room spun as fifty different hurts screamed for attention.

"You're all right, kiddo. Shh. Don't be afraid. It's over."

"Call the police, Cappy." The words took all Chris's strength. Her eyes squeezed shut.

"Already did. They should be here any minute."

Okay. Whatever you say. Any minute. Good.

"Ahh ... it's all right, sweet one."

Cappy's soothing voice did little to comfort the crying child.

"Is she all right?" Chris again forced her eyes to open. "Alaina? Sweetheart? Are you all right?"

In Cappy's tight embrace, Alaina lifted her eyes over Cappy's shoulder to meet Chris's gaze. The misery reflected on the girl's swollen face cut Chris to the bone.

But then, as tears coursed down her cheeks, the child gazed at Chris and ever so slowly smiled.

Mouth gaping, Chris tried to return it, but tears flooded her eyes, spilled down her face, dripped into the cut on her cheek and burned.

She pulled her shirt up and wept into it, then quickly used it to wipe her face.

Over the ringing in her ears, over Cappy's comforting words, she heard it. In the distance, growing ever louder, a siren wailed.

★★★

SHE PULLED A JAR OF strawberry jelly from the refrigerator and placed it on the counter next to the jar of mayonnaise. Her back ached, yet she quickly grabbed the bottles of maple syrup and ketchup and placed them on the counter too. Then the eggs. And the juice. The dumb juice. She pushed the fridge door closed, lifted a glass from the dish drainer, and poured the last few drops into the glass before crushing the carton and tossing it in the garbage. She leaned against the counter and sipped the tangy sweet liquid. Pink grapefruit juice cocktail had always been her favorite.

She glanced at the phone. Then forced her breaths to steady. Her baby kicked against her ribs, reminding her that she, or he, preferred to have Mommy relaxed and comfortable. Erin closed her eyes and whispered prayers for her little one, for her heart to slow its mad race, for her friends out there facing who knew what. She whispered the words aloud, yet spoke so quickly they made little sense even to her own ears. After a deep breath, she looked down and slowly rubbed her belly. "I know, my sweet little babe. I'm sorry Mommy's upset. But she'd feel much better if Cappy would only call her." She almost laughed. "Please be patient with me, my precious little one. Mommy's sorry. It'll be all right soon."

Her bottom lip trembled as she sipped the last of the juice.

Please, Lord, let it be true.

The refrigerator motor seemed to roar in protest as Erin pulled the door open again and grabbed what remained on the top shelf. She lowered everything to the counter and stopped, straining to hear the eerie sound that floated in the air over the fridge motor's hum. Far away. Yet getting louder. Closer.

A police siren.

Her eyes closed as she leaned forward and thumped her forehead against the cabinet door above her.

Lord . . . oh, God my Father . . . please . . .

★★★

Cars skidded to a stop outside. Red and blue lights strobed across the walls of the Walker's dining room. Chris slowly raised her eyes to watch them. Mesmerized.

Cappy still spoke softly to Alaina, trying to comfort her, trying to convince her the worst was over. Alaina still cried, sniffled, though her whimpering had eased.

Her father lay still on his back, eyes wide under his thick glasses, dazed. Maybe he too was mesmerized by the flashes of red and blue strobing across the walls of his house.

Chris couldn't move. Didn't want to move. Didn't even want to think about what might happen when the police walked up those stairs and looked into the house.

Movement to her right caught her eye. She turned her head. Saw a pair of shiny black shoes. Slowly lifted her gaze. Saw sharply creased navy blue trousers. A black leather utility belt. A holstered 9mm pistol. Handcuffs. Baton. Sharply creased navy blue shirt. A shiny badge. A name tag, but the letters were too small for her to read them. A man's face. A scowl. Brown eyes that quickly surveyed the room. Then met her gaze.

"What happened here?"

Her brain refused to process the question, let alone formulate an answer.

The officer turned to peer down at Cappy.

"We need to get this child out of here," Cappy said, her voice still quiet and soft. "Is an ambulance on the way? She needs to be checked out."

The officer grabbed the microphone by his collar and mumbled something about needing a bus at this location.

Yes. A bus. Chris looked away. *We definitely need a bus.*

"What do we got, Jim?"

Chris didn't bother to turn her head again to look.

"Domestic incident. Let's get the girl out of here."

"What about him?"

She glanced at Alaina's dad. His eyes blinked as he still appeared dazed.

"Who knows." Louder now. "Are you all right, sir?"

The officer loomed over Walker. Chris looked up at him.

"Is he all right?" the officer asked her. "What happened here?"

Chris swallowed. "He may have a sore throat. But he should be all right."

"Are you all right?"

How she hated that question. "Never better. You?"

The officer's brown eyes hardened.

"Um, sorry, sir. Yes. I'm fine." Gritting her teeth, Chris pushed up to sit straighter against the wall.

"What's wrong with him?"

"Sleeper hold."

"What?"

Walker started to move, started to roll, to push himself up.

"Stay still, sir."

Chris blinked. Glanced toward the door. The other officer, creased trousers and all, stood over Cappy and Alaina, trying to convince the girl to release her fierce grip around Cappy's neck. Alaina didn't seem at all interested in letting Cappy go.

"I said, stay still. Sir?"

Her eyes shifted.

Walker had rolled over onto his side, facing her, his eyes once again reflecting rage.

A spurt of terror lit up Chris's belly.

The officer tried to grab the man's arm to pull him back down to the floor away from Chris, but Walker had other ideas. He grabbed at Chris's foot. She pulled it away, but not far enough. He reached again and locked on to it, then pulled her toward him.

She let out a shriek.

The officer shouted for the man to relax, to release his grip. The man did not comply. In a tangle of arms and legs, Chris was suddenly caught in an ever-tightening net, grabbing at her, pulling her closer to the man's now flying fist. Trying to dodge it, her new collection of aches and bruises screamed at her from every direction.

The officer shouted a command that Walker only cursed away. His fist caught Chris's shoulder. His other hand held her wrist, twisting it.

Chris desperately tried to kick free, until hands grabbed her from behind and pulled her away. Grateful to be free, she tried to set her feet under her so she could stand, but the hands that had freed her now would not let her up. Roughly flipped over and tossed to the floor, Chris barely turned her head in time to avoid breaking her nose. Her sore cheek thumped off the carpeted floor. Stars sparked across the sudden blackness of her miserable existence.

She tried to draw in a breath. Felt like someone was standing on her back. She opened her eyes and blinked, but saw nothing through her mess of tangled hair. She heard Cappy shouting. Then a man's shout. Grunting. Walker's shout. More grunting. More shouting.

Oh, Jesus, please help me. What is … ? Cappy! What's happening?

As hard as she tried, she could not draw in a decent breath. On her stomach on the floor, her arms had been pulled behind her. She started to pull them back. Terror sliced through her so viciously, she gagged.

Her wrists were pinned. She pulled desperately to free them. Sharp pain across both wrists forced her to stop.

Handcuffed!

Oh, God! Oh, God! No!

★★★

"Don't do that. Stop it! Let her go!" On her knees, Cappy squeezed Alaina against her and tried not to yell in the girl's ear. "She didn't do anything. You don't have to arrest her."

A hand touched her shoulder. Startled, she turned her head. Two more officers stood at the door.

"Give us a minute to sort everything out, ma'am." The African-American officer squeezed Cappy's shoulder. "Let my partner take the child outside."

"Yes." She shifted her gaze to the female officer. Gave her a strained smile. Then turned back to Alaina and gently pushed her away. She kissed the girl's forehead. "Go with her, sweetheart. It's okay."

The female officer opened her arms to Alaina, and after a moment's hesitation, Alaina went to her.

Trying not to wince, Cappy forced herself up from the floor. She let out a deep sigh as the officer led the child by the hand down the stairs and away from the house.

The African-American officer pulled a small notebook from his shirt pocket. "Can you tell me what happened here, ma'am?" He glanced at Cappy, then began to write. "What is your name?"

A hint of kindness radiated from him. Cappy absorbed it, then looked at Chris. "Please don't arrest her. She didn't do anything!"

"All right, I hear you. But I need you to tell me what happened."

"I'll tell you what happened." Cappy bit her lower lip to keep from cussing. "She just saved that little girl. That's what happened."

✯✯✯

Breathe breathe breathe . . .

No use. What little air she could force into her lungs seemed to laugh at her. On her stomach, her lungs refused to fill. She coughed to clear her throat, then desperately swallowed to keep from throwing up.

She pulled on her wrists. The metal cuffs bit into her skin. Her shoulders stiffened. Started to cramp.

God, I can't—I can't take this!

Cappy's voice reached her, mixed in with all the other voices, commands, questions, curses. She tried to see what was happening, but her stupid hair covered her face. She tried to blow it out of her eyes, but couldn't draw in enough air.

Breathe breathe . . . breathe! Do it!

Oh, God . . . God, help me! Somebody!

✯✯✯

THEY NEEDED MORE CHEESE. SEEMED like they went through a lot of swiss cheese. Chris liked swiss. But sharp cheddar worked best for Erin.

She glanced at the phone.

The sirens had stopped, only to start again. Three, as far as she could tell. Not far away. Somewhere in Kimberley Square.

Enough. She slammed the fridge door closed, grabbed the phone, checked Isaiah's number, punched it in, then waited, praying to hear Cappy's familiar voice drenched in that glorious Hispanic attitude say, *"Hola, mamacita!"*

★★★

OUTSIDE, AT THE FOOT OF the stairs leading up to the Walker's front porch, Cappy's teeth ground. How could she make this nice policeman understand? She needed to be back in that house, to pull Chris out of there, to make them take off those filthy handcuffs. She tried again to go back up the stairs, but the officer—Richardson, it said on his name tag—stopped her. She glared at him.

"Ms. Sanchez, please, is there anything else you can tell me?"

She wanted to scream her reply. "I told you everything. And I'll tell you again. You don't need to handcuff her. Or arrest her. She didn't do anything wrong!"

"All right, all right. Let us sort this out first."

She turned away from the officer just as a strange ringing suddenly shattered the moment. Heart pounding, she looked down at the front pocket of her jeans, then reached inside and pulled out Isaiah's cell phone. Punched TALK. "Um ... hello?"

"Cappy?"

Erin. A deep swallow. "Um, hey there, *mamacita.*"

"Cappy, what's going on? I've been waiting to hear from you. Is everything all right?"

"Um ..." She glanced around. "Well ..."

"Cappy?"

"Let's just say ... it could have been worse." She walked a few steps into the Walker's front yard. "But don't worry, lady. We're all ... fine." Not very convincing. This wasn't going well.

"Cappy, please tell me the truth."   •

"Um . . . well . . ." She kicked the grass. "Erin, now, don't worry. Okay? Alaina is all right, and I'm all right . . . but I think it would be a good idea if you called Ben and Sonya. Have them come over to be with you. I'll call you in a little while. Okay?"

Ten seconds of silence. "Cappy, what happened?"

"Um . . . Erin . . . I think Chris has been . . . arrested." Cappy grimaced. "But she'll be all right. I'll make sure they take good care of her. It's all just a big mistake. Erin? Do you hear me?"

A full minute of silence.

Cappy peered up at the sky. Brilliant blue patches shone through the gray puffy clouds.

"Cappy?"

"Yeah?"

"Is she all right?"

Her eyes pinched shut as she lied. "Yeah, Erin. She's . . . fine." Her voice shook. "It's just a misunderstanding. We'll be home later. After we get it all figured out."

Silence.

"Erin? Try not to worry, okay? I have to go."

"Come home as soon as you can."

"We will."

"Call me. Okay?"

"Yeah. I will, Erin."

The line went dead.

Cappy pressed TALK to end the call, then wanted to crush the phone in her fist. She looked out toward the street where, in the back-seat of a police cruiser, her little nine-year-old friend sat crying beside the officer who tenderly cradled the child against her shoulder.

Cappy turned her gaze toward the house. The officers inside still leaned over Alaina's dad. Chris still lay on her stomach, hand-cuffed, on the floor.

"Ahh, girl . . ." The words left Cappy's lips in a whisper. "Give her strength, Jesus. Please. Give her strength."

THREE

SO LONG AGO. YET, WHEN it returned, it always felt like yesterday. The memories so vivid. The pain so real. So many days and nights spent lying on her stomach, trying to sleep, trying to heal. The deep throbbing fire across her entire back. So many horrible cuts, so many days of unbearable misery, so many nights of horrific dreams. Waking up screaming in terror, then screaming in agony, all of it so deeply rooted in the farthest reaches of her soul. She had tried to let it go, so many times. Had prayed so hard, had believed ... yet, at that moment, lying on her stomach on the floor of the Walker's living room, hands cuffed behind her, all of it came rushing back. Swept panic over her entire body with the force of a grand mal seizure. Churned her stomach into a frothy mess that threatened to explode any second.

God, please, God. Lord God. Please ...

Behind her, scuffling sounds, sounds of a struggle, the two police officers again worked to subdue Alaina's father over the curses he vented at them. His shouts, their shouts, more cursing ... something kicked her leg. Another kick. A shout. "Stop it, sir! Settle down! Get the cuff on him!"

"I'm trying!"

"Please?"

Did she speak the word aloud? She had opened her mouth and felt the word squeeze through her pinched throat, but did the word find voice? Did they hear it?

"What's your name, sir?"

Curses.

"Get him up."

"Yeah, right. Richardson, get in here!"

Chris pulled against the cuffs around her wrists. Tried to roll onto one shoulder so she could pull her feet up, to keep the men from stepping on her. Pressure on her shoulder built. She forced the word out again. "Please? Sir?"

"On three. Get him up. Watch his feet, Ray. Don't let him kick you."

Violent curses tore through her. Alaina's father's curses. Then a few of her own. She needed to get up. She worked herself up to her knees.

"Stay down, ma'am!"

Hands pushed her back to the floor.

"Don't move. Stay still."

"Please, I can't—!"

"Richardson!"

I can't take this! God, please, help me. Let me up!

"Sir, stop it now. Relax. I'm not telling you again." Grunting. A loud sigh of relief. "Just relax now. We'll take him in, Ray. Where's the girl?"

"With Mallory."

The voices and curses quieted as the men left the house.

Grinding her forehead into the carpet, Chris pushed back up to her knees. Hands on her back again forced her to the floor.

"Ma'am, I need you to stay down."

She bit back a scream. "I can't! Officer, please!"

"Just another second. Lay still."

"Please ..." Bile choked her. She coughed it up, then tried to swallow it down. Groaned.

"What is wrong with you? Just relax!"

Her mind spun. "I can't—please, sir, let me up. Please."

Hands grabbed her upper arm and almost pulled it out of its socket as she was lifted to her feet. Her knees immediately gave out.

"Stand up!"

Nausea roiled through her, dropped her to her knees. "Oh, God ..."

"All right. It's all right, ma'am. Just relax." The cop softened his grip on her arm.

Violent trembling shook her words. "I'm s—sorry, s—sir."

"It's all right. Try to control your breathing."

His command didn't make sense. Until she heard her breaths rushing in and out of her mouth. Too much air. Yet she couldn't get enough.

God . . . I'm sorry . . . please . . . help me . . .

"Sloan!"

The shout ripped through her. Her eyes pinched shut.

"Get in here. Quick. And bring your kit."

Breathe, breathe . . .

Trembling overtook her, clouded her mind, her complete existence. Still on her knees, she swayed, struggling against the bile burning her throat. Cold sweat broke out across her forehead, sending prickly chills racing through her entire body.

"Easy now. I've got you."

Gentle hands touched her back and shoulders.

"Take the cuffs off."

"Not a chance."

"Please . . ." The word barely escaped her throat. Another deep swallow.

The man beside her pressed his fingertips into the side of her neck. "It's all right. Try to relax for me. It's all right."

Chris clung to his soft voice, to each word he said.

"What's wrong with her?"

"She's all right. Just a little . . . overwhelmed. Take the cuffs off."

"Will she behave?"

"She's spent, Ray. What damage can she do?"

"She's done plenty already."

No . . . No more. Chris tried to lift her head. She couldn't. She sank down farther to the floor. Gentle arms caught her.

"Richardson, take off the cuffs."

Chris waited. Breathing. In and out. Ringing in her ears. Yet, she heard only silence — unbearable silence — for what seemed like forever.

"Ray."

"All right, all right. Whatever you say, Doc."

Clinking sounds. Her hands fell free. Relief trickled through her.

"Help me get her up. Let's get her to the couch."

Lifted to her feet, suspended between them, Chris tried to keep her feet under her as the men walked her to the couch. They slowly lowered her into it. Her eyes refused to focus. Her mouth gaped, gulping in the air. A hot tear slid down her cheek. She couldn't lift her hand to wipe it away.

"Yeah. She's all right. Thanks, Ray."

Rubber-gloved hands eased back the hair from her face. The rubber caught on the sweaty strands and pulled a bit. She struggled to keep her eyes open.

"Yeah. There we go."

"You'll be okay with her? I need to see what's happening outside."

"Sure. We'll be just fine."

Something suddenly covered her mouth and nose. She flinched back.

"Whoa, it's all right. Just a paper bag. Breathe into it. It'll help you breathe."

The bag covered her mouth again. Chris blinked slowly, watching the bag inflate and deflate with every breath. Quickly at first. Too quickly. Then, more slowly.

"That's it. Good."

Such a gentle, soothing voice. She squinted. Focused on the man's face.

His eyes met hers. A smile. "Hi there. I'm Jason."

Pale blue eyes. Soft. The bag inflated. Deflated. Inflated again.

"See? Didn't I tell you? That's better, isn't it? Just try to relax. I need for you to relax." His fingertips pressed again into the side of her neck. "Just try to calm down. That's it." After another minute, he pulled the bag away. "There. That's better."

Chris licked her lips, then tried to pull in a deep breath. Couldn't. Not at all. "Need to get out of here."

His eyes pierced her soul. "I know." He barely nodded. "But give it another second."

"No. Out of this house. Please."

"All right. Do you think you can walk?"

She nodded.

"Just a second. I'm going to put my kit outside. We'll go out and sit on the porch. Okay?"

She nodded. It was all she could do. She waited for him to come back. It took more than a few seconds.

"All right. Let's get out of here."

She forced her hands up to wipe the muck from her eyes and nose, the sweaty hair from her forehead. She winced. Her entire face hurt.

"Careful. Here." He handed her some tissues.

Chris wiped her eyes again, then blew her nose. The effort intensified the throbbing across her cheek.

"Are you sure you can walk?"

"Yeah." She stuffed the tissues into the front pocket of her jeans, then grabbed the man's proffered hand and allowed him to pull her out of the couch. To steady her.

"Not too fast. Just stand here a second."

Ignoring his last words, Chris pushed her feet toward the door. Outside, on the porch, she hung her head, dared not look at the swirling red and blue lights, at the chaos she had caused. She sat on the top step of the porch and closed her eyes, relishing the cool air on her face. Tried not to gulp it into her lungs.

"Easy now, or I'll have to get the bag back out."

She almost smiled.

"I'm gonna get touchy-feely here for a second. All right?"

"Yeah."

He palpated Chris's entire head. His fingers found every sore spot. "Let me take a look at your eyes." A click. "Just try to relax."

A pinpoint of light shot across her right eye. She flinched. Then across her left eye. She flinched again. Couldn't help it.

"All right. That's good. How's your headache?"

She blinked. Made a face.

"I bet. Any double vision?"

"No." A croak.

"Good." He reached into his kit and pulled out a blood pressure cuff.

Chris watched him wrap the cuff around her upper arm, then lift the stethoscope to his ears. He pumped the ball and the cuff tightened against her arm. She turned her watery gaze to take in the scene out on the street. Felt her pulse throb under her bicep. Saw an ambulance. Two police cars. Heard air hiss from the cuff. She blinked deeply, then squinted to focus. Cappy sat in the front seat of one of the cars, turned, looking into the backseat.

Alaina. Please, God, let her be all right.

Lights flashing, the first police cruiser took off down the street. Alaina's dad sat in the back, his head low.

What's gonna happen to him, Lord? She watched the car disappear around the corner. Wondered why she even cared enough to ask.

Velcro ripped, startling her. Her heart thumped as she watched the paramedic wrap up the BP cuff and stuff it back in his kit. "Will I live?" Almost a whisper.

He looked up, relaxed a bit, and smiled. "I'm sure of it."

Chris let out a weary laugh.

The man's smile faded. "I'm gonna work a bit on that cut on your cheek. Is that all right?"

"Yeah." The word almost didn't carry to her own ears.

"It's pretty deep." His gloved fingers dabbed a cold alcohol pad against her skin. "How'd it happen?"

Hey, I dodged the first one, didn't I? "Caught a backhand."

His wide eyes met hers. "He hit you?"

Chris only nodded. And gazed at the face a few inches from her own. "What did you say your name was?"

"Jason."

She glanced down at the name tag on his uniform. "Sloan."

"Yep, that's right."

The alcohol burned. She winced.

"Sorry."

"Don't be." She watched him as he worked. Studied his face. His dark brown hair. Thick dark eyebrows. Purposeful crop of three-day whiskers around his upper lip and chin. His smooth, fine lips. His long eyelashes. His gentle blue eyes. That suddenly caught her in the act. She looked away. Almost smiled. And said, "You've got a nice outside jump shot."

The man paused his work. His face softened with a smile. "I thought I knew you. You run the new gym for that church."

"You could say that." His smile filtered through her, warming her entire being.

"You've got a nice jump shot yourself. But you need to work on your defense. It's pitiful."

A breath burst through her lips. Her head throbbed with the exertion. She waited for it to ease. "I always thought basketball should be like football."

"What. Let someone else play the defense?"

"Yeah."

Jason Sloan laughed as he returned to his work, carefully cleaning the dried blood and dirt from the cut on Chris's cheek.

Chris closed her eyes, grateful for his gentle touch, and let the pleasant sound of his laughter settle her soul.

★★★

"Is she gonna be all right?"

Busy placing another butterfly bandage over the swollen cut on the woman's battered face, Jason didn't stop to look at his friend, Ray Richardson. Sugar Ray, everyone called him. Including his mommy, no doubt. Jason just called him Ray. Policeman Ray. Among other things. He pushed on the bandage to secure it. Eyes closed, the woman didn't move.

"Sloan?"

"Yep. She'll be fine."

"I need a statement from her."

"Not right now. I need to get her to the hospital." He wasn't surprised to see the woman's dark brown eyes fly open.

"Yeah. I figured that. We need to take the girl. So, we'll meet you there."

"Okay."

Those dark eyes stared at him. A whisper. "I don't need to go to the hospital."

Jason glanced over his shoulder, saw Ray walking away, then turned back to the woman in front of him. He leaned in closer. "If I don't take you, he will. He needs his statement."

"I'll give it to him. I'll tell him everything. But I don't need to go to the hospital."

"Chris?" A woman's voice.

Those dark eyes shifted. Jason wanted to smile. Chris. He thought that was her name.

"Cappy, what are you doing here?"

"You okay, girl?"

The two women embraced, then sat beside each other on the top step. Jason gathered up his garbage, pulled off his gloves, and closed his kit.

"You look terrible. You're going to the hospital, aren't you? Yes, you are. You're taking her, aren't you?"

He looked up at the friend. "Yes, I am. We should actually be going."

"Good. We're going too."

"How's Alaina?" Chris asked.

"She'll be all right. The paramedic said she had some old bruises, but nothing looking new. At least as far as he could tell. Mainly, she's just scared. They'll check her out real well at the hospital." After a second, the friend reached up and pulled Chris's head to her own. "She'll be fine, girl. Thanks to you."

"Cappy . . ."

"Believe it."

"Why are you here?"

Jason busied himself with his kit. Tried not to eavesdrop, but knew it was impossible.

"Erin called me."

"What? Is she all right? Where is she?"

"She's at home. And she's all right. Look, don't worry. None of this was your fault. Go to the hospital and get checked out. I'll see you there, okay?"

Jason watched Chris's face. His gut wrenched at the anguish he saw there.

"Take good care of her, all right?" Cappy flashed a smile at Jason before taking off down the stairs.

"I will." He gave Chris a small grin.

Yes, ma'am, I certainly will.

★★★

CHRIS COULD ONLY WATCH AS Cappy hurried across the Walker's yard to the police car parked in the street. Cappy climbed in the front seat. The car sped away, lights flashing.

A paramedic slowly stepped up the stairs. "What's up, Jase? Are we ready to go?"

Chris looked at Jason, saw his eyes gazing back at her. "You ready to take a trip?" he said.

Dread sickened her. Her eyes fell closed as her head lowered.

"Hey, come on. It won't be so bad." A pause. "Yeah, Coop, we'll be down in a second."

"All right."

She wanted to dry up into a tiny wisp and blow away on the breeze.

Jason's hand touched her knee. His fingertips gently raised her chin. "Wanna know a secret?"

She blinked open her eyes.

"In the ER nurses' lounge, in the freezer, they've got a box of fudgesicles. They're so good. I could eat the whole box myself. Let's go get us one."

Chris shook her head. "I don't want to go to the hospital."

Jason nodded slowly. "I know. But I'm afraid, at this point, you don't have a choice. If we don't take you to the hospital, we'll have to take you to the police station."

"Take me to the station, then. Please."

"You don't want a fudgesicle?" His eyes widened with feigned shock.

She wanted to bury her face in her hands and weep.

"Hey. Come on. We'll sneak in the back door. Head straight for the lounge. I know a fudgesicle will do you good. Call it good medicine." Jason held his hand out, palm up.

Chris stared at his hand. Then gazed up into his eyes.

"Shall we?"

She lifted her hand and placed it in his. Felt the warmth of his touch flow through her. Then the warmth of his smile.

★★★

No doubt about it. She was hurt.

The way her breath caught as he helped her stand, the way she swayed, then clenched her teeth as she stepped down the stairs. The walk down to the bus, then lifting her foot to climb into the back.

Jason wanted five minutes alone with the man who did this to her. That fat slob. That precious little girl—what was her name? Alaina? What a beautiful name. Beautiful kid. That fat slob's daughter. Terrorized. Crying in Mallory's arms.

Chris on her knees. Handcuffed like a criminal.

Some calls really grated his gut.

This was turning out to be one of those calls.

He guided Chris to the stretcher in the back of the ambulance and helped her ease down into it. Again, her breath caught. Until she lay back. Rested her head on the pillow. Finally let herself relax. A long, slow breath. Pushed out through clenched teeth.

Coop crawled in the driver's seat and slammed his door shut. "We ready?"

"Yeah," Jason said. "Take it slow, bro."

"You got it."

Chris's eyes were closed. Stayed closed.

Jason rubbed his face, then ran his fingers through his hair.

The ambulance pulled away from the curb.

He turned to look out the back window. Sometimes, after a call like this, it helped to see the crime scene fade as they drove away. Sometimes, nothing helped. He'd have to live with the pain in his gut. At least until the next call.

He noticed another police car had pulled up to the scene. They would secure the area until all the details had been hashed out, all statements and evidence collected. The house finally disappeared as the ambulance turned the corner. The police cruiser's flickering lights remained, reflecting in the windows of the neighbors' houses. Off the chrome bumpers of the neighbors' cars.

Jason turned his gaze back to the woman lying on his stretcher and wasn't surprised that her eyes were still closed, her head turned away from him. He knew she didn't want to talk about anything at that moment. At least not to him.

He reached into a built-in cooler and pulled out two small bottles of water and a hinged straw. He twisted off the cap of one of the bottles, pushed the straw down into it, then barely touched the back of her hand with it.

Her eyes opened at the touch. Her head turned.

He held up the water and she took it, saying thank you with a tiny press of her lips. He gazed at her lips a second longer, full and soft and the prettiest pink. He twisted off the cap of his own bottle and drank deeply. The cold water tasted sweet. Seemed to wash away the bitter taste of that house, of that first moment he gazed into this woman's bruised and bleeding face, at those dark brown eyes so full of terror. And pain.

His job. Every day. Always the terror and the pain. But this day . . .

"Thank you, Jason."

Her soft words startled him. "For what?"

"For your silence."

He studied those eyes. Barely smiled.

Chris stared at the bottle of water in her hand.

The bus rumbled on.

★★★

TRUE TO HIS WORD, JASON led Chris through a back door into the Emergency Room at Good Samaritan Hospital. His left hand gently at her elbow, he walked closely beside her, using his right hand to protect her from the swarms of people waiting for care, from the hurrying nurses and doctors trying their best to keep up with the flow. Chris let Jason lead her, concentrated only on breathing, trying not to notice the foul stench of hospital air.

It wasn't that Good Sam smelled bad. All hospitals, even the ones she had trained in and worked in, carried the stench of misery deep to Chris's soul.

Jason's hand on her arm. The warm glow radiating from it. Chris concentrated on that warmth. Kept her head low. Didn't look at anyone as she walked.

Deep in her heart, she trembled. She hoped, prayed, begged, and pleaded to the Lord—Erin's husband, Scott, worked at this hospital. He was here, just upstairs—if she saw him, if he saw her, at that very moment, she would die. Literally die.

Oh, Lord . . . I know Rinny's already called him.

Past the swarms of people, the bustle of the ER, Jason led her to a room halfway down a darkened hall. "Here we are," he said. He pushed open the door and looked inside. Then leaned back and gave Chris a smile. "Step into my office."

She walked into the room, relishing the silence and privacy as Jason closed the door. She sat in a chair at the table and pushed away a few magazines, then stared at the reddish bruises around her wrists.

Jason shut the freezer door, tore off a fudgesicle's wrapper, then presented the brown bit on a stick to her with overabundant flair. "For you."

She smiled and accepted it. "Thanks."

"I love these things." He sat beside her at the table and pulled his from the wrapper. "Somebody around here knows that. Every time the box gets low, somebody buys me another box."

Chris lifted hers for a bite. The freezing sweetness melted on her tongue, the pure ecstasy of the chocolate fudge carried her away.

Tears suddenly burned her eyes. She closed them quickly and rubbed her nose, holding her breath, trying to force the tears away. Heat rushed to her cheeks, enflamed her entire face. She blinked open her eyes and dared a glance at Jason. He sat beside her, to her left, facing the wall to her right. His jaw swished side to side as he seemed to be savoring his treat. He didn't look her way or say a word.

Chris swallowed deeply, then took another small bite of her fudgesicle. *Thank You, Lord*, whispered up from her soul.

Another bite of the frozen fudge, and she started to relax. The simple treat cooled her burning cheeks and throat, delighted her taste buds, carried her further and further away from the mess of her present moment.

Jason suddenly tossed his stick into a coffee mug half filled with someone's old coffee. He looked at Chris and grinned. "Didn't I tell ya? Don't you feel better? Medicine. That's what that is. Pure medicine."

Chris took another bite. And smiled as she savored it. Didn't look up at the man beside her. Couldn't.

"Well, I'm ready for another." He stood and rummaged through the freezer. "You?"

"Um, no." She forced strength into her voice. "Thanks. I'm still working on this one."

"Ahh. Yes. Patience is a good thing." He sat again at the table and tore his fudgesicle free of its wrapper. "But definitely something I lack. Especially when it comes to these things." He bit off a big chunk and grinned.

His grin was infectious. Chris returned it. Or tried to. Then allowed herself one quick glance down at his left hand.

She saw a simple gold wedding band.

Too bad.

The refrigerator kicked on. Its hum drifted across the room. Over the intercom, a doctor was paged to the OR. Chris thought again of Scott Mathis, MD. Wondered if all the good men were taken.

"How long have you played basketball? Since ... forever?"

She licked at a drip of fudge threatening to fall, then said, "Pretty much."

"My dad put a hoop out on our garage for my fifth birthday. It was the most awesome birthday present. Two years later he put up a huge light so we could play even after it got dark."

"That's cool."

"Yeah. My pop was cool."

Was? Chris glanced up.

"Do you have any brothers and sisters?"

A hint of wariness swept through her. She lifted her fudgesicle, said, "No," then took a big bite.

"Hmm. Too bad. I have three little sisters. They're the greatest."

She wanted to be polite and ask him about them, but didn't.

"Did you play basketball in high school?"

She almost choked as she tried to swallow. The sudden movement shot deep pains through her bruised ribs.

"You okay?"

She waited for breath to return. Barely nodded. Didn't raise her eyes.

Silence fell over the room. The refrigerator hummed. Voices filtered in from the hallway outside.

Chris finished her treat, but then didn't know what to do with the stick.

"Here, I'll take that."

She handed it to him, and he tossed it into the mug with his other one.

He turned toward her. "So. Did you?"

Chris licked her lips. "Did I what."

"Play basketball in high school."

Her heart started to pound. "No."

"Why not?"

She glanced at the door. The delightful sweetness lingering on her tongue started to sour.

"Man, I had so much fun in high school. Four years of varsity basketball. I played football and baseball too, but basketball's always been my favorite."

"I believe it. You're a good player." She only mumbled the words.

"Nah. Couldn't hack it in college. My high school was small. What did I know about big-time basketball? I tried to walk on, but didn't have a prayer of making the team."

Her hands started to shake. She pulled them under the table and clenched them into fists.

"Chris?"

She lifted her eyes.

"Are you all right?"

Her usual flippant reply to that vile question seemed out of place at the moment.

"You should get checked out."

"No."

"You need someone to stitch up your cheek, at least."

"No."

His eyes hardened. "Look, I know you're hurting." His studying gaze bore into her.

"I'm fine." She glanced again at the door.

"You're not fine."

She ground her teeth and looked away.

"You'll need to tell Ray you refused treatment, then."

"Fine."

"I know why you went into that house."

Her eyes quickly found his.

"I know what you did. And ... why you were so upset. Or ...
I think I do."

Bile burned through the last remaining remnant of the ice
cream in her throat. She swallowed deeply, forcing it down.

"Listen." A deep sigh. "Truth is, I don't know anything about
you. But, then again, maybe I do."

Her entire body tightened. Her headache throbbed. Breaths
quickened, keeping pace with her racing heart. She glanced again
at the door.

Silence filled the room. The refrigerator motor stopped. The
silence grew heavy.

Jason finished his fudgesicle and tossed the stick into the mug.
"How old were you ... when it happened?"

Chris's heart slammed to a stop. She knew her eyes were wide as
they gazed at Jason Sloan, yet she couldn't do anything about it.

He met her gaze. Slowly nodded.

Silence.

Lingering silence.

Jason's voice hardly broke it. "You were young, huh?"

Get out of here. You don't have to sit here. You don't—

"It's funny. Most of the time, it's the dad who's violent. At my
house, it was my mom."

Chris's mouth fell open.

Jason let out a laugh. "We loved it when she drank. She couldn't
hold her liquor one bit. It always knocked her out cold. That was
the only peace and quiet we had when she was around."

She couldn't slow her breaths. Or her heart.

"My dad was a great guy. When they divorced, we all begged
the judge to let us live with our dad. Mom didn't care. She wanted
to be free of us anyway."

She struggled to swallow.

Jason looked at her. His eyes softened. "Was it your dad?"

Screams ripped through her heart. *Who is this guy? Who does he think he is? Tell him to take off!* But yet, she focused on the man's gentle features. On his eyes. Such beautiful blue eyes. Concern, then pure empathy radiated from them. She could only stare. She had seen this much genuine concern only once before in her entire life. In another set of beautiful pale blue eyes. On the face of Erin Grayson Mathis.

Chris looked down, then barely—against all her better judgment, against everything in her system, against every word her own voice screamed at her—nodded.

The silence almost crushed her.

★★★

HE KNEW IT. THIS TIME, he was right. He wasn't always right. He wasn't too proud to admit when he was wrong. But this time, yes.

Yes, well, duh. It was only obvious. What he saw on this woman's face, in her eyes, it was as if she carried around a billboard the size of a Greyhound bus.

Though he wasn't always so willing to read the signs. Half the time, he hated to admit even to himself, he just didn't care about the people he helped every time he rolled out on a call.

So many calls. So many people with so many problems.

But this time...

Her hands shook as she reached up to rub her nose. She winced. But tried not to show it.

Jason's chest tightened. He hated watching her suffer. Seeing all her new bruises. And her old.

"Did she beat you?"

He almost didn't hear her words. Then wished he hadn't. "Not really. She *disciplined* us."

A questioning look.

"Technically, it wasn't a beating she gave out. She made that very clear. It was discipline. And we learned quickly. She didn't ... technically ... beat us."

"But she enjoyed it. And you still live with it. It still eats at you."

He wasn't sure he completely understood her meaning. Or

wanted to respond. He let out a deep sigh. "Sometimes."

Her eyes studied the table in front of her.

"You live with it. Don't you always?"

Her fingernail picked at a spot on the table. "I've learned to pray a lot."

Of course. She worked for the big church over on Kimberley Street. "Does it help?"

She nodded. Picked at that spot.

"How often . . . did he beat you?"

In a rush, she pushed away from the table and tried to stand, but lost her balance and fell back into the chair. Her eyes pinched shut. She leaned over and held her head in her hands.

Jason stood and reached out to her. She pulled away as soon as he touched her.

Slowly, he sat back down. Waited. Gave her time to decide her next move.

She took her time. Her breaths raced in and out of her open mouth.

Jason couldn't take it. "I'm sorry."

Breathless words. "Don't be."

"Please let me take you to get checked out."

"No."

"You may have a serious head injury. Or internal injuries. I'm worried about the way you're breathing."

"No."

"Chris, you need care!"

"No!" Her head turned. Her face burned with anger.

Jason found his own spot on the table to pick at. He stared at that spot, at the back and forth movement of his own fingernail, for what seemed like forever. He knew he couldn't sit here much longer. Coop would be looking for him. And Ray.

Yet, he didn't want to move. Didn't want to walk out on the woman beside him. He didn't want her to be hurting. Didn't want to hurt her. Didn't want to cause her more grief after everything she had been through.

So much at that moment he did not want.

He glanced at her left hand again. It bore no ring.

Maybe, what he really didn't want most of all was to have the woman beside him walk away, out of his life for good.

He thought about that. Really thought about it. And knew it was true.

★★★

"CAN I AT LEAST GET you some Tylenol?"

His words fell over her like a soft blanket. "Yes. That would be great."

"Give me a second." The paramedic stood and headed out the door.

Chris rubbed her temples. Tried to control her breathing. Dizzy with fatigue, all she wanted to do was go home and fall into bed.

No. She needed to see Erin first. *Oh, Lord Jesus, I need to see her. Please let her be all right. God, please. I'm so sorry about all this. Please help her be all right.* She dabbed her fingers at the thin bandages crossing the cut on her cheek. *Please don't worry, Rinny. Hear me. Please don't worry ...*

The door swung open. "Here we are." Jason held a bottle of water in one hand and a pack of Extra Strength Tylenol in the other. He handed them to her.

"Thank you so much." She accepted both with a smile. At least she hoped she smiled.

Jason sat beside her again. He waited as she tore open the pack, tossed the pills in her mouth, then chugged a long drink from the bottle. Afterward, he said, "I've got to go find Ray and tell him where we are. To find out what's going on. Stay here. You'll be fine here. Finish that. Drink it all. The bathroom's across the hall if you need it." He paused to smile. "I'll be back as soon as I can, okay?"

She swallowed one last time. Then nodded.

"Listen. I'm sorry I ..." His words ended, and he couldn't seem to find any more to say.

Chris wiped her lips with the back of her hand. Wanted to smile. "Do you know Scott and Erin Mathis?"

Jason's blue eyes widened. "Dr. Scott? Sure."

"You do?"

"Yeah. He's on duty today. I saw him earlier."

Chris tried to control the effect those words had on her. "You know his wife?"

"I've met her once, I think."

She smiled. "Okay. There's one very important thing she's taught me, among the bazillion things she's taught me since we first became friends. And now, I want to teach that one very important thing to you, Mr. Sloan."

His face reflected amused confusion. "Okay."

Chris paused a moment to organize her thoughts. "You see, when you care about someone—" She quickly bit her lip. "When you're *friends* with someone, you don't have to say you're sorry to them. Not for the dumb little things. Whatever you've said or done, if it's just a dumb little thing and you really didn't mean it, then it's okay. Don't say you're sorry. Unless you really need to say you're sorry. You know what I mean? Unless you did something really-really stupid and the word is really-really necessary. Then you've got to say it. Then it will mean what it's supposed to mean. Okay? Does that make sense?"

A grunt of laughter. "Um ... no."

Chris lowered her head and laughed.

Gentle fingertips raised her chin. "Yes." Jason's voice reached a sultry depth. "It makes perfect sense."

His smile melted Chris's heart all the way down to her toes.

"Doc Mathis has got a pretty smart wife. And you've got a pretty smart friend."

Tears rimmed her eyes. She tried to blink them away.

"I know where to find you, Chris. I won't let you get away." His fingertips brushed back her hair, tickled the side of her ear. Then he suddenly stood and walked out of the room.

Chris's mouth gaped. She slowly, so very slowly turned her head to stare at the door.

Um ... Lord? What just happened here?

In the man's absence, loneliness swept through her. It felt strange. Incredibly strange. Especially with that ring…

He's married, isn't he? Did he just make a pass at me? I think he did! Should I be freaked out? But I don't feel freaked out. I feel … I don't know. Strange.

But, then again, at that moment, what *didn't* feel strange? She leaned over the table and rested her head in her folded arms.

Oh, Lord. I'm sorry.

What a major mess. How could things have gotten so out of hand?

I should've listened to Rinny. None of this should've happened. Not like this. I'm so sorry.

Her loneliness swelled, then receded as quickly as it flooded her. Peace swept in and took its place. Complete peace. Quieted her soul. Her entire being. She closed her eyes. Gave in to her weariness.

My peace I give to you; not as the world gives do I give to you.

Real peace.

Thank You, Lord Jesus. I mean it. Alaina's gonna be all right. She's safe now. That's all that really matters. As long as Rinny's all right.

Sweet peace. As sweet as any fudgesicle.

She let herself laugh. One time. But it felt good to laugh. Especially with all that had happened. Especially with all she knew still lay ahead.

FOUR

DISHES STILL SITTING IN THE drainer, contents of the refrigerator still spread across the kitchen counter, Erin sat on the couch in her living room surrounded by concerned friends, engulfed in the warmth of their hugs and love. She waited again for her phone to ring, for news from Cappy or Chris or Scott. If it did ring, Ben Connelly would answer it. Or Sonya. Or maybe even Isaiah. Or Velda. Whoever wasn't sitting by Erin's side on the couch at that moment.

Ben and Sonya had arrived only minutes after Erin called them. Dropped everything to be with her. Not long after that, Isaiah Sadler called to ask why Cappy took off running down the street and why she had taken his new cell phone with her. And since she had taken off with his phone and Velda's burned-out house didn't yet have a phone, he and Velda had walked over to Velda's neighbor's house just to call Erin to ask, "Is everything all right?"

Erin told him what happened, Isaiah told Velda, and, a few minutes later, they both arrived at Erin's house.

And then Cappy called to say she and Alaina were on their way to Good Samaritan Hospital with Chris following closely behind in the ambulance. Hearing that last word almost caused Erin's heart to give out, until Cappy quickly explained that Chris was all right. The ambulance ride was necessary because all the police cars were already occupied. Not that there were a lot of police cars, of course. Just a few. One hauled away Mr. Walker and the other carried Cappy and Alaina, and another arrived just as their car pulled away, but that was all right. They were just there to secure the scene. Nothing serious or anything. Just to hold down the fort until they could figure out where Alaina's mother was. Which was no big deal, since she was probably just at work. Or maybe at the supermarket.

With everything coursing through Erin Mathis at that moment, she still wanted to smile. Talking to Cappy Sanchez through Isaiah Sadler's cell phone during the crisis concerning Alaina Walker and Chris McIntyre had been almost . . . comical.

"Cappy," Erin had said, "listen to me. I'm fine. Really. I'm not going to worry about this, because we've been through rough times before and the Lord has always taken care of us. I'm refusing to worry, okay? So, please. I need for you to quit worrying about me so you can tell me exactly what is going on."

Cappy agreed to those terms. Then proceeded to tell all.

But even after the brave pronouncement, each word Cappy said intensified the queasiness in Erin's stomach. Sitting comfortably on the couch, surrounded by friends, she tried not to worry about Chris and Alaina. Or Cappy. But it was impossible.

Even after calling her husband and hearing his soothing voice say he would try to find out how Chris and Alaina were, Erin still worried. What if Chris had been arrested? Just how bad did it get in that house? What did Chris do to get arrested? Was she really all right? Would she insist on being her usual stubborn self? Would she allow anyone to help her?

In the kitchen, Velda Jackson hummed quietly as she finished wiping out the inside of the refrigerator. Isaiah had already boiled water to make Erin a cup of tea, and was now pouring water into the coffeemaker to brew a pot for everyone else. Erin lowered her head and tried to concentrate on the voice she heard behind her. Sitting at the dining room table, Ben Connelly spoke to the police on his cell phone, though he spoke too softly for Erin to hear what he said.

Erin's outgoing breath carried a faint hint of laughter. Those new cell phones were proving to be quite an investment. Chris was next in line to receive one so she could keep in touch with Ben and Isaiah as she worked alone at the gym. *If only she had one now,* whispered up from Erin's heart. *If only I could talk to her. Where is she, Lord? Is she really all right?*

Beside her on the couch, Sonya Connelly squeezed Erin's hand and gave her a warm smile. "Why don't you lay down for a while, sweetheart? We'll let you know the instant we hear anything."

Such precious friends. "No. Thanks, Sonya. I'm fine. Really."

Sonya nodded. Then squeezed Erin's hand again.

Erin felt such peace in the presence of these special friends. Her brothers and sisters. She knew all their prayers would be answered. Alaina would be safe. Cappy would be safe. Chris would be safe. If only this moment would end.

But what would happen next? What would happen when this moment ended? When Chris made it home?

Erin closed her eyes as fear tightened its grip on her.

Please, Lord, I don't want to worry. I can't worry. It hurts too much to worry. Keeping her eyes closed, she rubbed her belly with her free hand. She needed to feel her baby's tiniest kick. To make sure her little one knew Mommy was trying to relax. Everything would be all right soon. Daddy would be home. Things would settle down. Soon. Very soon.

If only it were true.

I need to know, Lord. Is Chris really all right? Please, bring her home. Please.

She didn't want to think about what she knew was true. Yet, the question nagged her. Begged to be asked. Needed to be answered. If only in Erin's mind.

Of everyone involved in the horrible events at the Walker's house that afternoon, who would be the most affected by it?

Alaina, most certainly. But she was young and such a happy kid. She would heal as the memories faded. Her future remained bright. Full of hope.

It had helped to hear Sonya's assessment of Alaina's mother. When she offered firm assurance that Laurie Walker would do the right thing, Erin felt a little better. "Laurie is a good mother," Sonya had said. "She'll fight for Alaina. And Meghan too. She'll see that they move on from this awful time." Sonya continued to say that Laurie had been fed up with her worthless husband for a while. They had prayed about it one day after the women's Bible study at the church. "Of course," Sonya said, "I had no idea he was violent. My goodness. Poor child. Maybe now is the time for her to shed that man like a flea-infested jacket."

The metaphor still made Erin's skin crawl.

But maybe, in this case, divorce was the best thing. Even if Laurie Walker finished raising her daughters without her husband's help, that would be far better than raising them around the man who hit and terrorized them.

Erin drew in a deep breath. Blew it out through trembling lips.

Lord, please help Laurie do the right thing. Divorce is never what You want for us. But in this case? Please help her know what to do. Please keep her and her children safe.

Sonya seemed so sure about Laurie Walker. And Erin trusted Sonya. Laurie had friends in Kimberley Square. Family she could turn to for help. Yes, Alaina would make it through this ordeal. She would continue to grow and possibly even gain inner strength from it. She would at least know that her friends loved her. That her "aunt" Chris was willing to risk everything to save her.

Erin bit her lip as tears stung her eyes.

Thanks to Chris, Alaina would be fine.

Thank You so much, Lord. A deep ache tore through Erin's heart. *But, Lord? Will Chris be all right? Of everyone involved in the mess today, Chris will be the one to bear the agony of it. She'll be embarrassed, frustrated, even angry at how "out of hand" it all became. And even though she saved that precious child, she'll be faced again with her own past. With all of her own past abuse. When no one was there ... oh, Abba, Father ... when no one was there ... to save her.*

★★★

THE DOOR OF THE NURSES' lounge burst open, startling Chris so hard she lifted her head and pushed away from the table — her entire world went black.

A man's deep voice called her name, but she knew it wasn't Jason Sloan's voice. She waited another second for her heart to slow, her head to clear, for the myriad of sharp, deep aches to ease.

The voice again. "Miss McIntyre? Are you all right?"

Oh . . . how she hated that question.

"Sloan, why hasn't she been seen by a doctor yet?"

"She refused treatment."

Chris blinked open her eyes. Tried to focus on the scuffed tile floor by the officer's feet.

"She did, huh? Is that right, Miss McIntyre? Are you refusing treatment?"

"Yes, sir, I am." The words clogged in her throat. She coughed.

"Then you're ready to go to the station to give your statement?"

She glanced up at the handsome African-American officer. "Yes, sir, I am."

"Let's go then." He motioned for her to join him.

Chris pushed out of the chair, then had to steady herself against the table.

"Chris, please. Let someone check you out."

She lifted her eyes to look at Jason. Wanted to smile. But didn't. Her mood had soured.

"Is there still some debate here? Are you ready to go or not?"

Gritting her teeth, Chris straightened, then said, "I'm ready. Lead the way, sir."

Jason scowled, but said nothing.

"You finished with her, Sloan?"

"Yeah, I guess. Take her away." Jason's voice carried his disgusted defeat.

Chris gave him one last look. Hoped he would give her one too. But his blue eyes stared at the floor.

The policeman touched Chris's arm and guided her to the door. He allowed her to use the nurses' restroom across the hall and then, with a firm grip on her upper arm, led her out of the hospital to the waiting squad car parked a few feet from the entrance of the Emergency Room. He guided her to the car's passenger side backseat, waited for her to situate herself inside, then slammed the door closed.

Chris turned her head to see Cappy Sanchez sitting beside her.

"Hey, stranger." Cappy's smile wavered.

"Hey back atcha." Chris settled in and secured her seat belt.

Cappy grabbed Chris's hand and squeezed it.

Chris let her.

The car pulled away from the curb.

"Girl . . . please tell me you're all right."

Chris forced a smile. "Yeah, Cap. Good as gold."

"You look like death warmed over."

Her smile widened easily. "Well, thanks, woman. Awfully nice of you to say so."

"Did you get an X-ray? I bet that creep broke a rib, the way he was hitting you."

Heat radiated from Cappy's grip. Chris's smile dissolved into a firm press of her lips. "I'm fine."

"Why didn't you get any stitches?"

She pulled her hand away. Gazed out her window.

Cappy let out a Spanish curse.

Chris looked at her.

A deep sigh. "Guess I haven't exactly given up the colorful language, huh. Lord, forgive me."

"I think He understands. I let out a few today too."

"It was a day for cussing, if there ever was one. But don't tell Isaiah. He's been really nagging me about my language."

Chris couldn't imagine the kind old gentlemen nagging anyone about anything. But, then again, Cappy did like to use some very flagrant words in the days before she gave her life to Jesus Christ. In both Spanish and English. Some old vices were hard to break.

Old vices. Oh, Lord . . .

She laid her head back against the seat. Could almost taste the whiskey's burn on her lips. Her whole being craved the mindless stupor that would send this entire day into oblivion. The day and all its mess. The mess she made. And all her pain.

"Lord, help us through this." Just a whisper.

Please, Lord. Chris swallowed deeply. Turned again to Cappy. "Are you all right, lady? He laid one on you, that's for sure."

"Yeah. I'm all right. I bruise easily, so the man's toast. But nothing's broke."

"Is Alaina all right? Were you with her?"

"They took her to a different area almost immediately. I haven't seen her since. But I think his partner stayed with her." Cappy used her chin to point at the officer in the front seat.

Chris leaned forward, then regretted it. She had to wait for the pain in her side to ease. "Sir? Do you know how Alaina is? Is she all right?"

"I'm sure she'll be fine." The officer's eyes never strayed from the road.

"But you don't know for sure? Have you found her mother? Have you found any of her family?"

"Please sit back and relax. We'll know more soon."

"You can't even tell us if she's all right?" Chris struggled to control her tone. "Or if she's hurt?"

"Miss McIntyre, please sit back and relax."

She sat back. But she did not relax. She watched half a city block pass by her, then said, "Please don't call me *Miss McIntyre.* My name is Chris. You can call me Chris."

Thick silence filled the car.

Unnerved by it, Chris dared a glance at the officer. She saw a faint smile. And his eyes glancing up at her through the rearview mirror.

"All right, Chris. And I'll tell you what. As soon as we finish our paperwork, I promise I'll find out how she's doing."

"Are we under arrest?" Cappy asked.

We? Chris couldn't help giving Cappy a wide-eyed look.

"No. From what I've seen, neither of you will be charged."

Relief trickled through her.

"I just need to get your written statements, then you can go home. We'll need you to stay close for a few days. We may need you to testify when Walker's arraigned, but we'll let you know."

"He's being arrested then."

"Yes, ma'am. Considering the shoe print he left on your back, and his resisting arrest, he's definitely going to be charged."

Cappy let out a deep breath.

"Thank you, Officer." Chris's voice didn't quite carry the gratitude she felt.

"You're very welcome, Chris. And the name's Richardson. But away from the station, you can call me Ray."

She smiled. Then allowed a breath of laughter to carry up from her heart.

✯✯✯

Two sips of peppermint tea, and Erin needed to excuse herself to use the bathroom. The tea tasted wonderful. Just those two sips helped soothe her worried stomach. But her rascally daughter had chosen that moment to lounge on her mommy's bladder. Again. Silly girl. Mommy would have to mention that to daughter when daughter turned sixteen and demanded something outrageous. Like most sixteen-year-old daughters do.

Oh my.

Erin turned on the water and watched it splash over her hands. *What will she be like at sixteen, Lord? What should I do to keep her as sweet as the day she's born?*

She laughed as Chris's words, spoken only a few days ago, snuck back into her mind to haunt her. *"That's the problem with cute little puppies, Rinny. They usually grow into very big dogs."*

Erin had laughed then. Quite heartily. Until Chris added, *"And don't forget. Your daughter may be . . . your son."*

Oh my.

She turned off the water, then lifted her wet hands to her cheeks. *Lord, what do I know about raising a son? About as much as I know about raising a daughter.* She reached for a towel and dabbed it over her face. Stared into the mirror. At her pink splotchy cheeks. At the lines of worry etched across her forehead. At the lines of red streaking through the whites of her eyes. At the pale blue irises mixed with tiny flecks of jade green. At the perfectly round, shiny black pupils intensely staring back at her.

"I can see it in your eyes. You have definitely not lost your 'glow.'"

Her breath caught. Her reflection shimmered through a flood of burning tears.

Oh, Chris . . .

She covered her face with the towel and let her tears fall into its softness.

★★★

STAYING FOCUSED ON THE PAPER, on the words she struggled to write, became more and more difficult. Already it seemed the Tylenol had given out. Her head throbbed, along with her cheek, her entire face, the back of her shoulder, her side. If only her heart would stop beating so hard against her chest, maybe all of her throbbing woes would ease.

If only her heart would stop beating . . .

She blinked deeply a few times, then closed her burning eyes and rubbed them, careful not to touch the bandages on her cheek.

Lord, I just wanna go home.

She drew in a long breath and focused again on the words. If any of it made sense, only a few more paragraphs should do it. Why couldn't they take her statement verbally? Why did they insist she write it out?

Like writing a sick story. Or a lousy screenplay for an equally lousy B-rated movie. Villains and good guys. Oh, yes. But this good guy freaked out and lost it. Yes, the villain got carted away to the big house. But here sits the good guy, wondering if things could have been handled just a tad bit differently, wondering if the entire sordid scene could have been avoided in the first place.

A curse worked its way through her system. She clenched her teeth, refusing to let it find its way across her tongue.

Some stories should never be written. Especially if they were true.

And this sick story is definitely true.

She forced herself to remember every littlest detail, then finished her last sentence and signed her name at the bottom. Pushed the papers and pen across the table. Sat back in her chair. And waited. Alone. In the small, stuffy room.

Her stomach simmered. Her eyes fell closed. Her head bobbed. Blinking quickly, she wanted to shake her head to clear her muddled brain, yet didn't dare. Even the tiniest movement intensified the throbbing. She lifted her arms and folded them on the table, then lowered her head to rest against them. Let her eyes again fall closed.

Rinny ... please don't worry ...

Time passed. The door finally opened. Chris lifted her head, but couldn't open her eyes to see who had entered.

"Hold on. I'll be right back."

Richardson's voice. Chris waited. Forced her eyes to open.

He returned a minute later. Tossed a packet of Tylenol on the table. Lowered a Styrofoam cup of water beside it.

Tears flooded Chris's eyes. "Thanks," came out as a croak.

The officer gave her no response, just picked up her statement, lifted his foot onto a chair, rested his elbow against his knee, and started reading through it.

Chris swallowed the pills. Waited. Tried not to squirm. Tried not to move at all.

The silence lingered.

Richardson flipped to the statement's second page.

Chris glanced around the room. Then stopped. Even moving her eyes hurt. She let them close. Waited. The officer's booming voice startled her.

"Okay. This is all good. But there are still some unanswered questions."

She blinked open her eyes.

The man glared down at her. "I'm still a little confused about exactly why you entered the house." He waited. Continued to glare.

"Well, I certainly didn't want to. Not after seeing Mr. Walker through the screen door."

His face softened a bit, though he didn't speak. Only glared.

Chris swallowed. Then quietly cleared her throat. "I was heading home. But I heard him shout."

"You say here, he shouted, 'I said no.' You didn't hear anything else?"

"I heard his voice, but not what he said."

"Then you heard the girl cry out."

"Scream. I heard her scream."

The officer sifted through the papers in his hand. Then nodded. "Yes. Scream. Of course." A frown. "Did you think Mr. Walker struck his daughter? Is that why you entered the house?"

"I, um … I don't know what I thought. I just knew I had to get in there."

Another nod. "Okay. I'll buy that."

Good. Can I go now?

Another frown. "But why did he hit you?"

How do I know?

"Was it just because you were in his house, or did you say something to antagonize him?"

Keeping her face impassive, Chris slowly drew in a deep breath to calm her raging heart. Shooting pains across her ribs forced her to stop. She held the breath a second longer, then slowly let it out.

"You say here, you told him to 'back off.' Is that right?"

She stared at a scratch on the tabletop. "Yes, sir. I told him to back off."

"Is that why he hit you?"

"I don't know why he hit me."

"From the time you arrived at the Walker's house until the time we arrived, did you ever see Mr. Walker hit his daughter?"

She blinked. Continued to stare. "No."

"Why did you go over there in the first place?"

Her mind struggled to make sense of her tangled thoughts, to rein in the smart-mouth responses that needed to stay unsaid.

"You must have had a good reason. Did you suspect Mr. Walker was hurting his daughter?"

"Um ... yes. I guess. I'm not sure."

"You're not sure?"

She didn't look up at the officer. Didn't say a word.

"I'm going to venture a guess here, Miss McIntyre ... and say that you've never even met this man before today. Am I right?"

She wanted to dissolve away and disappear.

"Answer me, Miss McIntyre."

"Yes. You're right."

Dead silence.

Chris squirmed. "I've never met the man."

"You've never met the man, yet you suspected him of abusing his daughter?"

To dissolve away, to disappear, to die.

"How is that possible? Can you explain that?"

She could. But not in any way the officer would understand.

"Can you at least tell me when you first suspected him?"

"A few weeks ago. Maybe a month. Or two."

"A few weeks ... maybe two months. You can do better than that, can't you?"

Her lips parted to speak, but her mind refused to process anything she could say.

The officer pulled his foot off the chair and straightened. Towered over her. "Can you at least tell me *why* you suspected him?"

How could she answer that?

"Did you see him strike his daughter on a previous occasion? Did someone tell you they saw him hit his daughter on a previous occasion? Help me out here, Miss McIntyre. I'm trying to understand this."

She lifted her eyes. He stood there, waiting for an answer. But did he have any idea how absurd his questions were? He couldn't be that stupid, could he? She quietly cleared her throat. Spoke slowly.

Deliberately. "Don't you think if I knew for sure that he had hit her, or if I had *seen* him hit her before, I would have called you immediately?"

"Then why didn't you call us when you first suspected him?"

"Call and tell you what? That I had a feeling a man I've never even met was beating his daughter? Come on."

Richardson's face hardened.

"Look, I'm sorry. But if I would have called you this morning before I went over to his house, what would you have done?" Chris gave the officer no chance to respond. "Nothing. That's what you would've done. I had no proof. I needed to be sure. That's why I went to the man's house. I needed to see Alaina."

"If you would have called us first and reported your suspicions, we would have started an investigation."

Chris squelched a bitter laugh. And words she knew she dared not give voice. *When? When you got around to it? When she ended up half dead in the hospital?*

"We treat reports of child abuse very seriously."

I'm sure you do. It's about time somebody did.

"We would have prevented you from going over there. Alone."

She found a new scratch on the tabletop to stare at.

"Well, we would have tried, anyway."

A breath of laughter blew out her lips before she could stop it. She covered it with a cough. Refused to give in to the accompanying smile.

"Even suspicions, Chris. We take even suspicions seriously. Very seriously."

Okay, okay. Fine. Whatever you say.

"Weren't you afraid?"

She slowly gazed up at him, letting her eyes reveal her confusion.

"Floyd Walker is a big man. You say it right here yourself." He held up her paperwork and pointed to the spot.

She blinked. *Floyd?*

"And yet, when you heard him shout, you ran into his house?"

Richardson folded his arms and struck a thoughtful pose. "Now that just doesn't seem like a smart thing to do. Why didn't you run to a neighbor's house and call us from there?"

Another absurd question. She wouldn't waste the breath to justify it with a response. She started to shake her head to dismiss it, but quickly stopped.

"You're not made that way, are you, Christina McIntyre?"

Now his words made no sense at all. She allowed the growl she felt in her chest to play out on her face.

"I remember you. From last February."

Her eyes fell closed as her growl gave way to a cringe.

Richardson's soft laughter filtered through the room. "Now, don't worry. I'm not going to label you a troublemaker. Not just yet. It takes three innocent incidents to label one a troublemaker. At least in my book."

She dared a glance his way. "There will not be a third."

He tossed her statement onto the table. "Hey. In this neighborhood, who's to say."

A smile barely pulled her lips.

"I read your file, you know."

"I have a file?"

"Nothing major. Just a witness fact sheet. Vital statistics. You know." The man's brown eyes gave evidence he was playing with her. "I saw you were in the army. That you served during Desert Storm."

"Yes, sir. That's right."

"You didn't cause any trouble over there, did you?"

Her smile threatened to widen. She let it. Just a bit. "Only for the Iraqis, sir."

"Well, I guess I can allow that." More laughter. "I think you should go home, Chris McIntyre. You've put in a long day."

With a sigh of relief, Chris forced herself out of the chair. Slowly stood. Looked Richardson in the eye. "Yes, sir." Gave him a weary smile. "Thanks."

"Oh, by the way, I called my partner at the hospital before I came in here."

The words captured Chris's complete attention.

"Alaina is going to be fine. She displayed a few signs of previous injuries, old bruises and such, down her one side, like she'd been hit or kicked or something of that nature. But my partner said there were no indications of any recent injuries. And they were able to reach the mother. There's no reason why she shouldn't be able to take her daughter home in a few hours. After everything gets straightened out."

Each word eased Chris's miserable existence. "Thanks, Ray."

His right eyebrow lifted as his eyes narrowed.

"I mean, Officer Richardson."

"That's right. And don't you forget it." He let out a laugh, then headed for the door and pulled it open. "Oh, hey. Sloan told me you've got an adult basketball league starting up at that new gym of yours. Thursday nights, right?"

Chris couldn't hide her surprise. "Um, yeah. But it's only an open gym right now. The league won't start until next month. And it's real low-keyed. More rec league."

"He said Fire's already got a team entered."

"That's right, they do."

"Well, we'd better get our act together then, huh."

Chris gave him the warmest smile she could muster. "We can't afford real referees, so we're asking everyone to be on their best behavior."

The man let out a burst of hearty laughter. "I think we can contain ourselves."

"You'll have to put it in writing. Just because you're cops, we can't assume you'll behave."

"Just show me where to sign." Richardson's brown eyes shone. "And if you need me to arrest anyone for breaking the agreement, just say the word."

Chris laughed at his words, then followed him out the door and down the long hall toward the front door of the station.

Walking behind him, staring at the tiled floor as it passed beneath her feet, she vowed to the Lord Jesus, to Erin and Ben and everyone else she held dear, she would never again in any way, shape, or capacity return to this police station. She would never again see the inside of it. Not even if they held a Christmas party and invited her to place the star at the top of their Christmas tree. Never. From now on, she'd be on her best behavior. From now on, and for the rest of her natural life. Forever. Never again would she step a foot inside this place.

Right. And how long did your promise to Erin last? Fifty years, you said. You promised her you'd be boring for the next fifty years. And that lasted what. Three months?

"I'll see if Miss Sanchez is ready." Richardson stopped to hold the swinging gate open for her. "And then I'll take you both home."

"Thanks. That'd be—" The words stuck like glue in her throat. She stared across the room. Knew her mouth gaped, but couldn't pull it shut.

Cappy Sanchez stood at the front doorway of the police station beside two very familiar men.

Dread sifted through Chris's entire body. *Oh ... no.*

Scott Mathis. And Ben Connelly.

"But, then again," Richardson said, "I can see she is ready, and it appears you two already have a ride home."

Yep, it would appear that way. She gave Richardson no response. Still couldn't pull up her lower jaw. Her last few steps toward the front door and freedom drained every last bit of her reserve.

Richardson stepped up and shook hands with the two men. Seemed to recognize them both as friends. Cappy grinned at Chris, though Chris couldn't return it.

"Well, all right then. We'll let you know how Walker's arraignment goes." Richardson glanced at Chris and Cappy. "Should be sometime Monday. Or Tuesday."

Chris wanted to smile and thank the man, but she could only nod. He flashed smiles at everyone, then turned and walked away toward a row of cluttered desks. Chris watched him a second longer. Then slowly turned to her friends.

"Let's get outta here," Cappy said, her voice hushed.

Chris lifted her eyes just high enough to meet Ben Connelly's gaze. What she saw in his expression ... She quickly glanced away and wiped her tears as heat coursed through her face.

He walked up to her. Pulled her against him. Engulfed her in a warm and gentle hug.

Chris melted into his arms. Held her breath to keep her tears from falling onto his shirt.

"Come on," he said softly, "let's go home."

She pushed away and again wiped her eyes. "Yeah. Please." She dared a glance at Scott Mathis. Immediately hated what she saw on his face. His concern. The pain she had caused him. And Erin. Again.

Lord ... forgive me.

She couldn't look at him a second longer.

He held the door open for her. Didn't say anything as she passed through. His face bore only his concern. She whispered a thank-you, but wasn't sure if she even spoke the words loud enough for him to hear.

Ben's arm came around her as she walked across the parking lot toward his Explorer. He waited patiently as she eased herself into the driver's side backseat. Then gently pushed the door closed.

He steered the truck down one busy city street after the other. Chris stared at the back of his seat the entire way. She glanced once or twice out the window. Glanced once at Scott. Was glad he didn't look her way. Cappy talked a little about Alaina. Said words Chris savored. "They said she'd be all right. And that her mom came to pick her up."

Even after Cappy stopped talking, after Ben and Scott fell silent, Chris didn't say a word. Over the last few minutes of the trip, silence filled the truck like a thick, smothering fog.

The Explorer rolled on. Then turned onto Kimberley Street. Nervousness flooded Chris's belly. How could she face Erin? Or Sonya?

Ben pulled the truck into a vacant parking space in front of the duplex where all three of his passengers lived. He quickly shut down the engine and got out, then pulled Chris's door open for her. Smiling sheepishly, she forced herself out of the truck. Steadied herself against the door for a second. Pushed it closed. Turned. Glanced up to meet Ben's gaze.

He stood there, smiling timidly. "You're going to be all right, sweetheart." His voice cracked. "We'll see you tomorrow. You go home and get some rest." He leaned in and kissed the top of Chris's head. "You know we love you. And we're praying for you."

Her throat pinched shut. She couldn't speak one word, though she wanted to say so much. Her lips trembled as she tried to smile.

"Better believe it, lady." Cappy moved in close, her arms lifted out to her sides.

Chris pulled her in and hugged her as tight as she dared. "Thanks, Cappy." Just a whisper. "Oh, girl ..." So many things to say to this woman too, yet she couldn't force anything more through her aching throat.

"You go on now. I'll be home later." Cappy pushed away and turned to Ben. They gave Chris one last smile, then walked across the street to Ben and Sonya's house.

Chris stood and stared as they walked away. Didn't want them to go, yet felt a hint of relief trickle through her. She loved them for being so considerate. Appreciated all of her friends' love and concern. But even so, she didn't think she could absorb any more of either. She couldn't stand that they were all so worried about her. That they all were praying for her.

Well, that's what happens when you let things get so out of hand.

Movement caught her eye. She turned to gaze at Scott Mathis. He stood just a few feet away.

"Come on. Let's go inside." His voice was soft and he held his hand out, as if he wanted Chris to take it.

Lord, help me. She couldn't move. Her lips trembled as she swallowed deeply.

"It's all right."

"Scott ..." Fresh tears flooded her eyes.

The tender smile he gave her broke her heart. "Come on." A whisper. Soft as a breath.

She reached up and took his hand. Let him guide her around the Explorer to the sidewalk in front of their house.

Up on the porch, Erin stood, hands covering her mouth, waiting for them to reach her.

Chris pulled away from Scott and almost ran up the stairs straight into Erin's arms.

✪✪✪

The moment overwhelmed her. Terrified by the deep bruises on Chris's face, the bandages covering the nasty cut on her cheek, Erin's heart swelled with joy and so much love she could barely breathe. She held Chris as close as she could, which wasn't close enough. Chris started to cry against Erin's shoulder, hard, bitter sobs that shattered Erin's swollen heart into a billion jagged pieces.

"Oh, Rinny . . ."

"Shh . . ." Tears dripped down her cheeks and into Chris's hair.

"God help me, I'm so sorry." The words barely carried through Chris's anguished sobs.

"It's all right. Please . . . it's all right."

Chris sagged in Erin's arms. Pushed herself away. Then turned to face the street.

"Come inside." Erin gently squeezed Chris's shoulder. "Please come in and sit down." She glanced at Scott.

He gave her a nod, then headed into the clinic.

Chris slowly turned. Erin guided her through the front door into her living room, then steered her to the couch. They both sat gingerly and let out a deep sigh as they relaxed. Chris grabbed a few tissues from the end table and handed them to Erin, then grabbed a few more for herself. She wiped her eyes and nose before resting her head against the back of the couch. Immediately, her eyes fell closed.

Erin wiped her own face, then turned in the couch and pulled her left leg under her as far as she could. She leaned sideways into the back of the couch and stared at the battered face of her best friend. A scream threatened to wrench its way out of her. She wanted immediate answers to the zillion questions racing through her mind.

What happened to you? Did Alaina's dad do this to you? Why? How?

She bit into her cheek, then tasted the saltiness of her blood. She forced herself to relax. Her teeth to part. She wanted Scott to return, needed to draw comfort from his presence. She needed his strength. *And Yours, Father God. Please help us.*

She wanted to turn back time, back to that morning, to that moment when she let Chris go. Deep in her heart, didn't she know it was wrong to let Chris go? Chris had no business going to the Walker's house. But there was no way Erin could stop her once her mind was made up.

She stared at that bruised face. And waited. Sorted through her present moment. And she prayed. Pleaded for strength. For the right words to say.

Ever so slowly, Chris turned her head to look Erin's way. Then reached out and grabbed Erin's hand. "Are you all right, girl?"

Erin pressed her lips into a pathetic smile. Squeezed Chris's hand. Couldn't answer the question. Could hardly force breath through her throat.

She needed to throw something, anything, across the room. Preferably something glass. Something that would shatter. Something that would explode against the wall loud enough to wake her from this nightmare and allow her to see the light of the new day.

Fury swept into her blood, tangling with the fear and sadness already there. It coursed through her. Tore at her soul.

Chris's eyes fell closed again.

Staring at that face, Erin wanted to weep. She squeezed Chris's hand. Slowly leaned closer and brushed back the hair from Chris's forehead.

Those dark eyes opened. The faintest possible smile touched Chris's lips. "I'm all right, Rinny."

Erin swallowed hard to clear her throat. "I really wish that were true."

"It is. I wouldn't kid you at a time like this."

She let a smile surface.

"I need to know ... that you are too."

Erin tried to draw in a deep breath, though in her present position it wasn't a very deep breath. "I can't sit like this. My daughter's in the way."

"That's a nice problem to have."

Another smile. Erin pulled her hand from Chris's, straightened in the couch, and kicked her feet up on the coffee table. Her deep breath came easily. She enjoyed its refreshing release. "That's better."

"Has she been kicking much today?"

"Not more than usual."

"I bet she's mad at me for getting you upset."

"Nah. But she may still be wondering why her mommy's heart was beating so fast since lunch."

Chris lifted her hand to rub her eyes. "Rinny ..."

"Don't. Don't say it. You're home now, and that's all that matters."

"Let me say it. Please. I need to say it."

Erin turned her head to look at Chris.

"Please?"

"Okay."

"I am so sorry."

"Okay."

"Don't blow this off. I mean it."

"I know. Don't worry. I'm not blowing anything off. I know you're sorry, and it's okay."

"Really?"

"Yes." Erin straightened her head against the back of the couch and grabbed Chris's hand again. "*Absitively*. Which is short for ..."

Chris barely laughed. "Absolutely positively."

"Right. Give the woman a star. Just as long as it's not bronze."

"Please. Don't bring that up."

"Sorry." A giggle worked its way out Erin's throat.

Silence again filled the room. Complete silence.

"I'm just glad you're home," Erin whispered.

"Me too." Chris squeezed Erin's hand.

A moment later, the door between the living room and the clinic swung open a few inches. A brown-haired head poked through the opening. Brown eyes looked Erin's way. Then Chris's.

Erin lifted her free hand and motioned for her husband to join them.

With a smile on his handsome face and his black medical kit in his hand, Scott pushed through the door and sat on the love seat across from them. He lowered the kit to the floor by his feet, then leaned back and let out a deep sigh.

"Hey, baby." Erin gave him a wink and a grin.

His smile widened. "How are my three favorite girls?"

A faint breath of laughter spurted out of Chris. Erin turned to see a soft smile lingering after the laughter faded.

"What are you guys gonna do," Chris said, "when you discover your she is a he?"

"Hey, I've wanted a son since day one." Scott kicked his feet up on the coffee table. Played footsies with his wife for a second. "But it's my deepest desire to please my wife in all things. So I'm fully prepared to adore a daughter, should my he be a she."

More faint laughter. And at that moment, coming from a woman who had just survived one of the worst days of her life, Erin could not remember hearing a sweeter sound.

FIVE

THE MOMENT PLAYED OUT IN small talk, comfortable banter, gentle laughter. Erin sat holding Chris's hand, feeling not the least bit self-conscious. Chris was her sister in the Lord Jesus Christ. And the closest thing to a real sister Erin had ever known.

She would squeeze that hand from time to time and enjoy the responding squeeze Chris gave her. It became a lifeline in that moment, a necessity. She held on. Didn't want the moment to end.

But her eyes were drawn to the ugly contusions and abrasions on Chris's wrist. Ugly, but not as severe as her own had been a few months ago. Though the deep cuts and abrasions the bootlace tore into her wrists had long since healed, they left permanent hints of their existence behind. Chris's wrists were not as severely torn, but they were still torn, nonetheless. Erin wanted to rub a healing balm on them, yet didn't know of anything that would instantly remove the bruises and the pain. Only time would heal these wounds. Like the rest so evident on Chris's face.

Where else was she hurt? What else had she endured? What else was she still enduring? Alone?

"Rin?" Just a whisper.

"Huh?" Erin glanced up. "What? I'm sorry."

"We lost you for a second," Scott said softly.

Erin smiled. Didn't know what to say.

That same silence once again descended. Heavy silence. But this time it grew increasingly uncomfortable.

Chris squeezed Erin's hand. "Can you believe they wanted to arrest me? They slapped cuffs on me and everything."

Erin pulled Chris's hand up and held it in both of her own. She couldn't look up from the sight of them entwined. Chris's smooth skin. Darker than Erin's. Just a bit. A smaller hand than Erin's. Though much stronger. So much stronger.

"Rinny …"

"Did you, um …" Erin swallowed. "Did you let anyone check you out at the hospital?"

Silence.

She slowly turned her head. Chris would not meet her gaze. More silence.

"You didn't. Did you?"

"I'm fine. I told you that."

"I could just smack you sometimes." She pushed Chris's hand away, then reached up to run her fingers through her hair. Her teeth clenched at her outburst, and her poor choice of words.

"Could I at least take a look at that cut?" Scott leaned forward and rested his elbows on his knees. "Who put on the butterflies?"

Hesitation. Chris quietly cleared her throat. "The paramedic." She rubbed her nose. "Actually, I think you guys know him. Jason Sloan?"

Scott's face brightened as he smiled. "Sloan? Sure, we know Sloan." He looked at Erin. "You remember him, don't you, sweetheart? He played Santa that one Christmas at the children's party. And did a miserable job, I might add. His stuffing kept falling out."

Erin's faint smile trembled as her heart fell. At that moment, she didn't think it was possible to feel any worse, but hearing Jason Sloan's name dropped her lower yet.

"Do you mind if I take a closer look at his handiwork?" Scott waited for Chris's response without moving an inch.

"Um … no. I don't mind."

As he reached into his medical kit, Erin let her eyes close. Her stomach had turned sour again, stealing any hope of being able to relax. She heard Scott rummaging through the kit, pulling on his gloves, then moving closer to sit on the coffee table in front of them. She forced her eyes open. Saw him gazing at her. She quickly smiled, and made sure he knew she meant it. She smiled at Chris.

Then let it fade as she drew in a long, slow breath to settle her stomach.

Chris pushed herself forward to sit on the edge of the couch. Scott leaned in and closely examined her cheek. Erin watched him. Watched his face. Wondered if his tongue would appear as he fell lost in his work. Sometimes, and not just at work, when he concentrated intensely on something, a bit of his tongue would poke through his lips.

She watched her husband. And fell in love with him all over again. Watched his eyes. Let them draw her away into the warm abyss of total infatuation.

Scott worked. Erin watched him. Until her eyes once again closed.

Father God ... how I love this man. I love this woman too, You know that. But sometimes she makes me completely insane! I want to help her. You know I do. But when she gets pigheaded and won't let me — won't let anyone ... what can I do? What can any of us do?

"He did some fine work here." Scott spoke softly to his captivated audience. "Closed it quite nicely. And it looks clean. I think we can leave these in place for a little while longer. If we keep it clean, we may not need to put in any stitches." He leaned back and gave Chris a smile. "Keeping it clean means not shedding any more tears. Think you can manage that?"

"I certainly hope so."

"Good." Scott moved in close to her again. "Tell me about these contusions. You seem to have collected quite a few."

A soft laugh. But no response to Scott's request.

"Well? Don't be shy."

"What's to tell?"

"You know the routine, Chris. Help me out here. Let me help you."

Oh, Lord ... Erin savored her husband's words. Loved him that much more for saying them.

Chris closed her eyes as Scott palpated her entire head. "You guys worry too much. You know that?"

"To know you is to worry about you," Scott replied.

"Great."

"Get used to it." Scott glanced at Erin.

She wanted to kiss him.

Chris tensed. "Okay. That's a sore spot."

"It should be. There's quite a knot here."

She pulled away from his touch and ran her fingers through her hair. "Look. I really appreciate it." She gazed at Erin. "You know I do. But I'm fine. Really."

"If you say so." Erin's voice carried half the strength she wanted it to.

"Jason checked me out. Took my BP and everything. I've got a few bumps, but that's it."

Erin tried to smile.

Scott's lips pressed into a firm line.

"Really. And he seemed like a good paramedic. Actually, he seemed like a great paramedic. He knew what he was doing." Chris glanced first at Erin, then at Scott. "I've seen him at the gym a few times. Does he live around here?"

Scott's eyes met Erin's. A look of great sadness passed between them.

"He's married, though, huh. Too bad." A hint of a giggle. "Listen to me. Yeah, I checked out his ring finger. But only because there was something about him. He really seemed to care. And he was so sweet. Seems like all the good guys are always taken. It's not fair, actually. Can't a few of them still be single for us who are taking our time trying to decide?"

Erin's gaze fell to the floor. She wanted to put her hand over Chris's mouth to stop her nervous chatter. Wanted to change the subject and escape the misery of what was about to come.

"He'll probably get into trouble. He didn't ask for my insurance information or anything. I got a free ride to the hospital. Though all we did was eat fudgesicles in the nurses' lounge." A laugh. "He was really cool."

"He's a good guy. And a good medic." Scott's voice carried a heavy tone. "But he's not married. Not anymore."

Chris's mouth fell open. "What do you mean? He's divorced?"

Hearing the hope in Chris's voice, Erin prayed for a way to protect her, for a way to protect her own husband from the grief he was about to inflict. The grief he was already feeling. Jason Sloan had been one of his closest friends for years, before the tragedy that shattered Jason's life. For so long now, Scott rarely even spoke of him. Jason had pulled away from everyone and everything. He seemed to pull into himself, into his agony, and into his work. He left all his buddies behind.

"Scott? Is he divorced?"

"No." Erin said the word quickly, then waited for Scott's eyes to turn her way. She tried to give him a comforting look. "No, Chris, he's not divorced." She turned back to Chris. "His wife and unborn daughter were killed in a car accident about ..." Her mind went blank. She looked at Scott. "How long ago was it?"

He swallowed deeply. Pursed his lips as he considered the answer. "Two and a half years?" The question played out on his face as he gazed at Erin. "Almost three years ago? We hadn't been married long."

Erin nodded, then glanced at Chris. The expression on her face forced Erin to look away. Down at her hands. Her heart thumped. "A drunk driver made no attempt to stop at a red light. He hit them broadside, doing about fifty. Crushed the entire passenger side of the car. In all likelihood, she didn't even know what hit her. They said she died instantly." Her throat pinched shut as tears burned her eyes. "She was about seven months pregnant."

"No ... God, no ..." Breathless words.

Erin lifted her head. Saw utter misery on Chris's face.

"Come on, you guys." Her wide eyes swept over Erin and Scott. Back and forth. "That can't be true. Don't say that. Don't do this to me."

Scott slowly shook his head, then lowered his gaze to the floor. "I'm sorry, Chris. But it's true." Sadness choked his words.

Erin slid forward to sit on the edge of the couch, then grabbed his hand and lifted it to her lips.

Chris stood and walked a few steps toward the kitchen. "He was still wearing his ring." She sat at the dining room table and lowered her head into her arms.

Scott slowly stood and pulled Erin up with him. They both moved closer to Chris, yet kept their distance, not sure what she needed from them. Giving her space, yet staying close.

Prayers flooded Erin's heart. This moment, on top of everything that had happened that day . . . would it ever end? She finally moved closer and sat at the table beside Chris. "Are you okay?" She touched Chris's shoulder.

Chris lifted her head, yet covered her face with her hands. "It's not fair, Rinny." Just a whisper.

"I know."

"Oh, God . . . why something so senseless?" The heels of her hands pressed hard against her eyes. "He was so sweet to me. He cared about me. He really . . . cared."

"I'm sure he did. He's a sweet and caring man."

"Then why?" Her fists slammed the table. "Why, Rin? Why did they have to die?"

Erin could only shake her head. She lowered her hand to cover Chris's.

But Chris instantly pulled away. She jumped up and walked a few determined steps toward the front door. Then swayed a bit. Raised her hand to her head.

Scott moved in beside her to steady her.

Erin started for the clinic and was pleased to see Scott guiding Chris that direction. She held the swinging door open for them.

"I'm okay, guys," Chris mumbled as she walked. "Just a bit dizzy."

"Step into my office, m'dear," Scott said softly, "and we'll take care of that in no time." As he moved past Erin, he gave her a tender smile.

She quickly returned it, even as every part of her wanted to weep.

✶✶✶

They spoke soft words to her, words they obviously hoped would break through the misery she felt. Their words were heartfelt and comforting, yet not enough. Chris wanted to run away and hide, but the day had worked her over and left her completely spent. In her exhaustion, she begged the Lord to let her wake up from this nightmare, to look around and find herself in her bedroom ready to start the day.

If she could only wake up. Then her head wouldn't hurt. Or any other part of her. The birds would be singing. Cappy would be fixing breakfast. Erin and Scott would be sitting at their table sipping coffee and peppermint tea, enjoying their quiet Saturday morning. All would be well. Jason Sloan and his lovely wife and daughter would be leaving their house for another happy family adventure. Maybe a trip to the coast to hunt for sand dollars and eat clam chowder. Wherever they would go, whatever they would do, they would do it together. And what a good day it would be.

God? Is it even remotely possible all of this is just a dream? Please say yes. Please?

She hadn't endured one of her old dreams in quite a while. Her dreams now were mostly silly and strange. Showing up to a Stand To in a pair of pajamas. Jumping out of the Huey and flying away like a bird. The other morning she actually woke up laughing. Erin had worn fuzzy bunny slippers to church, and no one seemed to care. No one but Chris even seemed to notice.

Her dreams now were sitcoms compared to the torturous nightmares she used to endure. For weeks on end, she would dream every single night. She'd wake up screaming, drenched in sweat. Old faces, old words, old festering miseries. Memories refusing to fade. Old wounds refusing to heal. Old terrors and agonies returning night after night to push her closer and closer to the brink of total breakdown.

God, my Father . . . Jesus . . . thank You. Those dreams had gone away, ever since that night she became a Christian. *No, Lord, it was the night before that, huh. The night I slept so long.*

The night she smashed two of Erin's dresser drawers against the wall. The night she actually hit Erin across the face.

God ... help me forget that night too. This day and that night. Ahh ... what a mess.

She lay on the padded examining table in Erin and Scott's clinic with a towel and a soft ice pack covering her forehead and eyes. The darkness felt just as good as the ice. At least she didn't have to look at their faces. To see how she had upset her two best friends. Again.

Oh, God ... forgive me.

They didn't say much. Chris felt Erin's grip on her hand, that same grip as earlier, yet more intense somehow, more desperate. They had covered her with a heavy blanket to ease her chills from the ice. The freezing cold radiated through her head, eased her headache, helped her give in to her exhaustion and let it overtake her. The ice pack under her neck really hit the spot. The soft pillow did as well. She could easily fall asleep. But she couldn't sleep down here all night. And if she did fall asleep, she'd fall asleep hard. It would be next to impossible for them to wake her. Scott would have to carry her up the stairs to her own apartment, then tuck her into her own bed. Like he did that one night.

No. He was not going to carry her again. This arrangement, however comfortable, was just temporary. Just until she caught her breath. Until the pounding in her head eased. The ache in her side eased. And the awkwardness of the moment.

How did she get herself into such a mess? How could she put her friends through this again? *How am I supposed to tell them all how sorry I am? Oh, Lord, I'm even sorry about being sorry.*

Chris squeezed Erin's hand. Felt the immediate squeeze in return.

God ... somehow I have to show her how sorry I am. She won't let me say it. Maybe I can wash her dishes for a year. Do her laundry for the next decade.

All of it. Absolutely insane.

Why couldn't I leave well enough alone? Why did I have to push it? Why did I have to go over there? When will I ever learn?

And to think all of it started with four simple words. She wanted to laugh. Though it made perfect sense hours later in hindsight. Four simple words started everything careening the wrong direction and proceeded to ruin the entire day. And not just for her, but for everyone she loved. She let the words play out in her mind.

If you don't forgive . . .

Yes. Refusing to forgive. Refusing to pray about it. Refusing to obey.

Father God . . .

It was true, wasn't it? How could she expect her heavenly Father to talk to her and help her when she refused to listen to what He said? No wonder she didn't want to pray and ask for His guidance that morning about going to the Walker's house. How could she expect Him to guide her into matters involving other people's lives when she refused to follow His guidance about how she was to live her own life? And how could she now expect Him to step in and make everything right when she caused all of the entire day's mess by her own stubborn refusal to forgive? And obey?

But then . . . how could she love and obey a God who allowed an innocent woman and her unborn child to be so senselessly killed? A beautiful family just starting out, so cruelly and totally destroyed?

With her free hand, she pressed against the ice pack covering her forehead, pushed the frozen towel into the burning tears flooding her eyes.

God . . . please . . . forgive me. There's so much I need to learn about You. Don't be mad at me. Please help me learn. Don't let me go. I need You so much.

"Chris, please try to relax." Erin's voice softly carried the words. "Please don't worry about anything. This will all pass. Really it will. Please don't be afraid."

Chris lowered her hand and felt every word soothe the ache in her soul, though her tears still soaked into the towel and burned her eyes. Even as the ice penetrated her skull.

Erin released Chris's hand to press a wad of tissues into it. Chris smiled, then used them to blow her nose, grateful she didn't have to lift the towel to do so. She crumpled the wet tissues into a ball in her left hand.

"Trash can." Scott's voice.

Chris extended her hand toward his voice. Waited another second. Then opened her hand and let the ball fall.

"Two points."

She smiled. "Thanks." She heard the can make contact with the floor.

"No problemo, *señorita*."

"You know, love," Erin said, "you really need a new line."

"Hmm. Well, then, how would they say it in Russian? *Nyet probleminski, Christerina?*"

Laughter bubbled up from Chris's belly. She let it escape, then regretted it. The movement caused her headache to swell. And yet, the laughter felt good. Especially when it blended with Erin's goofy giggle. Sometimes when she giggled like that she sounded just like a kid at Christmas.

"Stick with Spanish," Erin said.

A breath of feigned disgust from Scott. "You don't like my Russian. I'm crushed."

"I like it," Chris said, though her voice cracked. "Don't listen to her."

"See? She likes it."

"But she gives bad advice." Erin grabbed Chris's hand again and gave it a tight squeeze.

"Yeah. Sorry, Scott. Don't listen to me. Always listen to your wife."

Deep laughter rumbled from Scott's direction. "Don't worry, Chris. That's one command already permanently tattooed on the walls of my tender loving heart."

"Oh, please," came from Erin.

More rumbling laughter. And a hint of that childish giggle.

Love. This is what it feels like. Oh, God, thank You for these two. I love them so much. What great friends. How can I thank You enough?

"Hey, Chris?" Scott's voice. "Is there anything else I can do for you? Please, just say the word and I'll do it."

Such gentle words. Her breath caught as her throat tightened.

"Do you need another ice pack anywhere?"

"No. Thanks."

"What have you already taken for the pain? Did Jason give you anything?"

"Yeah. He gave me a couple of Extra Strength Tylenols. Then the cop gave me a couple of regulars."

"Are they having any effect?"

She almost laughed. Didn't let it surface. "They would if I let 'em."

Scott did laugh. Quietly. "We'd better not give you any more yet. Let them work. I'll give you some PMs for tonight."

"Okay."

"Are you comfortable? How's your back? Do you want a pillow under your knees?"

Hot tears again burned her frozen eyes. "Yeah. That'd be great." As she swallowed down the lump in her throat, she heard shuffling. Felt the blanket being lifted just a bit. She lifted her legs. Felt the pillow slide in under her knees. When she lowered them, the stress on her lower back almost completely disappeared. "Oh, wow. Thanks, Doc."

"Just lie still for a while. Okay? Erin, are you all right? Do you need anything? I'll bring you some ice. Can you think of anything else?"

"I think we're good. Are you good, Chris?"

"Yeah. Really. I am."

"All right. I'm not going to argue. I'll be right back."

Footsteps. Silence. Erin squeezed Chris's hand.

A few seconds later. "Here. Chris?" Scott's voice. "Open your mouth and I'll give you some ice."

She opened her mouth, then felt a flat chunk of ice rest on her bottom lip. She carefully sucked it into her mouth, relishing the taste of it on her tongue. "Mmm. Thanks."

She heard a kiss. Was half tempted to raise the towel and take a look. But she resisted the urge. Dreaded the thought of moving even an inch. Of letting in even a hint of blinding light.

But the ice packs were definitely working. Or maybe it was the grip on her hand.

"I'm gonna go, Chris." Scott's voice again. "Lie still and rest. I mean it. I'll be back in about an hour and give you a hand upstairs if you need it."

She swallowed the last of the ice. "Thanks, Scott, but I'll be fine."

"I know you will. But I'll be here."

She smiled.

"I'll take a look at that cut and change the butterflies when I come back." A pause. "I won't be long, love. Don't let her get up. Make her rest."

"I will."

Chris heard a few more kisses. Couldn't force away her smile. Silence again fell. Another squeeze on her hand.

"Rinny?"

"Yeah?"

"He is *absitively* the most awesome man the Lord God ever created."

There was that giggle again. Yet ever so faint.

"And you ..."

"Don't say it, Chris."

"Come on. Please? You won't let me tell you how sorry I am for the mess I made of this day, so at least let me tell you how much I love you."

"You just did. Thanks."

"You're welcome. I think."

More giggles.

Chris drew in a long, deep, utterly refreshing breath. Let it out slowly.

"Want another ice chip?"

"Yeah." She felt it against her bottom lip, then sucked it into her mouth and savored it.

"Will you tell me now?"

A swallow. "Tell you what?" She swished the ice to the other side of her mouth.

"Well, you can start by telling me why you almost got arrested? And how your face came to look like hamburger?"

A laugh. Another swallow. "Didn't I tell you already?"

"Chris."

Another laugh. "Okay, Rin. But, before I do, please tell me if you're all right. I'm laying here all comfie-cozy, but if you're not, tell me."

"I'm fine."

"What are you sitting on?" Chris started to lift away the ice pack from her eyes. The light assaulted her.

"Stop. I'm fine. Put that back. Relax."

"Okay, okay."

"Now tell me. Or do you want another piece of ice?"

"No. I'm good with the ice."

"Good. Now tell me."

"All right, Rin!"

"And don't leave anything out."

★★★

Erin listened intently as Chris told her tale, then wished she had left out the part about Mr. Walker stomping Cappy, or when he swung his elbow back and hit Chris in the ribs. And the part about Jason using the paper bag to prevent Chris from hyperventilating. And the part about Cappy cussing. In Spanish.

She wished Chris would have left out a few other parts too, and told her more about what really happened. What was she feeling —what was really going on in her mind when the police forced those handcuffs on her? When she needed a paper bag to calm her breathing?

She knew Chris would never tell her the complete story or the complete truth about what happened in the Walker's house that afternoon. And if Chris would never tell, Erin would never know. A part of her was glad about that. And a part of her wanted to know everything.

And yet, as Chris flavored her sad story with lighthearted jabs at her own lack of good sense or her inability to duck twice when the fists were flying, Erin could only marvel. Here was a woman — a loving, caring woman — who willingly risked everything, her own health and safety and, to a certain extent, her very life, to help an innocent child. She didn't think about the danger or the consequences when she ran into that house to save that helpless little girl from the one man who threatened every dimension of that little girl's existence. Who else but a father could terrorize a daughter to the point of irreparable lifelong injury? Who else but a father could misuse a daughter's trust to the point of causing that daughter to die on the inside? Who else but a father could hurt his daughter so severely in the ways only he knew she could be hurt?

Mothers could sometimes be just as bad. But the father-daughter relationship? Nothing compared with that. Nothing reached as deeply into a little girl's heart as the tender care and undivided attention of her loving father.

And nothing destroyed a daughter more completely than when that loving father turned everything in her world against her.

Something tickled Erin's cheek. She reached up to scratch it. Her fingers came away wet. She reached for a tissue and wiped her tears away.

"You're awfully quiet, Rin."

"Just listening." She dabbed the tissue at her nose. "Go on."

"There's not much more to tell."

"Sure there is. What about Jason? You said something about fudgesicles? What was that about?"

A smile spread across Chris's lips. "He said they were good medicine. And he was right."

"Where did he find fudgesicles?"

"Crazy dude. He thinks someone buys them just for him and leaves them in the ER nurses' lounge. I didn't have the heart to tell him he was probably making some poor woman crazy by eating her private stash of goodies. He seems to think he's adored around the ER."

"Most paramedics do. That's because most of them are."

Chris laughed.

"He's a good man. I know it nearly killed him when …" Erin let her words fade. "And it nearly killed Scott when Jason pulled away. They've pretty much completely lost touch with each other. Scott hasn't talked about him in a long time. I don't think they even see each other anymore, except for when they meet up at the hospital."

"They were pretty close?"

"Yeah. As far as I can remember. One time I found them up on the helipad shooting baskets. I sat and watched them for almost a half hour before they realized I was there."

"What was his wife's name?"

Erin stared at the battered tissue in her hand. "Jessica. And they were going to name their daughter Elizabeth."

Chris lifted her hand to adjust the ice pack over her eyes. Then slowly pulled it off. Wiped her face with the towel. Then blinked open her eyes and squinted against the light. "Why do you think all of this happened, Rinny?"

Erin's reply was a whisper. "I don't know."

Chris turned her head. Dark bruises had formed under both of her eyes. The whites of her eyes were streaked with angry red lines. "Do you think all of this happened … for a reason?"

Erin slowly nodded. "Yes. I do."

Chris gazed at the wall. Blinked heavy eyelids.

"Someday we'll know why. When we're supposed to know."

"Did Jason and his wife go to church?"

"Not at Kimberley. As far as I can remember. But I think they did go somewhere."

"Do you think he still goes?"

"I don't know. But I think he may have let go of God just like he let go of all his other friends."

Those dark eyes closed. "Can we pray for him, Rin?"

The words warmed Erin's soul. "You bet we can." She quickly reached for another tissue.

"And I wanna pray for you too."

"For me?"

"Yeah." Chris again blinked open her eyes. "I'm worried about you."

"Silly girl. Don't be."

"Rin—"

Erin raised her hand and shook her head.

"You know something?"

"I know plenty."

Chris laughed. "No, Rin. Listen to me. You don't know this."

"Okay. Enlighten me."

Her smile lingered. "This is the truth. If you hadn't called Cappy, I would've been in real trouble. I mean it. I got in way over my head today. And Cappy saved my tookis. Which means—"

"If it wasn't for Isaiah's new cell phone—"

"Rin, if it wasn't for you! You saved me. You did it."

"I just made a phone call. God saved you."

Chris's weary eyes sparkled. "You can say that again."

Erin smiled.

"Hey, if I pray for you and Scott, will you pray for Jason? And Lainer too?"

She tilted her head. "But who will pray for you?"

The sparkle in those eyes flickered out.

"You are such a silly girl."

"Just pray, Rin."

Erin grabbed Chris's hand. Squeezed it tightly in both of hers. Gave Chris one last smile. Then closed her eyes and began to pray.

✳✳✳

After the unbelievable day, Erin didn't want the night to end. "You don't have to go. You can stay down here."

"I know." Chris slowly leaned forward and pushed herself out of the love seat. "I'd like to. Really." She stood and stretched her arms over her head. Winced faintly as her breath caught. Then lowered her hands and grinned sheepishly. "It's probably time for me to call it a night. And that's funny, 'cause I don't even know what time it is."

Laughing, Scott glanced at his watch. "A quarter after eight."

"Really?" Chris let out a grunt. "Feels like midnight. I'm definitely ready for bed."

"I'll come up with you." Erin started to push herself up from the couch.

"No, Rin. Stay put. Please? I'll be fine."

She froze mid-push. Gazed up at Chris. "You sure?"

"I'll be upstairs with my teeth half brushed before you even manage to get out of the couch."

Erin didn't appreciate the laughter coming from the man sitting on the couch with her. She relaxed beside him, then forced her face into a playful frown. "Oh, really?" She glared first at Chris, then at her laughing husband.

"Listen to me." Chris rolled her eyes. "That wasn't a very cool thing to say, was it?"

"Yeah, have a heart, Chris." Scott rubbed Erin's shoulder. "Don't make fun of my wife in her present condition."

Erin still glared. Though her lips twitched with a smile.

"I'm sorry, Rinny. Just think of it as another stupid thing I did today. Add it to my list."

Her smile escaped. She let it capture her entire face. "What list?" She leaned against her husband, felt his arms pull her to him, all the while she continued to grin at the speechless woman standing a few feet away.

Chris raised her fist and shook her index finger at Erin. "Stop that. I mean it." She shook it at Scott as well. "You two …" Her hand fell to her side. "I love you guys." She blinked. "I'm going to bed." She spun around and pushed through the swinging door, heading for the back stairs leading up to her apartment.

"Good night, Chris," Scott hollered as the door swung shut.

"Night, lady." But Erin's voice only softly carried the words. She turned to take in the warmth emanating from her husband's brown eyes.

"What a day, huh."

She let out a laugh that sounded exactly like Chris's grunt.

"Never a dull moment with her around."

"She has that way about her."

"Maybe that's what we love about her."

"Maybe. Among other things."

"And you. You have that way about you too." His hand gently caressed her cheek. "I cannot believe how beautiful you are."

"Oh my. Get real, bub."

"Now listen to you!" His smile danced in his eyes. "I'll not have that kind of talk, young lady. You hear me?" His fingertips lightly traced her lips. "If you keep talking that way, I'll have to shut you up."

"Go for it, bub."

"You asked for it."

She laughed as his lips touched hers, until her ability to laugh and then even to breathe were completely stolen away.

★★★

THE APARTMENT WAS DARK. CHRIS didn't turn on the hallway light. She slowly pushed the stair door closed, then stood by Cappy's bedroom door and listened. She heard a faint whisper waft her way from the living room.

"Is dat the boogeyman?"

A breath of laughter burst through her lips.

"I know it ain't da Avon Lady, 'cause she always rings da bell. And she never comes in da back door. No, suh. Only da boogeyman sneaks in da back door."

Chris sat on the couch across from Cappy's recliner. "Who told you that?" She kicked her feet up onto the coffee table and slouched low in the couch.

"My momma. She was a boogeyman expert."

"She was, huh?"

"And d'ya know what? The way she described him?"

"Big and hairy and mean?"

"Sounds just like Floyd Walker, doesn't it?"

Chris should have seen that coming a mile away, but she didn't. She cracked up.

"Yes, go ahead and laugh, brave one. For you have faced dat ugly monster … dat nasty ol' boogeyman … and you have sent him away to meet his just reward."

"You're a nut, Cap."

"Yeah, maybe. But I'm definitely not a flake. I'd much rather be a nut than a flake."

Chris's eyes closed as she laughed.

"It's good to hear you laugh, woman."

A sigh. "It's good to laugh. Thanks."

"Nah. Don't mention it."

She lifted her head. "How are you? How's the shoe print he left on your back?"

"Ahh, I'll live to fight another day."

"You wanna hear what I told Erin?"

"Sure."

"I told her you saved my tookis. Which is the truth, lady."

Cappy let out a grunt. "From where I see it, I showed up about nine seconds too late to save your tookis. When I first saw your tookis, it was flying across that ogre's living room."

"Oh. That? Just a minor setback."

"Yeah. Right."

Silence played out between them.

"Why were you sitting here in the dark?"

"Ever notice it's quieter around here when the lights are out?"

Chris considered that. "Yeah. I think I've noticed that."

"The lights make too much noise sometimes. I just needed to hear the silence."

Chris savored the words.

"He's in the silence. Have you noticed that?"

Her eyes filled with tears.

"He's not a God of chaos, but of peace."

She closed her eyes and felt her entire being relax.

"Though He does send a little chaos our way from time to time."

"Yeah. Why does He do that?"

"Who knows."

Laughter bubbled up from her belly. She let every bit of it escape.

"But I know this."

"Tell me, Cap."

"He loves us."

Silence again danced playfully around them. Chris laid still and let it wash over her soul like a cleansing, healing flood.

✯✯✯

IT WAS ONE OF HER husband's favorite songs. He used to sing it when they first met. "You Are My Sunshine." Erin kept blinking, hoping her tears wouldn't cloud the precious sight before her.

Stretched out across the couch, her husband's cheek gently rested against the bulge of their unborn child as his voice carried the sweet song perfectly in tune to their baby's kicking delight.

The moment overwhelmed her the same way it did every night when he sang the song to their little one and she kicked and danced with joy. Such a sweet way to end the day. Especially a day like today.

Sweetheart . . . it's so true. You'll never know how much I love you. Oh, please, Lord, tell him for me. Help me show him in every way.

More kicking. Scott laughed, his entire face beaming, yet he made not a sound. Erin slowly wiped her eyes.

"We're making Mommy cry again."

"Yes, you are."

"Is it okay that we're making Mommy cry?"

"Oh my, yes."

Scott lifted his head and smiled at his wife. Then lowered his cheek against her belly again. "Should we make Mommy really cry now? Should we show her our little secret?"

Erin felt her eyes widen. "Secret?"

Another kick. Another beaming smile on her husband's face. "Daddy's got a gift for Mommy. And it's a gift for you too, my little boo."

"A gift?"

Scott's eyes lifted to meet Erin's gaze. "Yeah. And after a day like today, I think it's a perfect time for some gift giving."

Erin certainly couldn't argue with that.

"Shall we trudge up the stairs so Daddy can give his two most precious gifts ... a gift?"

"You're silly, Daddy."

"Silliness abounds. Why not?"

She could only smile.

Scott pushed up from her lap and quickly turned to help her out of the couch. They locked the front door and turned off the downstairs lights. Then slowly worked their way up the stairs. When they cleared the last step, Erin stood for a second to catch her breath.

"Do you want to change first?" Scott's hand gently rubbed Erin's back.

"No, I want to see my gift."

Smiling, Scott led her down the hall to the nursery and stopped at the closed door. "Close your eyes."

She made a face at him.

"Come on. Please?" Oh, how his eyes pleaded.

"Don't walk me into the door."

His tongue clicked against the roof of his mouth. "You say the sweetest things sometimes."

"I get it from you." Erin laughed. Closed her eyes. After a second, she sensed he had opened the door. She reached out to feel the door frame. Let him lead her inside the room.

"Okay. Open them."

Slowly, so very slowly, Erin blinked open her eyes. She saw the nursery fully adorned with Winnie-the-Poohs and Tiggers too, just the way she had left it earlier that day. But there, on the floor by her glider rocker and matching ottoman, filled with the entire assortment of Christopher Robin's stuffed and happy friends, sat a gorgeously stained and perfectly detailed old-fashioned wooden cradle.

It was by far the most beautiful cradle Erin had ever seen.

SIX

"I HAVE A CONFESSION TO make."

Scott pulled off his socks and tossed them toward the clothes hamper. Then leaned back on the bed and laid his head across Erin's blanket-covered legs. "Yes, dear?"

Erin rubbed her belly with one hand, then pulled a piece of fuzz from the blanket with the other. She rolled it between her fingers. Tried to formulate her confession into something presentable.

"I'm waiting."

"I knew about the cradle."

Shock, then sadness played out on her husband's face.

"But I never dreamed it would be so beautiful! It's perfect, Scott. You did a beautiful job. You and Isaiah."

He slowly smiled. "Who told you?"

Erin remembered the day a few months back, sitting at the table in the basement of the church, sipping peppermint tea with Sonya Connelly while one of the worst storms in the history of Portland raged outside.

"Emily. She told you."

"No. It wasn't Emily." Not at first, anyway. Emily Sadler couldn't keep the secret any better than Sonya Connelly could. And Emily was Isaiah's wife.

"Isaiah didn't tell you." Scott's eyes bulged. "Did he?"

"No. Isaiah didn't tell me." Though she enjoyed the game of Twenty Questions, she didn't want to keep her husband guessing all night. "Sonya told me."

"Sonya? That fink! She told me she wouldn't tell. When did she tell you?"

"During the storm. I think she did it to cheer me up."

"The storm in February? Why did you need cheering up?"

Erin only grinned.

Scott gazed at her. Until, "Oh. Yeah. Never mind." A laugh. Then a quick frown. "You've known all this time?"

Still grinning, she nodded.

"Do you really like it, Erin?"

If her daughter hadn't been in the way, Erin would have leaned over and kissed his sweet lips. Instead, she reached toward him and waited for his hand to take hers. "Baby, yes. Oh, yes. I love it. It is absolutely gorgeous. And absolutely perfect. And she'll love it too." She couldn't resist pointing to her bulging belly.

Scott sat up and placed his hands on Erin's belly. Gently caressed it. Slid his hands to feel this little bump, then that one. She watched him, savored the sight, then slid her hands to the same spots, feeling the warmth his hands left behind.

She gasped. Both of their hands stopped over the spot where their baby just kicked. Her mouth fell open. "I don't think that was a kick."

Scott's eyes lit up. "Do you think it was her hand?"

They gazed at each other for a second. Erin bit her lip. Then nodded. She lowered her gaze to the sight of their hands together, over the very spot where their daughter—or son—just reached up to join a tiny hand with theirs.

"This is a moment, Erin."

She struggled to blink tears from her eyes.

"This is a moment ... I will never forget."

"I love you, Scott."

"Oh, baby ... I love you too." He moved in close to kiss her lips. Then crawled up beside her and pulled her into his arms.

They sat side by side for quite a while, leaning against each other, holding hands with their precious little one, singing happy songs to each other, and laughing as their little one danced.

★★★

"Baby?" A hand touched her shoulder. Shook her. "Wake up. You're dreaming."

Erin woke with a start. "Scott?" She rolled onto her back.

"You okay? You were dreaming."

She rolled the rest of the way toward him, onto her left side. Rubbed her eyes. "What?"

"You were dreaming. Sort of mumbling. I don't know what you were trying to say, but it didn't sound good."

"I was?" She fluffed her pillow and relaxed against it. Let out a deep breath. "That's so weird. I don't remember any dream."

"Really? Not at all?"

"I was mumbling?"

"You sounded pretty agitated. Like you were afraid."

"Huh. Wonder why?" She yawned. "Sorry I woke you."

"I was already awake. I can't sleep."

Erin grabbed her husband's hand. "Why not? Are you all right?"

"I've been thinking."

In the faint glow of the streetlight filtering through the blinds, she saw a clouded expression on her husband's face. "About what, love? What were you thinking about?"

"Not a what. A who."

She squeezed his hand. "Tell me."

"You should go back to sleep."

"No, tell me."

A deep sigh. "I don't know. I guess ... I was thinking about Chris."

The words surprised her, but only for a second. "Well, considering everything that happened today, that's understandable."

"Do you think she's going to be all right? I mean ... Erin, should we see about getting her professional help?"

She lightly kissed the back of her husband's hand. "Baby, I *know* she'll be all right. She belongs to God now. And she knows it."

Scott seemed to be carefully choosing his words. "Forgive me, sweetheart, I don't want this to sound cold. I know that's enough for God, and that He is definitely at work in her. It's great. But . . . do you think that's enough for Chris? Will she continue to let Him work? Or will she . . . run?"

"It's been four months. She hasn't run yet."

"I think she would have today if the dizziness hadn't stopped her."

Erin swallowed. Used her thumb to gently caress the back of Scott's hand.

"Do you think I'm wrong?"

"No." A whisper.

Scott drew in a sharp breath. "You really should go back to sleep."

"No. I'm all right. I want to talk about this."

"Are you sure? I mean . . . some of the stuff I'm wondering about may be none of my business anyway."

"Don't say that."

"I really do care about her, and I want to do everything I can to help her. I hope you know that."

"I do know that."

"I want to ask you something, but if you don't think it's my place to know, then just say so. I'll understand."

"Ask me anything, Scott. I'll answer it. If I can."

He fell silent for a moment. "Erin, why is there so much rage in her?"

A prayer whispered up from her soul.

"Can you tell me? Do you know? What would cause such a level of rage in her that she would slam her fists into the table the way she did? What caused her to reach that place where she smashed the dresser drawers against the wall that one night? What has she been through? Was it the war?"

"Slow down, baby . . ."

A faint growl. "I'm sorry."

"Don't be. But listen for a second. I think I know how to answer your question, but you really need to be sure you want to hear the answer. I'm not doubting your sincerity—I know you want to help

Chris. But when you hear what I've got to say, it'll change the way you see her. You'll understand her better, yes. But you'll wish you were never told. If you're told, Scott, you'll be committing yourself. You'll be past that point where you can turn your back on her and just walk away. You'll never be able to just *walk away*."

He chewed his bottom lip for a second. "Is it that bad?" He paused. "Is that what happened to you? When you found out about it? You knew you could never walk away?"

"Yes. That's exactly what happened."

"All those years. And all the times I tried to make you forget."

"It's why I needed to go to Colorado. After losing track of her, and then finding her again …"

"I'm sorry I gave you so much grief about that."

"You didn't know. And I didn't know how to explain it to you. We didn't have time. I'm sorry too, babe. That was a … difficult time."

"So when did you find out about … whatever it is we're talking about?"

Erin sighed. "If you can believe it, it was during a stupid game of volleyball."

A laugh. "What? When was this?"

"We were at Rafha, finally in place, waiting for the start of the ground war. The weather had just cleared. Someone had set up a net and we were just goofing around, playing some serious 'beach volleyball' in the Land of Sand." She let out a laugh. "There were four of us: Tim Boyd and Chris against Teddy and I. We played for quite a while. It was fun. Until …" She stopped.

Scott waited.

Erin didn't want to tell this story again. She drew in another deep breath. Slowly let it out.

"Are you sure you're all right with this? Do you want to just forget it and go back to sleep?"

She looked up at him. "Do you?"

His lips pressed into a firm line. "Maybe. If you're tired."

"I'm definitely awake now, and we've started something that will need to be finished."

"Ahh, baby … I'm sorry." He caressed her cheek, then pushed back her hair from her face.

"This is important, Scott. Especially after what happened today."

His fingertip lightly poked her nose. "The instant you change your mind, let's quit. Okay? We can certainly talk about this tomorrow."

"What I have to tell you, I'm only going to tell you once."

He squeezed her hand. "I understand."

"If we start talking about it, we're not going to stop until we're done. We can skip church tomorrow if we have to."

Against the pillow, he nodded.

"So I'll ask *you*. Are you sure?"

Scott grinned. "I've opened up a serious can of worms, haven't I?"

"Well …" Erin refluffed her pillow. "As long as you're willing to gather 'em all back up and put 'em back in the can, I think we'll be all right."

"Deal."

She smiled. Then tried to steel herself against what was to come. "You know what? I'm not going to start with the volleyball game. Let me establish a few things first."

"Works for me."

"First of all, you need to know … I never asked to be Chris McIntyre's friend."

A burst of laughter.

"It was Teddy's fault. He's the one who took me to the parking garage and put my gear down beside Chris's cot. And if it wasn't Teddy's fault, then it was Ben's, because he's the one who assigned us to the same unit. And if it wasn't Ben's fault … then it was God's. You know what? I blame Him entirely. Forget Teddy and Ben. And you know what else?"

More laughter. "No, baby. What."

"This won't be as hard to talk about as I thought, because all of this is God's fault, and you and I are just along for the ride. In the end, Chris will be well and healed and living a beautiful life of love and faith in the Lord Jesus. She's already so almost there it's not even funny."

"You're absolutely right."

"So." Erin traced her fingers across the hair on Scott's arm. "With that said, no one can blame me for becoming Chris's friend. It was meant to be. And no one can blame me for sticking with her all these years. Or putting up with her. I think we've already covered why that's true."

"Yes, I think we did."

"But here's the next thing I need to establish. After all this preamble, the truth is I still don't know that much about her. That should make you laugh, because you pointed this out to me several times after Chris first arrived here, and you were exactly right. There is so much more I *don't* know about her than I do know. And all I do know is what I've seen or what she's told me, which, when you put both of them together, add up to almost nothing." Her fingertips caressed the smooth skin on the underside of Scott's forearm.

"Are you okay with that?"

"I don't know. A part of me really wishes she would sit me down someday and tell me everything she's been through. And the rest of me is absolutely terrified that someday . . . she actually will."

"You're afraid if she tells you, you won't know how to help her deal with it?"

She felt the strong beat of his heart pulsing through his wrist. "I'm just afraid."

They lay in silence for a while. Scott's voice barely broke it. "If she ever does tell you, just the fact you're willing to listen should help her."

"I don't think she'll ever tell me. Not unless I ask her and really pester her about it. And I don't want to do that. But even if I did, she'd only tell me as much as she thought necessary. She wouldn't tell me everything. She will never forcibly expose to anyone what she endured as a child."

"But you think she'll volunteer it someday?"

"I'm hoping she will. In the meantime, I don't want to push her about it." A quick sigh. "I mean, like today. I had to practically beg her to tell me what happened. She didn't want to tell me, and she only did because she pretty much knew she had to. Then, when she did tell me what happened, she only told me exactly what she wanted me to hear. Nothing more, nothing less. No details she thought would bother me. Nothing glamorizing what she did. And nothing even remotely resembling what she really endured." Erin lifted her hand and ran her fingers through her hair. "She seriously makes me crazy sometimes, that's for sure."

Scott only smiled.

"But that's just it. She'd rather make me crazy than hurt me. She'd rather make me angry at her than have me feel sorry for her. She's always been like that."

"She wants to protect you."

"Why do you and her think I need all this protection? When she first got here, you two about drove me crazy with all your protection."

"But I'm not the one who throws dresser drawers across rooms."

Erin sighed deeply, allowing a soft hum to carry on the outgoing breath. "Yes, you are right about that."

Scott seemed to enjoy his little victory.

"I still can't believe she threw our dresser drawers across the room."

A peaceful silence fell.

"What did you think about her when you first met her? Was there any indication she carried such rage?"

"Well ..." Suddenly smiling, Erin went back to tracing the hair on her husband's arm. "Ten seconds after I first met her, she proceeded to call Teddy every nasty name in the book. And then some." She laughed. "You know? I could never figure their relationship out. They seemed to hate each other, yet they worked well together. It's like they fed off each other's hostility." As she slowly shook her head, the pillow rustled against her ear.

"So you didn't like her at first?"

"No, I liked her. Very much. Just because she cussed at Teddy didn't mean the man didn't deserve it."

"What was it about her you liked?"

"Her strength. Immediately. I know that's strange to hear, but that's what drew me to her the moment I saw her. I didn't sense a hint of fear in her. Even though I was terrified to be in Saudi."

"Terrified?"

"Okay, that may be a bit melodramatic. But I was scared."

"You know, she may not have acted like it, but I bet she was scared too."

"She told me one night, while we were looking up at the stars, that she was afraid of everything. And she meant it. I couldn't believe it. I mean, I had been in Saudi two days when I saw her rappel headfirst in a freefall from our airborne Huey. From that moment I was sure the woman wasn't afraid of anything. I actually wondered for the longest time if she had a death wish. I realize now that she almost sort of did. Thank God she didn't hurt herself. She did some crazy things, that's for sure."

"Like hanging by her knees from the rafter at the gym?"

A laugh. "Yep, just like that. Man. She had Sonya wondering too." Another laugh. "And like the time we turned back in the Huey to go to the Dustoff. As we turned, Chris stood on the skid and hung completely out, completely at the mercy of her restraint strap. If it would have snapped or if her vest would have slipped, she would have fallen. And died."

"Isaiah told me he couldn't believe it when she climbed up that rope into the rafters."

"I'm way past asking *why*, but someday I'd really like to ask her *how* she does the things she does. And did. I mean, wow."

"Why did she say she was afraid of everything?"

The memory of that starry night washed sweetly over Erin's soul. "She told me she was born scared. That she was afraid of God. Of what He would do to her next." The words still burned like fire. "That night as we talked ... that was the first time she started to open up a bit about her past. She trusted me that night, trusted our friendship, and started to let go a little. But as soon as she realized what she was saying, she clammed up and ..." Erin couldn't finish.

"And what?"

"She ran."

Silence.

"But you know what's amazing? Even though I have every reason to believe she endured a horrific childhood, ever since I've known her, she has taught me more about true childlike faith in Christ than anyone. Does that make sense? It's like I simply just love to watch her *live*. She lives life full and complete. With every fiber of her being. I wish I could learn to live that well."

"Yeah." A long pause. "Me too."

"I just wish ... oh, Scott." Erin rubbed her eyes as tears threatened. "I just wish her childhood could have been better. She has struggled her entire adult life to move past what she endured in her childhood. Yet, she can't. Because it won't let her. It sits on the fringes of her waking hours tormenting her, then waits for her to close her eyes so it can haunt her when she sleeps. At least I know it used to. She's so much better now that she's given everything to Christ. But I know it still eats at her sometimes. And I believe it's what triggers her rage."

"Baby ... what happened at that volleyball game? What did you see?"

She grabbed her husband's hand. Lifted it. Kissed it. Let it linger near her lips. "I saw the most horrifying and hideous sight I have ever seen in my life." She raised her eyes to meet her husband's gaze. "And you know I've seen some hideous things in my life. You have too. Things you'll never forget. It's the nature of our job."

He squeezed her hand and barely nodded.

"We were playing the stupid game just to kill some time." She moved his hand to rest against her cheek. "Tim set one up for Chris, and she jumped up and spiked it. It hit Teddy square on his big fat forehead." Laughter filtered out of her. "It hit him so hard it bounced all the way out of bounds and rolled under a Humvee. Oh man, it was hilarious. I about died laughing."

"I can almost picture it."

"Chris fell to her knees and was completely hysterical with laughter. And Teddy didn't like that. Not one bit. He ran at her and pretty much outright assaulted her. He jumped on her back and forced her face-first into the sand. I was so mad at him I wanted to write him up for it. I mean, it was just a stupid freak thing! He had no right to go after Chris that way."

He had no business going down that road . . .

Ben's words. His voice echoed through Erin's heart. So long ago. And so true. She drew in a slow, deep breath.

"What did you do?" Just a whisper.

The words embarrassed her. "I stood there, like an idiot. I just stood there while Teddy sat on Chris's back and laughed at her and threw sand into her hair. Oh, man, it was awful. And I did nothing to stop him."

"Don't say that. I'm sure it wasn't like that."

"Well, I do know I took a few steps closer, because I saw his knee move against her back. And when it did, it pulled her T-shirt up out of her pants." Breath caught in her tightening throat. She struggled to swallow. "Her T-shirt untucked . . . and I saw what I first thought was dirt streaked across Chris's bare back. Long lines of it. But then I instantly knew . . . it wasn't dirt." She gazed into her husband's eyes. "Scott, the lines on her back . . . were scars. So many scars." Her voice shook. "Every bit of her back that I saw was crisscrossed with them. I only saw it for a split second."

Scott's eyes pinched shut as his head pressed back against his pillow. His hand came up to squeeze the bridge of his nose. "Lord . . ."

"I couldn't move, I couldn't breathe . . . I just stood there, probably gaping like a fool, until she pushed Teddy off of her and stood. She turned around and coughed and spit the sand from her mouth . . . and looked straight at me. I'll never forget the look in her eyes."

"Did she say anything?"

"No. Nothing. She took one look at Teddy, then reached back ... and punched him on the mouth. I mean, she hit him so hard his feet flew out from under him and he landed flat on his back in the sand. She almost knocked him out. I'm still amazed she didn't break his jaw."

"Did she ever say anything to you about it?"

"No. We have never talked about that day. Well, I take that back. We did talk about it the night she came home drunk."

A small smile stretched her husband's lips. "Ahh, yes. I remember that night."

"She was drunk, which was the only reason I could get her to talk about it. She completely severed our friendship when she turned and walked away from me that day. The night she was drunk, she told me the reason she did that was because she knew I saw what I saw."

"She didn't want you to pity her."

"Or question or wonder or even lie and say I didn't see. Oh, that would have made her completely insane, if I would have lied about it or even pretended like I hadn't seen it. She definitely knew that I had."

"But why was that such a problem? Why couldn't she just talk to you about it?"

"Because she had never talked to anyone about it. Ever. Even now, I don't think she has ever talked to anyone about anything even remotely related to her childhood."

"Except you."

"Except me. But only on those few occasions when she unwittingly let her guard down."

"Or had it taken down by booze."

A grunt of laughter. Then long, weary silence. Erin finally released her husband's hand and rubbed her eyes.

"We should stop so you can sleep."

"I'm okay. Actually, I'm surprised I'm not crying. When I talked to Ben about this ..." She instantly regretted her words. "I'm sorry, babe. But I told Ben that night after I talked to Chris. When she was drunk." Her eyes closed as her heart swelled with sadness. "I'm sorry I couldn't stay and pray with you that night. When I went downstairs, I saw the light on at Ben's house. I really thought it was Sonya. That's why I went over. But when he answered the door … it almost felt like God had worked something out. As it turned out, He did. Ben and I talked about things …" She opened her eyes. "We had a good talk. And we prayed."

Scott gently lifted Erin's chin so he could look into her eyes. "Erin, I asked you to stay and pray with me that night, but I didn't really want to pray with you. I just wanted you close to me."

She saw a reflection of her own sadness in his shadowed eyes. She lifted her hand and touched his cheek.

"I was arrogant. And I was selfish. I wanted you to lie down beside me. Even if it meant faking a prayer about someone I didn't care about, you would have been beside me, and that was all I cared about."

Tears burned her eyes. She tried to blink them away.

"I'm sorry, love. I can't tell you how sorry I am."

"You don't have to be sorry. I walked out on you, remember? I could have stayed and tried to talk to you about it. I could have made you understand. At least a little." She wiped her tears to see him clearly. "We were both selfish that night."

"That's not true and you know it."

"What. You want to argue now?" A smile. "We're here now. We're talking. And I think we both understand so much more than we did. Not just about Chris, but about ourselves. And our place in this … work."

"The work of God. Right before our eyes."

"And it's going to turn out beautifully. I just know it."

"Do you think she and Jason hit it off?"

Joy flooded Erin's entire being. "She was definitely rambling about him this afternoon. Wouldn't it be something if they hooked up?"

"He'd be good for her. He's a good guy." Scott drew in a deep breath as he smiled. Let it out in a rush. "Erin, that night, when Chris came home drunk …"

A quick thought brought a grin to Erin's face. *We need a better way of referring to that night, Lord.*

" ... I asked you to pray with me." He picked up her hand and held it in both of his. "Tonight ... I'm going to ask you again. But this time I'll mean it. Okay?"

Her grin softened.

"Sweetheart, will you pray with me? About Chris? I mean ... after everything that happened today, I'll admit ... I don't like what happened today. Though she did so much for Alaina, in a way ... she still scares me."

"She scares me sometimes too."

"Should I be worried about that?"

"No." A laugh.

Scott swallowed deeply. "I do trust her, Erin. I really want to keep trusting her. And I want to be a part of what God is doing in her. If He needs me to help in any way, I want to help."

"You have been. You've been a huge help to her. She adores you."

"I just don't want to do anything to jeopardize that. I don't want to hinder what God is doing in her life."

"You won't."

"You sound so sure."

"I know you. Sometimes I think I know you better than you know yourself."

He cupped her cheek with his hand. "I love you. Do you know that?"

"Is that a trick question?"

"At this moment, I love you more than I have ever loved you in my entire life."

She gazed into her husband's softly burning eyes ... and knew every word he said was true.

★★★

A BIRD SAT OUTSIDE HER bedroom window singing his happy little twelve-note song. But that wasn't the problem. The little critter was just singing the song the Lord gave him. Singing it with all his might. Over and over and over...

And that same one bird singing that same one song seemed to sit outside Chris's bedroom window every single morning of every single day since spring settled over Kimberley Square. She normally wasn't bothered by happy little birds singing their happy little songs. But this morning, considering her eyes refused to open and her head felt skewered to her pillow with railroad spikes, she sadly realized she was starting to be bothered. Seriously. She wished that one particular happy little bird would unfold his happy little wings and take his unceasing twelve-note song of joyous praise somewhere else.

She dared a glance at her alarm clock. Blinked. *Oops.*

She had every intention of getting up in time for Sunday school. But since her clock already read 9:21, her good intentions would not be enough to get her to the church on time. She closed her eyes. Considered her options. If she forced herself out of bed within the next five minutes, she would still be able to make the main service. If, that is, someone arrived sometime within the next four to pull out the railroad spikes so she could move.

Ugh. Not again.

The last time she woke up feeling this miserable—just last February, actually—she had vowed to never let it happen again.

So much for a vow.

Being body slammed by the boogeyman was almost as bad as taking a header down the concrete stairs of the Kimberley Street Community Church.

She wanted to laugh at herself, yet didn't want to move, not even to laugh.

But she had to move.

With a heartfelt groan, she slowly rolled onto her back, then lifted a hand to rub her eyes and forehead. Carefully avoided the sore spots. Wanted to squish her fingers into her ears to drown out that insanely obnoxious, happy dumb bird.

Don't pick on the poor little thing. This is all your own doing. She blinked. Couldn't argue with truth. *Got myself stupid drunk. And now I'm hungover. Paying the price for stubborn stupidity.* She dropped her hand and let out a deep breath. *Wish I'd gotten whiskey drunk instead. At least then I wouldn't remember being stupid.*

It was a drag being hungover and remembering every single stupid, dumb thing she did. And said.

"Lord?" The word came out as a croak. She didn't force that, just whispered the rest. "Rinny told me Your mercy is new every morning. I like that. Because I need Your mercy so much." She studied the swirls of plaster on her ceiling. "And You know? I think it's just like You to always have a fresh batch ready and waiting ... for mornings like this when I wake up and realize I've used up every bit of what You've already given me."

The happy little bird sang his happy little song.

The most beautiful sound Chris had ever heard.

✯✯✯

SHE DIDN'T WANT TO CALL. And didn't want to lug her pregnant self up those stairs. She certainly didn't want to send Scott up, for once he climbed the stairs and knocked on the door of Chris and Cappy's apartment, who could tell what he would see?

Oh my, no. That is not an option.

She wanted to call. Wanted to climb those stairs.

She sat quietly at the dining room table sipping her tea and listening to the creaks and bumps of the big old house. If she sat in the clinic, she would be able to hear footsteps above her. If either Cappy or Chris were awake and walking around. She strained her ears, hoping to hear that familiar sound as one, or sometimes both of them, stomped down the outside stairs. So far that morning, all Erin heard were the bumps and creaks giving hints that her husband had finished up in the bathroom and was now in the bedroom getting ready to walk with his wife across the street to the Kimberley Street Community Church.

They still had a few minutes before Sunday school started. Even after Erin lumbered across the street, they would make it with time to spare. She closed her eyes and tasted the sweet, minty burn of the tea. Swallowed it down. Slowly lowered her mug to the table. Then encircled it with both hands, feeling its warmth radiate up through her arms to soak into her entire body.

So quiet. So peaceful. A beautiful morning. Cheerful birdsong. Brilliant blue sky.

So unlike the previous day with all of its chaos and worry. And so unlike that one night, when Chris smashed the dresser drawers against the wall of the nursery. Since that night, Erin had willed herself to forget, and the memory had almost completely faded from her mind. But the sounds of that night still echoed across the walls of her soul. The shattering wood. The screams of rage. The violent curses.

The sounds . . .

Why were they so hard to forget? Chris slamming her fists on the table. Such rage in her eyes.

Could it be, Lord? Could it be . . . the sounds . . . are what plague Chris? The sounds of her dad's rage? The sounds of . . . Erin's stomach clenched. *Oh, dear Lord God, they're what haunt her. The sounds . . . of being beaten.* Her mouth fell open. She stared across the room, yet could almost feel herself being taken back to that time, that place in the desert, that aid station where she and Chris spent so much of their time.

To that one particular day. Chris had stood by a stack of boxes checking and repacking medevac kits. Her hair was pulled back in that ever-present French braid. Sweat dripped down the sides of her face and drenched her brown general-issue T-shirt, so deeply tucked into her tightly belted BDU pants. Her sunburned arm reached up to turn off the radio one of the other medics had left blaring on a stack of boxes. "Sorry, Rin. But I can't take that kind of music." She said the words, then grabbed a water bottle and chugged a huge drink.

"What kind of music do you like to listen to?" Erin asked her.

"Well, unfortunately, not much. I don't like anything with a heavy beat. Or anything with lame, repeated lyrics. Some country music makes me violently ill. I think I'm allergic to it." Chris flashed a brilliant smile, then set back to work repacking the kit.

"Hmm. No heavy beat. No lame, repeated lyrics. I'd say that pretty severely limits your options."

That brilliant smile flashed again. "Yeah, I know. Pretty much leaves me with ... silence."

Silence.

Faint stomping.

Erin blinked.

More stomping.

Her breath caught as her head turned.

Chris? Stomping down the outside stairs?

Footsteps on the porch.

She forced herself out of the chair. Waddled to the front door. Heard a faint knock just as she reached for the doorknob. Pulled open the door.

Cappy. Alone.

Erin smiled. And knew it wasn't the caliber of smile Cappy would save and keep forever.

"*Hola, mamacita.*"

Yes. Now her smile beamed like it should. "Morning, lady. Come on in."

"I was worried about you." Cappy closed the door behind her. "Hope you slept all right last night."

Erin waddled back to sit in her chair. "Yeah. We did all right." She motioned for Cappy to join her at the table.

"Chris is still zonked. I peeked in on her just before I left, and she was snoring."

Warmth filtered through Erin's heart as she imagined Chris wrapped up in her colorful Navajo fleece blankets, snoring peacefully. "Want some tea?"

"Do we have time?"

"Sure." She started to push up from the chair, but Cappy's hand on her arm stopped her.

"I'll get it. Just tell me where the tea bags are."

Erin relaxed. "I think they're still out on the counter."

A laugh. "Well, they should be easy to find then."

Cappy's smile touched Erin's heart. She basked in the moment, savoring the sweetness of friendship, knowing the new day would bring healing and hope for them all. For the One they would soon gather to worship, the One who loved them before life even began, had brought them together in this fleeting moment of eternity for just that one purpose. To love each other as friends. As family.

More stomping. From the stairs behind her. She turned and saw the grinning face of the man she adored. Felt his arms softly surround her. His lips gently nibbled her neck by her ear. And he smelled so good.

Erin couldn't say a word. She felt her husband move away toward the kitchen, then closed her eyes and continued to bask as he playfully greeted Cappy with his unbelievably lame Spanish.

You're working in all of us, precious Father God. In ways we can't even imagine or will ever fully know. Not until we stand in Your presence. Then we'll see how far You've brought us. Then we'll fully comprehend how deep Your love flows. She held her breath as her baby squirmed into a new position. *That moment will be pretty spectacular. But it'll have to be, Lord. To beat this moment right here and right now.*

★★★

The shower washed her clean. She was clean. Inside and out. With the hope of a new day and the new mercies it would bring, she knew she would be all right. Yet, she struggled to shake off the dirtiness, the defilement of the events of the previous day. She slogged through her routine, brushed her teeth, then brushed her wet hair without even glancing at the mirror. An entire day had passed. And she had yet to look into her own eyes. To see what stupidity had wreaked on her face.

But the time had come. If she was going to church to worship the Lord and see her friends, she needed to look into that mirror.

And she needed to do it now or else she'd be late. She steeled herself with a huge, deep breath that stretched her hurting ribs. Let it out with a huff. Then slowly lifted her head and gazed at her own face.

A sharp pain shot through her stomach. *Oh. God.* She blinked. *Makeup. Lots of makeup.* She dug through her shelf in the medicine cabinet for her bottle of foundation. Liberally applied it over everything black and blue. She carefully peeled off Scott's butterfly bandages, then waited, praying the cut on her cheek wouldn't separate and start spewing blood.

She stared at it. Waited. So far, so good. She dabbed a little foundation around its pink edges. Winced. Yet felt a hint of relief. Jason had closed it beautifully. *Sweet man.* With a little luck, the scar it left behind would be only a trace of its former self.

You still should've had someone stitch it.

Nah. Just another scar to add to my collection.

She closed up the bottle of foundation and gazed once again at her face. Presentable. At least as presentable as she could make herself. She never was very good at applying makeup. Maybe because she never wore it.

Stalling only aggravated her nervousness. She drew in another deep breath, then cupped her hand under the cold water and sipped some of it. Blew out another deep breath. Hated herself with every passing beat of her heart. Hated what she saw in the mirror looking back at her.

Lord, I don't want to do this. I can't do this. I can't face these people. Not again. Not like this.

She tried to blink away her tears, but they fell anyway, smearing the makeup on her cheeks. She lowered her head and slammed her fists on the edge of the sink. *I can't do this! Lord?*

I'm here.

Breaths raced in and out through her open mouth. She closed her eyes and strained to hear any other sound, anything outside or inside or even whispering through her soul.

She heard her heart pounding. And nothing more.

Did she really hear the words?

She closed her mouth and swallowed, yet couldn't force down the ache in her throat. She cupped her hand again under the water and drew it to her lips. Drank deeply. Turned off the water. Grabbed a towel and wiped her hand. Then her lips. Then dabbed it against her eyes. Slowly looked up.

Dark brown eyes peered back at her. Long thick lashes. Tiny streaks of red. Hints of bruised skin underneath the layer of foundation. Yet she made no effort to apply more.

You are here, Lord. I have to believe that. I can't do this if You don't help me.

She waited. Hugged the towel to her chest. Felt her blood course through her body. Heard it throb against her eardrums. Felt it throb inside her skull.

"Lord Jesus ..." The faintest of whispers. "I can't do this. I'm sorry."

Her hair needed to be dried and brushed. The thought of the insanely loud dryer next to her throbbing head didn't sit well. She could braid her hair still wet. But, either way, if she didn't make up her mind and do something with it right now and then walk out the door in the very next instant and run across the street, she'd be late.

Staring into the pathetic eyes staring back at her, she couldn't move.

Jesus ... please. I'm so sorry. But I can't do this. I know this is stupid. Please forgive me. Again.

She pushed away from the sink, hung the towel on the rack, then walked down the hall to sit in Cappy's recliner. She pulled her feet up and turned to lean her shoulder into the recliner's soft back. It slowly rocked for a few seconds. Silence fell over the room.

My love ...

Tears burned her eyes as the words, as light as a breath, whispered through her soul. She went there, her hands reaching out to cling to the words, but they were gone. Only a faint echo remained. Enough to savor for another heartbeat of time. Before it too, faded away.

Her eyes fell closed as her heart slowed. Silence washed through her. A long, slow breath eased every lingering ache.

I'm here ...

A faint smile pulled her lips. Deep inside the recesses of her soul, she reached out to touch the words, laughing as her fingers passed through them, as they slowly dissipated on an ever-so-gentle breeze. She could almost see Him standing there. She reached out her hand to touch Him. And wept as He slowly pulled her into His arms. And held her.

SEVEN

A touch on her arm startled her instantly awake. Her feet kicked to the floor, but the recliner rocked forward and almost tossed her out. A hand grabbed her arm. Erin's hand. A quick laugh. "Easy, now! I'm sorry."

Chris blinked her eyes and forced in a breath. "Erin, don't do that! Are you trying to give me heart failure?"

More laughter. "No. I'm sorry." But she didn't sound sorry. Not with the way she was laughing.

"What are you doing here?" Chris instantly regretted her words. "I mean ..."

"Are you okay?" Erin sat on the couch.

"I think so. Give me a minute to make sure."

"Take your time."

Chris gazed at her a second longer. Then laughed.

A peaceful silence fell.

She flopped back on the recliner. Glanced at the clock on the bookshelf. "Is church over?"

"Not yet. Almost. I snuck out to go to the bathroom, then kept on sneaking."

"Scott's gonna wonder if you fell in."

Erin let out a grunt of laughter. Then patted her bulging belly. "He'll know I didn't fall far if I did."

Chris tried not to laugh, but with the sudden mental picture, she couldn't help it.

"You're up and dressed."

She sighed. "Yeah."

Erin smoothed a wrinkle in her skirt near her knee. Then picked at something and brushed it away.

"You look nice."

She glanced up. "So do you. You look great, actually."

"Makeup."

A smile. "Did your cut close already?"

"Yeah. For the most part." Chris lightly dabbed at it. Saw no blood on her fingertips.

"Put on another butterfly or two tonight before you go to bed. So it doesn't pull open."

"I will."

Another smile. "Sonya asked about you. She said for you to come over for dinner. We're all going to be there."

Chris sat up in the recliner. Turned slightly to face Erin. Rested her head against the soft back.

"Have you eaten anything yet?"

A whisper. "No."

"How's your headache?"

"Better." She slowly grinned at the expression on Erin's face.

"Will you come with me to Sonya's?" Erin's blue eyes pleaded.

"Sure."

"You will?"

"Sure, Rin. I may have skipped church, but I'd be ..." The word *stupid* stuck in her throat. Clogged the rest of her statement as well.

"You'd be hungry."

A breath of laughter unclogged her throat. "Yeah. That."

"She, um ..." Erin picked at another spot on her skirt. "Chris, Laurie brought Alaina and Meghan to church today. I'm sure Sonya will invite them to dinner too. I ..." She glanced up. "I just wanted you to know."

The words echoed across Chris's heart. Then warmed her. "Really?"

"Yeah. You should've seen Alaina. She looked *absitively* gorgeous. Wearing a frilly white dress."

Alaina Walker? In a frilly white dress? A sudden image of young Idgie Threadgoode standing at the top of the stairs in *Fried Green Tomatoes* forced a burst of laughter through Chris's lips. "Was she also wearing her high-tops?"

"Nope. Black patent leather shoes. With lacey white socks."

Unbelievable. Yet a cruel thought invaded Chris's mind. *Poor kid. First her dad abuses her, then her mom abuses her by making her wear such things.* She didn't know how to process the thought. So she let it slip right back from where it came.

"I think she enjoyed being all dressed up."

I would hope so. The tone of this thought disturbed her as well. "Did Sonya tell you what she's fixing for dinner?"

Erin didn't seem concerned by the sudden turn of the conversation. "She said she put a ham in the oven. And Ben peeled and sliced an entire bag of sweet potatoes this morning. So they've been simmering as well."

The thoughts invading her mind now were worth savoring.

"You want to head over? By the time I make it down the stairs and across the street, Sonya should already have the table set and everything dished out."

She waved her hand. "Come on, Rin. Don't say that."

Erin gazed at Chris. Her right eyebrow suddenly shot up.

Heat flooded Chris's face. She squirmed in the recliner. Then pushed herself up to sit on its edge. "Yes, Rinny, I remember what I said last night. And it was stupid. I told you that."

A smile. "Okay. It's forgotten."

Chris stared. "I love how you do that."

"Do what?"

"Forgive and forget." She glanced at the floor. "It can't be easy."

"With you? It's the easiest thing in the world."

Her eyes quickly lifted to meet Erin's.

"Now come over here and help me out of this couch."

She laughed. And quickly obeyed.

★★★

Her wet hair had dried into some interesting configurations. Perfectly flat where her head had rested against the recliner to wacked-out curly at the tips. But nothing a quick French braiding couldn't fix. She held a hair tie between her teeth and watched her fingers' progression through the mirror in her bathroom.

Her eyes slowly fell to meet her own gaze. She blinked. Continued to work.

To forgive. And then ... to forget. Her eyes closed as the words played out in her heart. How wonderful it would be to forget. To forget every bit of the ugliness, the tension, the anger. To forget every memory not worth remembering. To shed the past like a dead skin. And move on. To start a new day, someday, completely new.

Her eyes blinked open. Her breath strained as the blood started to drain from her upraised arms. Still, her fingers worked. Her hair lined up into something presentable. Though her headache demanded the lines not to be too tight.

Her eyes slowly lowered once more, as if a part of her wanted to finish the previous thought. To savor the newness those thoughts considered. The newness her entire being craved.

But I am new, Lord. You've made me new. I know that. And I cannot thank You enough.

And it was so true. She dropped her arms and pulled the braid around to finish it down to the end. Then wrapped the tie around it.

It is true, Lord Jesus. I'm completely new.

She tossed the braid over her shoulder and leaned over the sink to face herself once more. Peered into those familiar dark eyes. Heard a faint echo of her own rage spewed in the Walker's house that previous day.

Okay, maybe not completely new. But we're working on it, aren't we? I know You'll finish me. Someday ... I'll be completely new. The past will totally be gone.

Please, Lord, make it be true.

She pushed away from the sink, turned off the bathroom light, and headed for the hall where Erin stood. She took one look at the smile on Erin's face, the way it beamed out her eyes, the patience and pure love pouring out of it, and felt her heart soar.

This is ... Lord Jesus, this is You *standing here ... this beautiful and insanely pregnant woman ... the best friend I have ever known.*

She tried to smile but knew it trembled on her lips.

"Ready?"

She nodded and pushed open the stairway door. "Let me go first, okay?" She started down a few steps, then turned and looked back, smiling, as Erin followed. At the bottom, she opened the door and waited in the back hall of the clinic for Erin to descend the last stair and close the door behind her.

A breath of relief. "Thanks, lady."

"No problem." Chris led Erin through the clinic toward the front door, but stopped instead at the big front window. She stared at that brown house almost directly across the street. Ben and Sonya's house. Ham in the oven. Sweet potatoes simmering on the stove. Laurie and Alaina and Meghan Walker. She bit into her lower lip to keep it from trembling.

Erin gently squeezed Chris's shoulder. A whisper. "Take your time, Chris. It's all right."

She lowered her head and rubbed her eyes. Her hand shook.

Erin's hand slid across Chris's shoulder, gently rubbing from side to side. It made a soothing sound as the warmth of the touch filtered through Chris's entire body. She listened to the sound of it and tried to drive out the thought of what waited for her across the street, to drive out the memories of her own unacceptable behavior that deeply affected the lives of all those she was about to see.

"You know she'll make raisin sauce too."

She lifted her head and sniffed back unshed tears. "Huh?"

"Sonya. Raisin sauce. For the ham."

She allowed a hint of laughter to carry on her breath.

"You're going to be all right. Do you know that?"

Chris glanced away. Slowly nodded.

"You are God's now. And He will never let you go."

"I know, Rinny." Barely a whisper.

"What you did yesterday was not stupid."

Her heart slammed to a stop as her eyes quickly found Erin's.

"Do you hear me?"

She stared. Felt her mouth slowly gape.

"I mean it, Chris. So stop believing it. Don't even think it anymore. We all know what you did was … love. Pure love."

Trembling slowly overtook her.

"Love is not something you say, Chris. It's something you do. And what you did yesterday … was love in its purest form."

"Stop, Rinny."

"No. It's the truth. You need to hear it."

"No …" Chris lifted her arm and tried to dab at her tears with the sleeve of her shirt. "If you don't stop, I'll start bawling and ruin my makeup."

That childish giggle.

"Just don't say anything else." She tried desperately to regain her composure.

"Okay. I promise. I won't say a word."

And Erin kept her promise. She didn't say a word. But she stepped forward and pulled Chris into a tight embrace.

Chris lowered her head against Erin's shoulder and not only cried, but smeared foundation all over Erin's blouse.

★★★

The cool, late spring breeze carried the scent of flowers and freshly cut grass. Chris lifted her chin into it, let it wash over her burning face, then drew it deeply into her lungs, savoring the taste of it in her soul. Her eyes burned and her cheek throbbed, but with all the reapplied makeup, she felt confident the people she was about to share the afternoon with would see in her the best she could offer.

She tried not to watch as Erin, wearing a different blouse with her skirt, waddled beside her, as they made their way slowly across Kimberley Street. Only a few more feet to the front door of the Connelly's house. Chris could almost smell the ham as it baked in that oven, the sweet potatoes as they simmered on that stove.

"Lord. Lord. Lord."

She turned to Erin. "Are you all right?"

"I'm gonna kill Scott."

"Huh? Why?" Chris stepped up onto the sidewalk. "What did Scott do?"

Erin's face reflected pure incredulousness. "Look at me! What *didn't* Scott do?"

"Oh." Laughter threatened—Chris quickly tamped it down.

"I am so over this. I'm telling you . . ."

"I know, Rin. Two more weeks. Right?"

"Oh, thank You, God."

Chris couldn't help it. She laughed.

They slowly stepped up the few stairs to the Connelly's front porch. Erin didn't hesitate. Or knock on the door. She pulled it open, but waited for Chris to walk in first.

Chris gave her a quick look.

"I'm fine now. Just point me to Ben's recliner."

She smiled. "I can do that." She took a step toward the open door.

Erin gently grabbed Chris's arm. "Remember what I said. Okay?"

Chris swallowed deeply. "I always do, Rin."

"Good." A wink.

She walked through the door and was immediately greeted by the loving hollers and hellos of her friends. Cappy gave her a wave from the kitchen. Sonya immediately pulled Chris into a warm hug, then pushed her away and peered at her face.

From Sonya's expression, Chris knew she hadn't put on enough makeup.

Ben moved in behind his wife and put his hands on her shoulders. "Hi, Chris. Hungry?" His smile beamed.

"Hi, Ben. And yes, sir, I am." Chris wanted to hug the man, wanted to group hug both him and his wife. But she didn't move.

A cute little girl wearing the prettiest white dress suddenly stood beside Ben, almost hiding behind him. Chris glanced at the girl, then stared at her, eyes bulging, jaw dropping almost to the floor. "Alaina?"

The girl grinned, then lowered her head and turned slightly back and forth, her feet firmly planted beside Ben.

"No. You can't be Alaina." Chris reached out to place her hands on the girl's shoulders. "You're not Alaina! What have you done with Alaina?"

The girl let out a burst of happy giggles. "It's me, Chris! I'm just wearin' a dress!"

Chris forced her eyes as wide as she could. "No. Say it isn't so! Who did this to you? Who would do such a thing?"

The girl, still giggling, immediately turned to point over her shoulder at a pretty, blonde-haired woman. The woman's pale green eyes seemed to study Chris. But then softened with a smile.

Unsettled by it, Chris glanced away. Then gazed at Alaina. "She did this?"

"That's my mommy!" Alaina's entire face shone as she smiled. "My sister's here too. We went to church. We were lookin' for ya. Why didn't you come to church, Chris?"

Caught, Chris only smiled. Then slowly lowered herself to kneel in front of the child, her hands gently holding the child by the shoulders. "I'm sorry I didn't, Lainer. But I'm here now. And I'm telling you ... girl, you look beautiful."

The girl blushed and giggled. Then slowly reached up to touch Chris's cheek. "My daddy hurt you, huh."

Chris's heart about fell through the floor. Silence filled the entire house.

"Does it still hurt?" Alaina's fingertip gently traced the cut.

"No, Lainer. Not anymore."

"I was really scared, Chris." The girl's blue eyes peered at her. "But you're okay, right?"

Chris couldn't blink her tears away. One dripped down her cheek. "Yeah, sweetheart. I'm okay."

"I made you cry."

"You sure did. But that's okay. My friend Erin made me cry earlier too. I guess today's my day to cry."

"I cried yesterday. But I was really okay. I was just scared."

"I know, Lainer. And I'm sorry you were scared."

"Are you gonna stay and eat with us? Grammy Sonya made lemon pie and everything!"

"She did, huh?" Chris glanced up. Saw Sonya wiping her eyes.

"You sit beside me, okay? Will you sit beside me?"

Chris barely touched the tip of the little girl's nose. "You bet I will. I'll sit beside you. But you better not drink my milk."

"There's plenty of milk, Chris. Plenty for all of us."

Gazing at the precious child, Chris could only laugh.

"Come see my mommy!" Alaina grabbed Chris's hand and pulled her across the room.

Chris had no choice but to follow. She suddenly stood before Laurie Walker. Alaina threw her arms around her mother's waist.

Laurie returned her daughter's tight hug, then lifted a hand toward Chris. A soft voice. "Hello, Chris."

Chris gently squeezed the woman's hand. She smiled, though her brain struggled to formulate a response. "Hello, Laurie. I, um, almost didn't recognize your little angel." After one last squeeze, Chris released the woman's hand.

"It was her idea, if you can believe it." Laurie smoothed back her daughter's flyaway blonde hair. "She wore this at Easter when we went to my mother's church in Tualatin."

"I wanted to look pretty today too!"

Chris let out a faint laugh. "And you certainly do, girlfriend." Her heart slowed to a stop as Alaina pushed away from her mother and turned to throw her hug on Chris. Definitely a tight hug. Chris could barely breathe. Her hands encircled the child and held her close.

Alaina raised her head and looked Chris in the eye. "I love you, Chris. I love you forever."

The words sent her over the edge. She fell to her knees and hugged Alaina as close as she dared as sobs overtook her. She glanced up for only a second. Laurie Walker stood watching her, her hand covering her mouth as tears coursed down her cheeks.

★★★

SHE REFUSED TO LOOK INTO the mirror. Absolutely refused. The water she splashed on her face effectively washed away whatever foundation hadn't been already washed away by her tears. When she left this bathroom, the bruises on her face would be completely visible for all to see. But her face would be clean. And her eyes would be dry. She hoped.

She made the water as cold as she could. It felt so good on her burning cheeks, against her burning eyes. She splashed a few more handfuls, then grabbed the towel and patted her face dry. Then slowly, reluctantly, dared a glance into the mirror.

Her face glowed. Was that a good thing? Her dark eyes bore streaks of red. Yet not as bad as before. Had she finally cried herself out? Dried up the reservoir?

Please, Lord. Say yes. I cannot cry anymore. I mean it.

She fluffed back a few strands of hair that had escaped from her French braid. Then realized her headache had disappeared. When did that happen? Her stomach growled. With the smell of ham wafting through the house, no wonder her mouth watered.

So quit hiding in the bathroom and get back out there.

A tiny smile curled her lip. She hung up her towel and then headed out to the dining room, hungry and refreshed and ready to sit with her friends and laugh about . . . anything. At that moment, all she wanted to do was eat. And laugh.

Alaina had saved Chris a seat right next to hers. And Chris couldn't help notice the two tall glasses of milk standing side by side near Alaina's plate.

★★★

AS SHE FINISHED HER MILK and savored the memory of Sonya's lemon meringue pie, Chris glanced around the table and watched her friends talk and laugh and sip their coffee and tea. It was a moment she hoped would carve itself into the deepest parts of her memory, never to be forgotten. Sonya's heartwarming hint of that southern drawl turned her soft-spoken words into melodies. Ben's laughter seemed to thunder out of him, yet his gentle banter with his wife and friends reminded Chris of a softhearted grizzly bear. Gentle Ben. Literally.

Erin and Scott would drift away from the group's conversation from time to time to whisper sweet nothings to each other. Alaina's sister, Meghan, playfully argued with Cappy about who was better looking: a guy named Ricky Martin or some other guy named Marky Mark. Chris enjoyed watching their quiet argument play out, though she had no idea what either man looked like, or how the one ended up with two first names.

A sudden thought startled her—the image of a handsome man with a three-day growth of whiskers across his upper lip and chin, with pale blue eyes that shone when he smiled. She covered her mouth with her napkin to hide the joy that had overtaken her. Then hoped no one had noticed. Hoped with all her heart she would see that handsome man again soon.

Alaina tugged on Chris's shirtsleeve. Chris slowly turned her head. "Yes, m'dear?"

"Guess what." Her angel face bore a cheesy grin. "I gotta burp. Wanna hear it?"

A breath of relief trickled out of Chris. Yes, the little girl in that white frilly dress really was Alaina Walker. And the burp the girl proceeded to broadcast throughout the entire room was one of her best. Made Chris downright proud.

"Alaina!" Laurie Walker's eyes about popped out of her head. "You stop that! That's not polite."

"Goodness, Lainer," came from Cappy, "get any on ya?"

The girl only grinned. As did everyone else sitting around the table.

The moment slowly faded.

A few seconds later, after thanking their hostess with a kiss on the cheek, Ben and Scott meandered into the living room. Sonya, still glowing from being kissed on both cheeks, stood to start collecting the dirty dishes. Beside her, Cappy stood to help. A second after that, Erin reached out to help gather plates, but promptly received a slap on her wrist. Alaina gulped down the last of her milk and then turned to Chris and proudly displayed her dripping white mustache. As Chris tried not to laugh, Laurie Walker tapped her on the shoulder.

Startled, she turned to face the woman. Gave her a small smile.

"Would it be okay if I talked to you? Maybe outside?"

As full as it was, Chris's stomach flip-flopped. She swallowed deeply. "Um, sure." She tossed her napkin on the table and pushed back her chair. Then stood and followed Alaina's mother to the back door, glancing quickly back into the dining room at Erin before closing the door behind her.

Erin's firm look and tiny smile spoke courage straight to where Chris needed it. Everywhere.

Outside on the porch, she drew in a long breath and was rewarded by the sweet fragrance of Sonya's roses in bloom. So beautiful, she let her eyes follow the flight of a fat honeybee as it lighted on one of the rose's petals and seemed to lean in to give it a good sniff before darting away into the tangle of a rhododendron bush. Her breath hovered full in her lungs as she marveled. The rhododendron blossoms exuded the most brilliant red she had ever seen.

As brilliant as fresh blood.

Her breath released in a rush. She desperately pulled in another.

Laurie Walker stood with her back to Chris, her hands resting on the top of the deck railing. She seemed to peer out over the backyard, past the church's side parking lot, even past the trees lining both sides of the far street. Her dress ruffled a bit in the breeze. She reached up with one hand to push her hair away from her face.

Chris stood and watched her. Then hoped the woman would not turn around. She needed at least another minute to force away the terror pouring into her stomach and making it churn. She drew in one more deep breath and slowly let it out. As Laurie slowly turned around.

A smile. A pleasant smile. The type of smile that says, *"Nice weather we're having, isn't it?"* Or, *"Isn't it a lovely day?"*

Deep in Chris's heart, a part of her hoped Laurie would ask about the weather, so she could reply, *"Why, yes. It is, indeed, a lovely day."* She would enjoy a pleasant conversation about the weather since the sun shone brightly above them and there was hardly a cloud in the beautiful blue sky. But she knew it wouldn't happen. Talking about the weather was not the reason Laurie Walker brought Chris out to this place. To this place that still haunted her with memories of a night she would much rather forget.

Another pleasant smile. Though Laurie barely lifted her eyes to look Chris's way, Chris forced her lips to return it. Then backed up a few steps to lean against the deck railing. She noticed too late that she stood across the porch about as far away as she could get from the woman. It wasn't intentional. But it was a fact.

"I told you I wanted to talk to you, and now that we're here, I have no idea what I want to say."

Honesty. Chris liked that.

Laurie's eyes lifted to meet Chris's gaze. "I'm sorry. I don't want to make this hard for you."

Chris slowly nodded. "I know. Me neither."

Laurie started to cross her arms over her chest, but then let one arm fall to her side and grabbed her elbow instead. A much less imposing stance. Another smile. That failed in the attempt. "You must think I'm a monster."

Chris's jaw dropped as a rush of responses tangled in her throat. "No. I mean ... not at all." She pushed away from the railing and took a step forward. "I have never thought that."

The expression on Laurie's face conveyed her doubt about Chris's honesty. And then she spoke. And wiped away all doubt. "How could you not?"

Chris's teeth clenched. "Easy. I ..." She ran out of words. Her eyes held Laurie's a second longer, then had to look away. Down at the deck. Anywhere but at Laurie's face. So much for easy. How could she explain what she had seen in Laurie's eyes? That look of shame. And guilt. As far as she could tell, Laurie Walker was just as much a victim as her daughter was. Victims carried that haunted look in their eyes. Their aggressors didn't.

She let herself sigh. Long and deep. "Look, Laurie, I can't speak for anyone else, but I can speak for me. And I do not think you're a bad mother." She tried to smile. "I watched Alaina throw her arms around you this afternoon. I'd say you were a terrific mother. The proof to me is the way Alaina sees you. The proof ... is in Alaina's eyes."

Laurie seemed to struggle with that.

Chris couldn't believe she had actually said the words. She wondered where they came from. Her heart thumped.

A pair of chirping chickadees chased each other through the tops of the trees. She allowed herself one quick look. And enjoyed the fleeting sight.

"You, of all people, Chris ... have every right to think—"

"No."

The woman's eyes seemed to search Chris out.

"Listen. I don't want to be rude, but ... for me, this has never been about you. It's always been about Alaina."

Laurie stared at the ground. Then slowly nodded.

Chris's heart thumped so hard, she struggled to breathe. "Can we sit down?"

Laurie's eyes lifted. Softened. "Sure."

They walked to the back of the porch and dusted off two of the big deck chairs, then pushed them into the middle of the deck. They both sat with deep sighs. And then gave each other embarrassed smiles.

"Before another minute goes by, Chris, I have to say ... thanks. Thank you so much for what you did."

Chris squirmed for a second. Then jumped up to fetch the small table that matched the deck chairs. She placed it in front of her chair. Then sat back down and kicked her feet up onto it. "Ahh. That's better." She turned her head to look at Laurie, then smiled as the woman also kicked up her feet and slouched in her chair.

They sat for almost a full minute watching the chickadees. Chris whispered a prayer in her heart for her new friend sitting beside her. She hoped the woman was enjoying the moment. That she at least was enjoying the sweet smell of Sonya's roses.

"Alaina really loves you."

Chris's prayer dissolved into a cloud of warm fuzzies. "She's an easy kid to love." Her heart froze. Her immediate thought almost made her retch. *If the kid is so easy to love, then why did her father kick her around?*

She dared a glance at Laurie. Saw tears in the woman's eyes.

Chris wanted to disappear. "I'm sorry, Laurie."

Those eyes lifted. Blinked. "For what?"

"I love what I just said. And I hate it too."

Laurie's mouth slowly gaped. "You've been through it, haven't you?"

Chris stared into the trees. "Let's just say Alaina is easy to love, and I'm really sorry her father doesn't think so."

"He used to."

She dropped her gaze just an inch. Continued to stare.

"He used to love all of us. And then he turned."

"How long ago?" She closed her eyes for a second. "Don't answer that."

"Long enough for me to know he had turned. Not long enough for me to do anything about it."

Chris looked at Laurie. "That's a remarkable thing to say."

"It's the truth."

"Not everyone can see the truth like you just saw it."

"Not everyone is given a chance like I've been given to make things right." Laurie lifted her gaze to meet Chris's. "Thank you for giving me that chance."

"Don't thank me."

"Then know I am grateful."

Chris's heart melted. She slowly nodded. "Okay."

"Good."

They both settled back and gazed out over the trees.

"How did you know?" Laurie's voice shook.

Chris drew in a deep breath. She hated the image that replayed in her mind. Alaina's beautiful blue eyes filled with weariness and pain. The poor child holding her side and struggling to breathe.

"Did Alaina tell you?"

The words startled her. "No. Alaina never said a word."

"Then how did you know?"

Chris gave voice to her first thought. "I guess Alaina did tell me. She just didn't use words."

Laurie turned her head. "How did you hear her? When ... I didn't?"

Chris had no idea what to say.

"I wasn't listening."

She stayed quiet.

"I was in denial."

"So was I. I didn't act until weeks after I first ... suspected. And I hate to use that word."

"But I never acted."

"Look, Laurie." Chris turned to face her. "Maybe you do need to answer my earlier question. How long ago did your husband turn? When did he start hitting Alaina?"

A whisper. "A few months ago. I think."

"Then it hasn't been that long. I saw the first evidence of it. Only because ..."

Laurie waited.

Chris wished she hadn't started what she didn't want to finish. "Because I knew what I was seeing. Does that make sense? I saw what I saw, and I knew what it was." She softened her voice. "And then I saw it in you and knew for sure I was right."

"You saw it in me?"

"In your eyes. The first day I met you. When you came to church that one Sunday."

Laurie blinked. A whisper. "What did you see?"

Shame. "I saw you were hurting. You were hurting for your children."

"How did you … know?"

Chris straightened in the chair and gazed again out over the trees. "What I said earlier was wrong. This is about Alaina, but it's also about you too. But one thing's for sure, Laurie. This is not about me." She dared a glance. "I'm sorry. But please understand."

"You have been through it."

"And if it's not about me, then you can imagine I don't want to talk about whether or not I've been through it. Can we talk about Alaina? Please? What's going to happen to her? And to Meghan?"

Laurie sniffed. "He's gone. I won't have him back in my house."

"Is it really your house?"

Silence.

"You and the girls may need to be the ones to move out. Are you prepared for that?"

"I can stay at my sister's for as long as I need."

"Is that best for your children?"

Laurie glared at Chris.

"Simple questions, Laurie. You don't know me, but you know I like to stick my nose in where it doesn't belong."

The glare vanished. "And get it smacked for your efforts."

"Well, that part I don't like."

A pause. "Cappy told me he really hit you. She told me everything."

Chris didn't mind hearing that since Cappy didn't know everything to tell. "Has he ever hit *you*?"

Laurie fell silent. A long moment passed before she pressed open her lips to speak. "If he had, then maybe I wouldn't have lived the last few months in denial."

"Has he hit Meghan?"

"He's actually quite intimidated by her. If he starts yelling at her, she yells right back and runs away. She doesn't spend much time at the house." A bitter laugh. "But, then again, neither do I." Her voice shook. "Which has left Alaina alone with her father."

"Where she's an easy target."

Laurie wiped her eyes.

"Do you have any idea why he turned?"

"He lost his job. And he's gained so much weight recently. He struggles with diabetes. He doesn't control it very well. It makes him crazy."

Chris could attest to that.

"I hardly recognize him anymore. He's definitely not the same man I married."

I should hope not. Chris choked down the bitter thought. "Do you think he has the ability to change back into what he used to be?" As she said the words, they started to burn in her mind. Echo across her soul.

A long breath. "I don't know."

Does he have the ability? To change back? To what he used to be?

She wished she had never spoken the words. Was it even possible for a man to start out decent, turn into a monster, then turn back into the decent man he used to be?

Her dad's face appeared in her mind and a shudder ripped through her heart. His eyes bore into her. His dark hair needed to be combed. Like always. He opened his mouth to say something. Chris's eyes pinched shut, but the darkness only made his face clearer. Made his voice sound that much closer.

So. What about it, Chrissy? Is it possible for a monster to change back into someone decent and good?

She glared at her father. *Only if that monster really did start out decent and good. It wouldn't work if he was pretending. If being a monster was all he really knew. Or wanted to be.*

His face vanished. Chris blinked open her eyes. Then reached up and rubbed them.

She heard Laurie let out another deep breath. "I don't know, Chris. He would really have to change. Something would really have to make him change."

Chris turned her head. "God could change him."

Laurie nodded. "I believe that. If he'll let Him."

"Do you know about Jesus? I mean ... do you believe in Him?"

"I'm trying to. Between Sonya and my mother, I will. And soon. They've really been praying for me and telling me about Him."

Chris wanted to pray with her too. To tell her about Jesus. To make her believe. But words started to tumble in her mind, and the moment seemed to lose itself in the tumble. She grabbed a snatch of a thought. Gave it voice. "Believe in Him, Laurie. He is ... everything this world is not."

"How long have you been a Christian?"

She smiled. "Not very long. Compared to how long I've lived. And how much time I've let slip away."

"But you're here now, surrounded by friends. Christian friends."

"Yes. This is my home."

"Where are you from?"

"Colorado."

"Do you like it here?"

She thought about that. "Sometimes." Her smile widened.

"You're with good people. And you're just like them."

She blinked. Had no idea what to say.

The screen door suddenly slammed. An irritated whine. "Mom? Can we go now?"

Chris watched Laurie's eyes lift to the sky. Then quickly lower again. "Yes, dear." She turned to Chris. "It's time we headed out anyway. We're going over to my sister's tonight. I think we need to get away for a few days."

Chris nodded.

"I'm glad we talked."

"Me too."

Laurie pushed up from her chair, then turned to smile at her oldest daughter. "Go tell your sister."

The door slammed.

Chris slowly stood. Then debated if she should give voice to a sudden thought.

"Thanks, Chris. I really mean it."

"I know you do."

"I'd like to talk again sometime. If that's all right with you."

"Absitively."

Confusion swept Laurie's face.

"Yes." Chris nodded. "I'd like that very much."

"Good. You know, maybe I should stop by that gym of yours sometime. Alaina says it's *da bomb.*" Another rolling of eyes.

Chris laughed. "Well, I hope so. If that's a good thing."

Laurie started for the door.

Chris walked a few steps to catch up. "Um, Laurie? I, um ... I don't know how to say this. I mean, I'm still so new to it and all. But ... your husband ... I'm sorry, but I'm not even sure if I know his name."

The woman's eyes widened playfully. "You mean he had the nerve to hit you, but didn't even tell you his name?" A laugh. "Bill. His name is Bill."

Chris wanted to laugh, but the word struck her. Didn't the cop say the man's name was Floyd?

"Actually, that's his middle name. William. His real name is Floyd. After his daddy and granddaddy. But he hates that name."

She smiled. "Bill. I'll remember that."

"As long as you can forget what he did to you." Laurie's face flushed as she glanced down at her feet. She reached up to open the door.

"Wait. Um ..." Chris whispered a quick prayer. "Look, Laurie. This is no big deal. But you know your husband. If he really was a good and decent man, there may be hope for him. I only say that because God is pretty big, and if He gets hold of your husband's heart, He'll be able to change him. He'll change you too. And His changes are sweet. He makes even the dirtiest person ... clean."

Laurie's eyes flickered. Then shimmered with tears. "I do believe that."

"I'm still learning so much about Him, but if you talk to Sonya, I know she'd love to help you ... if you have questions or anything."

"Thanks, Chris. I have talked to her about it. And I will again. I promise. She's ... a good friend." Laurie's bottom lip quivered.

"And I think you are too. I'm glad I met you. I just wish it could have been under better circumstances."

Laughter bubbled up from Chris's belly. "Yeah. Me too."

Laurie's eyes stayed on Chris's a second longer, then moved to take in Chris's entire face. Paused on every black-and-blue mark. Lingered on the cut on Chris's cheek.

Chris glanced away.

"Thank you."

She nodded. Tried to smile.

"I'll see you again."

"I'll be around."

The woman smiled a second longer, then pulled open the door and walked inside to collect her daughters. Chris followed, heart pounding, her eyes searching for Erin. At that moment, she desperately needed the comfort of Erin's steady gaze.

Comfort. And joy. Just like the song. The joy of friendship. And of love. In that moment, Erin gave Chris all three. And almost swept her away.

Laurie tried to herd Alaina toward the front door, but Alaina needed one more hug from Chris before she would give in. Chris returned the girl's hug and said, "See you later, Lainer gator."

Giggling, the girl pushed away and said, "After while, Chris crocodile!"

Ten seconds later, the girl was gone, out the door with her mother and sister, walking down the sidewalk toward her mother's car. Chris watched from the window in Ben and Sonya's living room. Then felt a squeeze on her shoulder. She turned and saw a friendly face.

"What a cutie."

Chris laughed. "Yep, that she is."

Sonya yelled from the kitchen, "Who's ready for another piece of pie?"

Erin's hand squeezed Chris's shoulder again. "Can I fix you a cup of tea?"

Chris's heart slowed to its normal patter. "Yeah. That'd be great."

"Leaded or unleaded."

A smile. "Leaded. I think I could use the caffeine."

"Pie?"

"Absolutely not."

Erin laughed and headed for the kitchen.

Chris turned and stared once more out the window, hoping in vain to catch one more glimpse of that white frilly dress and the angel who wore it.

Her blood cooled as icy tentacles inched their way through her veins. The chill carried into her soul, where the warmth she just savored grew cold.

His face. So real. His eyes. His dark hair, needing to be combed. His voice. Taunting her with promises of change. *I can, Chrissy. I'm not a bad man. Just you see. I can be good and decent and kind.*

She dared not close her eyes. Though she could not close her ears. His voice ... just the sound of it. The vilest sound in her world.

I can change, Chrissy. Just you see.

Oh, God ... don't let me see him. Don't let me hear his voice.

She studied the azaleas in Erin's front yard.

Unless it's true. Unless he can change. You can change Him. Oh, Lord ... if there's even a chance ...

The flowers blurred. Then went black as Chris crushed her eyes shut.

No. No way. He will never change. He has never been good or decent or kind. Never to me, at least. She cursed away her tears. *No. Never to me.*

She spun away from the window, then glanced around the room, hoping no one noticed. No one looked back at her. No one had seen. She put a smile on her face and walked closer to her friends, to the dining room table where Erin had just poured a dollop of milk into Chris's tea.

EIGHT

SOMETIMES, JUST BREATHING THE AIR inside the sanctuary of the Kimberley Street Community Church brought her to tears. It carried its own sweet scent, the scent of wood polish and grandeur. Of hope. If ever there was a scent of hope, this was it. Combined with the fragrance of a hundred different perfumes and breath mints. Two hundred people singing with all their hearts to God, blending their voices into one sweet strain.

Chris laughed at herself, though no one heard her as the song carried heavenward. She didn't feel embarrassed to be the only one not singing. She figured the rest of the congregation would appreciate her not contributing to their impressive work of musical artistry. Her inability to carry a note would toss a clink into their fine work, for sure. That would be bad enough, but it would also most certainly embarrass Erin and Sonya, who sat on either side of her and sang as beautifully as anyone in the church.

So, see? I'm doing them all a favor, Lord.

As she read the words in the hymnal, she moved her lips and pretended to be singing. Sometimes she hummed along. But she fully intended to save her vocal experimentations for the quiet mornings at the gym when Margaret Becker's *Immigrant's Daughter* spun on the CD player, blasting musical prayers across the huge open room. It was okay to let loose then. Chris locked the doors and made sure no one could hear or see. She sang along and even stepped out a dance or two if the moment demanded it. Sometimes the love overflowing her soul did that, made her do the strangest things. But she didn't mind. It was as if her feet needed to step out and move. So she let them. And, as she did, she knew the One she loved was watching. She knew He was there. He was always there.

161

And every so often she could tell He was stepping out too, just letting the music move His feet as if He couldn't stop them any more than Chris could stop hers.

Side by side they stepped out. She was sure of it.

Incredible moments making the entire rest of her day that much sweeter.

The hymn they were singing carried out to its end. Another hymn was announced, along with its page number and the request to stand. Chris knew the routine and was grateful for it. The chance to stand one last time before the sermon usually gave everyone the ability to sit and listen to Pastor Andy until that final "Amen." But the last few weeks at this point in the service, Chris always felt terrible standing when Erin's feet were so swollen it was so much better for her to stay in her seat. The wide hole her absence created beside Chris sent trickles of loneliness through her entire being. Only Erin's joyful singing would lift her from that loneliness and make everything all right. Hearing Erin sing made everything right.

The new hymn was a rompin'-stomper, as Sonya's granddaughter Amanda would say. Chris read the words and moved her lips, then felt that wiggling urge in her feet which she quickly ignored. She glanced down and exchanged warm smiles with Erin, then continued to glance at her fellow hymn singers. She saw one or two who, like her, only pretended to sing and one or two who, like her, seemed as determined to ignore that wiggling urge to dance. And then she saw a few others who had given in to that urge and let it overtake them. To a certain extent.

She returned Corissa Foley's kind smile, then let her gaze drift to the folks in the back. She enjoyed all the joyous expressions on everyone's face even as she wondered why the author of the hymn chose to call heaven by that strange name. She knew a Beulah once. And that woman was so mean she could eat steel and spit nails.

Enough gazing around. She started to turn to read the next line of the hymn, but her eye caught on the sight of a man far in the back row. Her knees dissolved into jelly. Her heart froze into a solid block of ice.

She turned quickly and plopped down on the pew next to Erin. Stared straight ahead. A poke on her arm came from Erin's direction. She turned and saw a questioning look. She gave no response, but tried to close up her mouth. She smiled at Erin but knew it was a pathetic gesture.

Erin kept on singing. Chris again stared straight ahead. The hymnal in her hands just lay there. Her eyes made no attempt to read the words.

The hymn played out and still Chris stared. She knew her face had enflamed, her cheeks felt the same way they did after she helped set up the hospital tent complex in Dhahran. Under the intense Saudi Arabian sun that day, she suffered second-degree burns on her face and arms. But this moment ... just her cheeks were burned. She hoped.

Her head turned. She didn't want it to. But maybe what she saw — *whom* she saw — was gone. Maybe she didn't see ... *him* ... at all. Maybe she saw someone who only looked like him.

Nope. It was Jason.

She gazed over her shoulder at him as Pastor Andy started to speak.

Jason Sloan just sat there and grinned at her. Looking so fine.

Chris straightened but did not lift her eyes to the pulpit. Erin again gave her a poke on the arm. And a whisper. "Are you all right?"

Chris didn't turn her head but strained her eyes as far to the left as she could. She whispered out of the corner of her mouth, "Yeah."

Pastor Andy preached on about something. Chris didn't hear one word the man said.

Enough. She stood and politely excused herself down the pew to the outside aisle. Tried not to run from the room. Did not look up or even dare a glance Jason's way as she pushed through the swinging doors out into the foyer.

The doors slapped shut behind her. She stood there.

The front doors of the church were open, allowing the warm, early summer breeze to swirl the air in the room. She walked outside and felt a bit queasy, as she always did when she peered down the hard concrete stairs of the church. She could still feel the bruises each one made as she tumbled down them, as that big dumb Del crushed her against them when he fell on top of her and tumbled down with her.

What a moron.

She sat down on the top step. Drew in a deep breath. Then wondered why she sat there. What in the world had caused her to run out of the church?

A hint of Pastor Andy's voice filtered toward her, then disappeared. That seemed strange to her, until a presence suddenly stood over her. She almost let out a shriek.

"Hey you."

She knew that gentle, deep voice. She struggled to swallow down everything her heart was sending up her throat. Then slowly lifted her head. And smiled. "Hey back atcha."

"Mind if I sit?"

She slid over a few inches, then wondered why. The step was at least twenty feet long. Plenty long enough for two people to sit.

"Nice night, huh."

"Yep." The word was a peep.

Silence fell over them like a ton of bricks.

"This is a nice neighborhood. Better than mine."

Chris swallowed again, then scolded herself for being so childish. The man just wanted to talk. "Where do you live?" Nice, personal question right off the bat.

"Not far from here. But it's a much busier street. I hate it."

She couldn't imagine a street busier than Kimberley. Though, she had to admit, for a busy city street, Kimberley wasn't very busy at all.

"I'd love to live out in the country. I heard a rumor you're from Colorado."

She blinked. "Who told you that?"

"Are you denying it?"

"No. I am. I'm just curious who told you."

"Ray. I asked him."

So much for privacy. But not that Chris minded.

"What part?" Jason's arms rested over his knees.

"Near Ouray. It's in west-central Colorado. In ski resort country."

"In the mountains."

"You could say that." That was where most ski resorts were located. She smiled. "Where are you from?" Did she already ask him that? "Originally."

"Right here. I'm Portland born and bred."

"And you hate it?" She wondered if she should have squelched that thought.

"Nah. I don't hate it. I guess I'm just ready to move on."

She let her eyes linger on him a second longer, hoping his would lift to meet hers. They did. Suddenly. She blinked. Startled. His eyes carried a warm glow as he smiled.

"Maybe I should just move to a different neighborhood."

Like this one? She watched him. Liked what she saw.

"How do you like living here?"

"I love it." *I do?* Where did that come from?

"Good. I'm glad. There are some real fine people around here."

There sure are. She wanted to slap herself upside the head! What was this man doing to her?

"I see you didn't get anyone to stitch up your cheek."

Breath gushed out of her. She covered it with a cough.

"I thought for sure you'd let Doc do it. Or his wife."

"Nah. They seemed to have enough to worry about."

"It'll leave a scar, though."

She bit her lower lip. "You closed it really well. You're a terrific paramedic, by the way."

His smile caused the whiskers above his lip to dance. "Ray also told me you were in Desert Storm."

"What *didn't* Ray tell you about me?"

"Are you denying it?" A playful grin.

Chris laughed. "No. I was there."

"What was it like?"

She let out a deep sigh. "Hot. Cold. Sandy. Dusty. Dirty. Intense. Boring. Silly. Terrifying. Insane. Aggravating. Exhilarating." She glanced up. "I think that about covers it."

Jason's eyes fixed on hers. Stayed fixed on hers.

She blinked. "That's where I met Erin. And she's why I'm here. Funny, huh."

"And you're why I'm here." His eyes took in Chris's entire face. Then quickly looked down at the steps. "I'm sorry. I sound like a schoolboy."

She didn't mind one bit.

"I should probably be going."

Her heart missed a beat. "Why? You don't have to go."

Jason stared out over the street while he twisted the ring on his finger.

Chris let her eyes fall closed and whispered a silent prayer for help.

"I haven't been to church in a long time." The words carried a faraway tone.

"I'm glad you're here."

"You have a funny way of showing it. I mean, when I saw you practically run out of the church ..."

Her hand came up to hide her face.

"I was afraid I'd ruined your night."

"No. I was just a little ... surprised."

"I told you I knew where to find you."

She couldn't answer that. But she smiled.

"Are you hungry?"

"Not really."

"Do you want to go back inside?"

"Not really."

A slow nod. "Do you want to go get some ice cream?"

Chris studied the man's pale blue eyes, his fuzzy chin, his soft lips. A huge part of her wanted to say no, to politely excuse herself and walk back inside the church, or across the street, or anywhere away from the man. But another huge part of her considered the question. Heard the gentle pleading in his voice. And wanted to say yes.

"And I'm not talking about a fudgesicle at the ER. Let's go try about six of the thirty-one flavors."

She definitely wanted to say yes. Yet still couldn't believe the words crossed her lips. "I think I'd like that."

"Good. But we can go after church if you'd like to hear the rest of the sermon. I don't want to keep you from it."

"I missed this morning's sermon, so I guess I can miss tonight's too."

"You'll start backsliding if you're not careful."

A laugh. "No, my friends around here wouldn't allow that."

"Well, then, shall we?" Jason stood and offered Chris his hand.

She reached up and allowed him to pull her up. "I guess we shall."

✦✦✦

HER EYES. OR MAYBE HER smile. Something drew him to her. In the worst way. Yet how could he separate her from the woman he loved? The woman so brutally taken. He would blink and see her face. Hear her laughter on the wind. So many years. He had lived without her longer than they had been married. It wasn't fair. She was to be his life.

His life now felt more like walking death. He had died that day with her and their unborn child. The only difference was that he still walked around. And breathed.

But at that moment at Baskin-Robbins, standing beside a woman who drew him to her like a little kid to an ice-cream cone, he pulled in deep breaths and found himself enjoying the refreshing feeling they left behind.

To breathe is to live, Jase. Let yourself breathe . . .

He still couldn't believe he had drummed up the nerve to walk into that church. Sitting in the last row, he studied the back of every single head hoping to see the light brown hair of the one he came to see, the thick shoulder-length hair with a bit of a curl. He never expected to see it restrained in a French braid. At first he didn't think it was her. Not until he saw Scott Mathis sitting close by, sitting next to a woman who was most certainly his wife, Erin. She had remained sitting when the rest of the group stood to sing another song, and that was the moment Chris started to turn. She looked down at Erin, then out across the group, smiling from time to time. And she kept right on turning. Standing there holding a hymnal but not singing the hymn, she turned around and looked right at him.

When their eyes met, Jason's breath caught in his throat. But her reaction had been priceless. She had practically turned green, dropped to the pew, then jumped up and nearly sprinted out of the church.

You have a terrific affect on women, Sloan. They take one look at you, turn green, and go running in the opposite direction.

He folded his arms across his chest, leaned against the glass ice-cream case, and watched her. Wanted to razz her about taking so long to decide. The place was packed, people crowded around them placing and receiving their orders while Chris slowly studied each of the thirty-one flavors trying to make up her mind.

She could not have been more beautiful.

Except for the dark bruises under her eyes and that sickening cut on her face.

"What are you getting?" she asked him for the second time.

A laugh spurted through his lips. "Same as the last time you asked me. Chocolate peanut butter, apple pie, and cherry cheese-cake." He savored the sound of his favorite combination and the face Chris made when she heard it.

"How can you mix peanut butter with apple pie?"

He could only smile.

"Just give me two scoops of mint chocolate chip, please. On a regular cone."

One of the clerks nodded and immediately went to work.

"You're so daring." He wanted to pull Chris into his arms and hold her. Instead, he turned and placed his order with an orange-haired bored-looking clerk, then watched as she scooped it into the cone.

Ice cream in hand and a bite of it in her mouth, Chris looked at Jason and smiled. "Mmm. Thanks. This is great."

Her smile. His heart. "You're most welcome." He grabbed his cone, paid the clerk, then guided Chris outside away from the ruckus of the crowded store.

The sun was setting, casting traces of pink across the high clouds streaking the sky. Chris walked slowly to Jason's truck, then stopped to lean back against the hood. She took another bite of her ice cream and gave Jason another warm smile.

His heart absorbed every bit of it as he leaned back beside her and savored a mouthful of frozen chocolate swirled with peanut butter.

The sun slowly set as they ate their ice cream and talked.

Simple pleasures. How he had missed them.

★★★

She didn't tell him she knew about his wife and daughter. A part of her wanted to, but she simply didn't know how. And she probably didn't need to anyway. Jason seemed to enjoy talking about work or next season's new lineup for the Portland Trailblazers. The conversation drifted back to his work, until he asked Chris about her job in the army. His eyes bulged when she finally told him she had served as a helicopter medevac medic during Operation Desert Storm.

She was used to seeing people's eyes bulge when she told them that. But seeing Jason's reaction especially tickled her.

"Wow. Ray certainly didn't tell me that."

"Well, good. I was hoping he'd save something for me to tell you."

"And not just a medic — you worked on a medevac."

"Yep. A UH-1 Huey that earned herself quite a reputation during Vietnam. She was their Ticket to Paradise. And ours. I really miss her sometimes."

"That's amazing."

"It was a lot of fun."

"How did you get into that? Whatever made you want to become a medevac medic?"

She licked at her cone, letting the frozen sweetness linger on her tongue. Swished it through her mouth. Then swallowed deeply. In the process, she hoped Jason would forget his question and ask another.

He didn't. He chomped a huge bite from the cherry cheesecake scoop and waited for Chris's response.

She watched his jaw muscles constrict and relax as he chewed. Watched the whiskers on his chin move.

He swallowed. "You don't want to answer that?"

His voice was soft and carried not even a hint of impatience. She tried to smile. "I don't really know how to answer that. It's a long story."

"Maybe a story for another time?"

Her smile widened. She felt the cut on her cheek protest. "Maybe."

"Good enough." Another huge bite. He talked with his mouth full. "I rode on a life flight a time or two. Definitely exciting. So how'd you meet Scott's wife?"

Chris turned a bit against the truck's hood to better face Jason. "Ben assigned her to our crew. He was our commanding officer. Actually, we became a part of his brigade. Do you know Ben Connelly?"

"I've met him once, I think. Many years ago."

"He's a great guy." She bit into her cone and chewed. "When he put her with us, we became one of the few medevacs hauling an experienced trauma nurse and a medic."

"Did you fly a lot of missions?"

She swallowed and wiped her mouth with a napkin. "Keep in mind the ground war only lasted one hundred hours. We actually only ran one mission that could have been classified as a 'combat mission.'" The words still haunted her. She licked her lips and let the lingering taste of mint chocolate chip soothe away the ghosts.

Jason remained quiet, yet appeared intensely interested.

Chris savored the silence almost as much as her ice cream. It was as if Jason knew it was her story to tell and was completely comfortable letting her tell it. She smiled at him. Couldn't help it. "We ran quite a few regular missions, though. We flew quite a bit."

"I'd love to hear about all of it sometime."

"Definitely a long story."

"Another time, maybe?"

From the warmth filtering up through her, she could tell her smile carried the feelings she couldn't express but still wanted Jason to feel. "Another time. Sure. I'd like that."

★★★

She stood on the porch and watched his truck disappear down Kimberley Street. Even after it disappeared, she continued to watch it. Even after Scott headed back inside, she continued to stand there. On the porch. Next to Erin.

Two more cars passed by the house. And another. Chris still stared down the street.

"I think he's gone." Just a whisper.

But enough to startle her out of her daze. She turned to look at Erin. "Huh?"

"I think you had a nice night." A grin.

"Oh. Yeah. It was nice." Chris lifted her arms and stretched them above her head.

"I was wondering what happened to you."

A long yawn. "Yeah. Sorry I took off." Her arms plopped back down to her sides. "I didn't plan it, that's for sure."

Erin gave her a knowing grin. Then turned and walked through the door and into the living room to sit in her brand-new homemade wooden rocking chair. She let out a deep sigh. Rested her head back. Closed her eyes. Slowly rocked. And she smiled.

Chris sat in the couch across from her and kicked her feet up on the coffee table. "Girlfriend, that is the best rocking chair ever." It seemed to fit Erin perfectly. The dark stain brought out the wood's intricate grain.

"Mmm. Most certainly is."

A sweet silence fell. Chris enjoyed the sight before her. Completely soaked it in, hoping it would sear into the walls of her heart. A memory that would stay with her forever. Joined with the laughter from earlier that night.

She let her eyes fall closed, let the faint creaking of wood against wood, of rocker against floor, lure her to a sleepy place filled with the earlier laughter and the warmth of sharing that laughter with good friends. The rocking chair's unveiling. Along with its matching cradle.

"The cradle was supposed to be a surprise," Scott had said, his eyes brimming with pride at his handiwork. And with good reason. The chair and matching cradle were incredible works of meticulous care. "But Sonya ruined it. The little rat."

Erin quickly spoke up as she rocked in her new chair for the first time. "But nobody told me you were also building this. Oh, sweetheart ... I think I'm going to sit here and just rock until the Lord returns."

"Or Junior arrives," Jason had said with a smile.

His smile, Erin's tears of joy, Scott's chest puffed out like a peacock ... Chris cherished every image playing out in her mind.

Help me always remember this night, dear Jesus. And thank You for making it so special in so many ways.

Creak creak. Creak creak. Erin slowly rocked. Chris pushed open her sleepy eyes and watched.

Sadness tugged at her. Though vibrant and gorgeous well into her eighth month of pregnancy, Erin looked downright weary. She seemed drained by it, weighed down. Chris closed her eyes and whispered a prayer. She needed Him to hear. Needed Him to hold Erin and her child as close and as tight as He could.

She didn't need to cry. And if she stayed another second in the room, she would. She pushed up to sit on the edge of the couch.

Erin's eyes blinked open. She pressed her lips into a grin. "I could sleep right here."

Chris breathed a faint laugh. "Me too."

Erin's face darkened.

The silence grew unnerving.

"I'm worried about you." Erin stopped rocking.

Chris could only stare. She didn't like how the silence or the moment had turned on her. "No, Rin. You've worried enough. Stop."

Such weariness in that ever-so-faint smile.

Tears blurred the sight. Chris wiped them away with a little more force than necessary. "I mean it. I'm fine. I'm worried about you."

"Then we've worked ourselves into a dilemma, huh. Both worried about the other."

Scott suddenly pushed through the door of the clinic—startled Chris so hard she gasped as her heart nearly exploded in her chest.

"Hey, you two." He laughed at Chris as she grabbed her chest, then he leaned over his wife and kissed her neck. "Do you really like it? Did we really surprise you?" His entire face beamed.

Erin reached up and entwined her fingers in his hair. "Positively and totally entirely." She pulled him in for a long kiss.

Chris's heart finally slowed.

Erin released her husband. He straightened. Grinned. "Good." He looked at Chris. Continued to grin. "It was great to see Jason. You two are good together."

Chris closed her eyes as she laughed.

"It was nice to see him smile," Erin said.

"Nice to see him have something to smile about."

"Cut it out, you guys." Chris gave them both a grin, but knew she'd never hear the end of it.

"Bring him around again sometime." Scott glanced down at his wife. "Maybe we could double date."

Chris quickly stood. "I'm gonna pretend I didn't hear that."

Scott's laughter rumbled like distant thunder.

"Good night, you two. Rinny, get some rest. And don't worry." Chris pushed herself through the clinic door on her way to her apartment stairs.

Scott's voice bellowed from behind her. "She said, 'Right back atcha, lady,' whatever that means."

Halfway up the stairs, Chris kept plodding ahead, even as she laughed and slowly shook her head.

★★★

"So what are you worried about?"

Erin rocked and waited for her husband to sit in the couch. Then gazed into his soft brown eyes. "One guess."

"What. You think she's still . . ."

"Yes. Fill in the blank. All of the above."

"I was going to say messed up."

"That too."

Scott leaned forward and hung his arms over his knees. Then drew up one hand and rested his chin in the palm of it. "So we need to pray, huh."

"Always."

A resigned look.

"Feel like you're in this for the long haul?"

"Hey, babe. I'm with you. If you're haulin', I'm haulin'."

She grinned. "Alicia Renae."

Scott's eyes lifted to scan the ceiling. "Nicholas Stanton. After my great-grandpa."

Erin bit her lip. "Joseph Nicholas. After my father."

Scott lowered his gaze to meet Erin's once more. "Mia Abigail. After my great-grandmother."

"What was your other great-grandmother's name?"

"Rose."

"Hmm. How do you even know that?"

"She was quite a gal. Mom loves to tell stories about her."

Erin smiled. "I love your mom, by the way. Have you bought her a ticket yet?"

The expression on Scott's face told her he had not.

"Buy her a ticket so she can come see her grandchild."

"Will do. First thing tomorrow. How about your dad?"

"He'll be here on the twenty-fourth."

"I love your dad. It'll be great having him around. How long is he staying?" A hint of fear emanated from Scott's brown eyes.

"A week."

"And how long is your mom staying?"

"Two weeks."

"Great." He tried, but his enthusiasm came across totally forced. And fake. "I love your mom."

Erin restrained a burst of laughter. Then let herself fall into the depths of his gaze. "I love you, you silly boy."

A brisk nod. And a wink. "Right back atcha, lady. Right back atcha."

HOME AGAIN. EMPTY HOME. HE needed to get a dog or something. This thing of coming home every night to dead silence and dark empty space … If nothing else, from now on he would leave the light on when he left. The place would still be empty, but at least it wouldn't be dark.

But sometimes the darkness helped. The last thing he wanted to do was walk in the door and immediately be greeted by her smiling face, by all the pictures lined up across the fireplace mantel — the ones he refused to take down and store away in the attic in some musty box.

Come on, Sloan, maybe it's time. Get a grip, buddy. Get a life.

He cursed himself. Tossed his keys on the kitchen table. Slowly walked across the living room to the fireplace mantel. Pulled down one of the many eight-by-tens.

Like all the others, the picture in his hand reflected the most beautiful face he had ever seen. The fullest, softest lips. The most incredible deep blue eyes. From the first moment those baby blues glanced his way, his heart tumbled hind end over teacups. Completely sold. Never to look back. He had followed Jessica Marie Cortland around the playground like a secret agent. Watching her every move, then, when she turned his way, quickly looking the other direction and pretending to be innocently gazing off into space. Or talking to whoever stood close by. He never actually pursed his lips and pretended to whistle, but in his mind that would have been the one gesture to complete the lame scene.

Without his consent, his lips slowly stretched into a smile. Warmth radiated through his heart, long dead ... or so he thought. Staring once more, for the millionth time, at the picture in his hand, at the blonde hair carried by an unseen breeze, the laughing blue eyes glittering in the sunlight, the tender lips so gorgeous and sweet ... he could stare at it all night. Her face would never tire his hungry eyes. Would never satisfy the longing in his soul. The need, the necessity of touching her face just once more, of hearing her laughter resonate through his heart just once more.

No, a picture would never do. And pictures were all he had left. His beautiful bride. The child he would never know. Would never hold in his arms. Would never hear call out to him, *"I love you, Daddy."*

Jessica ... Jessica ...

Tears blurred her face. Warmth that had flowed now raged white hot, searing his soul.

God, it's not right! Why Jessie ... and my precious Lizzy ... God ... why?

The picture shook in his hands. He reached up to run the back of his left hand over his eyes. Hoping to clear his vision, to wipe away his tears.

His eye was drawn to the simple gold band around his finger. He pulled his hand away and studied the shiny smooth ring. Used his thumb to turn it. Round and round his finger. The ring he swore he would never take off.

Maybe it's time, Sloan.

The words sliced through him.

Maybe it's time to put everything away.

He gazed at Jessica's image.

Let her go. She'd want you to.

His teeth clenched. How did anyone know what she would want? How could he just let her go?

You know she wouldn't want you to live like this. You know she'd want you to live. To live and be happy. To grieve . . . and then to move on.

Move on. How simple that seemed. So simple to say. Next to impossible to do.

But what has your life become?

Staring at her picture for hours on end. Weeping into a glassful of scotch. Wallowing in loneliness, letting it slog through his body like blood. Dead blood. Thick and enmeshed in misery.

She wouldn't want you to live like this. She wouldn't like what your life has become.

Some things he couldn't deny.

This is no way to live.

He lifted the picture and placed it back on the mantel. Let his gaze drift down the long collection of memories capturing the happiness of their short time together. His beautiful princess, Jessica Marie Cortland. Her knight in shining armor, Jason Matthew Sloan. Brought together by the words, "I love you." Forever bound by the words, "I do."

Till death did us part.

Tears fell against his cheeks. But these he didn't curse away.

Baby . . . I miss you so much.

How could he ever let her go?

Take off the ring, Jase. You can leave the one picture on your nightstand. But put all the rest away. Do it. Do it now. You can do it.

His head slowly shook. *How? How can I?*

A new face appeared in his mind's eye. He blinked, then lifted his teary gaze to study the stones set into the chimney. A beautiful face. Though battered and sore. Such dark brown eyes, so dark, they almost looked black. Soft. Revealing. Even more so than that smile.

Chris . . .

His head lowered as he lifted his left hand. The ring sparkled. The gold shone, though it had lost some of its luster since the day his new bride first placed it on his finger.

Can I do this? Baby? Is this okay?

The silence carried a whisper of peace. He raised his eyes and glanced around the room.

Maybe I should move. Get out of this house.

Start with the ring, Sloan. Don't get carried away.

He wanted to laugh. *Can I sleep on it?*

Something broke through the peaceful silence. Gentle laughter. An echo of a faded memory. Her sweet voice playfully mocking. *"Just don't sleep* on *it, Jase. I mean . . . ouch! That would hurt!"*

His eyes fell closed as a smile worked its way across his lips. *Baby, you'll always be mine. Even after I take off this ring. And put your pictures away.*

Better believe it, buster. Forever. For sure.

His smile lingered as he rubbed his eyes. He wiped his wet hand across his shirt, then turned and started for his bedroom. But he stopped at the edge of the hall and looked back across his living room. He strained his ears to hear even a hint of her laughter, just a breath of the fading echo of her voice, but it was gone. He turned off the light and headed to bed.

✶✶✶

CHRIS'S EYELIDS FELT LADEN WITH sand. She closed them, then forced them back open. She needed to look at the trinket in her hand, the perfect half of the broken sand dollar, just a little bit longer. Needed to study its delicate design. To allow her heart to pine for the other perfect half. Wherever it may be. Somewhere out on that beach, perhaps. But, by this time, completely ground to sand. Nothing but grains of sand on a beach. Pounded by never-ending waves of the sea.

No. She knew exactly where the other half of this perfect sand dollar lay. It was buried under six feet of dirt in a cemetery outside Colorado Springs, under the gravestone with his name on it. *Travis Ethan Novak.*

Her love, her hope, and her future with him lay buried beside him. Only this perfect half shell remained. Half of the living creature that had died and been scoured clean by the sea. So amazingly beautiful in its intricate design.

And so corny, girl. Get over yourself.

She let out a laugh. Then ran her thumb along the rounded, yet jagged edge. *But I miss him. I miss you, Travis. We could've been good, boy. We really could've lived a good life.*

She sighed deeply, then placed the shell back in its place on her nightstand. Next to the gold earrings and the necklace Travis had given her. Next to her Bible and the picture taken at her birthday party last month.

She lifted the picture and drew it closer to her sleepy eyes. Forced them to focus on every grinning face. A wall of women. Side by side. Arms entwined like a daisy chain. Bettema and Cappy and Erin and Chris. The Four Warriors, as Corissa Foley called them. Sweet lady. And she was right.

Bettema so tall. Cappy so crazy. Erin so pregnant. And Chris so ... alive. And looking good. Even if she had to say so herself.

What a party that had been. What a complete surprise. But she would only turn twenty-nine once in her life, and last month at that party, she turned it.

Thirty. I can't be almost thirty. Wasn't I just almost twenty?

Another trickle of icy dread diffused through her veins. She chose once again to ignore it. Picked up her Bible to read a few more psalms.

The words drifted in and out of her weary soul. So powerful, yet so sweet. *Oh, taste and see that the LORD is good; Blessed is the man who trusts in Him! Oh, fear the LORD, you His saints! There is no want to those who fear Him.*

Sweet like ice cream. Mint chocolate chip. *Oh, taste and see ...*

Asking Erin, "How am I supposed to fear Him, when He turns right around and says, 'Do not be afraid'? I mean, what's up with that?"

"Reverence Him," Erin had replied. "But absolutely do *not* be afraid of Him."

"I know, Rinny. I know." Spoken with a cheeky grin.

And she did know. Very well.

She continued to read until the words blurred on the page. She rubbed her eyes, yet could not keep them open. Could not stay awake.

Another psalm. So beautiful. *In His hand are the deep places of the earth; The heights of the hills are His also. The sea is His, for He made it; And His hands formed the dry land. Oh come, let us worship and bow down; Let us kneel before the LORD our Maker.*

She wanted to kneel, yet didn't move. Sitting on her bed, the Bible held loosely in her hands, she gazed at her closet door, let her vision blur. The fake wood grain of the door completely swirled into fuzz.

It's late. Go to bed.

She blinked. Glanced at her alarm clock. The numbers read 10:34. Not so late. So why did she feel like a zombie?

What a day. Just the thought of replaying the memories of her day exhausted her. And she dared not even peek back further than this day. If she remembered the events of yesterday, exhaustion would plow her over like a bulldozer. She flat-out needed to forget the events of yesterday.

Yet, there was no way. Yesterday, today … it would all beat on the lid of her mind's eye begging to be let in, to replay every stinking, stupid thing she did. And said. And thought. And touched. And destroyed.

But Alaina's all right. Remember that. That's all that matters.

Was it?

She enjoyed her conversation with Laurie. And with Jason. What a treat.

You'd like him, Trav. He's a lot like you. Though he's not near as good looking as you. Wow, boy. What did you ever see in me?

A tiny smile. She felt it play out on her lips. Her eyes fell closed. Her head bobbed.

Go to bed.

She shook her head to clear it. Shuddered as the trickle of dread strengthened into a stream. Her blood ran cold. She knew why. Still chose to ignore it. Tried to pray it away.

Her prayers drifted into praises like the Psalms. Erin had told her to pray the Psalms. To compose her own. To open her heart and let what she really wanted to say to her Lord Jesus be said. In the language He longed to hear. The unspoken language of purest love.

"You feel it when someone loves you. Well, He feels it too. Let your hearts connect."

She wanted her love to flow heavenward. She wanted to open her heart and let it flow to her Lord …

She tried, but at that moment, couldn't open her heart. She couldn't open anything. No connection would be made. "Jesus, Lord, please hear what I can't say." Her prayer was a whisper. Her eyes did not close. Though they blinked, she forced them open. Again and again. "Please know that I love You. I'm so glad this weekend is past."

Tears stung her eyes. Burning heat flooded her cheeks. She lowered her head into her hands.

"Oh, God … You know I saw … *him* … today. Like he was standing beside me. Has he changed at all? Is there any way my dad … has changed?" She slowly rubbed her forehead, then ran her fingers through her hair. "I heard his voice! But it doesn't have to mean anything. I mean … so I saw him. Big deal. It doesn't have to scare me. Not if I don't let it. Help me to lie down right now and sleep. It's not like he'll be the one waking me up."

Her stomach lurched. A soft groan escaped her throat. She must be tired. Why else would she say something so stupid?

"Oh, God …" She couldn't take hearing her own soft cry. *Don't let me see him again. Especially tonight. I don't ever want to see his face again.*

Her lungs held her breath. Refused to let it escape.

But what if he's changed? What if he's not the same man I once knew?

She coughed to force her breath to flow.

No. Never again, Lord. I'm sorry, but I don't ever want to see him again. And please don't ask me to forgive him.

No. She dashed the thought from her mind. Wiped her eyes with the back of her hand. Felt the cut on her cheek pull. And remembered. She needed to put one of Scott's butterfly bandages on it. If she didn't, it would probably pull apart as she slept.

Her hand fell to her lap. The bandages were in the bathroom. Too far away. Too much of a hassle. *Sorry, Rinny.*

She needed to lie down and let the entire weekend disappear. To sleep, then to wake up in the morning and start a new week renewed and refreshed. A brand-new day. With the past two days forever buried and forgotten and gone.

A new day . . .

Would only come if she crawled into bed. Sleep would come fast. And would feel so good.

She placed her Bible on the nightstand. Ran her fingertips over the broken sand dollar. Watched the gold chain catch the light and flicker it back to her. Then reached up and turned the light off.

She pushed back the covers and crawled into bed, then curled onto her left side and felt her head sink into her pillow. She pulled the covers up over her head and tucked them under her chin so she could breathe.

Please, Lord Jesus. I'm Yours. This is Your place. You're here . . . A deep, soothing yawn. *Don't let him find me here. He hasn't yet.* Her stomach slowly relaxed. Her heart slowed. *Just let me . . . sleep. Mmm-hmm. Just . . . sleep. Please help . . . Rinny. I pray in . . . Thank . . . love . . .*

Darkness swirled around her. Then quickly pulled her under.

NINE

Swirling rays of light barely brighten the gloom. A room full of people. A familiar room. Terrible sterile smell. Much too warm. No windows. Shadows rise and fall against the bleak far wall.

"Well … hello, Chris. We've been wonderin' when you'd get here."

Ronny. Big Happy Ronny. The sweetest and biggest orderly in the hospital. Standing at his usual place at the end of the bed, gently massaging the small foot of the child lying on her stomach in the bed.

"Hey, Hap. It's been a long time." Her voice is her own which surprises her. A grown-up's voice. Soft. She studies the two small legs sticking out from under the white sheet. Watches Ronny's huge black fingers tenderly kneading the small white foot. Wants to cry even as she watches him. Wants to remember how good it feels when Ronny massages her feet. Wants to thank him so much for caring enough to bring one moment of bliss into the lifetime of agony she suffers in this room.

She doesn't say a word.

"Yes, indeed. Long time. But we've been waitin' for ya. We knew you'd get here soon."

A swirl of light lifts the gloom enough for her to see three faces. Three people sit on the vinyl couch against the far wall. She recognizes them immediately.

Ray Richardson. Dr. Johnson. Jason Sloan.

Her heart drops to the floor. She feels it fall, as if the

strings holding it in place have been suddenly cut. "What are they doing here, Hap? Who let them in?"

Ronny's round, dark face breaks into a wide smile. "Well, the nice police officer is here to find out just what happened to you. And Dr. Johnson says you're gonna be just fine. He was on his way out to get you a Popsicle. He knows how much you like Popsicles."

Especially the green ones. So cold and tangy and sweet.

"And Mr. Sloan's here 'cause he wants to see you. To see what you look like. To see if you're all right."

Panic sweeps through her. "Don't let him see me, Hap! Why did you let him in here?"

"He ain't gonna hurt you, Chrissy."

"I told you not to call me that."

"I thought you said it was all right." Ronny's big brown eyes are sad.

Did she? Ever? "No. You're not Raymond."

"Nah, Chrissy, I'm da Big Happy. Remember?"

She remembers. Blinks. Slowly turns to look down at the bed. Sees the white sheet spread over the small child. The sheet is propped up with books to keep it from falling against …

But still it is stained. The sheet must have fallen. Hints of brilliant red lines have ruined the clean white sheet, as white as snow. She turns to Hap. Yells at him. "Why did you let it fall?" Strange. She never yelled at him before. Dr. Johnson is the only one she's ever yelled at. Especially that first night when he let the sheet fall.

Ronny starts to cry at her accusation. Fat tears fall down his round cheeks. "It wasn't me, Chrissy. I didn't let it fall. You know I would never do that. I know it hurts you something awful when it falls."

"Stop it, Hap. Don't." She glances at Jason. Sees him listening intently. "Get them all out. Right now. Tell them to get out of here and leave me alone."

Ronny stops massaging the child's foot. He has stopped crying, but his face is very sad. "All right, Chrissy. I'm sorry. I'll tell 'em."

"Hurry, Hap. Please."

Shadows. Grumbles. She's suddenly alone in the room. She hears a faint noise. A whimper. The child under the sheet is crying. So quietly. Yet Chris hears every tear fall against the soft towel they have placed under the child's cheek. Drip. Drip. So many tears.

"Quit crying," she says. "Stop being a baby."

And still the girl cries.

"If you don't stop crying, he'll come in and give you something to cry about."

But that wasn't true. He was in jail. The nice policeman said so.

And still the child cries.

Chris rushes to the head of the bed. Grabs the top of the sheet and rips it back. "Shut up! Don't cry! You don't —"

Tear-filled blue eyes gaze back at her.

Definitely not her own. "Who are you?" But she instantly knows.

Alaina!

Sobs. A wail. "I just wanted to look pretty ..."

Hard darkness.

A gasp.

A cough.

Chris blinked open her eyes, then gulped in air. Again and again. Her heart thudded wildly. She peered across the room. Through the gray night and the faint orange glow from the streetlight sifting through her blinds, she saw her Heceta Head Lighthouse poster.

Okay. I'm in Portland. I'm home. She forced her breathing to slow. *But ... what was that?*

Let it go. Don't think about it. Just a dream. Let it fade.

She pushed back the covers and sat up in the bed. Rubbed her eyes. Waited for the swirling to ease. Then headed for the bathroom, desperately refusing to let the image of the crying child replay in her mind. She availed herself of the facilities. Then splashed her face with cold water. The cut on her cheek stung.

Easy. Don't pull it open.

She grabbed a towel and dabbed it against her face, then drew in a long, deep breath as her heart slowed its mad race inside her. She blinked as she slowly lifted her eyes. In her reflection in the mirror, through the dark gray night, only her eyes and gaping mouth could be seen.

The whites of her eyes. Streaked with red. White like the sheet. So clean and so soft. Yet, when it fell ...

Her eyes pinched shut.

Let it go and it'll fade. Think about something else. Think about ... Her eyes slowly opened. *Jason. Yeah. Think about that handsome man.*

What in the world was he doing in my dream?

She wanted to laugh, but didn't. She stared another second. Then tossed the towel into the sink and headed back to bed. Only a little past one. Only a stupid, crazy dream. Ronny was a sweetheart. Big Happy. Indeed. And Alaina was fine. It wasn't her crying. It wasn't her lying in that bed. No. Chris had made sure of that. Bore the cut on her cheek to prove it.

She crawled back under the covers and pulled them up over her head. Tucked herself in under the heavy fleece blankets she loved. The ones still faintly giving off the scent of wood smoke. Reminding her again of a faraway miner's cabin high up in the Rockies near a hot-spring pool and a stream that still carried a flake or two of gold.

A hum. *Thank You, Lord, for that place. And for this place. I can have two homes, can't I?* Warmth from the blankets started to radiate into her. *And thanks for "da Big Hap." He was a trip. And a total sweetheart. If it wasn't for him ...*

Her heart slowed. She drew in a deep yawn. Let it out in a huff.

Jason's face wafted across the darkness. His lips white with ice cream. As he chewed his cherry cheesecake. Waiting for an answer to his question.

Without Hap, Lord ... what would I have become?

She didn't even want to consider it. She was born to fly Hueys. And missed it terribly.

Thanks ... that Lainer's all right. She really is. I know it. It wasn't her in that bed.

She let that thought disintegrate too.

Lord Jesus ... please help Rinny ...

She wanted to continue the prayer, but it followed her thoughts and drifted away on the hush of her breaths.

And darkness fell.

Thick, miry darkness. Oily and shimmering.

Then sparkling. Glittering with brilliant flashes of light.

Sudden bright light. Illuminating the entire front room of her old house. It is exactly as she remembers it.

Again.

Oh, no.

How she hates this house.

And this nightmare.

Lord, no! Please! It's been months! I thought — !

Her dad's old chair. Threadbare and ugly. The hassock stacked with old newspapers, held down by a dirty dinner plate. Old *Reader's Digest*s and a bag of pretzels on the brick ledge in front of the fireplace. Beside his wet work boots that had long since dried. Empty Coors cans stacked on the cluttered bookshelf beside the chair. A few on the floor by the TV.

Yeah. Go ahead. Throw them at it. Like that'll make the Nuggets win.

She glances around. A hint of wariness worms through her belly. Maybe if she picks up the cans before he comes back … Where is he, anyway? Mrs. Anderson will be here any minute.

She blinks and stares at herself picking up the cans. She knows she's dreaming, yet can't escape it, can't wake herself up. The scene plays out again in front of her like it has a million times before.

Not again. God, no! Make it stop! Please, God, make it stop!

Her dad's footsteps rip terror through her. Her head turns. Sharp pains course through her stomach. Her eyes peer down the empty hall.

He's coming closer! Run away, stupid! Don't just stand there!

She stands there, empty beer cans in her arms.

Her dad appears. He stops his inevitable progression to his chair just long enough to give his daughter a good once-over. "Been drinkin' my beer again, Chrissy?"

Laughter echoes across the room. She shrinks back at the memory of the taste his beer left on her lips. And the beating he gave her after he found her and smelled it on her breath. The memory sickens her. She sits down at the dining room table while the little girl she used to be stares up at her dad.

Not so little. Soon to be fifteen. Almost big enough to drive. Big enough to stand up to her dad. If she dared.

"My, my. All dressed up, Chrissy. Where you think you're off to?"

She wants to scream at him, *"You know where! Don't make me say it!"*

She has to say it. He's standing there waiting for her answer. She keeps her voice sweet. Doesn't let her aggravation show. "Don't you remember, Daddy? Mrs. Anderson is coming to pick me up to — "

Pathetic. Of course he won't let her say another word. His bellows of laughter fill the house, yet nothing is funny.

And she stands there like an idiot, holding an armful of empty beer cans.

Some of the beer drips onto her pretty shirt. She wiggles the cans away from her chest and rushes to the kitchen to throw them into the garbage.

"And bring me some more while you're in there."

She watches him settle back in his chair. He kicks his feet up onto the hassock, but not before he kicks the dinner plate and the newspapers to the floor. She turns her head and watches herself load up her arms with cold, full cans of beer from the refrigerator. The sight makes her shiver as a chill races through her — the cans are cold against her bare arms. She glances inside the refrigerator and notices there aren't many beers left. That is never good. Icy fingers reach across her chest and squeeze her heart.

She hurries into the living room and allows her dad to pull one of the cans out of her arms. She tries to lower the rest to the end table beside him, yet one still falls, at which her dad turns and glares. "Set that one aside, Chrissy. And go get me another."

"There aren't many left."

"Just bring me another!"

She pushes the beer that dropped behind the others and heads back into the kitchen.

Why did you say that? Why did you tell him there weren't many left? Are you trying to aggravate him? In a few minutes you'll be gone with Mrs. Anderson, and he'll see he's out of beer. He'll go get some and that will be that!

Right. Sure. Get real.

She knows how this scene will play out, and suddenly wonders why she wasted her breath. She wasn't listening, anyway.

But maybe it wasn't wasted. This is just a dream. Maybe this time he will let her leave with Mrs. Anderson. Maybe she'll get to leave and go see the play and — but she knows.

This may be a dream, but it's a dream like all the others. So far. She has to find a way out before Mrs. Anderson shows up. Before Mrs. Anderson leaves without taking young Chris with her.

"You're not going anywhere. Go take off those good clothes."

She slaps the beer down on the table next to the others. "But, Daddy! You said I could!"

His eyes sour. "I'm changing my mind."

"You can't! She'll be here any minute!"

Stupid! Don't yell at him!

"And she'll leave the first minute after that." His voice rakes her stomach. "Now get. I'm trying to watch the game."

Stupid game. She wants to shout, *"They're gonna lose again anyway. They always lose. Why bother? Watch something else."*

She doesn't say a word. Only sits and watches herself storm into her bedroom and slam the door.

Stupid. You're definitely asking for it.

The doorbell rings. Chris's head turns so quickly toward the sound the entire vision spins. She races out of her bedroom to answer it. Opens it. Sees Mrs. Anderson, her favorite teacher in the whole world, standing at the door. Smiling.

"Hello, Chris. Happy Easter to you. Are you ready to go?"

Chris slowly turns to look over her shoulder at her father. Swallows deeply when she discovers he has already left his chair and is walking toward them.

Don't get up, Daddy. Just say it's okay from there. Let me go. Don't get up.

Her father grabs the door and opens it wide. Takes in the sight of the woman standing just outside. Up and down his eyes study her. She's wearing a flowery pink dress with ruffles and a broach on her shoulder. A flower of some kind. Made of gold. As far as Chris could tell.

But she blinks. Didn't Mrs. Anderson wear a blue dress last time?

The nice lady smiles at Chris's dad. Chris doesn't want her to. She knows her smile is wasted if it's directed her daddy's way. He only sees what he wants to see, nothing else. And he can't see kindness for anything. He'll twist her pleasant smile into something hideous. Then slap it back in her face.

"Hello, Donovan. It's nice to see you again."

Her dad shakes Mrs. Anderson's hand, though his upper lip has a slight curl to it. "You too, Alice. But I'm sorry you came all this way."

No, Daddy, don't say it. Just let me go.

Chris laughs. Turns her head away. She can't stand hearing herself beg. She searches the room for a way out. But, like in all the other times she sits in this chair watching this scene play out, she never finds it. There is no way out. No escape. The scene always plays out like a wound-up toy monkey. The cymbals clash against each other until the monkey gets tired and stops. Who knows when that will be? Maybe, if she prays hard enough, this time, it will be soon. Before …

She hears Mrs. Anderson's voice and turns to see that the woman's smile wavers a bit. "I'm sorry, Donovan, but I don't understand."

Don't make him repeat it. Just leave. So this nightmare can end.

"Chrissy can't go to your play. I'm sorry, but she's gonna stay home tonight. With me."

Why do you say you're sorry? You're so obviously not.

"Really? Well, okay, I guess. I'm sorry about that. I know she would really enjoy it. It is Easter, after all."

"I understand that, Alice. And I'm her father."

Just go. And thanks for trying.

Mrs. Anderson leaves. Chris stands at the open door of her father's house and watches the car leave a trail of cloudy dust as it heads down the long driveway.

Don't do it. Don't slam the door.

The car disappears. The cloud of dust fades. Chris suddenly turns and slams the door. The windows rattle.

Her dad raises his head, then his eyes to look at her. They narrow until they are just slits in his head. His mouth opens. Words grate out of his throat. "You're gonna live to regret that."

Chris looks around the house again, desperate for a way out, for a window, a door, a crack in the framework of this imaginary hell she finds herself in. The world buried in the vile depths of her mind.

She searches for it. There is still no way out. She sits locked in the horror of her life as she lived it.

God … please …

What are you praying for, Chris? You did this. You made him so crazy. Why did you slam the door? Why did you scream the words you are about to scream?

She knows the words, yet is helpless to stop herself from saying them. She lifts her hands and presses them against her ears as the curses fly. They bounce off her hands and she's glad. Just lame imitations of her dad's words. To curse at her dad is to speak his language. They mean nothing to him.

Or to Chris. It's the rest of the words she says that cause her teeth to grind. Her eyes to pinch shut.

"How could you? You monster! Don't you love me at all?"

No, don't ask him that. He'll answer you. He'll tell you the truth. And you won't be able to take it!

"You better rein in that attitude, girlie."

"No! You beast! I just wanted to go see a stinking play. What's so wrong with that?"

He stands from his ugly chair. Seems to loom over her. Every time this scene plays out, he seems to grow another inch. "Get to your room. Now."

"No, Daddy! I cannot believe you couldn't do this one little thing for me. I fetch your beers and clean your house —"

"Enough, Chrissy!"

Enough!

She tries to hide her face with her hands, but her hands refuse.

"NO!" More stupid curses. "You don't love me at all, do you? Is there anything inside you at all? Don't you care about me … at all?"

Her dad takes a huge step forward. His cheeks blaze. "If you care about your backside, you'll go straight to your room."

"Answer me, Daddy."

No, don't. Please! I can't take it.

"What do you want me to say?" His voice is a growl. His eyes bear down on her through fierce slits. "Should I love you? Why? Because of you my wife left. I loved her, Chrissy, but because you couldn't get along with her boys, you forced her out."

Her jaw drops against her chest as her heart freezes the blood in her veins. She tries to push out of her chair so she can run away, so she can at least run and hide in her bedroom. On the floor between her bed and her desk. To curl up there like so many times before. But she cannot move. She's mired in the dream. Worse than ever before.

Oh God, oh God …

The last time, the time before that — every time the dream plays out, after her dad asks her, *"What do you want me to say?"* he says something different. Every time his words cut to her core. But this? This is ridiculous!

But as crazy as it is, she can't keep herself from talking back. From screaming the words she can't bear to hear.

"How can you say that? You know how they treated me, Daddy!"

"Stop it, Chrissy. Go to your room."

"I was just a kid!"

Tears cloud her eyes, drip down her cheeks. She feels a sting, yet can't comprehend why. Or why her cheek is cut. He hasn't hit her yet.

"They were just foolin' around, Chrissy. You know how boys are at that age."

She sobs, but neither of them hear. They stand almost nose to nose, her eyes wide, his eyes narrowed into cruel slits.

"I tried to teach you how to defend yourself, but you're always so helpless. My little Chrissy. Always so helpless." His hand lifts. Touches her arm.

Chris shudders as his touch sends fiery slithers through her entire body.

"I told you to tell Tony to leave you alone. If you would've told him —"

She pushes him away. But he's too strong. Stands too close. "I did tell him to leave me alone!" His breath smells so vulgar her stomach turns and she gags.

His voice takes on a singsong tone. "Tony was a good boy. Jeffy was too. We could've been a nice family. But you had to —"

Her hand flies up.

No! Don't!

And slaps her dad's face.

Oh … God …

Hard. Enough to force his head to reel.

The palm of her right hand stings.

God … no …

He straightens. Blinks. Stares. His eyes are no longer slits, but are wide, gazing at his daughter. "I can't believe you just hit me."

Her body trembles, though she knows it was just a slap. Her hand was open. And he had taught her how to hit with a closed fist. Taught her well.

"I can't believe it! Should I be proud of the fact you just hit me? That I didn't even see it coming?"

She wants to run more than breathe. Nausea sweeps through her, yet she cannot move. Not even to draw in a breath.

"I didn't even try to duck it, huh." His voice carries a hint of laughter. "What kind of teacher am I? I don't even duck a pillow punch like that."

Her teeth clench. But that's it. She's helpless to do anything but sit and watch. As she stands and glares into the eyes of her dad.

She sees it coming, yet doesn't say a word. Doesn't scream or even attempt to move out of the way. Like so many times before, the scene slows as she watches her dad pull his right arm back. His hand curls into a fist that swings around and connects with the side of her face.

She winces and lowers her head, feeling the impact of the blow, yet doesn't feel near the pain she used to. But it hurts to watch her head rip around, her arms fly up, her entire body go limp and crash to the floor.

Hmm. Something different. Her head tilts as she peers at herself lying on the floor of the living room, as she notices how close her head came to hitting the corner of the brick ledge in front of the fireplace. Another few inches …

God … another few inches and it would've been done. Why didn't You finish it when You had the chance?

Silence. Eerie silence. Her eyes widen. She slowly glances around the room.

Where'd he go?

Stupid! You know where he went! Run! Run now!

She struggles against the mire. Can't lift her arms or make her feet move at all. Surrounded on all sides by it, as thick as cement and just as heavy, she can barely move an arm, but what good is that going to do?

Here he comes!

She tries to scream at the girl on the floor. Tries, but can't force in a breath. The mire crushes her. Words race through her mind, desperate for release. *Get up! Get up and run!*

The girl slowly starts to push herself up.

RUN!

Her eyes shift right. Her dad is in the hallway, storming toward the dining room. Heading straight for her! But he looks through her, as if she doesn't even exist.

I don't exist. He doesn't have a clue I'm here or that I can see him. That I can see everything.

So stop him! Quit being so helpless!

She struggles and pulls against the mire, but still can't move. Sobs overtake her. She sits and weeps, helpless to do anything but sit and weep and be helpless. Like so many times before.

No … no, no, no! God! Do something!

Her dad has the cord. He's gripping it so tightly in his hand his knuckles are white. His bicep bulges under his dirty T-shirt.

This is it, Chris. Can't you stop it? Make it stop! Wake up!

She sobs. Screams, thrashes in the chair. But can't break free of the mire. She lifts her arm just an inch. Is exhausted by the effort. Lets it fall back to her side. And cries.

Chris? Do something!

I can't … I can't stop it.

She's suddenly tossed aside with the rest of what lay on the table. The apples in the bowl fly and scatter. The two books she left there after doing her homework earlier that day. All of it sails past her. Hits the floor about the same time she does. Everything scatters across the floor.

He's clearing the table …

Whimpers.

God, please, make him stop.

A scream. Her own scream. Etched in her memory for fourteen years.

Her hands cover her face. Tears leak through her fingers like sand. *Let me wake up. God, please, I can't take this. I don't want to see it again.*

Thrown facedown on the table, the hard wood bruises her hips and chin.

God ... help me ...

Her new blouse is yanked up to her shoulders.

Chris gags. Her hand covers her mouth. Enraged, she jumps up, but the mire falls over her once more. She cowers against its weight, struggles to breathe as she's crushed beneath it. Darkness swirls as she lies frozen. Her chance to escape is gone.

A scream.

Don't scream! Just take it! Lay there and take it!

A cruel growl. "If you scream once more, Chrissy, you're really gonna regret it. I mean it."

She forces her hands up to cover her ears, but every sound reaches the deepest places in her mind.

Curses rent the air. Dragon breaths huff in and out of her dad.

A trembling cry. "Please, Daddy, no!"

Her heart and lungs seize. The whirl of the cord splitting the air is immediately followed by the loud smack as it lands.

Violent retching overtakes her, tosses her headlong into oily darkness. She breathes it in as she tries to scream, hears only the cord slice the air again and again. The whirl of it, the smacking sound as it lands wrenches her deeper into total darkness. She feels no pain as it lands, yet heaves at the sound of it, and thrashes as more of the warm, thick oil is sucked into her lungs. Slowly drowning, she feels herself falling. Only to hear another whirl and be jerked back up. Another smack. Another violent dry heave.

A writhing scream splits the air.

Brilliant light pierces her eyes.

Brilliant light! White-hot lances piercing straight through her eyes deep into her head. She gasped and cried out, then quickly covered her face with her arms.

"Chris?"

Her stomach in knots, she struggled to unwrap herself from her blankets, then ran to the bathroom and fell over the toilet. She vomited long after her stomach emptied, heaving and coughing as her vision swirled. Her heart spasmed as it struggled to pump frozen blood through her arteries. Hot tears coursed down her sweaty face, burning through chills that left her shivering.

Another violent heave. With nothing left to come up, her body tightened against it. When it eased, trembling overtook her. She cried between gulps of vile air.

Never. Never before had it ever hit her so hard.

Dear God, please—

Another intense heave. A desperate moment of agony as it tore through her. A gasp. A trembling whimper. "Oh, God … God, please …"

★★★

SHOULD SHE MOVE CLOSER? SHE wanted to try, but her feet would not move. The sight so terrified her, she stood in the bathroom doorway, mouth gaping.

Dry heaves hurt. Cappy wanted to cry. She took a step closer, but really wanted to run back and jump into bed. Vivid, hideous cries of agony had wakened her. She rushed to Chris's room, tore open the door, and ran inside. She just wished she hadn't turned on the light. But what else could she do? She had shaken Chris, yelled at her, called her name …

She would leave this light off. She could see through the gray darkness, and what she saw was enough. After a deep breath and a prayer for help, she slowly moved forward, then lifted the towel out of the sink and filled a glass with water. Chris would want to rinse her mouth when the heaves subsided.

Cappy held the glass and draped the towel over her arm. Then knelt beside her friend, her hands trembling so hard the water in the glass shook. She touched Chris's shoulder and marveled at what she felt. The muscle in Chris's shoulder felt like solid rock.

Another long heave. It seized Chris's entire body. Slowly let her go. Breath ground out her throat in a soft, trembling groan. She shivered. Spit. Gasped. "Don't touch me."

Cappy quickly lifted her hand. Then moved back a few feet to sit against the wall. She still held the water. The towel was still draped over her arm. She sat there. Didn't know what else to do but wait. And keep quiet. And pray.

Chris lifted a trembling hand to flush the toilet. The familiar sound struck Cappy as so out of place in that moment so completely unfamiliar.

She waited.

Still on her knees, still leaning over the toilet, Chris's eyes were closed. She didn't seem able to open them. Or willing. A gravelly whisper. "Sorry, Cap."

"Forget it." She couldn't believe the words squeaked out her throat.

Chris coughed. Groaned.

Cappy moved closer and handed her the water. A bit of it sloshed onto the floor. She dabbed at it with the towel.

"Thanks."

"Sure."

Chris took the towel and hid her face with it.

Cappy slowly pushed away again to lean back against the wall. She waited for Chris to rinse her mouth and spit. To drink a few swallows.

A hard, violent shudder racked Chris's body. The cup fell from her hand and clattered across the floor, splashing what remained of the water.

Cappy moved closer, then grabbed Chris and pulled her into her arms. Chris fell against her and cried. The towel covered her face. Muffled her anguished sobs.

Tears dripped from Cappy's eyes into Chris's sweated-wet hair. She sorted through the chaos in her mind for anything to say. Searched her heart for any answer. She heard a quiet voice hush her. And knew she just needed to be silent and still. To let Chris cry. And to pray.

⋆⋆⋆

CHRIS TRIED TO PUSH OUT of Cappy's arms, but fell back as the mire engulfed her. For a moment, she thought she still dreamed, then hoped it was true, that she wasn't really sitting on the floor of her bathroom crying on Cappy's shoulder. But the moment passed. She knew it was true. Cappy held her gently, as a good friend should. And didn't say a word. The best of good friends.

She bit into the towel and held her breath, fighting the moment, furious at her tears, yet wanting to cry forever. Another sob burst out, and she let it, but a hiccup soon followed and that ended it. She pulled in a deep breath and held it again. By the time she released it, her sobs had ceased. She dried her face with the towel and pushed out of Cappy's arms.

A sniff. She needed a tissue. And for the darkness to swallow her up.

Cappy touched her arm.

Chris pulled the towel away and dared a glance. The woman handed her a wad of toilet paper.

One of the best friends she ever had.

She blew her nose, almost gagged from it, then tossed the wad into the toilet. Flushed it once more. Cringed as the sudden explosion of water grated her nerves and intensified her headache. And validated the sad truth she did indeed sit on the floor of her bathroom by the toilet where she just deposited Sonya's incredible ham dinner. And that equally incredible mint chocolate chip ice-cream cone.

She leaned away from Cappy to rest against the bathtub. Instantly regretted the decision—the tub was unbearably hard. Chills raced through her as the freezing porcelain bled through her damp T-shirt into her shoulders. She wanted to pull away, to walk away, to run away as fast as she could. She sat there. And tried to summon the courage to look Cappy Sanchez in the eye.

The woman handed her that glass again. Full of cold water. Tears stung her eyes. She forced the word through her throat. "Thanks."

"Do you want some Pepto or something?"

So softly spoken, the voice didn't sound like Cappy at all.

Chris lifted her eyes. Gave her friend a smile. Or attempted to. She didn't know if she succeeded. But the words flowed easier through her throat. "No. Thanks."

"Anything?"

"No." If her lips weren't cooperating, maybe Cappy felt the smile in her heart directed Cappy's way. "You know what they say about a cup of cold water."

The woman slowly grinned. "Yeah. Cheaper than a Bud and ten times better for ya."

Laughter burst up from Chris's belly. The sudden movement enflamed her grated nerve endings. Her eyes fell closed.

"Just drink it, lady. Thank me later."

She lifted the glass and drew in a long drink. The water ignited the foul taste in her mouth and throat, even as its iciness soothed.

"I wanna go get Erin."

Her eyes flew open. *"What?"*

"Do you want me to go get her?"

"Absolutely not." Her teeth ground as rage lit up her belly. Gritted sharply from the lingering bile. "No. Don't even think about it." Her stomach burned.

"I think you need her here."

"No." She tried not to glare, but had no strength left for niceties. "Do *not* tell her a thing. I mean it, Cap. Just go back to bed."

The silence lingered.

She hated herself. Wanted to lie down on the floor and die.

"Are you gonna be all right? And don't lie to me, Chris. If you lie to me, I'll go get Sonya too."

She definitely glared. "Shut up, Cappy. Don't push this."

"I'm not trying to."

Her next breath seemed to pull in cleaner air. Fresher air. She drew it in deeply. Felt it soothe her entire being.

Cappy didn't move.

Chris let out her breath. Waited for the tingly sensation it left behind to fade. Then drew the cup to her lips and chugged every last drop.

Cappy didn't say a word.

The water sloshed in Chris's empty stomach. The fire flickered. And died. She lowered the cup to the floor. Slowly looked up at her friend. "You're the best. You know that?"

"I have the worst time trying to figure you out."

A weary laugh.

"Do you really think I can go back to bed with you sitting here like this? You must think I'm loco."

Another laugh. Slightly stronger that the first. "Help me up."

"Sit there another second. Make sure you're all right."

A sigh. "I'm fine, Cap. Really."

"You do think I'm loco. Well, I think you're loco too. And I *am* going back to bed. As soon as I'm sure you're all right."

"Just help me up." She started to push away from the floor, then let Cappy pull her the rest of the way up to her feet. Her legs shook. She swayed a bit. Grabbed the edge of the sink to steady herself. Waited for the stars to recede, the swirling to ease.

"There. You're up."

"Thanks."

Cappy still tightly gripped Chris's arm.

"You can let go now."

"Give it another second. Make sure."

"You sound like a broken record." But it took another ten seconds for Chris to see straight. She blinked. Looked up. "Okay. I'm good. Let go."

Cappy stared Chris down. Then released her grip on Chris's arm.

"Really. I'm fine."

Still Cappy stared. "Do you want to talk about it?" Just a whisper.

"No." Chris lowered her head. "But thanks."

"I don't need to go back to bed."

"Yes, you do. It'll make me feel better."

"Are you sure?"

"Yes. And sleep. Don't worry about me. I'll be fine."

"All right then. *Hasta mañana.*" She flipped a wave and started for the door.

"Hey."

She stopped and turned around.

Chris wanted to pull Cappy into a tight hug. To tell her so many things. To make sure Cappy knew how much she cherished their friendship, to help her make sense of what she had just seen. But in that moment, she couldn't move. Couldn't put the words together. She gazed at her friend. And smiled. A faint press of her lips. That was all she could muster. "Thanks, lady. I mean it."

Cappy's expression softened.

"And no, I don't think you're loco."

A smile appeared.

"But if you tell Erin or Sonya about this, I swear I'll gather up all that Latin polka music you've got and haul it straight to Goodwill."

"You wouldn't dare."

"You better believe I would. In a heartbeat. If I find out you told them."

"Oh, girl, you *are* loco."

Chris enjoyed the laughter gurgling up from her belly. She knew it left a real and happy smile on her face. The type of smile that would put Cappy at ease.

Even as a writhing scream echoed deep in her own soul.

TEN

Cappy's recliner called out to her. But Chris needed air. Lots of it. And a few billion stars wouldn't hurt.

She needed her jacket. And desperately needed to take a shower. But since it was 4:53 in the morning and Cappy had gone back to bed, she figured she could wait. Let the poor girl try to get some sleep. Before her alarm woke her up in two hours.

Please, Lord. Help her forget everything she just saw.

Chris lifted her jacket off the hook. Stuffed her hands into the sleeves.

Help me forget too.

As quietly as she could, she turned the dead bolt and unlocked the front doorknob. Eased the door open. Outside on the small landing, the early morning air chilled her to the bone. Yet comforted her. She stepped down to the middle of the stairs and stopped. Though the birds joyously proclaimed the new day, it was still too dark to see them. She sat down on the step and leaned back. Let her head rest on a step above her.

The sky was clear, but in her tiny patch of it, only a few stars shone brightly enough to be seen. The thick, ugly darkness returned to spread through her. It seemed to soak into her skin, to mix with her blood, to shoot straight to her heart. So thick, her heart worked twice as hard to pump it back out to her skin. So heavy, it seemed to crush her against the stairs.

Frame by frame, her dream flashed across her mind's eye. She couldn't pray it away, couldn't move from the stairs where she lay. She watched it play out.

Yet, deep in her soul, she heard a little girl's voice softly pleading. *Jesus. Jesus.*

"My, my. All dressed up, Chrissy. Where do you think you're off to?"

"Don't you remember, Daddy? Mrs. Anderson is coming to pick me up to —"

He didn't laugh.

Chris's eyes flew open.

In the dream, he laughed. But he didn't laugh. Not that day. He just blew her off. A huff and a gruff. He did that when he was drunk. And that day, he was drunk. He had been drinking all afternoon. Throwing his beer cans at the TV. Easter Sunday 1982.

But he did laugh . . .

The sound of it lingered in her mind. Loud, mocking laughter.

And he wasn't drunk.

In her dream, her father was completely sober.

He wouldn't have hit you so hard if he was sober.

He did in the dream.

In all the dreams, the hundreds of dreams, he was always drunk. Staggering. Slurring his words. But tonight he was perfectly sober. And still beating her . . .

She sat up on the stairs and wiped her eyes. Her headache swelled and throbbed against her skull.

This dream was just plain weird.

The little girl's voice whispered up from her soul. *Please, Jesus . . . help me forget.*

Her dad didn't know Mrs. Anderson. So why did he call her Alice? Was that even her first name? And why did she call him Donovan? How did she know his first name? Had they met before? Did she know him? And she still wanted to come pick her up?

What color dress did she wear that day? Chris wanted to laugh even as her eyes burned with tears. *Every dream it's different. I guess I'll never know for sure.*

So different.

That day he had softened when she asked if he loved her. "Of course, I do, Chrissy. Quit asking me that," he had said. But almost as soon as the dreams began, his words changed along with his tone. His voice became a growl as his words formed a question. Always that one question. Only in her dreams. "What do you want me to say?" And in each new dream, as if answering his own question, he would say something different and ugly and cruel. Each time he would lay out another reason why his original words that day were nothing but lies.

And now she had learned a new truth. Her dad hated her for causing his wife, Saundra, and her boys to leave. But she didn't cause it. Didn't he say how sorry he was that Tony had been hurting her? And Jeffy too?

She wanted to scream into the peaceful city's morning air.

Anthony and Jeffrey. Saundra's two little princes. In the three short years they were Chris's stepbrothers, they did nothing but terrorize her. Stole her toys. Commandeered her tree house. She took a beating one night when she complained to her dad about them. He took off his belt and let her have it right in front of Saundra. Just to show Saundra how much he loved her. And didn't love his own daughter. When the boys found out, they laughed at her. But later that night her dad kicked the boys out of the tree house he had built for her. Made it off-limits to them from that night on. Even after Saundra yelled at him for it. Even after the boys pitched a fit.

And then, a few months after that, when he caught Saundra's oldest little prince on top of his daughter, didn't he curse and yell at Saundra? Then demand she pack up and move out? That very same night Saundra loaded up her car and left, taking her two hideous sons with her. After they were gone, didn't Chris sit on her father's lap and cry while he held her? While he said to her, his voice soft and sad, "You're a good girl, Chrissy. You're a good girl. Don't be afraid, now. It's over. They're gone, and they won't ever hurt you again." He hushed her as she cried, and held her tenderly until she stopped crying. He told her he was sorry for everything that happened. He said the words. He didn't blame her for the divorce.

Did he?

Was it all just a lie?

She jumped up and nearly fell as she hurried down the stairs.

God, I can't take this!

The little girl in her soul was weeping.

She hopped off Erin's porch and stumbled into the street.

He did love me. He held me and kissed me that night and said he was glad they were gone. He said Saundra was a demanding witch. And her boys were spoiled rotten.

Chris had laughed against his shoulder as he spoke those words. Just a breath as she hiccuped and sobbed. But hearing his words stirred up the laughter. And she would never forget it.

Please help me forget . . .

She walked to the far sidewalk, then turned and headed slowly toward the gym.

The little girl's whine started to grate on her nerves.

She whispered aloud to shut her up. "Truth is, Lord, if he would've said that night what he said in my dream tonight, I certainly wouldn't have just slapped him. I would have laid him out." Her hands curled into fists. "He taught me how to punch. I would've shown him what a good teacher he was. I would've knocked him on his can. Broke his jaw. Then kicked him bloody while he was down."

Nausea swept into her stomach. Her steps faltered as she lifted her hands to her head. *Oh, God . . .*

Relax. Just relax.

She stopped at the street corner and let out a deep breath.

Please, God . . . Lord Jesus . . . The little girl's voice was now her own. *Precious Lord . . . forgive me. Please help me forget.*

A car stopped at the corner and hesitated a moment before continuing through the intersection. She watched its taillights flicker and disappear. Then walked. Straight ahead. Across the street. Aimlessly down the sidewalk. She suddenly stopped and stared at the streetlight's orange glow reflected in a car window.

Why didn't I ever notice how close my head came to hitting the fireplace? Did it really come that close? Or was the dream a lie?

She turned to look over her shoulder. Saw her house far down the street.

Kimberley Street.

She needed to go home.

She crossed the street to the far sidewalk. Pushed her fists into the pockets of her jacket. Walked with her head down.

It did, didn't it? The dream didn't lie.

Tears blurred the path under her feet.

That's exactly how I fell. And if I would've hit the … Oh, God … I would've died. He would've killed me. And I would've been dead.

She stopped and ran her fingers through her hair. Lifting her hands hurt. Her entire body hurt.

The little girl in her soul let out a wail.

God, if I had died that night … because I wanted to go see a play about Easter …

Her wail became a cry.

Jesus … Oh, Lord, You saved me. You literally saved my life. My eternity.

Cries and tears of joy.

You saved me … so I could know You. You knew I wanted to learn about You. You knew …

The street swirled. She reached out to steady herself against a tree. Felt the rough bark bite into her palms.

"My Lord … my Savior … my God." Slowly, between sobs, the words whispered out of her. "Please forgive me. Forgive me for all of this. For everything. And please help me forget. I need to forget. Help me to forget and move on."

The words soothed her soul like sweet music to her ears. *Yes, Lord God, to forget and move on.*

No. A breath of a whisper. *To forgive … and forget.*

Her blood froze. She lifted her head. Her mouth gaped.

If you do not forgive …

She pushed herself away from the tree. "God, please. I can't."

Forgive and forget and then … move on.

The words sliced through her. Yet the little girl laughed.

Chris heard laughter in her soul.

She listened to it. And cursed it away. Wiped the back of her hand over her eyes. Then almost ran down the sidewalk. She tiptoed up the stairs of her apartment, tiptoed down the hall to the bathroom. Tore off her clothes and let a long, hot shower cleanse away the dream and the stench it left behind. Quickly braiding her wet hair, she did not even glance at the mirror. She gathered up a few things and left the apartment before Cappy woke up, before any lights shone through the windows of Erin's or Sonya's house. She hurried back down Kimberley to the gym, unlocked one of the big glass doors, let herself in, then quickly locked it behind her. She turned on just enough lights to brighten the far corner of the floor. Unlocked her office and tossed the keys and her backpack on the desk. Grabbed her favorite basketball. Tightened the laces of her high-tops. Then shot baskets alone at the far hoop until she dropped to the floor over an hour later, completely exhausted. She lay on her back gasping for breath, arms out to her sides, listening to her thumping heart, staring up into the dusty rafters of the old warehouse. She lay there. Until her eyes slowly drifted shut. And she fell into a peaceful sleep.

✩✩✩

Faint squealing woke her, followed by the obnoxious squawk of a school bus's brakes. The diesel engine roared, then slowly faded away down the street. She blinked open her eyes and made sense of the telltale sign. It was eight o'clock in the morning on a school day. Another new week. And another bus full of happy Portland children were on their way to their private Catholic school across town.

Her eyes pinched shut.

Another new day. And what a delightful way to start it off.

She drew in a deep yawn. Slowly let it leak through her lips. Pushed herself up to sit. Rubbed the back of her neck. Her eyes. The back of her head where the hard floor had flattened her braid.

But still, that long on the hard floor, her back didn't hurt. Her headache was gone. The sleep had done her good. She could hardly believe it.

She pushed up to her feet, grabbed her basketball, and headed for her office. She sat in her chair and leaned back, turning the basketball round and round in her hands.

Hungry and tired and aching from her long night, sticky and stinky from her workout, she needed to go home, take another shower, have Cappy fix her some oatmeal, then go see Erin and wish her a nice new day. Okay, maybe not wish her a nice new day. But just go see her and say hi. Just go see her. Just go.

She sat. Rested her forearms over the top of the basketball. And didn't move.

Lord? What is happening to me?

She blinked.

Don't answer that.

She tossed the ball to the floor, then leaned over and let her head fall over her arms on the top of the desk.

Her fingers brushed the remote laying there. Without moving her head, she stretched one finger and punched the power button, then the button to play a CD. Didn't matter which one. Any one of the three on the changer would be fine. But not too loud. She pushed the volume button to lower the sound to an acceptable level.

Soft and quiet this morning. Nothing to rekindle her headache. But something to kindle the tiny flicker in her heart. Something to help it burn brightly once again.

A song started to play. Too loud. She tapped the volume button again. Too much of a heavy beat. Though she loved this song. The CD's title track. "Immigrant's Daughter." Great tune to savor on a much happier day.

She stretched her finger to push the track-advance button. Then clenched her hand into a fist and closed her eyes.

The next song's opening swirl of steel guitar sounded inviting, yet the beat ... still too much. *Sorry, Margaret.* Keeping her eyes closed, she stretched her finger once more to turn off the stereo. Thought she succeeded. Until a soft piano began to play. She must have hit the wrong button. The song was familiar. The piano so soft. She let it play. Let it filter into the depths of her soul. Then started to cry. Hard. The words became her prayer. A prayer she clung to with all her strength.

Jesus ... Jesus ... stay close to me. Please, Lord, I need You. You are my only hope. I've found my hope in You. Please ... I need You. Don't ever leave me.

★★★

Isaiah walked in as Chris swept the gym floor for Kay's one o'clock aerobics class. Sweet man. Chris couldn't explain it, and would never admit it to the man, but just laying eyes on him soothed her soul. So much like her friend Raymond. So gentle and loving and kind. Their dark skin seemed to glitter, to capture the light and reflect it back to her with such softness and warmth. Seeing Isaiah slowly meander across the floor in his work boots, baggy work jeans, and light blue checkered flannel shirt reminded Chris of Raymond so much she held her breath to keep from crying.

This is insane! She wanted to gouge out her tear ducts and throw them across the room. Never in her entire life had she cried so much. For the past five months, it seemed everything set her off. And she hated it!

And loved it.

She gave Isaiah a warm smile. "Hello, sir."

His smile. She savored it. "Hi ya, Chris. Workin' hard?"

She shook her head. "Nah. Just cleaning up a bit for Kay's class."

He nodded. Glanced over at the new set of old bleachers recently donated by a local elementary school. "You gonna work on them today?"

"I might. But I'd rather go outside and clean up around the lot some. If it doesn't rain."

"Spoken like a true Oregonian." Isaiah's grin quickly faded. "Lots to do around here."

She knew it wasn't true. In the weeks since the gym had opened, she almost felt guilty cashing her paychecks. Of her forty hours on the job each week, she probably only really worked about half of them. As far as real work went.

Isaiah's head slowly bobbed. "Yessiree. Lots to do. But it doesn't all have to be done today." His dark eyes glimmered under the multitude of overhead lights. "I was sent to tell you something. And to give you something. What do you want first?" A totally delightful smile. And the man still had a set of fully functional and clean white teeth.

"Good news or bad news?" Chris would play his game. "Something sour or something sweet?"

A rumble of laughter. "Well, depends on how you receive it. Keep in mind now, I'm just the messenger."

Heat slowly crept up the sides of her neck.

"All right. I'll just tell you. Ben and Sonya and Erin and Cappy all sent me to tell you they're worried about you, and if you'd rather just take today off and go on back home and get some sleep or to maybe go for a ride or something, maybe a ride to the coast for some fresh air or whatever, or if you'd like to go with Sonya to Wal-Mart and help her find some new comforters for the women's shelter, you're more than free to do so. Kay can certainly stay a few extra hours after her class, then Cappy said she'd come and keep an eye on the after-schoolers. Then I can close up. It wouldn't be a problem, Chris. For any of us. If you'd like, just say the word. And go. We want you to. If you'd like."

At that moment, hearing the words from anyone else would have infuriated her to the point of explosion. But staring into the sweet face of the kindly grandfather, she only felt sorry that he had been the one sent to pass along the news. She suddenly wished she held a shovel in her hand instead of the long floor broom so she could dig a deep hole right where she stood and disappear into it.

"Now, you don't have to. If you're feeling all right and you want to stay ... well, you can do that too." Sheepishness radiated from the man's eyes.

She didn't like her friends putting Isaiah in this position. Didn't like Cappy most of all. "No. I'm fine. I can work. But thanks for the offer."

"It really would be okay, Chris. I'd love to see you take the day off. Just go do something . . . fun."

She smiled. "This is fun. I can't believe I get paid for running a gym."

His lips pressed into a firm line. "Have you eaten lunch yet?"

"Um . . . yeah." A lie, but a necessary one.

Isaiah shook his head. "Well, if you're sure, I won't hound you about it. If you change your mind, just use this to call me. I've already set my number into the speed dial." A wide grin.

A cell phone.

Chris stared at it.

"Go on, take it. It's yours. You knew Ben has wanted to get you one too. And here it is."

"I thought he said it would be another month." Chris lifted her hand.

Isaiah dropped the phone in her palm. "Nah. He told me there was no reason why you shouldn't have one now. He got one for Sonya too. So now we're pretty much fully wired."

"Wired for sound." Chris turned the phone over in her hand, studying it. "But you know I don't have any idea how to use this."

"That's why I brought this." The man pulled a white booklet out of his back pocket and handed it to Chris. "Instruction manual."

She started to laugh. "Little light reading?"

"Over lunch. I'm buying."

Her mouth fell open.

"Soon as Kay gets here, I'm taking you to lunch. Okay?"

How could she say no to this man? She let a smile work its way across her entire face. Then frowned and shook her head. "All right, you terrible, stubborn man."

Isaiah's outburst of laughter ricocheted off the walls of the huge open room and hit Chris from every conceivable direction. It settled deep in her heart. A memory to savor for all time.

★★★

CHRIS TOOK ONE LOOK AT Cappy Sanchez and wanted to strangle her. Or maybe smack her upside the head with the ratchet she held in her hand. But she glanced at the children playing happily at the other end of the gym and thought better of it. The absence of Alaina Walker again tugged at her heart. She turned back to her work. Her teeth ground. Echoes of Isaiah's words filtered through her brain. Refused to fade. *Ben and Sonya and Erin and Cappy all sent me to tell you ... they're worried about you ...*

Against the wrench holding the nut in place, the ratchet wouldn't budge, yet she strained to tighten the bolt a bit more. Her palms burned inside their thick leather gloves. She heard what sounded like Cappy's laughter and felt her blood immediately boil.

She wanted to throw the ratchet across the room. Instead, she grabbed another bolt and stuffed it into another hole she had drilled into another clamp surrounding another bar of the metal framework of the small set of donated bleachers. One of the billions of holes. One of the billions of bolts. Stuffed into the holes and tightened by hand to reinforce the rickety old matrix of wood and steel. She attached a thick nut and spun it into the bolt. Dumb rickety bleachers. So far at the end of the gym, what good would they do? A lot of good, if a person only wanted to watch half of the basketball game.

Her hand cranked the ratchet. Clickety-clickety, the ratchet tightened the bolt. She focused on the clicks and let them settle her. Good, solid sounds. Sounds of work. Of doing something useful. Sweat. Earning her paycheck. Making the rickety old bleachers safer for the big heavy bodies that would lounge on them to watch the game.

Half the game. Unless they brought binoculars with them.

Another bolt. Another nut. Another clamp. Another hole. Squealing laughter from the twenty or so kids playing basketball and foursquare. And not one of them, Alaina Walker.

"*Hola*, girlfriend."

Her heart almost exploded in her chest. The wrench slipped, but she caught it before it left her fingers and dropped to the floor.

"What are ya doin'?"

She couldn't force her teeth to part. Or her lips. She stared at the bleacher's scratched metal bar she had gripped with her gloved hand. *What's it look like I'm doing?*

"I was in the neighborhood."

"Sure, Cap." The words were a growl.

"Well, I guess I'm pretty much always in the neighborhood."

"What do you want?" Chris turned to glare.

Cappy's face tightened into a frown. "What's up with you?"

Chris jammed another bolt into another hole. "Nothing."

"Look. Isaiah told me he talked to you."

She turned to face her friend. At least the woman she thought was her friend. "He did talk to me. And he told me you talked to him. And to Erin and Sonya and Ben. That's great, Cappy. Thanks a lot."

"What are you talking about?"

Chris drew in a sharp breath. Forced back the rage ripping through her. "Did you tell Sonya and Erin about this morning?"

Cappy's eyes bulged. "No!" Then bulged a bit more. "You think I did? I told you I wouldn't!"

Chris stared into those dark eyes. Almost as dark as her own. But not quite.

"I mean it, Chris. I did not tell them." Cappy shook her head. "I didn't need to tell them. They have their own reasons for worrying about you."

Chris only wanted to toss the wrench and ratchet, but they flew from her hand with enough force to slam into the tool chest and snap the lid shut. She looked up at Cappy as she pulled off her gloves. "Stop worrying about me. I'm fine." She stomped across the gym to her office and slammed the door behind her.

Cappy's thoughts were so loud Chris could hear them. *"Yeah. Right, woman. You're fine. You must think I'm completely loco."*

She lifted her foot and kicked over her filing cabinet.

***

Though he didn't really care for the dog days of sweltering temperatures that always seemed to lay Portland out for a week or two every year, Jason did look forward to clear blue skies and lots of summer sunshine. Playing on the beach. Taking his truck to Sand Lake when the sand was really dry and didn't stick to everything it touched. Eating hot dogs while watching Beaver baseball games. Oohing and aahing at the fireworks exploding overhead after the Fourth of July game.

May. Not quite summer, but almost.

He smiled at the thought, then slowed his steps and carefully leaned around the edge of the old warehouse the church had successfully converted into a fairly nice gym. His eyes searched the sprawling back lot for the woman his heart needed to see. The lady inside had said he would find her out here. Somewhere. Pulling weeds or raking or whatever needed to be done. As he glanced around, he noticed much still needed to be done.

He leaned a bit farther around the side of the wall and let his eyes follow a long patch of freshly weeded ground next to the building. A good thirty feet of turned soil lay ready for flowers or grass or a thick layer of concrete.

A smile slowly worked its way across his lips. His eyes spotted the woman who had weeded that soil. She still knelt over it, jabbing into it with a small hand shovel.

Girl. There you are.

She pulled out dandelions and other scruff by the roots. Tossed it behind her. And jabbed that shovel again.

His smile faded. Almost into a frown.

She didn't look very happy as she worked the soil. Didn't look like she was enjoying herself at all.

Jason pushed away from the wall and moved closer. Quietly. He didn't want to startle her. Then he felt stupid, because if he didn't announce his presence soon, she would hear his steps and freak out for sure.

He stopped and watched her a bit longer. She was so focused on her work, Jason could have waved his arms and danced a jig and she wouldn't have noticed. He started to call her name, but held his breath and just continued to watch. He relaxed. Standing there. Watching the woman jab her shovel into the dirt and pull out more weeds.

Poor weeds. She seemed to be yanking with vengeance. Not a happy weed puller at all.

He took a few steps closer. Quietly called her name. Then wondered if he spoke loud enough for her to hear. She didn't look up or respond in any way. Just continued to jab that shovel into the dirt. And yank. Until she reached up to wipe her forehead. The gloves she wore left a streak of dirt there.

He moved closer. "I see you . . . do you see me?"

The shovel spun in her hand. Immediately became a weapon. Jason froze.

Her eyes found his. Blinked deeply. "What are you doing here?"

He licked his lips. Tried not to stare at that shovel. At the way she held it. "I . . . um, didn't want to startle you."

The shovel came down. Jabbed again into the dirt. "Well, you did. About gave me heart failure."

Was she kidding? She didn't smile or look up from her work. Work she seemed to resume pretty quickly. "I'm sorry." He took a few steps closer. "That was a cool trick, though."

Jab. Yank. "What was?"

"What you did with that shovel."

She slowly pushed back to sit on her haunches. Let out a huff. "Think so? You should see what I can do with a full-sized shovel. I'm a regular shovel ninja."

Soft laughter rumbled up from Jason's gut.

Chris didn't laugh. Under the sweat and the dirt, her eyes were swollen. Puffy, dark bags hung from them. The cut on her cheek was still closed, which was a good thing, but it should have been covered to keep it clean. Jason hoped it wouldn't leave a nasty scar. He hoped he had closed it well enough to keep the damage to a minimum. But he never dreamed at the time she wouldn't have it stitched. If he had known, he would have been even more careful.

"What are you doing here?" Softly spoken, yet without warmth.

Jason swallowed deeply. "I bet you're starved."

"You'd lose that bet." She tossed her shovel toward a wicker basket and grabbed a bottle of water. Drew it up for a long drink. "I had a big lunch." She finished the bottle and tossed it toward the basket. Then picked up a handheld garden rake and started mixing the soil with it.

"Are you gonna plant flowers here?"

"Maybe." Nothing more.

"Looks ten times better already without the weeds."

Nothing. Raking. Mixing the dirt.

Jason sighed deeply. Then instantly regretted it when Chris's eyes lifted to lock onto his. Such hard sadness in the expression on her face. Such weariness. The sight wrenched his heart.

She sat back again. Grimaced. Then pulled her feet out from under her and sat on the ground. The rake spun in her hands. Playfully. Not defensively. She watched it spin. Didn't look up. "It was nice of you to stop by. But I'm afraid I'm not good company right now."

Jason walked the rest of the way to her and sat beside her. Not too close. He eyed that rake warily. "Are you a rake ninja too?"

A tiny smile. "I've been trained by the best."

"Thanks for the warning."

Her eyes softened.

"So. You're not hungry. But there's always room for ice cream."

"No. Not tonight." She tossed the rake toward the basket. It clanked against the shovel.

"You're about ready to call it a night, aren't you?"

"What time is it?"

His eyes searched her bruised wrists. He saw no watch. He quickly glanced at his own. "Seven thirty."

"I still have a half hour. The gym closes at eight tonight."

"We can go after that. After you get cleaned up." Breath stuck in his throat. Why did he say that?

She pulled off her gloves and tossed them as well. One landed in the basket. She didn't see it land. "I'm sorry, Jason, but I don't want to go out tonight. I'm tired."

"You look it." A curse slipped into his thoughts. Was he trying to make her mad?

But she smiled. Barely. "Thanks. At least you're honest."

"You want honesty? You look terrible. Can I at least walk you home?"

"Don't hang around here for a half hour just to walk me home."

"Why not?"

She let out what sounded like a growl. Then suddenly pushed herself to her knees. Hesitated.

Still hurting … Jason quickly stood and reached out to help her up.

She yanked her arm away. The extra movement almost caused her to lose her balance. But she recovered, stood, then pushed her fists into her lower back and stretched.

"Can't you quit a little early? I'll walk you home."

"Please." She turned and struggled to pick up her tools.

Jason moved in to help. Gathered up her water bottle and glove. Put them in her basket. He reached out to grab it, to lift it, to hand it to her, but she grabbed it first. Then slowly lifted her head to look at him.

"Thanks."

He couldn't move. Didn't know what to say.

A faint smile. "I mean it. I'll see you later, okay?" She started walking toward the gym's door.

Jason lightly touched her arm.

She stopped and spun around. Glared at him.

His heart raced. "Are you all right?"

Her jaw muscles clenched as her teeth ground.

"I mean, forgive me for caring about you, but you don't look all right. You look terrible, and—"

"Yes, and thanks again for saying so." She turned and headed for the door.

Jason ran a few steps to catch up. "Wait a minute. I need to tell you about Walker. Or have you heard?"

Chris stopped and slowly turned toward him. "Heard what?"

"He's been arraigned. His bail was set at fifty grand. He's not going to post it. He'll stay in jail until his trial."

"And that's good news?"

"I thought it was."

"Well, it's not." Again she turned.

"He resisted arrest. And took a swipe at one of the guards trying to book him."

Nothing. Chris was almost to the door.

Jason quickly caught up to her. "Hey, come on! What is your problem?"

She turned. "My problem?"

"Walker hit you. Kicked your friend. And his kid."

"Thanks for reminding me."

Another curse ripped through his head. "Look, whatever your problem is, can't you talk to me about it? I care about you." He softened his voice. Reached up to tuck a stray strand of hair behind her ear. "I'm worried about you."

Her eyes narrowed into an angry glare. "Don't. Worry. About. Me." She turned and pushed through the gym's door.

Jason's mouth hung open. His eyes burned. He squeezed them shut. Then peered again through the glass doors.

Just what was that? How could she be happy and pleasant one night, and mean and hateful the next? Was he wrong about her? Was he wrong to worry about her? But how could he not worry, after what he just saw? Was he a fool for even considering that she may be the one? That maybe there was hope for a relationship?

He lifted his left hand and stared at the pale skin encircling the base of his ring finger. All that day, every time he saw it, it terrified him. But now, white-hot rage bolted through him.

You're a fool, Sloan. Look at you. To think this woman was the one. To think she was worth laying down your first love.

His hand clenched into a trembling fist. He glanced once more through those glass doors, then turned away and stormed to his truck. As soon as the engine roared, he jammed it into gear and floored the accelerator.

The squeal of tires perfectly capped the moment. He cranked up his stereo and let a steel guitar's familiar whine carry him down the street.

★★★

No, no, no, no, no!

In her office bathroom, leaning against the inside of the door, Chris lowered her head a few inches and slammed it back against the wood.

You are so stupid! Go after him! Don't let him get away!

She spun around and tore open the door, then ran out of her office and down the side of the gym to push through the glass doors. She looked right. Left. And heard a loud squeal of tires spinning out.

Her heart missed a beat.

Don't go!

She ran toward the street as Jason's truck disappeared down Kimberley Street.

She turned and forced the scream in her throat back down into her gut. Felt it wrench her throat in its fight to break free. Her eyes pinched shut as she staggered back toward the gym. And still the scream raged.

ELEVEN

THE BIG CHURCH FLASHED BY on his left. He knew he needed to slow down, yet couldn't seem to move his right foot. His truck raced on. Into heavier traffic. Closer to downtown. He slammed on the brakes and skidded to a stop at a busy red light. He stared straight ahead as cars passed. As pedestrians walked in front of his truck. He ignored their angry glares.

He stopped, didn't he? So what if he had laid a little rubber in the process? He'd lay a little more as soon as that light turned green.

He tapped the steering wheel. The commercial on the stereo aggravated him. He spun the dial to find another station. Heard only stupid songs and more commercials. Flipped the power button. The sudden silence hit him like a fist in the gut.

He sat back in the seat. Revved the engine. Saw the other light finally turn yellow. He waited to pop the clutch and take off the instant his light turned green.

Green. His feet went to work — the engine of his truck coughed and died.

Fitting.

He quickly started it, then sped through the intersection. But, a minute later, he turned right at a cross street and coasted the truck into an empty parking space. He shut off the engine, then sat, just listening to the silence. To the whisper. Deep in his heart. His precious bride whispering straight to his soul.

Turn around . . . go back.

He didn't move. His heartbeat slowed. Breaths filled his lungs.

To breathe is to live, Jase.

His own soft whisper blended with hers. *To live . . . is to love.*

A faint smile left his lips trembling.

He slowly reached down and turned the key, then drove away from the curb. He headed back down Kimberley Street. To that gym. And the woman who drew him to her. The woman he needed to love.

*** ✦✦✦ ***

A KNOCK AT HER OFFICE door. Cappy's voice. "All's clear. Do you want me to lock up?"

Chris looked up from the soapy lather on her hands and met Cappy's gaze. "Yeah. Go ahead."

Cappy leaned against the bathroom door frame. "You're done, aren't you? Aren't you heading home?"

"Not yet. Pretty soon."

"Why? What more is left to do?"

Chris chose to ignore both questions. She picked at the dirt under her fingernails.

Cappy shifted to the other door frame. Her head tilted as her arms crossed her chest. "Come on, Chris. Let's jet this coop."

A twinge ripped through Chris's stomach. Warm water washed the suds from her hands. "You go ahead. I'll be home later."

"How much later?"

She looked up and desperately tried to smile. "Just go, lady. Lock up and turn off the lights, okay?"

Cappy slowly shook her head. Then heaved a deep sigh and pushed away from the door. "All right. Fine."

"Hey." Chris bit her lower lip and grabbed a paper towel as she waited for Cappy to look back at her. It took a few seconds. "I need you to know something."

Another sigh. This one sounded a bit dramatic. "What, Chris?"

"I need you to know how much ..." The words hung in the air. Chris tossed the paper towel into the garbage. And slowly started again. "Cappy ... thank you. I mean it. And I'm sorry I yelled at you."

"I didn't tell them, Chris."

"I know you didn't. And I appreciate it."

"I wanted to. And I still do."

"I know. Someday ... I'll tell them."

Cappy's right eyebrow lifted.

"I will. I promise. After ..."

A grin. "After *mamacita* pops?"

Laughter burst up from Chris's belly. "Yeah. Something like that."

"Okay. But in the meantime ... I'm still worried about you." Cappy lifted her hands, palms out. "Just let me be worried."

Chris slowly nodded. "Okay."

Cappy's expression grew serious. "I'm still new to this ... like you, I guess. About trusting God ... and praying. But ... do you want me to pray with you?"

Chris glanced away and held her breath to fight back tears. She shook her head. "No. Not right now." She knew the first word of Cappy's prayer would start her bawling. And she couldn't take that. Not again. "But thanks. Really. I mean it."

"I'll pray *for* you then. I can do that without your permission."

A grunt. "Get out of here, Cappy."

"*Adios, hermana.*"

"Right back atcha, lady."

Chris shut off the light in the bathroom and walked over to her desk. She lifted one of the papers there, then glanced up as the lights in the gym flickered out. She heard keys jangling in the glass doors. Then heavy, refreshing silence. She listened to it, felt it fall over her, and savored the moment. Until she glanced down at the booklet on her desk.

How would she ever figure out how to work that stupid cell phone?

She sat at her desk and sorted through the rest of the accumulated material on her desk. Stuffed some of the papers into files in her filing cabinet. Tried again to corral some of the disarray she found there. Tried not to cuss herself out for kicking it over.

The sound of an occasional passing car seeped through the thick concrete walls of the gym. It seemed to confront the silence for just a second, only to surrender and be swallowed up.

But the silence could not compete against the ringing in Chris's ears. The thump of her heart.

The sudden loud pounding on the glass doors.

She jumped. Held her breath.

Loud knocks on the glass.

Her heart nearly burst. She pushed away from the cabinet and stood, listening.

"Chris?"

The word barely reached her. A man's voice.

Her racing heart skipped a beat. She grabbed her keys and hurried out of the office, but slowed and stayed close to the gym wall as she approached the glass doors.

"Chris?"

Oh, Lord . . .

Loud pounding. The man would break the glass if he continued.

Chris walked up to the door and held up her hand. And gazed into the fierce eyes of Jason Sloan. She froze solid as she stared.

"You gonna let me in?"

His smile sent a tickling giggle into her belly. "We're closed."

"Oh, really? Well, then I guess I'll have to come back later." He playfully started to turn.

No, wait! Chris quickly unlocked the door and pushed it open. Stood there.

"Oh. So you're . . . not closed?"

Not for you. "I can make an exception."

"Good. Because I brought you a present." He proudly displayed a small bag. "But you'll have to let me in to get it."

She backed up a few steps.

"I'm glad I decided to knock." He walked inside. "But a part of me was hoping you'd already be gone."

"I'm just finishing up." She watched the door swing shut

226

behind him. Quickly relocked it. Tested it to be sure. Then turned and found herself face-to-face with Jason Sloan.

Face to chest. The man was tall.

Chris slowly looked up. Saw his eyes drinking her in. The sight stole her breath.

"I'm glad you weren't gone." A husky whisper. "And I'm glad you washed your face."

She wanted to smile. To laugh. She could only gaze into his eyes.

"I really want to kiss you."

She blinked. Backed up a step. The door clanked as she backed into it.

"Maybe later?"

Heat enflamed her cheeks. "We'll have to add that to the list." Head down, she walked toward the office. She heard him following. She sat in the chair behind her desk and watched him sit on the old love seat Isaiah had donated to the cause. A comfortable addition to her office. She enjoyed watching Jason make himself comfortable in it.

He looked up at her. "You've got a nice little deal here."

"Yeah. It's a fun job."

"As much fun as flying Hueys?"

She lowered her gaze to her desk. And smiled.

"That's on our list too, right? For things to do later. We need to talk about when you flew Hueys."

"Yeah. Later."

"Good. I want to hear all about it."

She gave him another faint smile.

"Oh, we better eat what I brought before it melts." Jason opened his bag and pulled out a pint of ice cream. He stood up and handed it to Chris. Then dug through the bag and handed her a plastic spoon.

Mint chocolate chip. Her mouth watered at the sight.

Jason sat back on the love seat and pulled his own pint and spoon from the bag.

"Thanks, dude." Chris's voice shook.

"No problem. Like I said, there's always room for ice cream."

She let a faint laugh carry her smile, but felt it quickly fade. She opened the ice cream and tasted a small bite. Though it was sweet and cold and minty chocolaty, it didn't taste near as good as it should. She tried another bite. Swallowed. It seemed to sour in her throat on its way down.

She cursed herself. There was nothing wrong with the ice cream.

"So, if I may ..." Jason chewed a mouthful, then swallowed. "May I ask you why you were in such a foul mood earlier? No. Wait." He straightened on the love seat. Glanced at his watch. "Tell me first why you're still here at eight thirty."

Was it that late already? She lifted another tiny bite of ice cream into her mouth. And didn't look across the room at the man waiting for an answer to his question.

The silence lingered.

"Fine. Forget that." Another huge spoonful of ice cream entered his mouth. He talked as he chewed. "Can you tell me if you'd like to go see a movie?"

She struggled to swallow. "Yes." Dared a glance his way. "No."

His chewing paused. Then resumed.

"I'm sorry." Chris drew in a deep breath, hoping it would ease the burn intensifying in her stomach. She put down her spoon and tightened the lid back on her ice cream. "I'm sorry, Jason. This is really good, but I'm not hungry." She glanced at him. "Thanks, though. I mean it. It was a nice thing to do."

His spoon carried another load to his mouth, but he smiled with his eyes. Chewed. Swallowed. A pause. "Can you tell me why I shouldn't take you home right now?"

The words caught her by surprise. Then frightened her. She didn't want to go home. Yet she couldn't think of anything more wonderful than falling dead asleep in her bed.

Jason lowered his spoon, then pushed the lid on his ice cream and put it back into the bag. "Come on. I'll take you home."

"No." The word popped out before she could stop it.

Jason looked at her.

"I mean ..."

He stood and walked around the desk to sit on its edge. He towered over her. "You need to go home, Chris. Let me take you."

"I will. When I finish up here."

He touched her arm.

Everything in her system screamed at her to pull away from his touch. She didn't move.

His hand curled under her arm. Started to pull her up.

"Jase, don't." But she let him even as the words slipped through her lips.

Breath gushed out of him.

She quickly looked up. Then stood face-to-face with him. Eye to eye.

His gaze seemed to falter, to struggle as it studied her face.

Too close. Chris gently pushed away. Then reached to grab her ice cream. She turned to put it in the freezer. Ben's contribution to the office. With a microwave on the way.

Home away from home.

"Chris."

She glanced over her shoulder. Was relieved to see Jason still sitting on the desk.

"Please tell me ... why you're so weary."

Her hand lifted to cover her mouth.

Jason stood and walked closer. Gently touched her shoulders.

"It's been a long day." The words blurted out her trembling lips.

"That's not what I mean."

Her thoughts tangled. "It'll have to be."

His hands gently massaged her neck. She melted into his touch. Yet didn't move. "Maybe you'll tell me why ... later?" His voice was so soft.

She struggled to pull in a breath. Could only nod.

"Let's go. My truck's right out front."

Her hand curled into a fist and pushed her upper lip hard against her front teeth. She pulled it away to let two words escape. "I can't." Curses cut through her.

"Tell me why."

"I can't."

He gently turned her. Then lifted his hand to smooth her forehead. "We have much to talk about later."

A breath of laughter blew through her lips.

"Tell you what. Let me take you home. And when you get home, go straight to your room, jump into your sleepers, and then into bed. Don't brush your teeth or anything."

Her eyes slowly lifted to meet his.

"Go to the bathroom right now. Get that out of the way. And maybe . . . take your hair out of your braid. Brush it out. It'll make you feel better. I'll wait. Then we'll go. Sound like a plan?"

She wanted to say so much. To say yes. But she couldn't force her lips to cooperate. She barely nodded.

His intense gaze softened. He moved in close and kissed her forehead.

Chris quickly pulled away and headed for the bathroom.

★★★

"THIS IS THE PLACE, RIGHT?" Jason knew it was, but from the expression on Chris's face, a doubt crossed his mind.

"Upstairs."

"Well then, run up those stairs and do exactly what I told you."

She sat in his truck and stared at the dashboard.

He shut off the engine, then turned in his seat to face her. "Please tell me."

A faint laugh. "She says that."

"Who does?"

"Erin."

Jason waited. Content in her presence. Even as his heart ached for her.

"I can't face her."

The words were so soft, he barely heard them. "Who, Chris?"

"I need to see her. I haven't seen her all day."

Erin. Had to be. Jason strained his brain to remember everything he knew about her. And instantly knew she would understand. He let the thought carry. "Won't she understand?"

Chris slowly lifted the saddest eyes he had ever seen.

He swallowed down the sudden lump in his throat. "I know she would. You need to get some sleep. She would want that."

"She's worried about me."

"I'll go tell her not to worry."

Surprise, then a hint of hope flickered in her sad eyes. "You will?"

"Sure. You go upstairs and sleep. I'll go tell her you're fine. I'll make her believe me." He couldn't resist adding a playful smirk to his words.

Breath rushed out of her as her head fell back against the seat. "That would be so cool. Please tell her I'm fine."

"Well, I hate to lie to her."

A deep breath this time. In and out. "Then don't. Believe it. And make her believe."

"Okay. I will. Come on."

They left the truck and walked side by side up the wide stairs onto the porch. Chris headed past the clinic toward the outside stairs leading up to her apartment. Jason watched her go. She stopped at the corner and turned to look over her shoulder. "Thanks, Jase. I mean it. I mean . . . I really mean it."

His heart twisted and danced wildly in his chest. Hearing her say his name like that . . . he grinned. "Go."

"Going. See ya." And she went.

Jason heard her footsteps climbing the stairs. He waited another second. Then knocked on the door of Scott Mathis's house. The porch light came on. The door opened. He took one look, and gave his old friend a smile.

"Jason! Hey, buddy!"

"What's up, Doc?" He stepped into the house and enjoyed Scott's smart-aleck response. Across the living room, Erin sat in her rocking chair. Jason's heart reached a level of happiness it hadn't known in a long time. "Hi, Erin."

Her smile brightened the entire room. "Hey, Jason. What a surprise!"

"I'm not disturbing anything, am I?" He glanced at Scott.

"Just a little cuddly coo." Scott pointed Jason to the couch. "Can I get you anything?"

"No. Thanks. I can't stay long."

Erin started to smile, but her eyes lost their focus as she tightened her grip on the armrests of the rocking chair. "Oh my. That was a good one."

Scott's face beamed. "We've decided he's a he. Only a he could kick like he's kicking right now."

"You should feel this." Erin's voice was breathless.

Jason's happy heart froze. "Um ... no. Thanks. That's okay."

Scott grabbed him from the couch and pulled him closer. "Come on, buddy. Don't miss this."

Jason gazed into Erin's eyes, pleased to see her nod and smile. "Here." She took his hand and pressed it over a spot on her huge belly. "There. Feel that?"

Jason's heart burst. Tingles of the explosion glittered through his entire being.

"I think he did." Scott let out a laugh.

"You should see your face right now." Erin's soft voice trembled.

"You should feel my heart right now." Jason gazed into Erin's pretty blue eyes and struggled to breathe.

Another sharp kick. He watched Erin's belly move. Felt another kick. And then what felt like an arm. Or an elbow. "Wow." He glanced up. "You can't tell me that doesn't hurt."

"Sometimes he catches a rib. But right now he seems content to keep his kicks away from any vital organs."

Jason could only smile.

He pushed back to sit again on the couch and savored the joy still radiating through him. And he probably stared at his friends like a drunken fool. Drunk on the moment.

The moment played out. Small talk dissolved into looks of concern. Erin could tell Jason brought important news. He saw it in her eyes.

He leaned forward to sit on the edge of the couch. "Erin ... yeah, I'm here because of Chris. She's upstairs hopefully already asleep in bed. She's totally beat. She really wanted to come see you, but ..." The words ended. Jason wondered why he had talked himself into a corner. "I saw her at the gym and brought her home. And sent her to bed. I told her I'd talk to you. I told her ... I'd tell you she was fine. She doesn't want you to worry about her. I told her I'd tell you ... and make you believe it."

A knowing grin appeared on Erin's face.

"So. Believe it. Chris is fine. She's sleeping. But I'm sure she'll see you tomorrow. Don't worry about her. She really doesn't want you to worry."

"She doesn't want anyone to worry."

Jason stared. Then slowly nodded. He glanced down at the floor.

"But we still worry."

He lifted his eyes to look at her.

"She's worth it, Jason."

His eyes locked on hers. And in those pretty blue eyes he saw a glimpse of Erin Mathis's heart. And instantly knew she had also been drawn. He let her words echo through him. And knew she was right.

Yes, Erin. He gave her a slight nod. *She is.*

✯✯✯

That happy little dumb bird's joyful twelve-note song of praise reverberated across Chris's eardrums. She pushed open one very sleepy eyelid and tried to focus on her alarm clock. Her eyes pinched shut. A grumbling growl rumbled up from her chest and drowned out the happy little bird. The sparkling darkness swirling across the backs of her tightly closed eyelids overpowered the brilliant sunlight pouring through her bedroom window.

Tuesday. To make it to work by ten, she needed to get up some-time in the next two hours. If she wanted to eat breakfast and take a shower, she needed to get up in the next hour. If she wanted to eat, take a shower, and see Erin before work, she needed to get up sometime in the next three minutes.

Another long growl. Though she did blink open her eyes.

With her head buried deeply in the pillow, only one eye took in the splendor of the new day. Brilliant sunshine. Bright swatches of reds, blues, and greens adorning the fleece blanket tucked under her chin. Florescent green numbers beaming from her alarm clock. 7:44.

Good morning, Lord Jesus. Can you turn off the sun and stop time for another hour please?

Her gaze drifted to the book on her nightstand. The deep maroon leather with bright gold lettering. *The Holy Bible. Christina Renae McIntyre.*

Written Word, spoken Word, living Word. Jesus. The Living Word of God.

Her eyes closed, though the image of Pastor Andy remained, his open Bible draped over his palm, his soft eyes peering intently at the small group gathered in his dad's living room for the Tues-day night Bible study.

Tuesday night . . . She pulled up her hand and rubbed her nose. Then rolled onto her back and rubbed her eyes and forehead. *Make this day go away.*

Can't hide up here all day, girl.

She dropped her hand and gazed at the ceiling. Studied the swirls of plaster. Familiar swirls. Lately it seemed she spent a lot of time staring at the ceiling. As if trying to make sense of the swirls. As if trying to make sense of the mess her life had become.

Things were fine before Alaina, weren't they, Lord? I mean . . . life was good. Setting up the gym, hanging out at Rinny's . . . And Alaina's fine. It's a done deal. Her dad . . . well, her dad will never hurt her again. Thank You for that, my Lord.

It was enough to have Alaina safe.

A thump. Steps down the outside stairs. Cappy heading off to work.

Cappy. Lord, I've been so hateful to her lately. Forgive me.

The words sliced through her. She drew in a breath that quickly became a deep yawn. Then pushed back her blankets and sat on the edge of the bed. She turned off her alarm clock. Lightly touched the half sand dollar on her nightstand. Let her fingertips trail down the smooth leather of her Bible. Felt an urgent need to pick it up. To hold it close. To read again about Jesus. About His love.

Lord … The word whispered through her as soft as the lightest breeze, yet she knew He heard it and waited for her to say more. But she couldn't say anything more. She couldn't look Him in the eye. Her head lowered. She studied her fingers. Her voice again whispered through her. *I don't know what to say to You. Except … I'm sorry.*

Echoes of Erin's voice drifted into her soul. All the hours spent reading the Word together, praying together, learning and studying and asking questions and having them answered.

She'll just tell me what I already know. To trust You. To follow Your guidance. How can she tell me anything else? She wants me to know You. I want to know You. But the more I learn …

I forgive you …

She propped her elbows on her knees and lowered her head into her hands.

I can't, Lord. I can't say those words. Not to him.

How can you live … without forgiveness? Forgive as I forgave …

Oh, Lord … I know You forgave them when they … but I can't. I can't do it, Lord. I'm so sorry.

Silence.

Dead, ear-ringing silence.

Jesus?

The silence of death.

Lord, please! Don't leave me!

He'll never leave you or forsake you, Chris. Read it for yourself. Right here.

The words appeared in her mind's eye. Erin's finger pointing out the verse. *I will never leave you . . .*

You can trust Him, Chris. He'll never leave you.

She clung to the words. To Erin's voice.

But, Rinny, what if I don't do what He asks? What if . . . what He asks . . . is too hard?

The silence overwhelmed her. She jumped off the bed and hurried to the bathroom for a long shower before getting ready for work.

THE WRENCH. THE RATCHET. ANOTHER clamp. Another bolt. Another nut. Turn and click. Click and turn. Good solid clicks. Good solid turns. Over and over and over. But these reinforced bleachers would stand the test. Only a few more bolts to tighten and turn.

Then what would she do?

She needed to stay busy. To keep the dark silence from returning. To keep Erin's smile in her heart. The laughter they shared only an hour ago, when the baby danced in Erin's womb to their pitiful rendition of "Jesus Loves You, Little One."

A made-up song just for the babe. The priceless memory . . . already it was fading.

Chris tried to hum it as she worked. Even her hum faded into silence.

Unnerved, she peered down to the other end of the gym and realized Mr. Dungrass and his basket-shooting cohort, Mr. Foley, had stopped to take a water break.

Well, no wonder it got so quiet. She wished they'd get back to their game. As she grabbed another bolt and stuffed it into another hole.

Maybe later she could sand the old polyurethane from the thick wooden seats of the bleachers and lay down a fresh coat. That would be a good thing to do. Simple and time consuming.

To ensure no spectator took a splinter in the tookis. *That's a caring thing to do for someone else, isn't it, Lord? Ben would approve of that, wouldn't he?*

Silence.

Only clicks from the ratchet. And pumps of blood in her heart.

Until the faintest wail lifted from deep in her soul. *Lord Jesus … please talk to me!*

Something bumped into her leg and startled her so completely the wrench squirted out of her hand and fell to the floor. The jangle dulled her eardrums.

A basketball.

Smiling, she bent over to pick it up, then drew in a breath to tell Mr. Dungrass it wasn't polite to scare her half to death, but the sight of a dark-haired, good-looking man standing in front of her stole her breath and left her gaping. An especially good-looking dark-haired man. Wearing a three-day growth of fuzz on his chin and upper lip, a pair of ratty jeans with a black Portland Trailblazer T-shirt, and a bright toothy grin.

She still couldn't breathe.

The man held out his hands for the basketball. "Wanna play?"

She tossed it to him. "I'm working."

"Yes, you are. I can see that." Jason glanced around the gym. "But I don't think anyone will mind. Maybe we can take on the grumpy old men in a friendly game of two-on-two."

Chris forced her head to turn away from the sight of him. "Don't say that. They're not grumpy old men."

"Well, now … I happen to know Myron Dungrass, and he can be a grumpy old codger sometimes."

Chris laughed, but quickly squashed it.

"Come on, let's take 'em on." Jason stepped backward while he dribbled flamboyantly.

"I'm not playing two-on-two with them. And quit showing off."

"Come on then, little lady. Show me what you've got."

She stood another second watching the crazy fool, then, against her better judgment, pulled off her gloves and joined him.

They shot baskets for a while. Then played Horse with the grumpy old men and were soundly trounced. After agreeing to Jason's demand for a future rematch, the men said their good-byes and left. Silence fell over the gym in their absence. Chris almost hated to see them leave.

Jason dribbled the ball between his legs. "I think they cheated." Then twirled it on his finger. "Old men shouldn't be able to make the shots they were making." He grabbed the ball and tucked it under his arm. Then flashed a wide smile at Chris.

She tried to return it. Knew she failed miserably. She headed for her office.

"Where ya goin'?"

"I need a drink." In so many ways.

"Got any ice cream left?" More dribbles as he ran to catch up.

"Spoil your lunch." Chris pulled two bottles of water out of the fridge. Handed one to Jason.

"Which we should go out and get."

She chugged a long drink, then regretted it as the iciness radiated across the back of her throat.

"Let me take you out to lunch."

"No." She couldn't look at him. "Thanks." She sat at her desk.

"Come on. I took off work. So can you."

"Yes, and why did you do that?" She dared a glance his way.

He lounged in the love seat. "I was hoping to take you to the coast."

"Um ... I don't think so."

"Why not?"

"I can't just leave!" And she couldn't reign in her growing frustration.

"Why not? Someone will hold down the fort for you."

"I don't want someone to hold down the fort for me." *Or do my job.*

"A trip to the beach would do you good."

She jumped out of her chair and headed for the bleachers.

"Now where are you going?"

"Back to work." She sucked in her cheek and bit into it as she walked, desperate to control the anger sweeping through her. Which only increased her anger.

Lord God ... what is wrong with me?

"Will you wait a second?"

The touch on her shoulder sent her over the top. She spun so quickly Jason almost ran into her. He slammed to a halt, then stood and stared at her.

A billion thoughts demanded voice. She tasted salty blood pouring from her cheek.

"What is this?" Softly spoken.

She turned and walked closer to the bleachers, then reached down to grab her gloves. She pulled them on, then grabbed the wrench.

"Chris?"

"You should just go, Jason. Before ..." She stared at the shiny metal length in her hand.

"Before what?"

Her eyes fell closed as trembling overtook her. "Please, Jase ..."

He touched her again. Lightly. On the shoulder. "Don't pull away. Let me touch you."

Panic stunned her. She couldn't move.

The warmth of his hand radiated through her shoulder. Another touch. Lightly. On her other shoulder.

Too much. She squirmed away, though the bleachers hindered her escape. Terror zipped through her belly as she realized she had conveniently trapped herself in a corner.

"All right. I won't touch you."

"Just go." Her voice shook.

"No."

Someone needed to burst through the doors of the gym, grab one of the basketballs off the cart, and start making some serious racket. Anyone. Anything to shatter the silence drowning her.

"Can we go back to the office and talk?"

His voice weighed heavier than the silence. She dreaded to hear what he would say next.

"Can you at least put that wrench down?"

Not what she expected. A nervous laugh tried to spurt through her lips. She squelched it in her throat.

"Okay. We'll stand here and talk. And you can hold the wrench."

"I don't want to talk."

"We're going to."

She tapped the end of the wrench against the palm of her hand.

"You need to talk. Talk to me. I'm a good listener."

"Then listen to me. I am not going to stand here and talk to you. So just leave. Or I will."

"Where will you go?"

Anywhere. Everywhere.

Lies. She couldn't leave this place.

"Let's go to the coast. Right now."

"If you say that again, I'm gonna smack you with this wrench." She didn't look to see if Jason believed her. Didn't look inside herself to see if she really meant it.

"Are these safe to sit on?"

She glanced at him. He pointed at the bleachers. Her outgoing breath sounded more like a grunt. *They better be.*

"Let's sit. Just hang out for a while."

His voice was starting to wear her down. And she hated him for it. She needed air. She allowed herself to draw in a long, full breath. Held it another second. Then slowly let it out as quietly as she could.

Jason made a show of stepping up to the middle row of seats. He gingerly sat, then lifted his arms and pretended to test his weight against the wood. "Seems safe." He leaned back and clasped his hands behind his head, then stretched his legs out and crossed them at the ankles. He let out an exaggerated, "Ahh . . ."

Chris really wanted to smack the man upside the head.

"You do some good work, Miss McIntyre."

And you're a jerk, Jason Sloan.

Another lie. She couldn't fool her own heart.

"Come join me."

No thanks.

"Fine. Stand over there. Big deal."

The flippant tone of the words enraged her. She moved closer to him even as her entire system screamed at her to make her escape. "Will you just go? Please?"

A smirk. "Nope."

She threw the wrench against the far wall. The clatter electrified her eardrums. Her hands covered her ears as she turned her back and cowered against it.

The man touched her again. Just on the shoulder. A gentle touch.

She screamed at him. Her voice echoed across the gym. Foul words. Words she learned from her dad. Words she despised. She struggled to glance Jason's way.

His wide eyes flickered. A hint of fear. Or rage.

Chris stepped away. Then quickly turned. "Don't touch me! You said you wouldn't touch me!"

"I'm sorry."

"Don't you dare be sorry. You're doing this on purpose."

The look in his eyes was too much for her to take. She stormed to her office and slammed the door, then grabbed the first thing she could find and flung it against the far wall. It shattered into a billion pieces. Terror exploded inside her.

Ben's brand-new cell phone. Disintegrated.

The office door slowly opened. A soft voice. "What did you just kill?"

Trembling threatened to drop her. She couldn't move to sit down. "My brand-new cell phone." The softness in her words surprised her. That they continued, surprised her even more. "Ben just gave it to me. It was charging on the counter. I hadn't even used it yet."

A small laugh. Quickly covered by a cough.

"It's not funny." Just a whisper.

"No. It most certainly isn't." Spoken without a trace of sincerity. The door opened until it tapped her foot. Jason's hand reached in to guide her away from the door.

She let him touch her. Walked where he led. He guided her to the love seat. Sat her down. Sat beside her. Not too close. Chris slouched and rested her head back against the seat. And closed her eyes.

Jason let out a deep sigh.

They sat in silence for a long while.

Until a whisper barely broke it. "I know what this is about. Do you want me to tell you?"

Chris summoned the strength to respond. "No."

"It's about two dads."

"Didn't I just say no?"

"Alaina's dad ..."

"Please, Jase." *I can't take any more.*

" ... and yours."

Her eyes flew open.

"Am I right?"

She sat up.

"Now ... just relax."

Like that was even a remote possibility.

"Can I ask you something?"

"Are you asking me just to aggravate me?" She gave him a strong glare. " 'Cause if I say no, you're just going to ask me anyway."

"Have you ever talked to anyone about your dad?"

Breath stuck in her throat as her mouth fell open.

"See, I asked the question, but I know the answer. I knew it Saturday when we talked. You've never talked to anyone about your dad. Well, Chris, it's about time you did."

She told him what she thought of him. The words she chose would have made her dad proud.

But then Jason tossed a few her direction. Just to play with her mind. She could tell he didn't mean it. But he meant his next words. "You need to talk about it."

"Don't tell me what I need."

"It's eating you alive."

She turned away from him. Her gaze fell to the shattered cell phone scattered across the floor by the bathroom.

"Right now. You're gonna spill. Give it up, Chris. Let me help you."

"I did give it up." The words left her lips. She cringed at how stupid they sounded.

Jason gave her no smart-mouth reply, though she left the door wide open for him to do so. A few seconds of silence passed. Until he said, "Then you need to give it up again."

Her eyes closed as tears flooded them.

His hand touched her, spread wide across her back, between her shoulder blades.

A scream wrenched her to her feet. She backed away as far as she could from him, cursing at him almost as much as at herself.

He slowly stood. But moved no closer.

A stare down played out between them. Though Jason's eyes were soft, Chris forced hers to glare as hard as they could. Her teeth clenched so tightly they ached.

"What did he do to you?"

Her jaw dropped. "That's none of your business!"

"It became my business the minute I looked into your eyes."

The words slammed her. She backed up a step to lean against the wall.

Jason took a step forward. "You reached out and grabbed me with your eyes that day. I'm here. I'm yours. And I'm making this my business. Getting you through this is my business. Whatever he did to you . . . can be forgotten."

Her words grated her throat. "Do not stand there and say that to me."

"Do you want me to sit?" Keeping his eyes fixed on hers, he turned slightly and pointed to the love seat.

"Do you think this is funny?"

"No, Chris. Not at all." Another step forward. "It's killing you. I've known you for three days, and I can see how it's killing you. I can see how much you've died. You want to know why? Because I saw you alive the other night." His voice started to shake. "You were staring at all those flavors ... and you couldn't make up your mind. You looked just like a kid in a candy store."

"Stop it, Jason."

"Your eyes sparkled in the light. You have the most beautiful eyes—"

"Stop it! Shut up!" Chris's back ground into the wall. The coolness of the concrete tempered her rage just a bit.

"You're dying. This, whatever it is, is killing you. No wonder everyone's worried about you."

She grabbed the water bottle on her desk and hurled it at the wall by his head. A scream. "Get out of here! Get out!"

He lowered his hands and straightened, then stared her down. "Tell me what he did to you. You said he beat you. How?"

"You think I'm gonna tell you that?"

"Lots of dads use their fists. Did he use his fist?"

Chris stood and gaped at the man's unimaginable gall.

"Lots of dads use their belts. Did he use his belt?"

Screamed curses. "How dare you ask me that!"

"What did he use, Chris?" Jason's intense gaze matched his shout.

Her mind short-circuited. "The cord!" The word sent her tumbling. "He used the cord! All right?"

Confusion swept Jason's face. Then unbearable pity.

"No!" She rushed for the door.

He stepped in front of her. Blocked her way.

"MOVE."

"No. Tell me the rest."

Her head lifted. Her eyes burned as they peered into his. "There is nothing else to tell."

"I don't know what you mean by a cord. An electrical cord?"

Her teeth clenched. "Yes, Jason. But not just any cord. *The* cord. He made it special. Just for me."

A deep swallow.

Searing heat boiled her blood. She growled her next words. "Move out of the way or I'll move you."

"Don't. You've come this far. Tell me the rest. How often did he beat you with this ... cord?"

"This is a game to you."

"No. God, no."

"A pathetic game, Jason. I'm sick of it."

"And I'm sick of what this has done to you. I know it's killing you. I hate that."

"You're insane."

"I'm totally drawn to you, Chris. I ... I think I'm starting to fall in love with you."

The words knocked her back a step. "You are insane! You fool!"

"Stop that! Because I care about you?"

"You don't even know me!"

"I know enough."

Laughter, bitter as bile, burned her throat. "You know nothing."

"Then tell me."

"I can't tell you." She drilled her eyes into his. "But I can show you." Over the top and out of control. She couldn't stop herself. Or the screams coursing through her.

He blinked.

"Yeah. You better make sure you want to see. 'Cause I'll show you what's killing me. I'll show you what he did to me." Darkness crowded the room. Her words muffled in her own ears. "And I'll show you why you're a fool for even thinking about falling in love with me."

Definite fear in Jason's eyes.

"Get out of the way."

"No. Show me."

"MOVE!" She pushed him with all her might.

He caught her arms and tried to pull her to him.

Screams and curses rent the air as she struggled to break free. A step back. Another.

"I'm here, Chris. Show me."

Insanity ripped through her. Trembling against it, fighting back a surge of nausea, she gave in to it. To his pathetic pleadings. To the current pulling her under. She let it carry her deep into the darkest place she had ever known.

She gazed into his eyes, so full of concern and pity. Then turned around and lifted her shirt as high as she could. She waited, unable to breathe but making sure Jason got a good long look, then pulled it down and rushed at him, shoving him out of the way. She tore open the door and ran out of the office, then through the gym's glass doors out into the middle of the empty weed-covered back lot.

✯✯✯

Bright sunshine.

Birds singing.

Fresh, cool air drifting on a light breeze. Carrying hints of honeysuckle. Of forest. Of rich soil recently turned.

Gorgeous purple and red rhododendrons in full bloom. Green leafy hardwoods. Tall Douglas fir. Clear blue sky above. Ladybug in the gravel below. Just trucking along. Oblivious.

Chris eased down into a crouch for a closer look. She watched the fat little bug climb up on a rock and counted the black spots on the brilliant red wings. She carefully touched the rock where the ladybug sat. Held her finger still. Waited. And smiled. The cute little critter crawled onto her finger and continued trucking. Up past the middle knuckle. On her way to parts unknown. Chris pushed back up to stand, then drew the little lady closer to her eyes.

Tiny feelers. Even tinier legs. Pulling that red round load across the back of Chris's hand.

Unbelievably beautiful. Equally hilarious.

Without warning, the bug fluttered away. Chris watched it go. A bit of gentle sadness tugged at her. She gave the critter another smile, then lifted her hands above her head and stretched. The stretch overwhelmed her, captured every muscle in her body. She breathed deeply of the sweet-smelling air. Laid her head back. Peered through the trees, past the blue sky, up and up until the breeze made her eyes water and she let them fall closed. Her arms reached higher. Her heart thumped. Warmth cascaded through her.

The moment swept over her. Left her washed and wrung out, clean. She couldn't fathom it. Had never felt anything like it before. She remembered the insanity, the rage, the unbearable shame. She thought she could run away from it. Like so many times before. *Forget it. Forget him. Let him go. Get out. Move on. Start again.*

She ran hard. Straight into the moment. Seeing everything so clear. Sweet. Clean. New.

Straight into the arms of her God.

But, Lord? What have I done?

Her hands lowered to her face and hid her eyes from the moment. She rubbed her eyes. Then her nose. Her forehead. Her fingers moved up to work their way through the tangled mess of her hair.

What if he's gone? Her hands fell to her sides. She stared at the gravel beneath her feet. "No." Just a whisper. "What if he's still here?"

He left. There's no way he stayed. Not after all that. He's long gone.

She couldn't blame him. Would never blame him. If she ever saw him again.

Please, Lord Jesus. Don't ever let me see him again.

But she needed to go back to keep an eye on the gym. To pick up the mess in her office. To call Ben and tell him what became of his brand-new cell phone.

A slow, deep sigh left her unbearably weary. She turned and headed back to the gym. A few steps from the door, she stopped and looked over her shoulder at the place that had held her.

Like so many times before, she had run away from the darkness. But always before, never far enough. It always found her cowering in some corner. But this time ... she ran straight into the light. Brilliant sunshine pouring down from above. Warming her cheeks. Scouring away all traces of darkness. Carrying it away on the fresh, cool breeze. Nothing dark remained. Only the brilliance of that new moment. It tested the waters of her heart as she slowly pushed through the doors of the gym.

Still quiet, so quiet, in the cavernous room. But not silent. Not like before. Hints of birdsong and passing cars seeped into the gym. The overhead lights hummed. Their brilliance were no match for the light of the moment. But would do. In this place. Her home away from home.

She pushed her feet toward the office and watched the floor slowly pass by as she walked. She dreaded lifting her eyes and seeing the place where darkness fell. Maybe she could rearrange the office. Put her desk against the far wall, move the fridge to —

Jason Sloan stood just inside the office, in the exact spot Chris shoved him into when she ran. He stood and stared back at her, his eyes flickering with emotion.

Chris felt every bit of his sadness, of his pity and concern, and his fear. Every bit of it stirred her weariness into chaos. Not one muscle in her body could move. Not one thought registered in her brain to help her figure out what to do.

His eyes ... slowly softened. His sadness and pity and fear ... dissolved into pure love. Radiating from those glimmering eyes, it traveled the short distance to the one standing in its way, and completely obliterated her.

Unable to dodge it, to run from it or deflect it in any way, Chris stood there and took it. Absorbed every tiny bit of it.

She couldn't move or breathe or even think of a word to say.

Jason's lips trembled as a hint of a smile played across them. His eyes softened that much more.

Oh ... God ...

His hand slowly lifted. Reached out to her. Palm up. Inviting her in.

Chris stared at that hand. Watched the strong fingers tremble as they stretched toward her. Her eyes lifted. Locked onto his. Couldn't look away. Didn't want to look away.

But she still couldn't move. Her mind sputtered in the chaos, in terror and unimaginable joy. She managed to whisper from her heart, *Lord? What do I do?*

Two heartbeats later, the breath she drew in tasted as sweet as the honeysuckle breeze. She heard a whisper lift up from her soul.

Let it go. Let him in.

His eyes. His trembling smile. His hand. Still reaching out for hers.

She stood too far away to touch him. To take his hand. To let him pull her in.

And he didn't move.

Lord, help me.

Chris stared at the man's hand. And then took three painfully slow steps toward him. On the last step, she lifted her hand and placed it in his.

Warmth washed over her as Jason closed his hand around hers. She glanced up into his face. Into eyes so tender and brimming with love.

He pulled her to him. Wrapped his arms around her.

Chris melted against him and held onto him for a long, long time.

TWELVE

Sitting in the love seat, Chris nestled against Jason's soft shoulder. His warmth continued to soak into her. The light in her soul continued to burn away every trace of the dark. Her eyes remained closed as Jason's hand gently rubbed her forehead, soothing away every last semblance of terror and shame. At that moment, she couldn't imagine anything sweeter than the sound of her own heart pumping blood through her body. Lifeblood coursed through her. Life that was truly and finally alive.

To be forgiven and cleansed and taken in by the Father God through the life and blood sacrifice of His precious Son. To feel His Son's heart beating deep in her own soul. To feel joy lifting up from her heart even as it coursed this new life into the deepest marrow of her bones.

To be surrounded by such incredible friends in a place she called home. Not just friends, but family, and who would remain family forever and ever as they shared eternal life with their Lord in His presence, in the spectacular home He built for them all.

To be held by a new friend. A friend who was kind and gentle and real. Who knew when to stay silent. And when to make himself heard. To be loved by a man who had seen the absolute worst in her. In every way. But loved her. Still. After seeing. After hearing. So much Chris wished she could take back.

So far they had come in just a few days. His gentle touch on her shoulder as she knelt handcuffed in Walker's living room. His gentle touch now, as she sat curled up against him in the love seat of her office. Gentle caresses. Like she had never known before.

A light kiss on her forehead.

She savored the tingly warmth it left behind.

The faintest of whispers. "Are you asleep?"

A trembling smile tugged her lips. "No." They had been sitting for so long in sweet silence, she wasn't surprised by his question. "I don't wanna sleep. I don't wanna wake up and find this has all been a dream." Now there was a subject better left dead.

"What have you been thinking about?"

She considered her response. "About how ... I can't believe how my life has changed."

"Since you moved here?"

Her eyes fluttered open for a second, then closed. "Since I met Rinny. That was the start of it. And now ..." She paused on purpose, just for the fun of it. Waited for him to ask for it.

"And now?"

"Now that I've met you."

His silence tickled her. It played out for another minute. Until he said, "I can't believe how hard I've fallen for you. In three days."

"Well don't ask me to explain it. I did everything I could to dissuade you. You're a stubborn cuss."

"I'm the luckiest cuss in the world to be sitting here with you in my arms."

The words almost didn't register, they were so loco. She pushed away to look him in the eye.

His eyes revealed nothing amiss. Only tenderness.

She sat back in the love seat. Instantly felt her temperature drop with the absence of his arms around her.

His head tilted. "What?"

She shook her head.

"Try to tell me."

She glanced across the office. "I can't." A deep sigh. "I mean ... I just can't take this all in yet. It's too big."

"Then don't. Save it for another time." He held his hand out, inviting her back into his arms.

She accepted the invitation.

They sat in quiet stillness for a long while.

Chris hated to break the stillness. Her voice barely carried her words. "Jase? What do you believe ... about God? Do you believe Jesus is His Son?"

A long breath hushed out of him. "Yeah. I mean, I did. And I'm starting to again. But there for a while it was really hard."

She looked into his eyes. "Because of ... your wife?"

His smile softened the sadness she saw there. "I figured Scott told you. You didn't seem too concerned that I wore a ring."

"When I first saw it I was seriously bummed." She cuddled against him. And could not believe how comfortable she felt in his arms.

"Did you notice I took it off?"

"Yeah. That had to have been hard."

"Especially after you screamed at me."

She covered her face with her hand. "Oh, man. Please forgive me." Then pushed up again to look at him. "You've got to know how sorry I am. For that, and for what I said today."

"It's forgotten, Chris. Every word."

"Forgive me, first. Then forget it."

"Oh. Is that how it works?" A huge grin. "Okay. I forgive you for ... something ... but I can't remember what it is."

Laughter bubbled through her. She fell again into his shoulder.

"Will you forgive me?"

"For what?"

"For pushing you so hard."

A deep breath helped settle her thoughts. "You cared enough to push."

"I didn't want to hurt you. And I know I did. But I had this feeling you were ready to be done with it. You've, um ... you've never ..." His voice faltered.

"No. Never. To all of it. I've never talked to anyone about my past."

"Never? Not even to Erin?"

"A little. But she's never asked me to talk about it more."

"It hurt to see you so ... angry."

"I never would have said to Erin what I said to you. I would've just left and never came back."

"Then I'm glad you said what you said."

"I'm not."

"I'm glad you're here in my arms and not on your way out of town."

"Okay. I'll give you that."

His arm squeezed her against him. His head lowered against hers. A whisper. "I'm not happy about what I saw ... but I'm glad you showed me."

A shudder raced through her.

Jason must have felt it. He hugged her tightly. "I'm not glad you showed me, but I'm glad I saw it. I hope that makes sense. I can't explain it."

Chris swallowed deeply. "Yeah. It does."

"I will never push you again. But I want you to tell me everything. Don't think anything is too ugly or hard. Talk about it. Please? So you can continue to let it go. Does that make sense?"

She grabbed his hand and held it in hers. "You've seen the worst of it. My dad really did try to be a good dad."

Jason's voice hardened. "How can you say that?"

"Hey. My mom and dad never married. But he took me in when no one else wanted me. I have to give him credit for that."

"But what made him ... so cruel?"

"Booze. Life. He lived a hard life. And the Nuggets never won."

A grunt of laughter.

"Don't laugh. They were the highest scoring team in the league, but still lost most of their games. Used to drive him crazy. That, and the fact he used to bet on them."

"Not very smart."

"My dad was smart. It was sad he let his life fall into something he couldn't control."

"When did he take you in?"

"I was four. My mother had overdosed, and my grandmother couldn't take care of me anymore. She had trouble getting around.

It's a pretty convoluted story."

"That's all right. There's nowhere else I'd rather be."

"Poor man."

Jason laughed softly.

"My grandmother was pretty cool. I adored her. But I was a little much for her. She used to tell me I blossomed into rambunctious childhood after a silent start. It wasn't until years later, just before she died, that she explained to me what she meant." Chris shifted a bit against Jason's shoulder. "She told me I was a good baby. That I never cried or made a sound. I was content to just lie in my crib and wait for a bottle or to be changed."

Except for the few grainy photographs, the image of her grandmother's face had long since faded from her mind. She regretted that again as she held onto the woman's words. "She told me I used to suck on my fist. And that I would just look around with my big dark eyes, takin' in my world." She savored the memory of her grandmother's voice. "My mom was a heroin addict. Things got pretty nasty right after I was born. I guess I just learned not to cry."

"You know ... there's a reason why babies don't cry."

"Yeah." A deep sigh. "I know."

Jason squeezed her against his chest.

"Dad took me in and treated me right. I was too scared of him to act up, and he was scared of me in a way too. So we got along fine. He built me the coolest tree house. My friend Eddie and I would play up there for hours. His dad worked the night shift a lot, and my dad watched TV a lot, so we had it made. But one day my dad brought home a wife. And I instantly had two stepbrothers. Ugh." She shuddered. "That's a time I would much rather forget."

"Not good, huh?"

"One could say that. A story for another time. But they got a divorce—thank You, Lord—and after that my dad started teaching me how to defend myself. He taught me how to throw a punch, and how to take one. Not that he ever hit me." Her throat tightened.

"Interesting how you tacked that on at the end."

A laugh. "No. He slapped me around once or twice, but never outright hit me with his fist. Not until … that night."

Jason leaned in to kiss the top of her head.

"He hit me that night and let me have it with the cord … because I hit him. Slapped him. But I rung his bell, that's for sure." Her heart started to race. "Up to that point, he only used it on me twice before. Once for drinking his beer. Oh, man. That was stupid." She shook her head against Jason's shoulder. "That was the second time. The first time … not long after the divorce, he used it just to show me what it felt like. In case I thought about acting up. I think I had left my bike out too many times or something. Actually, I don't really remember what caused him to make it. Something set him off, but of all the things I do remember and have carried with me all these years, that eludes me."

"He probably didn't have a reason. He probably just made it to—"

"No. I don't think so. I must have set him off. Somehow."

"I don't believe that. What would cause …?" A long growl. "And what do you mean by 'he made it'?"

Chris heaved a long sigh as her stomach started to burn, as a prayer whispered up from her soul. "He cut about a two-foot length from an old outdoor extension cord that didn't work anymore and wrapped one end with about a half roll of duct tape so he could get a good grip on it."

Vicious curses.

"He gave me one across the back just to let me know how it felt." She lowered her voice to mock her dad's, to lessen the sting of the words. "'That's just a taste, young lady,' he said. 'Now you know what you'll get if you ever …' But I forget the rest. It's so weird I don't remember what I did. I remember everything else."

"It's sick." Jason squirmed. "I mean …"

"I know what you mean. And I understand how you feel. But at the time, his methods proved very productive. I didn't give him any trouble, and we got along fine."

"I know you're saying what you think I want to hear."

Chris resisted a sudden urge to push away ... and run.

"I'm sorry. Go on."

"Don't be sorry."

"Okay. I'm not. Not really."

She almost smiled. Grabbed his hand and squeezed it.

"Did it ... cut you like that every time?"

Her stomach lurched.

Jason must have sensed it. "Don't answer that. I'm sorry."

"No." She swallowed hard to force down the bile burning deep in her chest. "It only cut that last time. He was so drunk, he didn't know how hard he was hitting me."

Jason gently pushed Chris up, then stood and walked across the office.

Chris leaned back in the love seat and closed her eyes, then lowered her head. *Please, Lord Jesus ...*

"All right, Chris. I hear you."

Her eyes opened. She slowly lifted them to meet Jason's gaze.

"I hear what you're saying. You don't want to blame your dad for what he did to you. But someone's to blame. And it most certainly is not you."

"I'm not saying it was my fault."

His expression told her he didn't believe her.

"All I'm saying is that he didn't just beat me because he wanted to. He let me have it when I deserved it. And that last night ... I deserved it."

"How many times did he hit you with it that night?"

Her head shook as a shudder raced through her. "I don't know."

"From what I saw—!"

Her eyes pinched shut.

Jason's voice softened. "From what I saw, he hit you a lot."

"You only saw half of it." Just a mumble. But she cursed herself for saying it. And hoped Jason didn't hear it.

The string of quiet obscenities told her he did. He heard every word.

She did not want to open her eyes. The silence completely unnerved her.

Jason sat again beside her, then picked up her hands to hold them in his. She looked up to meet his intense gaze. "You will forget. So help me, Chris …"

Forgive … and forget.

The words sifted through her. Hovered over her vile memories like a blanket of fire, willing to burn them to ashes to be blown away by the wind. If she let them.

She blinked and the image disappeared. Only the word lingered on the fringes of her soul.

Forgive …

Jason rubbed the backs of Chris's hands with his thumbs. "How did you survive it? Who helped you … survive?"

The depth of anguish she saw in his eyes tore at her heart. She tried to give him a smile. Felt it widen as her memories took her back. "There was a policeman who held my hand for hours. And my favorite teacher visited me every day. I ate a ton of lime Popsicles and swallowed a ton of painkillers. But it was 'da Big Hap' who saved my life." She watched confusion play out on Jason's face. "Da Big Hap was da biggest African-American angel I've ever seen. He was an orderly, but he knew more about doctoring than any of the doctors I had. He used to sit with me and talk to me. For hours. He would massage my feet with those huge hands of his. I'd cry because it felt so good. For at least a little while, I couldn't feel anything but his hands rubbing my feet. He'd go away and I'd cry for him to come back."

Jason's eyes glimmered. He glanced away and blinked deeply.

Chris reached up to caress his cheek. "He used to tell me stories about when he was in the army. In Vietnam. You see …" Her lips pressed into a grin. "The man used to fly helicopters in the war. Medevac Hueys. And he'd tell me stories that blew my mind. He once hung out the door by his restraint strap and held onto the barrel of a soldier's rifle while that soldier hung by the rifle's strap. The LZ got so hot that was all he could do. The soldier stretched his rifle at Ronny, and Ronny grabbed it. I believe it too. That was something da Big Hap would do."

"Ronny."

"Big Happy Ronny. That was all I ever knew him by."

A faint smile. "Have you ever seen him since?"

"Only in my dreams."

Jason seemed to absorb the words. He put his arm around Chris and pulled her against him. They leaned back again in the love seat as a peaceful silence fell. Jason's voice softly broke it. "How long were you in the hospital?"

"A week."

"Then … what?"

"I went to foster care. More of a medical group home. I stayed there for six months, until they sent me to another home."

"What was it like?"

Chris placed her hand on Jason's chest. His heart thumped against her palm. Matched her own.

"Later. Tell me later."

"No, it's okay. The first month in the group home I could only stand or lay on my stomach. So that made things … difficult." Her mind drifted to that time and place. Standing at the window of her bedroom for hours, watching the other children shoot baskets at a makeshift hoop. Lying on the bed while Clara hummed songs from her childhood and carefully rubbed salve over every cut. So patient and kind. Gently rubbing in the soothing medicine while Chris struggled with the pain, the touch, the reality of her life at that moment. "From there I went to live with a family who already had four foster kids. They were nice, but by then all I wanted to do was …" She almost didn't want to say the rest. The Kirbys thought she had lost her mind when she told them her plans.

"Don't leave me hanging, girl."

A laugh. She lifted her eyes to gaze into his. "Well? Can't you figure it out?"

A hint of a knowing smile.

"All I wanted to do by then was join the army and fly Hueys."

"Da Big Hap created a little monster."

Her laughter continued long after she tried to rein it in. "Yeah. You could say that. But I'll never regret it. The army was good to me."

"And you were good to it."

She stared into his eyes as her hand on his chest absorbed the beat of his heart.

"You know I'm dying to hear about it."

Her gaze lowered to take in the strong features of his face. "I'd love to tell you."

He grabbed her hands. "Tell me on the way to the coast. Today. Right now." He started to pull her up.

She resisted his pull. "What? I can't, Jason."

"Sure you can. Make the call." His eyebrows lifted. "Please?"

The magic word. Chris started to smile, which started her laughing, which caused Jason to pull her to her feet and into his arms.

★★★

THE SUNSET COULD NOT HAVE been more beautiful. The night, perfect in every way. Happy stories of flying Hueys. Much-embellished stories of Desert Shield. Much left unsaid about Desert Storm. She would tell him the rest later.

Her belly stuffed with the best mushroom swiss burger and onion rings she had ever eaten, Chris leaned against Jason's shoulder as he drove his truck over the coast range toward home. For the most part, he drove responsibly, until he'd take a hand off the wheel to pull her more closely against him. They had spent hours walking the beach, finding agates and gnarled bits of wood polished smooth by the pounding surf.

Joy and peace melted her heart into a gooey mess. She had prayed all afternoon, prayed as the sun hid itself beneath the jade swirling water, and heard her answer as the last rays of pink slowly faded from the clouds.

To forgive and forget. And then to move on. From the deepest corners of her soul to the lightest wisps of hope tickling her imagination. In the silence of rolling tires, whirling wind, and soft breaths of the one she leaned against, a picture painted itself across her mind's eye as vivid and sure as any she had ever seen. A picture of traveling east through Boise and Salt Lake, through Grand Junction, across Colorado to the city where she was born. To the house she used to live in. To the man she used to call Dad.

She would go and look the man in the eye. Once and for all. She would stand straight and tall and say the words to him. Words she never dreamed she would say to him in a hundred million years.

"Dad, I'm here to tell you ... I forgive you. For all you've ever done to me. For whatever reason you did it. I forgive you."

The words would end there. She wouldn't lie and tell him she loved him. Right now loving him remained unthinkable. But she had a feeling her Lord could live with that. The rest, if there was to be more, would come in time. But she would start with forgiveness. With obedience to her Lord's command. And if her dad had changed at all, if he had turned from what he was to a more good and decent man, then maybe there was hope for rekindling a relationship. They were both adults now. She didn't need to fear him anymore. She didn't need to cower from her past.

Still, the thought of it stirred up the burger in her belly.

Oh, Lord, if I do this ... You gotta go with me. You gotta do this through me. I can't chicken out and turn around without seeing him after traveling all that way.

Her eyelids were too heavy to push back up. She let them stay closed. Let the hum of the tires lull her away. Let the warmth of the shoulder she leaned against flow into her, into her blood, straight into her heart.

✲✲✲

Asleep against his shoulder, Chris's breaths bordered on outright snores. Jason didn't want to move, not even to lean forward enough to turn the key and shut off the rumbling engine. Orange light flooded Kimberley Street with an eerie, synthetic glow.

Definite snores now. Long breaths pulled in. A hush as they escaped.

Jason drew in his own long breath, let it wash through him softly, let it remind him of one simple truth. He was alive. And the love in his heart ... his breath slowly washed out. Only to be replaced by another. He turned his head and pressed his cheek against Chris's soft hair.

A prayer whispered up from his soul. It felt strange. Unfamiliar. It had been so long. Yet the prayer was familiar. He had prayed it so many times before as he held his love and watched her sleep. As the babe in her womb grew.

The prayer lifted to heaven. And he let it go. Simple thanks for the one he held in his arms. For the love making his heart soar. But a new prayer whispered up. Words that wrenched his soaring heart. *Oh, God ... please don't take this one from me. She is precious ... and she is Yours. Make us both Yours. Make her ... mine.*

He kissed the top of her head. Her hair tickled his lips.

She stirred awake. Then quickly sat up. "Oh. Are we home?" A deep yawn and a stretch.

Smiling, Jason turned the key. Silence quickly descended.

"We are home. Oh my. I fell asleep." Chris turned and gave Jason a wide-eyed look.

"Perfectly all right. We had fun, didn't we?"

Her eyes softened. "A perfectly *fantabulous* night." Her smile captured her entire face. "Thank you, sir. It was just what I needed."

Jason couldn't breathe. Her smile ...

"Those were *absitively* the best onion rings I have ever eaten. We'll have to go back to that place."

"You got it. Anytime." The streetlights glistened in her eyes. "You are so beautiful."

She quickly looked down. Rubbed her nose. Then unhooked her seat belt and turned in the seat to face him. Her eyes wouldn't look at him. "I need to thank you for today. For ... everything."

"No, you don't."

"Because of you, today, and tonight . . . I really think I'm gonna be all right. Which sounds weird to say, but I think you know what I mean."

He cherished the words. "Yes. I do."

"Jase, I need to do something. Right away. But I don't think you're gonna like it." She met his gaze. "I need to go to Colorado."

His heart slammed to a stop.

"Right away. If not tomorrow, then Thursday. I need to go and come back before . . ." Her eyes sparkled with unreleased laughter.

Anger coiled deep in Jason's belly.

"Well, I need to be here for Erin. That's all there is to it. But I need to go too. So it'll be a quick trip. Not more than a week, tops."

"Why?" The word ground out of him.

Her smile faded. "I think you know why."

"I know what you're talking about. But I don't understand why. Why would you even consider it?"

Her chin lifted just a bit. "I need to see him. To look into his eyes. And forgive him."

Breath gushed out of him so hard he coughed. "This is crazy."

"I don't think so." Her smile disappeared completely.

"You do not need to forgive that man. You do not need to see him. Ever again. Just forget him! Forget everything he did to you."

Her head slowly shook. "Be honest, Jase. Do you ever think I'll be able to forget?"

"Then don't forget. Just let it go. Good riddance."

"I can't keep that kind of . . . poison . . . in my system and be a Christian. Please try to understand. Being a Christian means everything to me. The more I learn about Jesus and who He was, and is . . . I don't just love Him, I adore Him. And I need Him more than I need breath. More than I need my life."

"Okay, fine. I hear you."

"I can't love Him and hate my dad at the same time."

"Then don't hate him! Just forget him!"

"I can't forget anything or let anything go or move on from anything in my past until I forgive. No regrets. No grudges. No

263

hatred lingering in the outer limits of my being." Her hands waved to display the limits.

Jason turned and stared at the lights in the window of the house across the street.

Her hand gently touched his arm. "If I forgive my dad, there may be a chance ... he'll forgive me. That would be so cool."

His mouth fell open as his head quickly turned. "What?"

"If I can tell him about Jesus, he may listen. He may be saved."

His teeth clenched. "Some people are beyond hope, Chris. If you see him, you're putting so much of yourself at risk. You have no idea what he's become. He may be ten times worse than he was."

"I need to find that out for myself. I need to look him in the eye."

The thought of her beautiful dark eyes even glancing in the direction of her deranged father sickened him. He quickly unhooked his seat belt, then pushed out of his truck and slammed the door.

He gulped the night air into his lungs.

"Jason, please." Chris moved around the truck to stand in the street with him.

He turned and walked a few aimless steps toward the back of his truck.

"Do you want me to move on? To be able to love you? Or anyone else, for that matter?"

He spun around. "You know I do."

"Then let me do this. Don't be afraid. I'll be fine. I'll be home before you know it. And we'll both cuddle a newborn baby ... and dare to look ahead at our future."

The words stunned him.

A faint smile. Chris slowly folded her arms across her chest. Lifted her eyebrows.

Jason shook his head and turned away. But he couldn't keep a smile from stretching his lips.

Her arms came around him. Her head rested between his shoulder blades. "I'll be home before you know it." He felt her lips press against his back. Then nothing as she pulled away.

He turned and stared at her. She stared back. Five seconds. Maybe ten. His own voice scolded him. *Pull her in! Hold her! Kiss her! Right now!* He didn't move.

She pressed her lips into a faint grin. "I'll call you when I get back."

Jason stood and watched as Chris climbed the stairs of her apartment and pulled the door closed behind her.

A few seconds later, he climbed back in his truck and started for home.

★★★

OH ... YOU SHOULD'VE KISSED HIM. *He definitely was acting like a boy needing to be kissed.*

Chris stopped her toothbrush mid-swish and glared at herself in the mirror. Then laughed and resumed. So what if he needed to be kissed. He didn't get a kiss because he was acting like a jerk.

Spit. Rinse. Spit.

Maybe, when she came home, if he quit acting like a jerk ... She covered her face with the towel.

Lord, help him understand. And help me! Please ... this is all so out of hand I can't stand it.

I need to talk to Rinny.

Yes. She would call Ben first thing in the morning and ask for the next week off. Then spend the rest of the day with Erin. Go to prayer meeting tomorrow night and pray, pray, pray. Then leave first thing Thursday morning.

Sounded like a plan.

She pulled the towel away. Stared into her worried eyes.

Lord? This may be it. If not ... please let me know. Okay?

She gave her reflection a weak smile, then hung the towel on the rack and headed to bed.

★★★

Erin rocked in her rocker and basked in the moment. Sunshine and sweet fresh air. Chirping birds. A peeking squirrel. Pleasant smiles and waves from her neighbors as they passed by on the street. Hugs and warm greetings from her patients as they walked past her into and out of the clinic. Constant kicks and squirms in her belly. Her little one seemed to be enjoying the moment almost as much as his mommy.

And it was just what she needed. So long cooped up in the house, the porch swing just not comfortable anymore, Chris had said to her, "Well, let's take your rocker out onto the porch." And thirty seconds later, she did.

A simple gift of friendship. A day of moments Erin would always cherish. Her hands moved across the huge bulge of her belly, feeling every kick and wiggly squirm. *Almost, my sweet love. It won't be long now. Mommy will hold you and kiss you and tickle your little kicking feet.*

She turned her head and gazed into the darkest brown eyes she had ever seen. Eyes so deep, so expressive, so full of life, of joy and hope. Just a hint of the peace transforming her friend's life. A transformation so beautiful and awesome, she had to look away and blink to keep her tears at bay.

She rocked and rocked, then felt another kick. She wanted to stand up and do a little dance. She filed that desire away for a later time. A time when she didn't carry a child the size of a watermelon in her belly.

"He's really kicking again, huh."

She lifted her eyes and met her friend's radiant gaze. "I think he wants out."

"Well, tell him to wait at least another week." Chris leaned forward on the porch swing and touched Erin's belly with both hands. "Listen here, you. If you even think about arriving when your aunt Chris is away ..." She glanced up at Erin. "Just relax in there. Make yourself comfortable. As soon as I come back, then you can ..." Another glance. And a sheepish grin.

Erin pushed up her right eyebrow.

"Let's just say you can arrive then." A giggle. "We won't tell your mommy how Aunt Cappy said it."

"And how did Aunt Cappy say it?"

Chris's grin. From sheepish to smug in two seconds flat.

"Never mind." Erin didn't really want to know anyway. Who could possibly imagine how Cappy's mind worked?

A good solid kick.

Chris's eyes almost popped out of her head. "Oh, man! That was a good one!" She knelt on the floor and stared at Erin's belly. Her hands found every spot where the little feet kicked.

Erin's heart swelled until she thought it would burst.

Though a bit of her trembled at what lay ahead. The sight of Chris's smile first thing that morning brought a depth of joy to Erin's heart that had been missing the past few days. But then came the news. Chris had smashed Ben's new cell phone against the wall. Had yelled and screamed at Jason. Then sat with him and told him everything. He took her to the beach where she prayed and received her answer. She asked Ben for the next week off so she could go to Colorado. And Ben said yes.

Overwhelmed, Erin had rocked as Chris sat in the love seat, leaning over the armrest, telling her news. They both cried when Chris said, "It should have been you, Rin. You should have been the one I told everything to. I should have trusted you enough to share this with you . . . weeks ago. Maybe even years ago."

Erin gently dismissed the words. The important thing was that Chris talked. That she talked to Jason could not have delighted Erin more.

But still, a part of her trembled as she sat in her rocking chair out on the porch, as Chris knelt with her hands poised, waiting for the baby's next kick. There would come a day when Chris would share all of her secrets with Erin. And that day would be one of the worst days of Erin's life.

And one of the best.

Her eyes closed as her heart reached out to her Savior. She handed Him every fear and concern for her friend. She watched as

He took them all, as He smiled and then carried them away. She watched Him go, knowing they could not be in better hands. Then she blinked her eyes open and gazed into the face of pure childlike wonder. Though it radiated from eyes still bruised, from a life still so weary from a past so cruel.

Erin's heart whispered to her, and she turned inward to look.

Her Savior held out His arms to give her a gift. She strained to make out what it was. But suddenly it engulfed her. Stole the breath from her lungs.

Hope. Sweet and undefiled.

She struggled to breathe. Gazed back into Chris's face.

"You okay, lady?"

She nodded. "Yeah. I'm fine." And for the first time since that day in that parking garage outside Dhahran, Saudi Arabia, when Teddy Brisbaine threw Erin's gear down on a cot beside this dark-brown-eyed woman, she knew Chris would be fine too. After a lifetime of reliving old wounds, in the next week, whatever Chris faced, one thing was for sure. She would come home completely healed.

Deep in Erin's heart, she threw her arms around her Lord Jesus Christ and hugged Him with all her might.

★★★

PRAYER. LOTS OF PRAYER. IF the butterflies attacking her stomach meant anything, she needed it. But with the hands of her best friends upon her, she told the butterflies to get lost. Nothing could stand between a child of the Father and His love for that child. Nothing seen or unseen. Nothing in heaven or on earth.

And Chris stood before Him, His child, holding out her arms for more of His love. Even as she knelt in silent reverence and felt the hands of her friends upon her.

Ben's deep voice prayed for Chris with authority and grateful confidence. Behind Chris, Velda Jackson repeatedly whispered, "Amen," and, "Thank You, Jesus."

Chris cried like a baby. She knew everything Ben prayed for, everything she asked for would be given her. Her trip would bring her back to these people, her real family, a new and different person.

At least … she hoped it would.

The prayer ended and her family hugged her from all sides. She absorbed and returned every one. And tried not to laugh as she realized she probably left a tear on everyone's shoulder.

***

The meeting ended, and Chris headed for Erin's house with Bettema, Cappy, and Scott where they all planned to eat ice cream and hang out. She longed for the company of her newest ice-cream-eating friend. As she stepped through the doors of the big church and gazed out over the street, her eyes latched onto a sight that almost dropped her once again down those hard concrete stairs.

Jason Sloan. There he stood. Leaning against his truck. Arms folded across his chest. Peering up at the crowd exiting the church.

Well.

It was a slow trip down the stairs with Erin blocking things. But Chris didn't mind. She knew to treat these stairs with healthy respect. And she wasn't in any particular hurry anyway.

Make the man wait. That'll teach him for being a jerk.

Step.

But why is he here?

Step.

Why? Are you kidding?

Step.

Wonder if he's still mad.

Step.

He better not try to talk me out of anything, Lord.

Step.

Another step.

Chris's group gave Jason happy waves, then headed toward Erin's house. Chris didn't wave. She walked up to the man and stood in front of him, waiting for him to say the first word.

He grinned. Didn't say a word.

Chris folded her arms across her chest and grinned to match his stance.

Finally, his lips parted. A word. "Hey."

"Well, hey back atcha."

"I was in the neighborhood."

"Glad to hear it." She struggled for impassivity.

"Are you still leaving?"

"First thing tomorrow."

His eyes flickered. Glanced away. "I can't change your mind?"

"Are you here to try?"

He blinked. "No. I'm just here to find out what's up."

Chris pushed up her right eyebrow.

"Fine. Well, can I give you a ride to the airport?"

"I'm not flying. I'm driving."

"What? Why?"

"Because I'd rather drive."

Jason pushed away from his truck. "You know what? Fine. Drive."

"All right, I will."

His head tilted as he looked at her. "Can I at least give you something before you go?"

"Depends on what it is."

A slight nod. His eyes studied something out over Chris's shoulder.

She waited.

Then gasped as Jason suddenly moved closer, placed his hands on the sides of her face, and pulled her into the most intense, yet gentle kiss she had ever received. She received it. Then returned it. As her heart spun wild cartwheels in her chest.

✲✲✲

THE FIRST BOWL OF MINT chocolate chip did not cool the fire in her heart. Nor the burning in her cheeks. So she dipped herself a different flavor. Orange vanilla this time.

She still laughed at herself. She had stood in the middle of Kimberley Street completely paralyzed. Her eyes refused to open. Until Jason's truck started up. Startled by it, she blinked to focus. And saw a wide grin on the man's face. "Be careful," he said, before gunning the truck and taking off in a cloud of fumes and dust.

She had explained to the others that Jason needed to leave. But she didn't tell them the rest. That he came to make a point. And he made it. And Chris knew she would carry that point with her every day for the rest of her life.

★★★

UP BEFORE DARK, BUT NOT before the early birds, she turned to give the apartment one more look before heading out the door. Cappy still slept. But her teary hug and kind words of hope the night before still warmed Chris's soul. Chris placed the card on the table where Cappy would find it. Then smiled as she realized she was just about to walk out that door.

It didn't seem possible. To have come so far in five short months. But this trip ... she needed to make this trip. And she needed to get going. Right now. So she could come back.

She quickly reached into a pocket of her backpack and checked again to be sure Ben's replacement cell phone was there. It was. This one, she would cherish. It would be her lifeline over the next week. She pushed TALK and heard a strong dial tone. Then clicked it off and tucked it back in her pack.

Enough stalling. She let out a deep sigh. Then slipped quietly out the squeaky door. And headed for Colorado.

★★★

RUBBING HER EYES, CAPPY PADDED to the coffeemaker in the kitchen. Sun up, birds doing their thing, she needed the dark brew to make her do her thing. But a white square of something leaning against the bowl of bananas on the table caught her eye. She stopped and picked it up.

A card. From Chris.

She opened the envelope flap and pulled it out. Opened the card. A folded check almost dropped out. She grabbed it. Then read the card's message.

Cappy, this is what I owe you. But I'll never be able to repay you for what I really owe you. Thanks, hermana. You are truly my sister. I love you. Chris.

She opened the check and let out a laugh.

PAY TO THE ORDER OF CAPRIELLA SANCHEZ. ONE HUN-
DRED FORTY AND 00/100 DOLLARS.

Chris's elegant signature. A smiley face on the note line.

A seventy-five-dollar debt with a dollar-a-month interest for sixty-five months. Paid in full. All because Cappy had three queens.

She laughed again and stared at the check.

Vaya con Dios, hermana, her heart whispered. *I love you too, sweet friend.*

THIRTEEN

RETRACING THE ROUTE SHE AND Erin had taken from Colorado five months ago felt a little strange. And with the sun in her eyes, Chris almost wished she could turn around and go home. She weaved her Explorer past the big rigs and RVs, pushing the speed limit to the max, trying not to think about anything but the road before her, the scenery flying by, and the music filtering out of the stereo. She didn't realize the irony behind the first cassette she had chosen to play on her journey: *Along the Road*. But when Margaret Becker sang the pretty song, Chris couldn't help laughing. And let the cassette play again.

The road rolled out beneath her. Beside her, the mighty Columbia River flowed to the sea. The music played as Chris sang along. Songs of praise and thanksgiving and hope. Prayers for strength. For wisdom. Holding on to that hope. Never letting that hope fade. Another hour. Another hundred miles. Time to change the tape.

The Dalles. Hermiston. Stop in Pendleton for gas and a bathroom break. Just like the last time she passed through the town. LaGrande, Baker City, state line, Idaho. She felt a twinge seeing the *Welcome to Oregon* sign in her rearview mirror. But she pressed on. As Out of the Grey sang "The Shape of Grace." Which reminded her. She needed to call Erin.

She pulled into a motel in Ogden just as the first stars peeked out above her. She tossed her suitcase and backpack on the bed, then plopped down beside them and tucked one of the thin pillows under her head. She pulled out the cell phone and pressed the first number on the speed dial. The drone of the road hummed through her as she lay there, as she waited to hear who would pick up and say, *"Hello?"*

Erin.

A smile worked its way through her weariness. "This is me, is that you?"

"You got that from Cappy."

"Does she say that? She must have got it from me."

The sound of Erin's laughter. Her soothing voice. Chris relished the small talk, and laughed hysterically when Erin recounted her entire day as a nervous mother-to-be lugging around what felt like a watermelon in her belly. She laughed, though her heart ached with pity. "Soon, Rinny. Just hang in there a little while longer." *But not too soon, Lord. Please help her wait until I get back home.*

But yet, another jolt of pure terror shot through her as she dared again to think of what Erin faced in her delivery. She pushed up to sit on the bed and dangled her feet over the edge.

She told Erin about the deer she almost hit in eastern Idaho. And about the incredible sunrise and how it had lit up the sky with at least a billion different shades of brilliant. She talked about the high gas prices, and revisiting their bathroom-break place in Pendleton. With not much more to talk about, she let out a deep sigh, but instantly regretted it. Even with nothing to talk about, she dreaded hanging up the phone.

"So you'll be there tomorrow night sometime, huh."

"Yeah. Not too late. I'm hoping to be early enough to call him. To give him some warning, you know? I'll just have to wait and see."

What else could she do? All day she had flatly refused to think about what she might find when she arrived at her dad's house. But the truth was, she didn't even know for sure he still lived in the same house. She hadn't talked to him or heard a word about him in over ten years. A part of her curled up inside at the thought her dad might not even live in Colorado anymore. He might have moved on years ago. And this trip might be a complete waste of energy and time.

Yet, she knew her dad loved Colorado, and would be hard pressed to leave. Wherever he was, she would track him down. She wouldn't think about what might be waiting ahead. She would cling to the hope bubbling inside her. This trip would not be a waste. She would stand before her dad. And say the words she needed to say.

As Chris finally pushed the button to end the call, Erin's last few words echoed through her. The soft voice. The image of Erin out on the porch, rocking and smiling as her hands caressed the bulge that would soon be her newborn baby, a tiny infant wrapped in blue flannel blankets and nestled deeply in her arms.

Chris squeezed her eyes shut. Prayers flooded her heart, then lifted one by one to her heavenly Father, carried to Him by her Lord Jesus, where He laid them at their Father's throne. Prayers for her best friend and the babe soon to be born. Prayers for the rest of her family she left behind in Portland. Prayers for Jason. Prayers for the dad she would soon see again.

"No matter what happens, Chris, Jesus will never let you go. You are His. You live in Him, and He lives in you. He loves you so much, and He's so pleased you're making this trip. You're making it in obedience to Him. When I see you again, girl, I'll look into your eyes and see how He's healed you. You'll be completely healed. It'll be ... well, let's just say I can't wait to see you again."

"Rinny ..." A whisper. "Lord Jesus ... thank You ..."

She laid back down and let her tears fall into the pillow as prayers lifted from her heart to the Lord.

★★★

CROSSING THE STATE LINE INTO Colorado made her smile. Yes, Portland was home. But this was ... *home.* Colorado simply ran in her blood. It called sweetly to her in a language all its own. Imploring. Enticing her to stay awhile. To lose herself in the majesty of the Rockies. To soar with the eagles on the alpine currents of crystal clear air.

She resisted the enticements. This trip wasn't about soaring with eagles. She had strict orders. Get in, accomplish the mission, and get out. Get home. Cuddle a newborn infant. And be that infant's aunt.

Ouray. Raymond. Liz and Sid and that hot-springs pool behind that ruined miner's cabin that used to be home. All of it called to her as she sailed past the Highway 50 exit off Interstate 70 in Grand Junction. She considered her options. And thought maybe she could schedule a quick trip that direction on her way home. Right now, she needed to stick to her plan.

But the closer I-70 carried her to Denver, the plan started to worry her. What if her dad had moved on? He had family in Kansas and a brother in California. At least he did. If Chris picked up that phone book and did not find a *McIntyre, Donovan* or any other McIntyre she recognized as her own, what would she do?

At the moment, she couldn't do a thing. So she pressed on, pushed the worry from her mind, and sang with all her might as Margaret Becker's *Soul* poured out the Explorer's stereo.

★★★

FIFTY MILES TO GO. SHE passed one creeping big rig after the other up the long incline taking them to the edge of the Continental Divide. From there it would all be downhill. Straight into Denver.

Chris's stomach twisted itself into one huge knot.

Another long, slow, deep pull of air into her lungs. She held it until the strain worked against her. Then slowly, so slowly, let it leak through her pursed lips, puffing her cheeks, stressing the healing cut just a bit. She reached for another cassette, then stopped and stared at the road coursing beneath her.

"Lord? Shouldn't we talk about this? I mean ... we're almost there."

Forty-five miles. Then forty.

"Okay, Lord, we need to talk about this. I need to get this straight in my head. I'm expecting him to be home and to welcome me in with a smile on his face. Is that a productive expectation?"

She grabbed her watered-down Pepsi and drew in a big drink. *Forget expectations. I just hope he's changed.*

The thought disturbed her. So she gave it voice. "Has he changed, Lord? I mean, if he hasn't, Jason may be right." She missed Jason. Enjoyed the lingering image of him playing out in her mind.

"What I mean is . . . I may be walking up to the door of a complete monster." She did that a few days ago. Did she want to do it again? "No, that's not right. He really wasn't a *monster*. At least not when he was sober." And when he slept.

Chris squirmed against her seat belt as her stomach twisted sharply. *Please, Lord, don't let him be drunk.*

"But You know what, Lord? He may just be a completely different man. He may be married. He may even have children."

She needed to filter her thoughts better, before they found voice. She pulled over at the next exit to walk around and relax. It wasn't good to drive while her hands shook. And rage boiled her blood.

Stupid thought anyway. After her dad's best efforts at raising her landed him in jail, why would he want to have another kid?

Her fingers ground into the steering wheel. Didn't she leave that concept at the off-ramp rest stop?

"Lord, if my dad has more kids, I trust You to protect them. End of story."

Thirty-two miles. Then thirty.

But who was this man she was going to see? Who was Donovan McIntyre back when Chris knew him? He was a drunk. A heavy equipment operator. Worked for the road crew. Then as a truck driver. Then as a bouncer in his favorite bar. Talk about the perfect job for a violent drunk.

He had one older sister. Two younger brothers. The youngest, Davey, was killed in Vietnam. Chris's dad would never talk about him, but she knew her uncle's death was part of the reason her dad refused to sign her army underage enlistment permission paper.

Another rabbit trail she refused to traipse down.

Her uncle Darren was a sweetheart. Was he still? Though, like all the rest, he had turned his back on her and ignored his big brother's behavior, he had at least taken the time to see her before she left for the army. He didn't exactly offer any apologies, but he did give a hint of insight into what formed his big brother into the dad he turned out to be.

At the time, Chris didn't much care. Hueys were calling her, and having to wait the extra year to enlist was unbearable. She had put her dad and all her horrible memories in a big box and left it in her closet. Someone would find it there, a big empty box full of invisible misery, and they would fill that box with good stuff like old sweaters and books, or maybe even load it up with toys for Goodwill. Didn't much matter to her what happened to the box. As long as it left her possession.

She only wished she could peel off her scars and leave them in the box too.

But that day, Darren McIntyre told his niece about his sister, the oldest of the McIntyre siblings. Their father, Chris's grandfather, died in a mining accident and left his distraught wife to care for their four young children.

Chris's great-grandfather had taken them all in and raised them as his own. And treated himself to his daughter's daughter any time he pleased. As the oldest son, Donovan tried to protect his sister, only to be beaten down for his efforts.

Hearing the story didn't mean much to Chris then. But as her Explorer quickly chewed up the miles between her and her dad, she racked her brain for any clue left by her uncle Darren to help her make sense of who his brother had become.

Darren idolized his big brother. Called him Donny. A name Chris would never again even dare repeat. She called him Donny one time. And her mouth had been slapped so hard she spit blood into the sink for ten minutes.

She forced her thoughts away. "Only You know, Lord. Only You know who he was, who he is, and who he will become. And only You know why."

He had put up a basketball hoop for her. And built the tree house. He bought her the coolest bike and taught her how to fish. He taught her how to defend herself from boys like Tony and Jeff. She learned much from her dad. And, despite her best efforts to forget them, she still carried fond memories of those moments when he really did act as if he loved her.

She had cuddled in his arms. And bounced on his knee. She watched so many Nugget games with him from 1977 to 1980 she could name every player on the team and ramble off most of their individual statistics.

But there was only one Nugget stat that mattered. Did they win? Then it would be a good night. Did they lose? Then stay alert and hide out in the tree house if necessary.

She used to love sleeping in her tree house. Especially when it rained.

★★★

Twenty miles. Fifteen.

Which was no big deal. She had plenty of time to find a motel and take a long hot bath before she sat on the bed and pulled out that big phone book. Made that simple call. The call . . . that would be weird. But she needed to warn him. Give him time to stew. And give herself time to abort the mission if she needed to. To abort and run home as fast as her cowardly feet could carry her.

Ten miles. Five.

No big deal! First motel she found, she'd pull in and get a room. Go into that room and fill the bathtub. Water hot enough to soak into her bones. She'd keep the light off. Soak in the dark. And just pray.

That was her plan.

★★★

"Try to relax, will you?" Scott handed his wife a mug of peppermint tea.

Erin's lips trembled as she pressed them into a smile.

"She's fine. And she'll be fine." He leaned in to kiss her lips. "And she'll call. Don't worry. Now drink your tea. And finish your dinner."

"Is that an order, sir?"

"A direct order that stands until she comes home."

"A direct standing order, hmm?" Her smile tightened into a smirk. "You've been talking to Ben."

"Just eat, soldier. And don't give me no lip."

Erin gave him some lip. Two of them. As she pulled him in by his shirt for a long kiss.

✯✯✯

Her wet hair up in a towel, soft sweatpants and T-shirt keeping her warm, bare feet glowing red from the heat of the bath, Chris sat on the bed, let out the deepest sigh of her life, and pulled the Denver Metro Area White Pages onto her lap. Huge book. A bazillion names and phone numbers. But she was only looking for one. She walked her fingers to the *M*s and read down the long list of McIntyres.

Darren and Joyce. That was it. No D., Don, Donny, or Donovan.

What did it mean? Was he gone? Unlisted his number? Was he even still alive?

A grunt of bitter laughter spurted out of her. Wouldn't that be her luck.

One call would answer it all.

She pulled the phone to the bed beside her. Lifted the handset. Punched nine for an outside line, heard the second dial tone, then punched in the number that would make her uncle Darren's phone ring.

She heard it ring. Three times. Five.

He wasn't home.

A "Hello?" sent terror splashing into her belly.

Her voice shook. "Um ... hello. Uncle Darren? Darren McIntyre?"

It was.

"I'm your niece. Chris. Chrissy is what my dad always called me."

Icy silence froze the line.

"Um, do you have a minute? I'm sorry to bother you."

He said he did have a minute. More than one, actually. And that he was surprised to hear her voice.

"Yeah. I'm sorry this is such short notice. But I'm in Denver. And I'd, um ... I'd like to see my dad."

Silence.

At this rate, it would be a long night.

"Where are you?" His voice still carried his surprise. "Do you want to come over here?"

Not really. She wanted to see her dad, not her uncle. "Um, I really appreciate it, but I'm only here for another day. I've, um ... lost track of Dad. Did he move?"

"He's living out in Golden now."

She swallowed. Golden. Not far. "He is?"

"Yeah. He had his number unlisted when he moved." But Uncle Darren proceeded to produce not only his big brother's phone number but his address and directions that would take Chris right up to the door. "He should be home tomorrow."

They both knew the odds of Donovan McIntyre being home on a Friday night.

"He's working out at Pollard's now."

Meant nothing to Chris.

"He's driving one of the big quarry trucks. He really likes it."

Feels like a big man in his big truck. No wonder he likes it. "I'll try to call him tonight. I definitely want to call him first." Why did she say that? She needed to thank her uncle and hang up the phone.

"Um ... Chris? Are you really sure ... you want to see him? It's, um ... been a long time."

She struggled to swallow.

"It may not ... be a good idea. You know?"

She did know. But what business was it of his?

"He's remarried. And seems quite happy."

The words stunned her. "Remarried, huh. That's good. How many does this make for him?" She needed to hang up the phone right now.

"This, um ... this is his third wife."

The question clogged her throat, but needed to be asked. "Any kids?"

"No. They don't have kids. I mean, Nellie does, but he's in his twenties. Lives back east somewhere."

Her eyes closed. *Thank You, Lord.*

"So ... you're really gonna go see him?"

"That's the plan, Uncle Darren."

"Why? If you don't mind me asking."

She did mind, very much, but still answered his question. "I have to."

"Is something wrong?"

Hasn't something been wrong for the last twenty-nine years? "No, nothing's wrong. I just need to see him."

"Anything I can help you with?"

Her teeth clenched. "No. Really. Thanks, though. I appreciate it."

"How have you been, Chris? Where are you living now?"

She told him.

"That sounds great. I'm glad to hear you're ... all right. And I wish you the best of luck. I mean ... you deserve it."

How awkward was that? "Thanks, Uncle Darren. You've always been ... sweet to me. I appreciate it. I mean it."

"You were a sweet kid, Chris. Don't let anyone tell you otherwise."

She really needed to hang up before she started bawling in his ear. "Thanks. And tell Aunt Joyce I said hello."

"Oh, she'd scold me if I didn't at least get your phone number. Can we call you some time?"

Tears burned her eyes. "Sure." She gave him her number. And her address.

"Thanks. And thanks for calling. Donny'll be glad to see you." Now her uncle needed to hang up before he said something else he'd regret.

"Good night, Uncle Darren. And thanks again."

"Good night, Chris. Take care."

She hung up the phone. Then stared down at the words she scratched on the motel's notepad. Numbers. Directions to her dad's house.

Her head lifted as a pent-up breath escaped. "Well, Lord, we've come to that moment. I can almost hear the drumroll now." She wanted to crumple the paper in her hand and throw it in the garbage. She glanced around. Heard Denver's Friday night bustle carry on outside her motel room window.

Just call him, tell him you'll see him tomorrow, and go to bed.

Not a bad plan.

THREE HOURS LATER, SHE LAY back on the bed and fought back tears. She had punched in the number so many times, only to hear it ring and ring and ring. Her dad obviously was too cheap to buy an answering machine. She had called the motel's front desk to make sure the phone worked. It did. She called the lawyer advertised on the cover of the yellow pages. Heard his answering machine.

Her phone worked perfectly.

Her dad and his third wife were not home.

She tried calling for another two hours. Until she drifted into a fitful sleep.

"CALL HER CELL."

"I hate to do that. It's late."

"Will you sleep if you don't?"

Erin pondered that.

"Will she mind if you call?"

She pondered that too.

"If you answered no to either question, call her." Scott lifted the phone off the nightstand and plopped it down on the bed.

"You can be so demanding sometimes." A playful smile. Erin picked up the handset and tapped in the number she had already memorized.

"Demanding, maybe. But always right." Scott stood and pulled off his shirt before climbing into bed.

Erin gazed at him as Chris's weary voice said, "Hey, Rinny!" At that very moment, her little one kicked her soundly in the ribs, stealing her breath. But she didn't mind. With what she saw and what she heard, she didn't have much breath left to steal.

✴✴✴

HEARING THE STRANGE RING OF the cell phone almost gave her a coronary, but hearing Erin's voice made everything right. Chris talked with the side of her face buried in the pillow and listened to another hysterical recount of Erin's day. She fell asleep with prayers of thanksgiving whispering up from her soul, and slept hard. She awoke rested, then sipped orange juice as she reread most of the book of John. After her shower and a meticulous makeup application, checkout was still an hour away. She sat on the bed and stared at the phone, needing to make that call.

Again.

She tried to make that call so many times last night she didn't need the slip of paper anymore. It had been tossed after the fifty millionth time she punched in the number. His address and the directions to find his address were now ingrained in her being. She picked up the phone. Whispered another prayer. Punched in the number. Waited. Two rings. Five. Seven. Nine.

And he still wasn't home.

A shadow fell over her. But then she heard her dad's voice. And the thin ice she'd been standing on shattered beneath her, dropping her into a freezing lake of boiling water.

"Wrong number."

She panicked. "Wait! Dad?"

Thick eerie silence filled the line. Ten, fifteen seconds of it. Until, "Chrissy? Is that you?"

Not how she imagined this moment would play out. Her eyes pinched so hard she saw stars. "Yeah, Dad. It's me."

Five seconds this time. "Well, I'll be. Why are you calling me? Are you all right?"

Oh ... that question. Completely vile, coming from him. "Yeah, Dad, I'm all right. I was just wondering ..."

"Where are you? What are you doing?"

"Well ..." She needed to lay out her plan and hang up the phone. "I'm in Denver. And I'd like to come see you. I talked to Uncle Darren last night, and he gave me your number and address. Will you be home in a couple of hours? Is it all right if I come see you?" She took a breath. Could not believe she forced the words out.

"Yeah. I'll be home. You talked to Darren, huh? How'd you get his number?"

Loaded question. Did he think she carried around her uncle's phone number and not his? "Phone book." Simple truth.

"Okay. Well ... yeah. I guess. Come on over. Did he tell you where I'm at?"

Of course he did. "Yeah."

"Think you can find it?"

He still loves to rub my nose in it. "Yeah. It's been awhile since I've been to Golden, but I'm sure I can find it."

"Well, then, come on over. I'll see you in a couple of hours." The line clicked in her ear.

Silence.

Breath gushed out of her.

And it was done.

She didn't move. Couldn't breathe. The maid knocked on the door. Then let herself in. The chain lock snapped tight. The maid bumped her arm on the door.

"I'm still in here."

"Sorry! So sorry!" The door slammed shut.

"Yes, I'm still here. And I should have my head examined. Could you tell room service to send up a shrink, please?"

Silence.

Lord? Are we ready for this?

She stared at the colorful pattern on the curtains blocking all hints of the new day.

You can do this. We'll do it together.

The words ... just a whisper. The most beautiful words she had ever heard.

★★★

SMALL HOUSE. SIMPLE. SMALL YARD. Beat-up Ford F-350 pickup parked in the driveway.

Big truck for a big man. Too bad he didn't take better care of it.

Didn't the man take care of anything?

Okay, Lord, I need Your help here. You need to control my thoughts and open my heart to the possibilities. She parked beside her dad's truck, careful not to block either his exit or her own. *There may be a possibility he's changed. If so, I'd love to talk to him about what You've done for me. Give me that chance, if possible. If not, then just help me do what I came to do.*

She finally reached down to turn off the Explorer's engine.

And please, if You could ... help me know exactly what that is.

She pushed open the door and stepped out. Turned her ankle a bit on the loose gravel.

Great. Perfectly fitting.

"Bought yourself a Ford, huh?"

His voice. Overwhelmed by the sound of it, Chris slammed her door a little too hard. But her smile came easily. Even though she had yet to look into her dad's eyes. "Yeah. This one followed me home, so I kept it."

"Buy it used?"

She walked closer to the house, watching her step, trying to ignore her aching ankle. "Nope. Brand-new."

"Ahh." He was pleased. "That's my girl."

Too bizarre. She glanced up. Met his gaze for a split second.

His eyes raked her over. Then he turned and headed into the house.

Chris swallowed down the bile in her throat. She did not want to process what she saw in his eyes. "Nice place." She stood in the doorway, not sure she wanted to follow him inside.

With a loud grunt, her dad flopped into his easy chair. Not the same easy chair of her dreams; this one looked almost new. And reclined. No ottoman with stacks of old newspapers. "Well, come on in and take a load off. Tell me why you're back in God's country."

She bit her lip to keep from laughing aloud. The empty Coors cans scattered about turned her stomach. She sat on the couch beside him. Both the couch and his recliner faced the TV. An Atlanta Braves baseball game was in progress. "Like the Braves, now?"

"I like whoever's playin'." A wide grin. "Wanna beer, Chrissy? There's plenty in the fridge."

"No thanks." She stared at the TV. Knew his eyes were upon her.

"What. Too proud to drink a beer with your old man?"

Easy ... She turned and gave him a smile. "No. I just don't drink."

"Lost the taste for it, huh? Wonder why?" A cruel sneer.

Her stomach roiled. She needed to leave.

"Well, hey. It's all right if you don't drink beer. Lotsa women don't drink beer. I just don't know any of 'em." He let out a hearty laugh.

Well, now you do. The game went to commercial.

"It's good to see you, Chrissy." His voice carried a strange softness.

Her heart leaped as she saw the matching expression on his face.

"I mean it. You've really ... grown up."

She couldn't pull away her gaze. She took in his eyes, his nose, his dark hair, and whiskery face.

He looked old. Gray. And as beat-up as his truck.

"Do you hate me, Chrissy?"

She blinked, stunned by the question.

"You have every reason to."

"I don't hate you." The words flowed too easily. But they were true.

His eyes flickered. Studied his daughter. Then turned back to the TV. "So, tell me what you've been doing with yourself."

She pulled in a deep breath and tried to relax. "I'm living in Portland now. Working at an inner-city community center."

"Sounds nice." He didn't hear a word she said. "Doncha miss the mountains?"

"Yeah. Some."

"You know those two dimwits you helped send up still haven't gone to trial yet."

Her eyes bulged, but no other part of her moved. She forced her words out slowly. "Really? Haven't heard that."

"The dunces. I can't believe they went up there after you."

He knew she lived in Portland. He knew everything about her. "You've been busy, Chrissy. I'm proud of you."

She really needed to leave.

"But it looks like you didn't duck the last one."

Her eyes fell closed.

"How'd you get cut?"

"Took a punch." She turned to look him in the eye. "But I ducked the first one."

His smile slowly widened into an outright burst of laughter. "That's my girl."

Right now. She needed to leave.

Commercial. He turned slightly in the recliner and gave her his full attention. "So, tell me why you're here. You didn't come just to make a social call. Did ya?"

She couldn't take his searing gaze. "Yeah, I did. Sort of. There are a few things I'd like to say to you." Her eyes burned as she looked into his. Though her smile wasn't fake. "I needed to see you again."

"Well, here I am."

Yes, you certainly are.

"And I'm listening."

Accomplish the mission and get out. Her smile wavered. "I just wanted to tell you ... that I'm over everything that happened. I'm done with it."

"Good. Glad to hear it."

"I mean it, Dad." Cruel thoughts tried to find voice, but she squashed them. Listened to her heart. Continued to let it speak. "I'm here because I need you to know ... that I don't want to blame you for anything anymore. I forgive you, Dad. I mean it."

His gaze didn't waver a bit. "Really? That's great, Chrissy. You know what? I forgive you too."

Her heart dropped to the floor.

"I forgive you for everything. Wow." He patted his chest with both hands. "That really makes me feel better!"

Her eyes studied the dirty carpet.

"Listen, Chrissy. I was hard on you growing up. But looking at you now, I can see you took it well. You were a good kid. And it looks like you still are. So go on home and do your thing, and I'll stay here and do mine." He turned back to the game. "Oh, wait." He jumped out of his recliner. "I've been saving your stuff for you. All these years. Can you believe that?" By his smile, he seemed quite pleased with himself. "Wanna come get it?"

"No. I need to get going."

"Come on! It's your stuff! Some of your old books, a few of your dolls ..."

She played with one doll as a child. Did he keep it all these years?

"Come on, Chrissy." He headed for the hallway. "Just up here in the attic. There's two boxes full of stuff. I couldn't take throwing them in the garbage."

She pinched the bridge of her nose and tried to pray away the headache threatening to explode.

Her dad stomped up the attic stairs. Chris slowly pushed herself to her feet and followed him.

"Here's one." Bent over beneath the low ceiling, her dad slid a box toward her. "I'll bring the other."

"Okay." The box in her arms, Chris carefully back-stepped down the narrow stairs. She carried it into the living room, then stood and waited for her dad to join her. Though the house was different, so much of it was the same. It even smelled the same. And she couldn't wait to leave.

Her dad carried his box into the living room, then gave Chris a somewhat sheepish grin. "You don't have to go so soon, you know. Nellie will be home in about an hour. She'd love to meet you."

Chris smiled. Then slowly shook her head. "No. That's all right."

"Said what you came to say, huh."

She stared into her dad's eyes. Could not figure out what she saw there. Or what to say in reply.

"Well, I guess this is good-bye, then." He pulled open the door and carried his box out to Chris's Explorer.

Chris followed, her brain in total chaos. Her dad waited for her to grab her keys and unlock the back door, then he opened it and slid his box in. Chris slid hers in beside it, then slammed the door shut. She lifted her gaze to meet his.

"I'm glad you stopped by, Chrissy. And I meant what I said. You really look great. All ... grown up."

She couldn't resist. "You've gotten a little gray."

Hearty laughter rumbled out of him. "Yeah. What's a man to do?" His eyes softened. Almost sparkled.

Chris savored the sound of his genuine laughter.

"Are you taking forty back?"

She struggled to make sense of his question. Route 40. Up through Steamboat. "Um, no. Seventy. I want to stop in at the station and say hi to Sid and everyone."

Her dad nodded. "Same difference, I guess. Either way, you've got quite a haul ahead of ya."

She didn't know what to say.

"Well, I'd better let you get to it." He released a deep breath and gazed once more into her eyes. His head tilted. "Did you mean what you said, Chrissy? About forgiving me?"

She nodded. "Yeah, Dad. I meant it. I need to move on."

"You've been through it, kid. But you turned out all right."

The words fell over her like gentle rain. "Thanks." She lifted her hand to touch his arm. The touch froze the blood in her veins. But when he grabbed her hand and squeezed it, her heart soared.

"Drive careful. If I'm ever up Portland way, I'll look you up."

"I have a feeling you know where to look."

A slow grin. He released her hand.

"I'll see ya, Dad. Take care of that wife of yours." Chris gave him a warm smile, then turned and stepped into the driver's seat of her Explorer. She started the engine, pulled the door closed, then rolled down the window.

Her dad leaned in for a closer look. "Get good mileage?"

"Yeah. It does all right."

His head slowly bobbed. He had that pleased look on his face again. "Well, Chrissy, I wish you well."

She gazed into his eyes. "Do you mean that?"

He cussed. "Sure I do. I hope you live a happy life. You got yourself a boyfriend?"

A laugh spurted out of her. "Yeah, I do. I've got a terrific boyfriend."

"You be sure and invite me to the weddin', then. I'll be there."

"I'll let you know. Take care, Dad." She pulled the gear-shift into reverse.

Her dad stepped away as the Explorer started to move. "You too, Chrissy," he said. "You too."

★★★

So. Whaddya think, Chrissy? Was it worth it?

Twenty-five hours of driving for fifteen minutes of his time. A couple smart-mouth remarks tempered by a couple moments of what appeared to be genuine concern. A couple boxes of musty junk that already stunk up the inside of her Explorer.

The moment overwhelmed her as she drove through Golden, Colorado, on her way to I-70. Too tired to control it, too wigged out to explain it, her giggles escaped into the wind blowing through her open window. And why not. She had accomplished her mission and was on her way home.

She looked her dad in the eye. And forgave him. He tried to flick it back in her face, and succeeded, but also accepted her forgiveness and let it stand. He didn't beat it down. He didn't blow it off. He accepted it. And he was forgiven.

The word radiated through her. Carried the warmth of her laughter to the deepest recesses of her being.

Precious Lord, we did it! And it's done. Thank You so much, Lord, Jesus ... my sweet and precious Lord.

Her Explorer again chewed up the miles between Denver and Portland, and even though she toyed with the idea of stopping for a visit in Ouray, she needed to see Erin. She decided to press on tonight as far as she could. Maybe even sleep in her truck. If she pushed, she'd be home by late tomorrow night. That suited her just fine.

But as her truck rolled along, curiosity ate at her. The musty smell emanating from the back wouldn't let her forget that two boxes filled with stuff from her childhood waited there for her to peruse.

She coasted up the off-ramp at the Bakerville exit and parked in a lonely spot near the trees where no one would see her or care about her business. She climbed out of the truck and lifted the back door. Stared down at the two boxes stinking up her afternoon.

She pulled one toward her and peeled back the strapping tape. The tape was so old it had turned yellow. She lifted the box flaps, then stepped back. Just a step. Peered inside the box. From a safe distance.

Clothes. Malodorous clothes that were way too small. But a tickling giggle worked its way through her belly. These were clothes she adored when she was nine, maybe ten. The Denver Broncos T-shirt she wore to bed off and on for what, five years?

A doll. The doll. The one she had left outside for a week, until her dad yelled at her and called her "ungrateful." The doll had been a gift from her aunt. The aunt she didn't even know. If her aunt would have taken the time to get to know her, the woman would have discovered Chris hated playing with dolls. Given her a Tonka. Or some kind of ball. Any kind of ball.

Though this doll, Mrs. Beasley, was a good doll. And after Chris brought her inside and cleaned her up, she found a home for her right beside her bed. Gave her a pat every night before going to sleep. Along with that teddy bear she loved and the stuffed monkey with the dumb grin on his face.

Childishness swept through her. She picked up the box and dumped it out on the gravel, hoping a dumb grinning monkey would fall out. Or that one special teddy bear.

Only more clothes. Some she didn't remember ever wearing.

All of it went back into the box. Once she made it home, she'd swing by Goodwill and give them everything. Even her Denver Broncos T-shirt.

She picked up the other box. The old tape peeled easily. Unable to contain herself, she upended the box and let everything fall to the gravel. She picked through more clothes, mainly clothes. No monkey. No teddy bear. Too bad.

She straightened and stretched, then let out a deep sigh. Two boxes of stinky garbage. And her dad had seemed so excited to give them to her. He had saved them for so long, never knowing when he'd see her again. Never knowing if she'd ever return to get them.

A twinge of sorrow shot through her.

It was a nice gesture. She'd give him that.

She lowered her head and let her eyes drift over the pile of clothes. "I'm not ungrateful, Lord. Thank You for this simple, dumb thing he did for me." She wanted to laugh, but her eye was drawn to something bright orange in the pile of clothes. She pulled back an old dress she never wore and stared at a long orange snake. She jumped back a step as her shriek scared her more than the snake. But the snake didn't move. And was much too … orange. Spotted with brown.

Chris kicked the dress away. Saw the end of the snake. Wrapped with gray duct tape.

Her scream became a retch. She turned away, fell to her knees, and threw up until she nearly passed out.

She tried to stand. To run. Her knees wouldn't carry her weight. She took a few steps, then fell again and convulsed with dry heaves. Handfuls of gravel came with her as she stood, and the pain in her palms infuriated her beyond anything she'd known. She threw both handfuls at a Dead End sign. Her eyes darted to the freeway, to the on-ramp just down the hill, to the pile of musty clothes lying near her truck. At the boxes, so lovingly packed and stored away. All these years.

Curses wrenched her throat. "How could you! You *are* a monster! Oh, my God! Lord, help me!" Violent weeping almost forced her to her knees. She wanted to drive away, to leave everything where it lay for whoever happened to stop by. They could have it. They could have it all.

No. Not all of it.

Oh, God …

She gagged at the thought of touching the hideous thing. The brown spots had to be her own dried blood. The tape that her dad carefully wrapped around the end of it still shone brilliant gray against the old pair of jeans beneath it.

But no one could take it. No one could touch it. Ever again.

She scrambled up a small hill into the trees and dropped to her knees, then began digging with a stick, her fingernails clawing away the dry, packed ground. She dug a hole about a foot deep. Then tossed the stick away and painfully pushed back up to her feet.

Her heart raced, sending scalding blood coursing through her. She picked her way back down the hill and slowly moved closer to the pile of clothes. With just her thumb and forefinger, she grabbed the very end of the grip, lifted it, then refused to even glance at it as she carried it up the hill to the hole. In thirty seconds, the hole was filled. She stomped the dirt to pack it. Dropped a large rock over it. Then stepped back. And knew. The cord would stay buried for the rest of all time.

✯✯✯

SHE KEPT HER TRUCK IN the passing lane and pushed it up the steep incline to the top of the Continental Divide. It seemed to know how badly she wanted to fly.

Hints of mustiness remained, but wouldn't last as the wind whipped her hair into a tangled mess. She wished the wind would cleanse away the dirt on her hands, the dirt buried under her fingernails. The bile on her breath sickened her. The taste of it lingered even after she guzzled her Pepsi. She had savored the icy sweetness, but now her stomach burned worse than ever. Miles from nowhere, she pushed her truck on. Two things mattered. Cover the distance. Get home.

You've forgiven him. Now ... forget him.

She tried to swallow, but shuddered against the vile taste in her throat.

Relax. Just relax. Breathe the Colorado air.

Forget him. Forget him. Forget him. Forget it all.

She smacked the steering wheel. "How, Lord? After this?"

Her thoughts jumbled into a chaotic mess. Curses blended with prayers until nothing connected into anything. One truth drifted up through the chaos. Her Explorer carried her home. She held on to that thought with all her might.

And entered the Eisenhower Memorial Tunnel. Crossed the Continental Divide. All downhill from here.

The tunnel seemed to drag on forever. Though all the illuminated signs read SPEED 50, the flow of traffic remained steady at sixty-five. Chris didn't mind.

The wind roared as blood throbbed against her eardrums. Deep, booming throbs of blood. Her heart struggled against the confines of her chest.

Forget him. Forget him. Forget it all.

Right. So simple. Just forget.

Daylight assaulted her as she exited the tunnel. Her Explorer picked up speed. She stayed in the far left passing lane. Glanced at her speedometer. Eighty-five miles per hour. But her speedometer only went up to eighty-five.

She did not lift her foot from the accelerator. Not until the road started to turn. Growling, she tapped the brakes as her truck took the first turn, then accelerated, but quickly hit the brakes again through another turn.

She glanced back down at her speed. The needle danced against the limit, as if it begged to reach farther, but was held back by an unseen hand.

What am I doing?

Faster. The grade of decline pushed seven percent. And lasted for miles. She had already passed one run-away ramp for big rigs with failed brakes.

There was nothing wrong with her brakes.

Her fingers tightened on the steering wheel as a sharp right turn loomed before her. She eased her foot off the accelerator and hugged the inside line of her lane as cars in the other lanes slowed. Out of the turn, her Explorer continued picking up speed. Easily over a hundred miles per hour by now. She saw a U-Haul truck passing a semi in the inside lanes and gasped at how quickly she ran up the back of them, how they flashed by on her right and disappeared in her rearview mirror.

How fast are you going, Chris?

She couldn't think. Her grip on the wheel tightened into a death grip. Her eyes hardened. Back and forth she steered through the turns, her vision clear, focused only on the thin strip of road in front of her.

One-ten, one-twenty, easy. Maybe even more.

This fast ... these turns ... you're gonna roll over.

A rollover would finish it. Crash and burn. And die.

Yes. This fast, for no other reason.

And why not. She'd never forget what she saw, what she touched, what she buried in that hole. She'd never forget what her dad did to her. She couldn't wash away her scars; she'd wear them the rest of her life. And if she had any hope of a future with Jason, he would need to see them all. Top to bottom. And after he saw, Chris would have to make him forget how they were laid across her, one by one. They would both have to forget so they could move on.

Ridiculous. Insane. And impossible.

The only way to forget ... is to die.

Forgiveness. Like peace, just another fantasy. How did one forgive a monster? And once a monster, always a monster.

This was her moment. If Jesus really loved her, He wouldn't like it, but He'd understand.

Right now. No other cars around. Turn the wheel hard. Or don't. Either way. It'll be done.

I'm sorry, Jesus. Please understand. I can't take any more. I need it to be over.

The engine whined as it teetered near its breaking point. Her eyes became part of the road. Her hands, part of the steering wheel. Her arms, her entire body struggled to control the truck, to keep its tires safely positioned in that outer lane. While convincing voices screamed at her to do it. Turn the wheel. Don't turn the wheel. Let it be done.

A wail lifted up from her soul. Cut through the angry voices. A little girl's cry. *"Daddy ... please!"*

Tears blurred her vision. But if she closed her eyes for even a second, she'd die.

"Please ... Daddy ... save me!"

She closed her eyes tightly. Blinked them open.

Keep 'em closed. Just let it happen. It'll finish itself.

"You'll be the best aunt, Chris. I can't wait for you to hold her."

Her heart slammed. "Oh, God ... Rinny ..." She spoke the words aloud, but they blurred into nothingness. The road, the trees, the sky above. All blurs. The cars she passed. The tears in her eyes.

"Rinny! Oh, God!"

The road ahead straightened. White-hot needles pricked her hands, her arms, her shoulders. The way she breathed made her arms shake. Only a matter of time. The wheel would turn. And she would die. She struggled to remain perfectly still as her heart pounded again, so hard she heard it throb against her eardrums.

"Jesus! Lord! I can't do this!"

She lifted her foot and gently touched the brake pedal.

Please, God ... I'm so sorry ...

The Explorer slowed. But she dared not even think about glancing at the speedometer. She knew she still traveled well over a hundred miles per hour.

God, forgive me. Please forgive me.

The truck slowed a bit more. A quick look. The speedometer needle moved. Eighty. Seventy-five. Chris blinked deeply as the engine's whine eased. Seventy. Sixty-five.

Exit 205. Silverthorne. Dillon. One mile ahead.

She glanced over her shoulder, saw the way clear, then steered toward the far right lane to exit. The same cars and trucks she had passed now passed her. Her truck coasted down the off-ramp. Coasted through the right turn at the intersection. Coasted down the Blue River Parkway. Coasted through the right turn at the next intersection. She suddenly found herself in the parking lot of a Wendy's. She steered into the last space beside a small stand of evergreens. Shut off the engine. And sat with her foot still pressed firmly on the brake.

Violent trembling overtook her. She started to sob. Which infuriated her. She slammed her fists on the steering wheel. "God, why? Why can't it be done?" Screaming the words only tore up her throat. She slammed the wheel again. "Why won't this end?"

Out of the truck, she kicked the door closed and walked a few steps toward the trees.

"I hate him! Why can't he leave me alone?" Her scream carried across the intersection below her. The cars continued merrily on their way. Oblivious. "God, please." Sobs left her breathless. "I don't need to know why. I just need it to end."

She leaned against the door of her truck and slid down it to sit on the ground. She covered her face with filthy hands.

"Jesus ... I don't wanna know why. I just want You to take me home." Bitter sobs. "I wanna be with You. I'm so tired of this. Please ... I can't take any more." A motorcycle rumbled through the intersection. Muffled her cries. She struggled to breathe, to clear the bile from her throat. "It was always about how much I could take. Like a game for him." Her hands pressed against her eyes. "He wins, okay? He wins. Just let it end."

Let him win. Let him go.

"I just wanna go home. I need to see Rinny." She lifted her head, but her vision swirled. "Oh, God ..." Dizziness hit her from all sides. She lay down on the hard ground and closed her eyes. "God ... just let me die."

Rest.

"Yeah. Just let me rest here a minute." A faint whisper. Loud ringing in her ears. "Please don't let me puke again."

Rest, My beloved.

"Oh, God ..." Her stomach cramped as the aroma of french fries wafted her way. "Father God ... don't let me go. Stay close to me ..."

I am your Father.

"My Father ... my God ..."

I will never leave you.

"Never ... I believe that."

Believe ... and rest.

"Forgive me."

Forgiven ... and forgotten.

"Oh, Lord ... thank You." Gentle sobs overtook her. As the world hurried on around her.

★★★

HOME.

She lifted her head and blinked deeply to focus. The trees beside her seemed to protect her. To comfort her. Blue sky shone through them. She wiped her eyes. "Yes." Just a whisper. "Lord? Let's go home." She forced herself up, then eased into the driver's seat of her truck, laid her head back, and closed her eyes.

A pleasant thought broke through the swirling nothingness in her mind. Her eyes slowly opened. "Yes. Oh, yes." A long hot bath. A nice big bed. She leaned forward to start the truck, then lifted her hands to the steering wheel. Her fingers ached when they curled around it again. Trying to ignore all her aches, she drove north through Silverthorne and found a motel. She didn't have the strength to carry anything but her purse into the room. She flopped on the bed. Forgot all about her bath. Barely kicked off her shoes. Fell asleep in her clothes. And slept.

✶✶✶

THE FIRST TWINGE CONCERNED HER. Sharp twinge. In the area she expected to feel a twinge. In about two weeks. Not tonight. Not this early.

The second twinge stole her breath. Clenched her teeth. Stronger than the first. And much more worrisome.

The third twinge left no doubt. These weren't just any old twinges. These were contractions.

"Scott? Sweetheart?" She reached for her phone and punched in Chris's cell phone number. Heard about twelve rings before the nice lady said, "Your party is not answering."

No kidding! Erin wanted to punch the nice lady in the nose. But as she hung up the phone, another contraction struck, paralyzing her in its agony.

"Scott? I need you!"

Oh, Lord ... Lord? Let's not do this now, okay? Please?

✶✶✶

EXPLOSIONS AND SIRENS. LOUD VOICES. Chris forced her eyes to open. Obnoxious neighbors. Stupid television. So loud, the paper-thin walls shook.

She glanced at the alarm clock on the nightstand. Saw the numbers 8:42, but couldn't comprehend how that was possible. Didn't she just lie down? And where was she, anyway? Her head felt like it had been stuffed with packing peanuts. Her mouth tasted worse than she ever remembered.

She pushed up to sit on the bed. The room swirled. She let it. Watched it. Heard her voice say, "Whoooaahh." Wanted to laugh. But couldn't. Not yet.

She tried to push her fingers through her hair. Failed miserably. The incredible mess on her head needed to be shaved off.

She needed her bath. Her comfie sweats. And a good night's sleep.

She staggered outside to her truck. Struggled to unlock the door. Pulled out her backpack and her half-eaten bag of pecans. Slammed the door. Staggered back to the room. Just as her cell phone rang.

Panicked, she tore open her pack to find it. Grabbed it and punched TALK after the eighth or so ring. "Hey, Rinny!"

"Hey to you too." Scott's voice. "Where are you?"

Chris's knees gave out. She plopped down on the bed. "Silverthorne. I think. What's up?"

"It's time, girl. How soon can you get here?"

The words completely blew her away.

★★★

SHE WANTED TO THROW THE phone against the wall. Again.

"How could they do this to me?" She hadn't even taken her bath yet! "Okay, this is not funny." She stuffed the phone back in her bag and tore off her clothes on her way to the shower. "Lord? Aren't You God? What do You have to say for Yourself?" Giggles threatened to explode, but she forced them back down. "This is serious! You know I'm at least twenty-four hours away!"

She took a quick shower, brushed her teeth, painfully brushed out her hair, then quickly French braided it. Fifteen minutes. How many contractions in that time?

Oh, Lord ...

Her stomach hurt, yet she skipped to her truck, threw her backpack inside, and raced back to that freeway. She laughed and prayed aloud until her throat gave out. Then she just prayed in her heart. As she pushed her truck on.

✦✦✦

If the cell phone survived this trip, she would be amazed. Again she wanted to throw it. But she only squeezed it. Violently. As her teeth crushed together. As she pulled the gas nozzle away from her tank and stuffed it back in the pump. Screwed on the gas cap. Shut the little door.

She wanted to scream. Tears stung her eyes. She grabbed her receipt from the pump and slid into the driver's seat, then started her truck and laid a little rubber on her way to the I-15 on-ramp.

Nine hours. And hearing Erin's voice after nine hours of labor only confirmed what Chris thought would be the case when the moment of truth finally arrived.

She wanted to laugh at herself even as she wanted to cry. Bazillions of women down through the ages have borne the pain of childbirth. A baby would be born. The agony would be worth it. All forgotten when that little one arrived.

But she didn't want to know about it. Didn't want to see it. Didn't want to hear it. She couldn't take it. Not for a second. Not when it was Erin Mathis in agony.

She swallowed a sip of ice-cold chocolate milk. Hummed with delight as the thick sweetness descended through her. Better than Pepto Bismol and cheaper too, she sipped her medicine and tried not to think of her best friend in agony.

"I'm sorry I'm being stupid, Lord. But right now I'm almost glad I'm in Utah. I know You're with Rin. So that's that, I guess." She grabbed a cassette and stuffed it into the stereo. Waited to hear which one she had grabbed.

I'll just sit here and listen to a little music.

302

Simple House. Very cool. Her hand tapped out the beat on the steering wheel.

I'll just sit here and drive and rock out with Margaret for a little while, okay? You stay with Rinny ... and hold her hand for me. Please? Like You held mine back in Silverthorne. Like You're holding mine ... right now.

Oh, Father, my Father God, Lord Jesus, thank You for holding our hands.

★★★

Scott dialed the number. Then winked at his wife and headed out the door. Erin pushed the phone more tightly against her ear and whispered a prayer for the one about to pick up. She needed to hear that voice. To share some incredible news.

Two rings. A click. The roar of the road. But no hello. Not a word.

A smile worked its way across her face. She almost laughed. "This is me, is that you?"

Still nothing.

Her smile wavered. "I'm here, are you there?"

"Yeah, Rinny. I'm sorry. I'm here. Are you ... all right?"

Joy swelled her heart until she thought it would burst. Laughter carried her simple words to the one she knew would cherish them. "I'm a mommy!"

FOURTEEN

PORTLAND'S SKYLINE SIMPLY GLITTERED. THE cool, midnight breeze smelled like home. Chris parked her truck, then ran across the street and through the Emergency entrance of Good Samaritan Hospital. Her stomach quaked at the sterile smell, at the memory of her previous trip through the ER. She stepped into the nearest elevator and waited for it to stop at the maternity ward floor.

As it stopped, her stomach dropped. Just a hint of that old familiar feeling she once cherished. She missed that old Huey helicopter, her Ticket to Paradise. Smiling a bit, she headed down the darkened hall, searching both sides of it for the room she needed to find. She heard a newborn's cry. Poor little guy. He didn't sound very happy.

She slowed to a stop and listened, wondering if the poor little guy was her niece. She'd know soon enough. Just as soon as she found the room. She knew the number but had no idea how to find it.

She headed for the nurses' station but slowed to a stop and gazed into the large waiting area. There, on a vinyl couch all spread out and sound asleep, lay the handsome paramedic, Jason Sloan. Over the cry of the newborn, Chris heard faint snoring. Her smile widened as warmth flooded her. She tiptoed closer. Wanted to laugh. The way the man slept, she doubted he was going anywhere for the next hour at least. Which was good. She'd definitely be back. She couldn't wait to look into those eyes and hear that low, sometimes sultry voice. To fall into those arms and be kissed by those soft lips.

I'll be back, Jase. Soon. I promise. Just as soon as I see Rinny. And my niece. She blew him a heartfelt kiss. "I'll be back, love." The whispered words tasted strange on her tongue. Sounded strange in her ears. But sweet. Oh, so sweet.

She gazed at him a second longer, then headed once again down the hall. She stopped at the nurses' station, but found it deserted. She continued down the hall. And soon found the room she was looking for.

The door was open.

She couldn't go in. She stood outside, her heart thumping. A prayer filtered through her. A prayer of thanksgiving. Of pure adoration. After all she had been through, to be home again with her real and eternal family, to think ahead to what each new day would bring, she could only stand amazed, humbled, overwhelmed that One so great would call her His own and give her this new life. This was, indeed, her new life. A life more wonderful than she ever could have imagined even a few short months ago.

Her bottom lip trembled, and she held her breath to force away tears. She hadn't even walked in the door yet. Couldn't she wait to cry at least until she looked into her best friend's face? Until she saw her tiny new niece? And held her?

She forced her feet to carry her through the door. Laughter immediately rumbled up from her belly. Her hand quickly covered her mouth.

The tuckered-out brand-new daddy lay sprawled out on a recliner, his head lolling to one side, his mouth open as snores resonated from the back of his throat.

Chris turned her head to take in the sight she knew would blow her away.

That smile. That face. That voice. "Hey you."

That little bundle of flannel nestled deep in Erin's arms.

"We've been waiting for you."

Breath failed her. Words, thoughts, even hope of moving closer.

Erin only smiled. Until a tiny hand reached toward her. She looked down and laughed as it latched onto her pinky finger.

Too much. Overwhelmed, tears filled Chris's eyes. Her hand still covered her mouth. She moved a few steps closer.

"I told you she would get here," Erin whispered to her tiny daughter. "Mia Renae ... my sweet one ... would you like to meet your aunt Chris?" Her eyes lifted. Glimmered in the faint light.

Chris sat on Erin's bed and stared at the infant. Bright-eyed, the babe seemed to stare back at her for a few seconds. Then slowly found her mother once more.

Too much. All of it. A sob threatened to escape Chris's throat. She turned to look at Erin … gazed at her as tears dripped down her cheeks. No words would express it. Nothing could express what coursed through her at that moment.

Way too much.

She carefully leaned over and touched her cheek to Erin's. She tried to whisper, "I'll be right back," into Erin's ear. The words left her lips, yet she couldn't stay for one more second to make sure Erin understood. Chris pushed up and quickly left the room, pressing her fist against her lips to keep back the sobs threatening to explode.

Wandering aimlessly down the hall, she heard the bell of an elevator and the swish of its doors. Two nurses gave her a concerned look as they walked out of it, but Chris tried to ignore them. She glanced up to see which way the elevator was heading.

Up.

She snuck inside. The doors swung shut.

She pushed the button that would take the elevator up as high as it could go, then wiped her face with her shirt and tried to steady her breathing. The doors swished open. A set of sliding glass doors stood directly in front of her, leading out to the roof. Glancing up and down the hall and seeing no one, she moved closer and held her breath, wondering if the doors would open and allow her access outside.

They swished open.

She barely smiled. Then walked through and far enough out to take a look around. The helipad lights burned brightly. A basketball hoop had been situated next to a few picnic tables. She pictured Scott and Jason there, shooting baskets as Erin watched. She pictured a life flight helicopter landing, dust flying in its own version of a Dustoff. She lifted her head and blinked deeply.

Stars filled the clear night sky. Brilliant. Twinkling. In her space of sky, no moon lit the night. Only stars. A quabozillion stars.

She fell to her knees as her sobs escaped. Too much love. Too much joy. Too much magnificence displayed across the midnight sky. Yet just a glimpse. Just a hint of His ways. Just a taste of what waited ahead for those who loved this big and gracious God.

Abba, Father. My Daddy God. The thought was too wonderful. Too sweet to comprehend.

Jesus ... Jesus ... Why? Who am I? Why would You ... love me? Why would You die ... for someone like me? Why do You continue to give me ... so much?

From the depths of her soul, a melody filled her. Her hands lifted to reach toward the sky. On her knees in that place, the song flooded her, and she whispered along as her lips trembled, as tears fell down her cheeks from eyes gazing into the spectacular midnight sky.

I am counting the stars on Your blackened sky
You call them all by name, You know them all by sight
In this sea of lights I sense Your majesty
And I break at the thought that One so great
could care for me
I am counting the mountains that I've laid at Your feet
And I'm reduced to tears when I think of how
You've moved them for me
In this storm of life You've been my safe retreat
Through the wind and the fire You always were
there to carry me
No greater honor could I ever find
Than the privilege to love You for the rest of my life
Who am I, Jesus, that You call me by name?
What could I ever do to be loved this way?
Who am I, Jesus? In Your eyes, tell me, who am I?

The question echoed through her, until she heard a faint reply. *You are Mine, My precious child. Forever ... you are Mine.*